THE GOLDEN MIRROR

THE GOLDEN MIRROR

BROOKE FISCHBECK

First Printing, 2021

For Mom and Dad, my first heroes.
With love, your favorite daughter.

Contents

Part One: Sun

What is the lamp which lights up men, but flame engulfs it, and wolves grasp after it always? She lights up every land and shines over all men. Those are wolves, one going before the sun, the other after the moon.

—A German riddle,
The answer being the sun.

One Going Before the Sun

Rain shook the world as the Queen laced a silver comb through her hair.

The rain pounded relentlessly against the cold stone walls, as if threatening to destroy the entire castle. Lightning flashed like glimpses of day. It lit up the night for a moment before falling away, returning the castle to a grim darkness. Haunted echoes of daytime come alive for a fraction of a second. Thunder followed, the most loyal companion. It resonated through the town below the castle, shaking the sky like some far away giants bellowing terrible cries of loss. The thunder roared over the dusty plains of the kingdom, roared over the cold night, and roared across the roof of the castle. Perhaps the thunder was trying to warn the slumbering residents inside the palace. Perhaps the thunder simply wanted to cause chaos.

Queen Callista did not care for any of this because no matter how powerful the rain could be, she knew she was stronger than any storm. Deep within the castle, far below the slumbering servants and royals, the Queen sat before her vanity. The storm could not reach her here. No one could. Only she knew of this place that hummed with the blessing of every dark thing the world had to offer.

An ornate mirror sat before her, small in stature and thin, but something told Callista that it went deeper than any human could see. It had a golden frame with tendrils that snaked their way across the stone walls like twisted strands of sun. The whole room buzzed almost, but this mirror pulsed and danced. Things laced with the magic of the Old Ones often had energies that one could *feel*.

Callista set the comb down and stared in the mirror. Gazing back at her was glass, beautiful and powerful. Her reflection. She looked for a long moment, admiring her dark skin, high cheekbones, and slender nose. She stared into her reflection and thought, *There is no one more entrancing than me.*

She wanted to be sure, however, as she always did.

Right as she was about to begin speaking, she heard a clattering sound from behind her. She whirled around, prepared to furiously chastise a servant, but saw nothing. The door to the chamber was slightly askew. Maybe she had left it like that. She had to have left it like that; yes. But she could have sworn she saw a glimpse of the bluest eyes she had ever seen. And felt something that reeked of...nevermind. Imagination could run faster than rivers. No storm or prayer could reach her here.

"Dark one, here, on the wall, who is the fairest of them all?" Her voice rang out musically, echoing in the deep chamber and against the stone walls. The thunder stopped for a moment as if waiting patiently for the answer.

The mirror's silver surface changed suddenly, swirling into a deep ebony color. Then it returned to the Queen's reflection once more.

A silky voice came from the mirror. It encompassed the whole room with its majesty, as if no other sound could dare be louder than it.

"You, my Queen, are fair, it's true, but the Sun's Child is a thousand times fairer than you. This battle for beauty has long been won, for even you cannot outshine the sun."

Callista's calm smile twisted into a hauntingly pretty sneer. Her fist crumpled into her scarlet dress, leaving half-moon marks on her palm. She had known this would be coming. What she hadn't known was how soon it would be. Her fingers dug deeper into her hand, stifling down the hot red anger rising. It was time for everything she had ever wished for to fall into place.

The stars would align for her soon indeed. No, the stars would *bow* to her.

She composed herself and stood, a tight-lipped smile back in place. She had to get back upstairs, to the ballroom. The children were entertaining guests from another kingdom. Her new husband didn't like to be kept waiting.

But Callista knew of patience. Just a little longer, and everything she had been working towards would be hers. She offered up a silent message, looking upward and digging her nails deeper into her palm. *Everything I do is for you, my love.*

The Queen turned and left the chambers.

Drops of blood dripped from her palms.

2

A Flower in the Wind

Princess Kyra raced through the gardens, outrunning the wind itself.

She passed through hedge mazes and flower beds, twisting marble sculptures and budding tulips of all colors. It had been raining the night before, and she wanted nothing more than to be outside and *breathe*. Nothing like the crisp air of morning to chase all the night's thunder out of her mind.

Kyra jumped over a marble bench, her blue dress billowing out behind her. She secretly hoped the dress, a birthday gift from her stepmother, got snagged and ripped.

Once she had sprinted around the width of the castle, she collapsed in a heap in a patch of grass that overlooked the town. Her breath came in heaving gasps, and she relished the cold air on her cheeks. The sun smiled down on her through a thick layer of clouds, like an old friend teasing her. But no, the sun did not force the clouds to part just yet, and with every passing second the wet grass seeped into Kyra's clothes, making her shiver. The sun did not seem to be in a very pleasant mood. She sourly rolled over.

I," she breathed heavily, "forgot how much I detest running." Her eyes locked on the clouds above. *Gray eyes, like storm clouds,* her step-mother, the Queen, had sneered at her once. *How ugly.* Kyra turned away from the clouds, the familiar blade of hatred spiking in her.

Her good mood returned as she looked out over the dust-ridden hills of the kingdom of Aazagonia and at the little people bustling around like ants on their hill. It calmed her to see so much energy in one place, bringing life and vigor despite the bleak landscape of ash and dryness.

Nothing could dull her good mood now, because she finally smelled what she had come here to smell—the bakery down in the village had awoken. The bakery had risen like the bread it baked and was now cooking up delightful pastries that Kyra would most definitely *borrow.* The other contribution to her mood was the castle to her back. Whenever the tall stone towers and the ever present stares weren't in her view, she was happier. Kyra hated everything about the stupid castle with its irritating, watching gaze. Well, maybe she liked one thing about the castle. And that one thing would be by her side in five, four, three, two—

"Kyra!"

Kyra propped herself up with an elbow and turned to see the approaching girl. Her step-sister, Princess Juniper.

The so-called Sun's Child.

Kyra couldn't help rolling her eyes every time someone referred to Juniper by that name. Juniper was the kingdom's beloved darling, kind, gentle, and Sun-like, apparently, while Kyra was oh-so lovingly called 'Moon's Child.' It made her nose wrinkle in disgust. She loved the people of Aazagonia, sure, but they could be so primordial in their favoritism of Juniper. Welp, maybe it had something to do with Kyra's manners. She hadn't exactly been a pleasure to the kingdom.

The favoritism began the second Juniper and her mother moved into the castle. At the presenting ceremony, Juniper had worn a pink veil over her face, and when it came time for her to introduce herself as the new princess, the whole crowd, gathered in the town square, had gone silent.

As the six-year-old girl had walked behind her mother, she had suddenly tripped.

Chuckles abounded, mocking and cruel. The watchful people of Aazagonia had made their decision, it seemed. The new member of the royal family was a disappointment. Kyra remembered scornful eyes and muttered insults. *She's done for*, Kyra had thought with a frown.

Yet Juniper had kept going. Head ducked low and blush peeking through her veil, she had stepped out in front of the crowd with an awkward shuffle. The crowd paid no attention, laughing and leering at the frightened girl. There was no way for Juniper to redeem herself. Kyra found herself wishing she would.

Then the new princess had said:

"Hello. Nice to meet you all. I am Juniper."

The girl raised her veil off her face.

Juniper was more beautiful than a flower in the wind.

Ever since that day, she had been worshipped as a goddess walking amongst men.

The twin names of Sun's Child and Moon's Child had wandered their way into the dialect of the kingdom in the weeks after the presentation. It was simple. Kyra was the night, Juniper the day. It just made sense.

The sun was bright and warm, true, but for their world, it had greater meaning. It was believed that an ancient sunbeam hidden in the farthest reaches of the world was the creator of all light magic. And dark magic...that came from something worse.

Now, Juniper squatted down next to Kyra, careful not to touch the wet grass. She had her hair tied behind her head in a low knot, a few tightly wound curls popping out. She was wearing a long lavender dress that accented her dark skin and eyes. She looked like her mother but somehow seemed...softer. If her stepmother was chiseled out of hard stone, Juniper was made from warm charcoal.

Kyra's head lolled backward to meet Juniper's gaze. "You're late."

"Pity."

"You missed the sunrise."

"There will be more." Juniper smiled, though her heart did not look in it. "If there is one thing I have learned about the sun, it is that it rises every day whether or not I watch."

"Whatever. Why were you late?"

"A servant stopped me. Mother wishes for us to meet her in the throne room. Something important, I think, because your father will be there too," Juniper said, a rogue curl falling from her bun. There was no doubt about it; her sister was gorgeous. Kyra had known this from the moment they had met. Juniper was six and Kyra was seven when Juni's mom and Kyra's dad had first married. Whispers had abounded from the moment little Juniper had lifted her veil, whispers of how she was even more beautiful than the Queen herself. The whispers continued today, especially now that they were older. Juniper was going to turn seventeen in the summer, and Kyra would be eighteen in winter.

"Wouldn't want to keep our dear parents waiting, then." Kyra rolled her eyes and stood.

They began walking towards the castle doors, winding their way up the grassy hill and away from the river at its base. Kyra had not stepped foot in the river since a fateful day she remembered as clear as dawn.

Juniper bit her lip, staring at Kyra, who pretended not to notice. "Kyra, you have to remember to hold your tongue in there, alright? My mother is in a bad mood, so if you go in there and make her even more upset, I think she will...I think she will take it out on you."

"Good. I've gone without getting in trouble for far too long. About time to shake things up."

"Come on, promise to behave? Please?"

"Don't think I will."

"Does your stubbornness have no end?" Juniper asked.

"Fine. I promise to be a good little girl. Only because you're asking so nicely, Sun's Child." Kyra felt the corner of her mouth quirk up.

Juniper returned the smile. "Thank you."

"So whatta you reckon this is all about?" Kyra said as they passed through a small doorway on the side of the stables. Horses neighed and whinnied as they passed, tossing glaring looks at Kyra. Last week, she may or may not have devised an elaborate plan that involved attempting to train them to buck off the Queen as she rode the next day. Unfortunately, it didn't work.

The sisters exited the stables, entering a connecting stone hallway that led to the throne room.

Kyra wondered if maybe her dad and the Queen were splitting up. She said a quick prayer hoping it would come true. It would make her life a whole lot easier. Every birthday, shooting star, and four-leaf clover wish came down to the same thing every year: The Queen out of her life. For good.

"I think it is something bad," Juniper said, dark eyes trained on the ground. "Something about you and me."

"What do you mean, 'something about you and me?' We're perfect angels!" Kyra batted her eyelashes to emphasize her innocence.

"I do not know if that is true. For you at least."

"Rude."

"All I really know is that Mom is upset at something...and it is most likely you."

"Can't argue with that one," Kyra said glumly. A memory flashed before her of Callista screaming at her when she knocked over her waterglass a few days ago. She shuddered, Callista's screams echoing in her ears like the roaring thunder from last night.

"We are here. Stand up straighter, smile, and...." Juniper opened the door to the throne room, beaming like a ray of sun.

Kyra put on her own half-smile as she walked forward. The throne room was her least favorite place in the castle, partially because it was so fancy, and partially because it was where you could most often find Callista.

The room was long and wide, with a red carpet rolled out in the middle. Gold and red flags decorated the ceiling. Guards in cleanly pressed uniforms stood on either side of the long carpet, standing at attention. Kyra often wondered if they were statues, as they never seemed to move. Then one would blink or twitch slightly and she'd jump, sprinting down the rest of the carpet. Though one time, she had accidentally punched a guard in the face when he startled her...yet another time she had disappointed the Queen.

Marble swirled across the floor, gleaming like sunken treasure as it clouded over the ground. Portraits lined the walls, one for each ruler of the country since its founding. They all stared down in disgust at Kyra. She stuck out her tongue at one that looked especially rude, an old man with a sour expression and a tall crown. Her great-great-great-great something or other.

The thrones were gilded in gold and scarlet, sunlight and blood. Aazagonia was founded through war; it was only fitting that their nation be reminded of it where their rulers sat.

On one throne sat Kyra's father, a tall and sturdy man with smile lines around his eyes and tousled blonde hair that looked grey in some lights (though she would never dare say that to him.) Normally, he would send a warm smile toward Kyra when they locked eyes, but now, he just stared down at her in disdain. She shrunk into herself more and hastily looked away. Gone from his eyes was any promise of home. They resembled Callista's wicked gaze more and more each day.

He didn't love the Queen. That Kyra knew. But she also knew fear could corrupt quicker than love. Behind the cold stare, Kyra could almost find echoes of the man she had known. The father who had watched the fireflies dance with her so long ago. But maybe that man was gone for good. Maybe she was searching for a ghost long passed.

Queen Callista was draped across the other throne like a snake perched on a rock, bathing in the sun. Her crown was nestled in her curls, shining in the light from the window in the ceiling. The skylight above wrought warped lines of sun across her neck, accenting a silver necklace glittering across her high collarbone. People all around said Callista was the most beautiful thing they had ever seen. Kyra was less kind. She had reason to be.

"Daughters," Callista began, eyes shining. Kyra thought, *I am not your daughter.*

"Mother," Juniper said, bowing her head slightly. "Father."

Kyra felt a quick jab in her rib cage and knew Juniper meant for her to give them a greeting.

"Hey." Kyra tossed up a little wave.

A flicker of annoyance crossed the Queen's face before it turned back to stone. She said, "You must be curious as to why I called you here today."

"A little," Kyra said easily, not intending it to sound sarcastic, though most of what she said came off that way. Disappointment practically emanated off of Juniper at the moment. Knowing this, Kyra tried to keep her mouth shut from then on.

"Kyra, your father and I have decided to send you away to the Winter Palace. For good."

3

The Huntsman

"Under different circumstances, we might have allotted you harbor here..." The Queen hesitated. "But I understand you were caught stealing crown jewels from my closet."

"I did not!" Kyra growled, heat flaring inside her. She would scam, she would disrupt, even steal—but she would never be accused of something she didn't do. Lying was her worst enemy. "I live in a castle, for sunbeam's sake, why would I need to steal?"

"One of the maids saw you doing it." Callista's eyes were slits. "Why would she lie about such a thing?"

Kyra bet it was that lying snitch Andrea from the upper chambers. Andrea always hated Kyra for making such a mess—and there was that one incident with a hornet's nest—but Kyra had never thought Andrea would frame her for something she didn't do.

"Father!" Kyra pleaded, already done trying to plead to her wretch of a stepmother. "You believe me, don't you? I don't lie! Juniper, tell them I'm not lying!"

Juniper froze at the mention of her name like a deer caught in headlights.

"Don't." Her father spoke up. "Callista found the jewels in your nightstand."

Callista raised a necklace from her pocket, making it gleam in the light from above. The necklace sneered down at her, holding her fate between gilded green jewels.

Eight words from her father hurt more than any of Callista's eloquent and thought out words. She wasn't special. Her future seat on the throne would eventually be passed over to Juniper, of course, she knew that, but never in her wildest nightmares could she believe they would send her away for stealing jewels. Ugly jewels, at that! This had to be some sick joke.

The look in her father's eyes told her it wasn't.

Silence enraptured the room. Kyra stared up at them with wide eyes. She couldn't believe what she was hearing. Her own parents were sending her across the world. She didn't cry. Didn't shed a single tear. All she did was stare up at them, meeting their eyes. So they knew what exactly they were sending away.

Juniper spluttered beside her, not knowing what to say.

"You mean to tell me," Kyra began, voice steady and slow, "that you're sending me across the world because I stole jewels? Which I didn't even do! Father, mother—" —calling Callista *Mother* physically hurt her, but Kyra suspected it hurt Callista more—"You can't be serious. Obviously, I'm a wreck sometimes. Don't get me wrong, I get that part, but why are you sending me away?"

Her dad sighed, "If you're sent away for a time, maybe you'll learn to be less of a 'wreck' as you call it. It's not even that you're a wreck, it's just that—"

"What? You don't love me?" Kyra calmly asked. "You hate your daughter so much that you would send her as far away as you can?"

Callista's mouth turned up at the corners. Kyra wouldn't have called it a smile, so much as a predator's smirk before landing the kill. The Queen said, "Of course we love you." Never had a lie been so obvious.

Kyra shook her head in disbelief. "When am I leaving?"

"The servants have already packed your things."

Her jaw dropped. *Now?* No heartfelt goodbyes, no reminiscing, nothing? She clenched her fist at her side, speechless.

Juniper spoke suddenly. Her voice was quiet. "I am going with her."

Callista seemed taken aback by her daughter's brazenness for a moment. But only for a moment. Regaining her composure, the Queen said, "Very well." Kyra noticed something off about her tone. She sounded deliriously happy, like a woman whose every dream was being accomplished. But why would she be overjoyed that her favorite was being sent away? None of this made any sense.

The King and Queen shared a look. The King said at last, "I don't see why not. If the girls want to be together, that's fine by me."

Kyra could see Callista clamp her mouth shut in a silent gloating. Her gaze roved over the two of them, catching on Juniper. Kyra took in her loveliness and knew the Queen was watching her, too, unsaid words echoing between them. People whispered that Juniper was more beautiful than the Queen, yes, but they also whispered that Callista was jealous of her daughter's looks. Kyra watched in curiosity as Callista's small smile returned. She said, "Then it's decided. Both girls will go to the Winter Palace."

Juniper cast a worried look over at Kyra, but all she felt was...off. Something was wrong. Why was the Queen acting so strange? Then again, she *was* a wicked tyrant snake woman, so there was that. Can't try to understand evil. Kyra held back a snicker.

"Come say goodbye, girls," Kyra's father said; a kind look in his eyes as he stood up with open arms. Kyra and Juniper raced over to him, and he enveloped them in a tight squeeze.

"Goodbye, father," Kyra whispered into his chest, though she wasn't sure he could hear her.

Callista stood when the hug was done. Juniper walked over to her and put her arms around her. The Queen snaked her thin arms around her daughter, though it looked to be a hug with little affection. However, when Callista stared at a space just past Juniper's head, a space that held a portrait on the wall of Juniper as a small child, holding a pink lily in her hand, her eyes widened slightly. She smiled.

Kyra caught eyes with Callista as the latter pulled away from the hug. The odd look was still on the Queen's face, and it made Kyra take a step backward against her will.

The Queen sat down hurriedly, as if to ward off any advances at a hug from Kyra. As if. Kyra would sooner jump off a cliff into a pit of venomous snake-sharks.

"Goodbye, Kyra. I am sure we will meet again soon. Perhaps we will both be changed for the better." The Queen gave an eerie smile. A tilt of the head. Then nothing.

Okay, what? Did the Queen just—did the Queen just *apologize* to Kyra? Her whole world felt like it was spinning off its axis, as if gravity had somehow been upended.

Kyra blinked. "Totally. I hope so, too. Changed for the better and all that. Yeah. Later," said Kyra hurriedly, before reaching out to give her mother a shake.

As Callista reached a slender hand out to Kyra's, Kyra took the opportunity to see the necklace on her stepmother's collar. She could see it clearer now. It was a silver chain, with a charm of a raven. Kyra froze. The raven was a symbol of the fae. The Dark Ones. The ones who had created dark magic, who lived in the darkness of the North Forest. Ravens were associated with the fae, but why would her mother have a necklace of it? Kyra narrowed her eyes. Maybe it was a fashion statement. Yes, that had to be it. A hideous fashion statement. Yet it still made her blood run cold, as if freezing water had been injected into her very veins and arteries, filling Kyra up until her whole body was nothing but a statue of ice.

She forced herself to move, one foot in front of the other, away from the towering thrones of her ancestors.

With a final nod at her father, Kyra began walking down out of the throne room, Juniper right by her side.

She didn't look back, but somehow she could feel the gaze of her stepmother boring into her as she exited the palace. The watchful eyes of all the portraits seemed to follow her, too, as if remarking on how much of a disgrace she was. Holding her head high, she internally stuck her tongue out at each and every one of those pretentious old guys frozen in time.

The sun was starting to set as the two girls walked out into the courtyard of the palace. The promise of dusk had awashed the stones surrounding the hedges in orange-yellow light. Light from the sun's rays had melted onto the cobblestone floor, coloring everything gold. Her shadow was the only darkness.

Kyra glanced up at Juniper, who was standing a little ways away, hugging herself tight and staring at the floor.

"Juni," Kyra said. "You don't need to come with me. I'll be fine on my own. I always am."

Juniper gave a weak smile, eyes never leaving her own still shadow on the floor. "You would not make it five feet without me." The smile disappeared as quickly as it came. Kyra swallowed hard and stepped away, not knowing what to say. She still had that odd feeling, like something was horribly wrong. Nothing should've been wrong. In fact, she realized, she should be happy! She was getting away from the awful castle at last, away from the Queen and responsibilities, too. Yet something deep within her understood the wrongness of it all. The raven necklace flashed before her eyes.

They waited in silence, making their shadows into warped versions of themselves, stretched long and short and penetrating the orange light of dusk.

Finally, a carriage pulled up around the hedges, black and haunting. Dust rolled around its wheels, flanking the horse's legs. Dust was the foundation of Aazagonia, as well as its downfall. Many a storm had laid waste to the villages, yet one could not simply pick up a kingdom and move it. So on dust the kingdom stood.

The carriage had luggage piled on top, so Kyra took a wild guess that it was the one taking them to the Winter Palace. She got inside, not even sparing a look back at the castle.

Kyra let her mind wander back to the weird raven necklace on the Queen's neck. She felt the hair on her arms stand up, goosebumps running down them. It was from the cold, she told herself, not because she was scared. She was not afraid of anything, let alone a stupid necklace. Just 'cause it symbolized the Dark Ones meant nothing. Besides, for all she knew, the fae weren't even around! Nobody had seen one in years! They were up in the cold North as always. She rubbed her arms and the goosebumps fell away.

They sat in silence as the carriage rumbled down the path. Kyra started tapping her fingers impatiently, swinging her legs left and right. She sat up, trying to get a look at the driver to no avail.

"It has been two minutes. Could you try to sit still?" Juniper asked.

"That goes against my very being." Kyra jumped up on the seat, balancing best she could. Juniper shot her a look, eyebrows still raised, just as they hit a bump and Kyra went flying, banging her head on the roof of the carriage before falling into a heap on the floor. The two dissolved into fits of laughter, and Kyra didn't even notice when the carriage rolled to a complete stop.

"Uh-oh." Kyra sat up. "You think it was 'cause of me?"

"Do not be vain," Juniper said. "Not everything is about you."

"Everything should be."

"Oh, shut up."

"Never."

Just then, the door to the carriage swung open, and Kyra was face to face with....a boy. Maybe her age, perhaps a little younger. He had caramel skin and almond-shaped eyes that slanted upwards prettily. Xiangshian eyes, the kingdom far south. He wore a simple green long-sleeve, with a brown leather vest and black pants. A knife hung at his waist, silver and sharp. The garb of a huntsman, not a driver. Kyra met his eyes. She decided to find out.

"Are you the one who was driving? You look barely old enough," she huffed.

"Yeah." The boy stood awkwardly, hunched as if trying to shrink into himself. "I'm sixteen." Not old enough to be a huntsman, then, but he could've been an apprentice.

"Goes to show you that a sixteen-year-old should not be entrusted to drive. That bump almost made me fly into the next kingdom over."

"Sorry," he said. "You're the princess. Kyra."

"And you are?"

Silence ensued. Kyra watched as the boy shoved a lock of hair out of his eyes, gaze darting to Juniper. His mouth dropped open a bit as he saw her, and Kyra smirked. The Sun's Child usually had that effect on people.

Kyra said, crossing her arms and lifting her chin, "If you would stop gawking at my sister, you could tell me your name and why you stopped driving."

"I'm Luca Takahashi." The boy—Luca—blinked rapidly as if faced with a bright light.

"Well, you know me."

"I am Juniper." Juniper nervously stuck out her hand.

Luca shook her hand, then slid it back down to his side hurriedly. "I'm supposed to take you into the forest. The Queen wants you two to see something," Luca said, gesturing out behind him. Kyra then noticed the tall green trees that reached high above, the moss and dirt-covered ground, and the smell of the crisp air and foliage.

The Southern Forest. Her favorite place in the world. The gentle wind beckoned her through the leaves of the tallest trees, as if inviting her to adventure. She breathed in the brisk night air and stepped out of the carriage. Anything that needed to be seen there surely couldn't harm her. Juniper cautiously stepped out behind her.

"Should we trust this boy?" Juniper murmured to Kyra.

Luca stood a little ways away, scratching the back of his head. He took the knife out of his scabbard, fumbled with it for a second, then let it drop.

Kyra grinned as he awkwardly grasped at it. "It's safe to say we're gonna be ok."

Narrowing her eyes, Juniper nodded slowly. Luca's gaze was trained on the forest, the same green as his shirt. It made his eyes look even darker. Almost black. She watched as he started walking into the treeline, not even waiting to see if they'd come. It was odd that he didn't ask for them to follow. Then again, maybe he didn't need to.

Luca trailed his way into the dark, a speckled ant against a backdrop of green. He looked incredibly small next to the trees.

"I mean, come on. He looks harmless!" Kyra said, already taking a step forward.

Juniper's gaze was thoughtful; her eyes dark. "Looks can be deceiving, Moon's Child."

They followed him into the forest as day slipped into night.

4

Into the Wild Wood

Kyra had never seen someone so horrifyingly incompetent in all her life.

Luca stumbled his way through the forest, tripping over almost every branch they passed. He dropped the poor knife in his hand four times (Kyra had been counting) and yet, Juniper was still voicing her worries about the boy to Kyra.

Every. Two. Seconds.

"He is going to kidnap us," Juniper said for the millionth time, eyes large.

Kyra sighed. "He's not gonna kidnap us."

"But what if he does?"

"Then we get kidnapped."

Juniper stared at her with an open mouth, then clamped it shut.

Kyra walked up next to Luca. Maybe she could get some more information out of him.

"Where are you taking us?" Kyra asked.

"I, uh, we're almost there." Luca's gaze shifted to a nearby tree.

He almost tripped over yet another log, but Kyra quickly reached an arm out to stop him from falling. Luca looked up at her in surprise. "Thanks."

"You don't get off that easily. Now you owe me a life debt," she joked.

Luca didn't reply. He just shook his head. Was that the beginning of a smile she saw?

"How much further?" Juniper called from behind.

"We're here," Luca said, giving a quick nod to the surroundings.

Kyra looked around. It was nothing spectacular, just the same old trees and plants. There was nothing that the Queen would make them get out of the carriage to see. The forest was completely dark now; night had fallen in its full fury. She had always liked nighttime better than day. *Moon's Child.*

She wondered if the Northern Forest looked like this, all quiet and serene. If it really was where the faeries lived, she pictured it as wild and dangerous. She rolled her thumb over her fingers, thinking that she would like to go there sometime. Juniper often told her that she was attracted to madness, to danger and risk. Kyra loved that label. It made her seem more of a hero than she was. Kyra was a million things. She was reckless and stubborn and dim and maybe even a little brave.

But she was no hero.

She *was* drawn to things that weren't safe. Something deep within her always was, as sure as rivers flowing to the sea. It was an ache within her that longed for more, that was hungry for things that were beyond her understanding. An ache that her sister said would kill her one day if she wasn't careful. *Let it come,* Kyra thought. *I am more than ready.*

She breathed out and could see the wisp of cold breath as it disappeared in the forest, whirling white against a backdrop of black. As the breathtaking beauty drew Kyra into a stupor, she let everything else—her worries, her thoughts, her memories—fall away like that breath. It was as if everything she had been thinking was suspended in the air before her eyes.

Caught up in all of this, Kyra didn't even realize that Luca was no longer by her side.

She didn't realize much of anything until she heard Juniper's scream. It almost sounded as if Juniper was singing. A bird caught in a snare.

Kyra whirled around as soon as she heard it, a waterfall of blood roaring in her ears.

Juniper was standing as if frozen, mouth open in an unfinished scream. Luca stood over her, wielding his knife right above her heart. Ready to plunge it deep within.

Kyra's mind begged her to move, but her legs stayed frozen.

The moonlight fell on them through the trees in blades. They looked like something out of a storybook, a tall tale. Not out of real life. This couldn't be happening. Kyra blinked as if that would make it go away. When it didn't disappear and the nightmarish figures still remained before her, Kyra sprang into action.

Before she could punch the living daylights out of Luca, however, his knife clattered to the floor. Luca crumpled, falling to his knees. Juniper collapsed, too, tears watering the ground like rain.

"What," Kyra said, able to form words now, "just happened."

She stormed forward, grabbing Luca by the collar and yanking him to his knees. Moonlight framed his freckles. Little stars amidst a sea of fear.

He said, voice rough and hitched, "She made me do it."

Kyra dropped him, and he fell to the floor, arms banging on rock instead of cushioning his fall. The boy was not skilled in the art of protecting himself. Not like Kyra was.

"She?" Juniper looked incredibly small on the floor, tears still falling. "Who is *she*?"

Luca looked Kyra in the eyes for the first time since they had met. "The Queen."

The words struck Kyra like a boulder.

Callista...her stepmother...the Queen.

"Liar!" Juniper yelled. Kyra couldn't recall the last time she had heard Juniper raise her voice.

"I-I'm not. I'm n-not lying," Luca said, hiccupping between words as tears fell fast.

"My mother would never enlist someone to murder me!"

Luca's face twisted in misery. "She-she said...she said you would get in this carriage, and I would take you out into the forest and kill you. I'm only the huntsman's apprentice. I've never killed a person before! I couldn't do it...I couldn't kill you. You have to understand. I never wanted to hurt you. I don't want to hurt anything, ever. My parents need the money. That's all. I-I'm so, I'm so sorry!"

Kyra didn't fully register his words. She breathed steadily and tried to tally up the facts. Her parents had been planning on sending her away. Fact. But the Queen had actually wanted to kill her. Also fact. But why would the Queen want this? Her daughter's death?

Then it struck her.

Of course the Queen wouldn't care if they died. Of course. Kyra was nothing but a hindrance and a wreck. It made sense that the Queen would want her gone. Juniper's beauty was something the Queen had long been jealous of, and the girl was the spitting image of the Queen's dead husband. It made sense. It made Kyra's stomach roil, but from a logical perspective, it made perfect sense. Kyra couldn't bear to think of it in any other way. At least she had been right; at least Luca was the huntsman's apprentice. At least she had that.

"Get up. You're sniveling like a baby." Kyra extended her hand out to Luca. He took it and she launched him up.

"You're not angry with me?" Luca asked.

"Uh, why?"

"Because I tried to kill you," Luca said, eyebrows scrunched together. "Because you almost died."

"Right! I guess I'm a little peeved at that."

"Peeved?"

"*Peeved?*" Juniper shrieked in hysteria.

"Peeved," Kyra agreed and began pacing. "It's not your fault the Queen is a monster. Anyone would have done the same in your place, except we got lucky that you're a decent human being." Then she wondered...the Queen wouldn't have entrusted just anyone to kill her daughters, especially not the huntsman's *apprentice*. She would have wanted someone experienced. So why send a weakling like Luca? That didn't make sense, not at all.

It struck Kyra then that she had been very close to death. Luca having a heart was simply a stroke of luck. If the Queen wanted them dead, that was going to be very hard to get around. Callista had an army, a kingdom, even, at her disposal. She started thinking of where she and Juniper could go, and oh, right *Juniper*...

"How are you doing?" Kyra asked Juniper, bending down next to her sister from where she sat on the floor, curled up into a ball like a scared kitten.

Juniper wiped the tears from her eyes with trembling hands. "I have seen better days."

"Shake it off," Kyra said, and Juniper stood. Kyra immediately realized that wasn't the best thing to say because hot anger flared in Juniper's eyes. Hey, at least she wasn't crying anymore.

"Did you just tell me to *shake it off*? Our own mother is trying to have us killed! How are you not upset? What are we going to do? We have nowhere to go! I almost died a few minutes ago, andifyouthinkforonesecondIammgoingtoshakeitoff—"

"With all those brains of yours, you'd think you'd understand that speaking requires breathing. Slow. It. Down."

Juniper stopped talking, harrumphed, and crossed over to Luca while Kyra began pacing again, her mind once again turning to how they were going to get out of this, if there even was a way. Had her father been in on it as well...? Nope. Not going there. Too much to unpack.

Hearing Juniper and Luca conversing, though, gave Kyra something to focus on instead.

"We'll need a horse..." Luca was saying, "We can't go back to the carriage. The Queen will be looking out for that. It has the royal emblem. We—"

"We?" Kyra spun on her heels to face him. She stalked up to him, pointing her finger in his face. "*We* will not be going anywhere. Juniper and I will figure this out on our own. You can just...scram. I don't know. Run along. Shoo." Kyra waved her hands away.

"We cannot send him off on his own! If the Queen finds out that he did not kill us, she will kill him too!" Juniper exclaimed.

Kyra mock smiled. "And how's that my issue, exactly?"

"We cannot leave him at the mercy of the Queen!" Juniper looked horrified.

Kyra shot a quick glance at Luca, who was watching the exchange with a trembling lip. He looked like a fluffy baby bunny just hearing a curse word for the first time. How was this guy in training to be a huntsman? If Kyra ever made it back to the castle, you know, without the ruler wanting to kill her, she was going to have a serious word with the huntsman in charge.

Kyra said, putting a comforting hand on Luca's shoulder, "I guess I was a little harsh. Luca, you can come with, no problem. Just promise not to try to kill us again, 'kay? Otherwise we'll have a problem."

Luca grinned, though it wobbled. "Promise."

"Now tell me your amazing plan."

"I was thinking we could get a couple of horses and flee to a different kingdom. Like Maiike or Xiangshu. Somewhere where the Queen can't find us," Luca said, looking out over the forest. What lied beyond beckoned with equal daunting and hope. Hope for a new life, free of the Queen's wrath.

"So we flee. And then what? We live the rest of our lives as muskrat farmers?" Kyra said, annoyed.

Luca said, "That's really not a thing."

"Okay, fine, what about cows? Wanna be a cow herder until you're seventy?" Kyra crossed her arms. "Wanna live on a conjoint farm with me until you die of boredom or me strangling you?"

"I like cows," Juniper piped in with a weak smile. "They are rather cute."

"Is that really what you took away from that?" Luca asked.

A plan was forming swiftly in Kyra's mind, and though her plans were rarely good, this one seemed like it might work. Bits and pieces of the puzzle were slowly coming together like clockwork. And if it was clockwork in her mind, then the midnight bell was ringing loudly as her idea resonated inside. *Time for a heck of a miracle,* she thought.

"We'll find a horse. Ride to a completely different kingdom across the world. Then go our separate ways and lie low for a few months. Juniper can be a cow herder, Luca can be a professional annoyance, and I'll marry a hot prince who lives in the jungle fighting monkeys."

"Or something like that." Luca was grinning now. Kyra liked it way better when he was smiling than when he looked like he was going to pass out. The smile was a little lopsided on the end. Like a half-moon rising.

"I shall herd cows *and* find a handsome prince, thank you kindly. I pass on the jungle monkeys, however," Juniper added. "But where will we find a horse?"

Echoing through the trees came a miracle.

A horse's footsteps could be heard on the mossy floor, click-clacking on rock and dirt. The sound of salvation. With this horse, they had that sweet promise that was a little bit of hope.

The first thing Kyra noticed was the horse itself. Its mane was black as rushing rivers at night, with a single streak of auburn through its back. The streak shone bright like embers cooling on a fire, and Kyra imagined it as the horse of a great ghost king, fit for the fae of legends.

The second thing she noticed was the boy.

He, simply, looked like a distraction.

The rider had sharp features, and an amused expression, as if the whole world had some inside joke with him. His hair was black like the hours of the night when the only people who were awake were people up to no good. He was wearing simple clothes and looked to be about her age or a little older. She noticed that his lips were moving and was torn back into reality. The distraction had already distracted.

"What are you staring at?" The boy was saying, looking down at her with a raised eyebrow.

"I'm not staring!" Kyra scowled.

"You most certainly were staring," said the rider.

"I could say the same thing about you."

"I'll tell you right now that I wasn't staring at you. And if I was it was only because you're pointing that knife at me." The boy shrugged calmly.

She hadn't even realized she was still holding onto Luca's knife. She tossed it at the huntsman, who caught it after a few seconds of fumbling. Good, at least he didn't impale himself, though that wouldn't be too bad, either. She could hear Juniper's voice in her head saying, *We do not hope for impalement, Kyra.*

"I wasn't staring either, is that clear?" Kyra said, swallowing hard.

"Crystal." The rider kept his grin.

Another boy came into the clearing then, this one with a blue-sky smile and tan skin no stranger to the sun.

Kyra couldn't shake the feeling that she had seen him before. His clothes were more elegant, a white flowy long-sleeve and red jacket with black pants. Clothes that would be seen on someone higher up in a court. Kyra wondered who these two people were and why they were all alone in the forest. Then again, they were probably wondering the same thing about her, Juniper, and Luca. The newcomer looked at the black-haired rider, then said, "Oh, Cal, there you are. I thought I lost you." He looked around quizzically at Kyra and the others. "Hey-o. Cal, who are your new friends?"

Cal. The black-haired boy's name was Cal. An annoying name for a pestering boy.

Cal shrugged. "Not sure. They were just standing here as I rode through. The crazy girl in the front here was waving a knife at me."

"I was not—" Kyra began, but was cut off by the blond rider.

"Don't wave a knife at my servant! That's awfully rude, you know," the blond boy said angrily. "Do you know who I am?"

"Do I strike you as someone who cares? You must have read me wrong. Come on guys, let's get out of here," Kyra said, and turned to Juniper and Luca, who were watching the whole exchange with wide eyes.

Juniper did not wrench her gaze from the wavy-haired boy, gaping in silence.

Kyra shook her head, exasperated. Sure, the boy was handsome, but there was no need to give up that card quite yet. And then Kyra realized the stare went beyond acknowledging his looks.

The look on Juniper's face was the look of recognition. That was not the look someone gave to a stranger. As if from a half-remembered dream, Kyra heard a lullaby that her real mother sang to her long ago. *In dreams we find our hopes, our fears, the lives that we left behind.*

"That's Prince Julian of Maiike," Juniper whispered, so only Luca and her could hear.

Oh. *That* Prince Julian. *Sunbeam above*, Kyra chastised herself. His kingdom was the richest in the whole world, allied with her own kingdom for as long as she could remember. That was why he had looked so familiar. They had met on many occasions from the time they were little. Her father had once told her that would be the man she would've married, if Aazagonia hadn't fallen from its former glory. Now, Prince Julian was going to marry some other princess, and Aazagonia's alliances had faded, along with its wealth. While once Aazagonia was a kingdom built upon the gold and riches of their ancestors, now it was a memory of a time long forgotten. A time of great wealth for Aazagonia...and also great magic. *Magic.* Why did her mind always return to that? She sometimes imagined she could feel it in the rays of the sun, could touch it in the damp grass...could hear it somewhere below the castle, where she swore something dark and old lurked.

"Prince Julian's parents would report us to the Queen," Kyra said quickly and quietly, "We can't let him know who we are."

"What if he remembers you?" Luca asked.

"From what I remember of him, he won't." As if supporting her point, Julian distractedly ran his horse into a tree with a dopey-looking smile.

Juniper nodded, her eyes still trained on the prince.

"But what if?" Luca asked. "You two aren't very ordinary."

"Oh, really?" Kyra's voice dripped in sarcasm, thinking of the past hour's events. "I wasn't aware!"

She then turned back to face Julian and Cal, who were both staring quizzically. Cal had jumped down off his horse and was giving a hand to Julian. Julian tossed a look at Luca, quick and unamused, before his gaze landed on Juniper. His jaw dropped a little before he composed himself, raking one hand through his blond curls.

"Sunbeam above," he said. "You are as beautiful as every pattern on a butterfly's wing." Julian crossed over to Juniper, bowing deep and low. When he came up, he had Juniper's hand in his and planted a slight kiss on it. "As beautiful as a princess."

Kyra dug her fingernails into her hand to keep from snickering. The irony was too much. She saw out of the corner of her eye that Cal was watching as she hid the laugh, and he had his head cocked in question. Kyra forced it down once she saw him looking.

Luca nudged her in the ribcage, murmuring, "They have horses."

Oh. Right. The plan. The distractions were well on their way to distracting.

This was better than she had hoped for...if Juniper could just charm Julian enough, they might be willing to give up the horses. Kyra wasn't sure Juniper could do that, though. The girl's acting skills were decidedly below par.

"Thank you," Juniper was saying to Julian. "Uh, that's very considerate of you. If I were a princess—which I am not."

"What my sister means to say is you aren't so bad yourself," Kyra jumped in.

"Sister?" Cal asked. His gaze made her uncomfortable, like he was looking into her very soul. If he was, she supposed he would see a heck of a lot of stolen pastries and darkness. But mostly the pastries. She called it a 4:1 ratio of pastries to darkness in her soul.

"You two don't look alike," Julian said, looking between Kyra and Juniper. It was true. The two girls were night and day. Yet another aspect of their nicknames come to haunt them. Juniper was all sweet, heart-shaped face and dark skin, while Kyra was all...gangly. Julian took this in, then said, "Wait a second. Do I know—"

"We're step-siblings," Kyra interjected, not wanting him to continue down that path, and she realized her voice was a little too enthusiastic and loud. She lowered it a notch before continuing, "Different parents. My mom died when I was little, her dad died when she was little, and now we're here! A happy, happy family," *Our mom is trying to kill us, and our dad's imprisoned.* "So beyond happy!" *Please don't remember us, oh please...*

"Yes, very happy!" Juniper tried to smile, but it looked more like she was going to throw up than grin. "The happiest of all happies! If you looked up 'happy family' in a dictionary, our picture is surely beside it!"

"That's cool," Julian said, looking distracted. "Did I mention I'm a prince?"

"Once or twice," muttered Luca truthfully. Kyra elbowed him in the gut.

Julian took no notice of Luca doubling over in pain. "Well, I am. Prince Julian of Maiike, and this is my servant, Calais. Cal, shake their hands for me." Julian light-heartedly punched him in the arm. As Cal went to shake Luca's hand, Julian said to Juniper, "It's pretty cool. Cal does anything I want; it's what you get when you're a prince. Like your own personal lapdog. Except he doesn't bark. That'd be pretty cool if he barked. I guess that's rude of me to say he's a dog. In fact, he's more like a friend. He's a very good friend to me; I'm not sure I'm easy to put up with." He paused, latching onto Juniper's arm with intimacy. "Are we having a moment? I think we're having a moment."

Cal rolled his eyes as he stuck out a hand to shake Kyra's. She took his hand in his and tried not to make eye contact as she was oddly aware of the heat rising to her cheeks. Kyra squeezed his hand extra tight as a show of strength, smiling wide and fake. Cal just squeezed back equally as strong. Taking notice of the fact that ever since she had touched him, electricity seemed to be frying her inside out, she quickly tried to bring her focus back to the plan.

"We need horses," Kyra blurted. All eyes turned to her.

"That's such a perfect coincidence," Jules said, eyes lighting up with excitement. "We have horses!"

"Any way we could take them?" Luca asked.

"Take them? I dunno about that...I need them to get back home...but maybe you guys can ride with us to wherever you need to get to!" Julian said, as if that were the best idea in the world.

"That's a great idea!" Kyra said, enthusiastically urging him on. "A super fun field trip!"

"Absolutely not," Cal interjected. "No field trip. Jules, we don't know these people, and your mom wanted you to get back in time for the ball. She'll kill me if you aren't."

"Remember, Cal, I'm the prince, not you," Julian said, pushing back a lock of blonde hair. "And I say that they can ride with us. We'll need another horse, though. Unless someone wants to carry the small boy."

Luca sourly crossed his arms. "I'm not that small."

"Yes, you are, and it's adorable," Kyra shot back angrily. "And I don't think that will be necessary. As long as we walk back into town, you can buy us another horse and we'll be on our way!"

"Hold up, crazy," Cal said, holding up a hand for emphasis. "The prince isn't just going to *buy* you a horse. Do you have any manners?"

"Much more exciting things in life than manners. Plus, I was raised by a pack of dancing wolves. So I never got around to it."

"I have so many questions."

"Kindly direct them to the wolves."

Juniper miraculously got the hint that the conversation needed desperate saving. She said, "Will you buy us horses, please?" in her voice that sounded like if he didn't do as she said, she would burst into tears. Though that probably wasn't too far off from the truth.

"Sure, why not? Can't do much harm." Jules shrugged with an easy-going nod at her. Cal groaned.

Kyra darted a quick look of celebration at the others, silently doing a conga line in her head as she feigned indifference.

"Then let's go." Kyra gave a look of goodbye to the forest. It was not one of sadness.

She knew she would return soon.

5

Birdsong

"That's when I drove the sword right into the dragon's heart," Julian said proudly, "And since then, everyone calls me the Dragon Warrior. So everyone knows I'm the best at fighting. I have a good singing voice, too, but that comes less in handy than a sword when slaying dragons, don't you think?"

"I should think so," Juniper said shyly. Despite herself, Juniper was engrossed in the story. It sounded like something out of all the books she had read growing up, where dashing heroes adorned in silver and gold rescued princesses from evil witches or dragons. The kind with happy endings. The kind that Juniper knew would come her way soon, if only she kept hoping.

The group was walking to the village at the base of her castle. The town sat as if kneeling to the great towering palace, humble and meek in comparison. Juniper felt much the same.

Kyra, Luca, and Cal were walking ways ahead, squabbling over something or other. Juniper and Julian strolled behind them, one of Jules' hands resting on the horse's neck. He stroked lazy patterns in its mane, and Juniper desperately wished she wasn't afraid of the horse kicking or biting her so she could pet it, too. So she just watched it in an awed silence, watched as Julian the Dragon Warrior spoke of creatures and quests and things so beyond her world that she felt like she watched through glass.

Sometimes she felt like she watched the entire world through glass, separate and apart and revered like some goddess of old. Maybe things could've been different if she were more like everyone else. But she wasn't. She was *beautiful*. That's what people called her. She had come to despise that word more than anything else in the language. Beautiful meant no one cared what you said or did. Beautiful was its own type of cage that felt as if the bars were closing in on her with each passing day. Every time someone cooed at her, calling her that word, the cage pressed tighter. Beautiful. Not brave or smart or kind. If only the world could see beyond the glass. She could show them that she could be more if only they let her.

For now she allowed herself to be caught up in Julian's story. Juniper said, intrigued, "The prophecy you mentioned earlier? What did it foretell?" She had read up on prophecies recently and knew they were few and far between. Only the fae or dragons could give them, due to the powerful dark magic in their veins.

Julian seemed pleased that she was so invested in his story. "I dunno...my dad said it went like: 'A prince with the blood of silver and death will be the one to bring Cemeflient's dying breath.' Pretty cool, right? Cemeflient, that's the name of some ancient dragon or something. Sounds like a pretty lame enemy. Wish she was named 'Death Ultra Mega Knife' or something cooler."

"I think it very cool," Juniper said. Why couldn't she have a prophecy? One without dragons, of course. Maybe she could have a quaint destiny that involved a large library or a trip to the seaside.

"What about you? What's your family like? Your sister seems pretty lethal."

"Kyra is kind, in her own way. Once you get to know her, you shall see."

"I don't want to get to know her," Julian said, flashing her that lopsided smile. Something inside Juniper felt a slight tug.

"Of course," Juniper said, looking at her feet in disappointment. Of course Julian wouldn't want to be around them more. She shouldn't have wanted to be around him more, either. She was going to be on the run for who knew how long. Yet if that little tug inside her had its wish, she would never leave Julian's side again. *Dangerous, tugs are*, Kyra would say. *Lovely*, Juniper thought instead.

Jules cocked his head at her, eyes brighter green than the trees around them. He said, "I want to get to know *you*."

It was at that precise moment that Juniper fell hopelessly and utterly in love.

Fireworks ricocheted in her skull as pixies danced around her vision, and she knew at that moment that this must be what love felt like. Julian was a hero and a prince, and surely he was the one who would rescue her. Already she pictured a white and gold wedding where her dress was floor-length and his hair was gelled back.

Once the fireworks faded away, she realized that Julian was staring at her expectantly, and she had been gaping in shock for a solid two minutes. Sunbeam above, she must have appeared to be a nutcase.

"Are you okay?" Julian asked.

Juniper blinked at him, suddenly forgetting every word she had ever learned.

She was saved from having to say anything by Kyra shouting, "Hey, lovebirds, we're here!" She waved her arm for them to join her at the top of a hill, where the forest had melted away and left a dust-ridden plain. There sat Aazagonia, her beloved kingdom. She had lived there as both peasant and princess, and the people had been kind in both times. Juniper looked down from the top of the hill, the wind rustling her hair and threatening to pull her braid from its knot. A stray curl fell from its perch, and she hastily brushed it back into place. Messy hair meant an hour-long lecture from her mother. But her mother wasn't around then, was she?

The kingdom was awash in the darkness of night. Swirls of dust blanketed the sky with each gust of dry wind. The same old thatched houses and muddy farms opened their arms in welcome. But something was different. Every night before bed, Juniper had cast blessings over the citizens while she looked out the window of her room. The town had never looked like this. Light glowed gently in the windows of every house and was especially bright towards the castle. Bright, warm light that had to be candles...but why so many?

She walked up beside her sister, who was framed against the dark sky in moonlight, the rigid frame of a warrior. Her hair was blowing in the wind, but Kyra did nothing to brush it away. She just stared out at the town below with a stony expression. A vengeful expression. Juniper often wondered if she could knock on her sister's forearm and hear a clang of metal.

"I know a place we can get a horse quick," Kyra said, trudging down the hill.

"I do, too." Luca tried to match her pace.

"Swell! We're going to my place."

"Of course we are."

They made it off the grass and onto the familiar dirt path that Juniper and Kyra had treaded a million times after roaming in the forest. The days when the Queen didn't care about their whereabouts. Those days were few and far between, but Juniper treasured them. Days of sunlight and laughter in the trees, days that could've been normal if they had normal parents. You know, not the kind of parents that wanted to have them murdered. Juniper swallowed hard thinking about it, tears suddenly filling her eyes. She couldn't quite grasp it all. How could her mother, the one who had helped her when she had fallen, the one who had been there for her, how could she enlist someone to assassinate her?

She thought of the days when her mother had taught her to play the violin, when she would sit patiently by her side for hours on end to help her get it right. Juniper would play and play and the Queen would smile down at her like she was the light of the world. *You look so much like your father, Juni-tree.* In her heart of hearts, she would never understand why this was happening. When Luca had raised the knife high in the air, she had been frozen like an ice sculpture, unable to move. Feet planted firmly on the ground and mouth open in a silent cry. A real hero, starring in a noble, grand story of faeries and dragons, would silence the enemy with a look. A hero could fight for herself.

But Juniper had long ago accepted that she was not brave enough to be a hero like the ones she read about.

They entered Aazagonia in the dead of night, so Juniper wondered why there were so many candles lighting the town. She marveled at the sight as flames danced in the streets, casting flickering shadows everywhere she looked.

"Are you sure the horse stables will be open?" Luca asked. "It's midnight."

"I'm sure," Kyra answered, but she was clearly distracted. Juniper walked up next to her, keeping her voice low. She knew her sister despised any sign that her intricately crafted walls had cracks. Cracks that Juniper knew like the back of her hand.

"Are you alright?"

Kyra responded easily, "I'm always alright."

"Mhm."

"All this fire, all this light is weird. I've never seen Aazagonia like this. Something really big must've happened. Hey, you think the Queen died?" Flames danced in her sister's eyes. Something about it made Juniper shrink back. That, and the mention of her mother.

"No! I don't think she died. If she did, people would be rejoicing in the streets." The words felt like a betrayal. "It wouldn't be so...empty." Juniper shuddered as she looked around. Not a person was to be seen. Every wandering soul in the kingdom was gone like mist disappearing in sunlight.

"You're right. I'm sure there would already be songs composed celebrating the Queen's death. In fact, I ought to think of one myself. That could be a promising career for me. A travelling bard preaching the wretchedness of the Queen." Kyra smirked, and pulled her hood up. "Well, we're almost at the square. Put your hood on. I'm not sure you're aware, but you're pretty famous here, Sun's Child." She winked.

Juniper pulled her black cloak's hood up, thankful for the shield between her and any eyes that could be watching.

They passed an extra bright candle, and she could feel the heat of the fire on the back of her hand. Wanting to curl up beside the light but knowing she had a purpose, Juniper forged ahead. Every step, every second brought her closer to understanding why the world had turned upside down. Suddenly she got the feeling that she needed to say something to Kyra, to warn her or tell her good luck, but she wasn't sure what for. It was a nagging impulse that wouldn't go away as they entered the town square.

"Kyra?"

"Yeah?"

"Be...be careful. Do not do anything foolish."

A flash of concern crossed Kyra's face before melting away into a mocking grin. "Me? Do something stupid? Never."

Juniper had a feeling she was going to disregard those words in an instant.

A memory flashed through her mind, a memory of Juniper and Kyra in the great library of the castle. It was a place that had always made Juniper feel safe, with its towering shelves of books and its warm sunlight filtering in through the stained glass windows. The light had been a protector, illuminating the dusty air and separating shadow from shelf. Kyra had been sprawled across a table, complaining about being cooped up in there, but Juniper was perfectly content. Their mother had found them there, though, and had interrupted their perfect moment of peace. That was the memory. Sunlight and dusty shelves and the loud, angry shouts of her mother. She didn't know why that memory came to her. It made her shiver in the muggy air.

Their odd group rounded the corner and entered the square, past the familiar cobblestones and shops. Hope, she thought, was the way to happy endings. Hope for rescue. Their group could get a horse—and then be gone, whispers and rumors of long-forgotten princesses following them as they went.

And so, two princesses, a prince, a page, and a huntsman walked into the square. That sounded like the beginning of an awful joke she would never get the nerve to tell.

When she entered the square, she froze.

It was adorned in the same lights that decorated the town, oranges and yellows and reds lighting up the small area in bold colors. Even though it was the middle of the night, it almost looked to be a garish, warped version of day.

A huge crowd of people flocked in the center, all wearing shades of green—the mourning colors of Aazagonia. A stage was at the front of the square, across from where Juniper stood. Her heart jumped into her throat as she surveyed the area. The answer was obvious, wasn't it? It was obvious what was happening around her, but she couldn't think why. The dots wouldn't connect. The grievers, the candles, the green.

"It's a funeral," Kyra said slowly, a muscle in her jaw twitching. The only thing betraying her otherwise stony demeanor, the crack in the wall.

Juniper felt sick. Of course. It was a funeral...for them. She was supposed to be gone right now; the villagers were mourning *her*. Her breathing quickened as she closed her eyes in shock. She was being grieved before her eyes, because at that very moment, the entire world thought she was dead. Every person she had ever met, every stranger who had given her a quick smile, her friends from childhood, all were in this square, weeping and grieving for a girl not yet dead. It made her feel hollow and very alone. Almost as if she *were* dead.

She felt a light touch on her shoulder, a spot of warmth in the cold night. Julian. He said, eyebrows knitted together in concern, "Who died here? Did you know them?"

Still not able to speak, Juniper shook her head hastily. Julian's hand retracted, and with it, the warmth.

Kyra coughed, and when she spoke, her voice sounded as if nothing had happened. "Julian, hand over some gold coins. Luca, come with me. We're gonna go buy a horse. Juni, if you'd like to take our two new friends and pay your respects to, uh..." she paused, fumbling for words, "...to whoever passed on, now's the time."

Juniper nodded and joined the villagers adorned in green, not caring if Julian and Cal followed. By the time she looked back over at Kyra and Luca, they were gone.

She felt sorely out of place, with her lavender dress in a sea of forest-colored coats and gowns. The black cape around her shoulders helped her feel a little less inconspicuous, but she still couldn't shake the feeling that people were looking. As she joined the crowd, she heard Cal and Julian whispering to each other.

"It is not polite to speak during a funeral," Juniper chided.

"Sorry," said Cal, the page boy, and he looked it. "But...who is this for?"

As soon as the words left his mouth, Queen Callista entered the stage. Juniper had to fight to keep from gasping. Her mother was adorned in beautiful green silks, accenting her dark brown skin. Bright red lipstick was painted on her lips, standing out against the black of night. Beautiful in an inhuman sort of way. In a way that made her seem far off from the crowd, and from Juniper. That made it easier. She said a silent thank you that Kyra wasn't there to see their mother on the stage. Juni was pretty sure she would fist-fight her right there and then.

And though that would have been fun to watch, it wasn't the time.

She heard Julian suck in a breath as he saw Callista. "She's gorgeous." Then he turned and looked at Juniper, casting a quizzical look. "You know," he said, "I met the royal family a long time ago. There were two daughters. You look a lot like—"

Quickly cutting in, Juniper said, "I told you, you are not supposed to talk at funerals."

Her stepfather had entered a little ways behind the Queen, a dark hood shadowing his face and casting sunken bags under his eyes. She pulled her hood tighter over her face, hoping her parents wouldn't catch her eyes and recognize her.

And then, Callista spoke, breaking the spell of silence. "The death of my daughters has shaken me and my husband to our core."

"Woah, the princesses died?" Cal asked. "That's terrible."

"Awful," Jules said thoughtfully, his gaze still trained on Juniper with that suspicious look from a moment ago.

"Do not speak at—"

"Funerals. Got it." Julian did not try to speak again, but he still stared in question.

The Queen, after letting her words sink in, said, "It is a horrible thing to have not just one, but both of your children ripped from you at once." A silver tear trailed down her cheek. "I'd say it's the worst pain in the world. But, the people of Aazagonia are strong, and we will not let the death of our beloved princesses shake us. My husband and I will rule on through these dark times. Being that the king is too heartbroken to continue ruling, my title has now been promoted to sole monarch of the crown. I share the burden of these sorrows on my shoulders as I take responsibility for ruling from the king. It will be me alone through these trying times, as my husband is simply too full of grief at these tragic events. I am now your only ruler. Your new monarch. In these trying, dark times, it is comforting to know that the kingdom is in good hands. My hands."

A collective groan could almost be heard amongst the villagers.

Juniper's mother was now going to be the sole ruler of Aazagonia. The King was no longer going to rule...so this was why she had done what she did. To take the crown for herself. That was what she was after, in the end. Power. Juniper wanted to scream. Callista would not be a gracious regent.

"I am heartbroken, too, of course, but I have found the strength to go on. My coronation will be held at the Winter Palace, as all coronations of Aazagonia have been held for generations. I hope you all can find the light, too, as we piece together our shattered souls from the remains of our loss," Callista said, her face wracked with sadness. Juniper watched in shock. Sunbeam above, where did Juniper get her horrible acting skills from, as it was certainly not her mother.

But underneath the grief, she swore that her mother was smiling.

The Queen turned to exit the stage, and then a flash of gold and pink jumped up on the stage, candlelight illuminating her long-limbed figure. The figure stood with her hands clenched in fists by her side, her face a mask of fire and anger.

The Moon's Child.

Oh no.

6

Left Off Blazing

Kyra stared at her stepmother, hostility building in her with each passing second. Anger snaked up her spine, it boiled in her stomach, and it gnashed its red-hot teeth in her blood. Rage was a white flame flaring within her; it had been her guide since birth. It was a call stronger than any song, wind, or wish. Rage was her burden—the burden she bore with all the heat of every burning star above.

Callista was trying to rule Aazagonia for her own. The Queen was a tyrant, even when she didn't have full power of the crown. When she had shared it with Kyra's father, she still was a cruel and uncaring dictator. The king balanced her out; though he had faults of his own, he did not let Callista be unkind to the people. Kyra shuddered to think of what kind of ruler Callista would be without the king by her side.

And Kyra was not about to let that happen.

The Queen's face showed a flash of—was that approval—before dissolving back to its mask of seriousness. Kyra took a moment to wonder if she had got that trait from her. The trait of being able to mask what they felt by a look. Though they weren't blood related, some things could be taught. Kyra hoped that her stepmother had taught her nothing else.

"You're a liar!" Kyra shouted. She pulled her hood down for dramatic effect, her tangled gold hair spilling out in waves around her.

She heard the crowd of villagers gasp, murmurs echoing among them all.

Their Moon's Child raised from the dead. A ghost returned.

Callista sneered. It made her look reptilian. She didn't look surprised or even upset. She looked almost pleased. Yet her words did not match that look that she had of a conductor arranging the pieces of an orchestra, a director staging a play that was going perfectly as planned. "You cannot be standing before me."

"Well, I am, so hah," Kyra said tauntingly. That didn't sound all that impressive, so she added, "I'm harder to kill than you might think. Six lives. Like a cat." Kyra held her hands up to her face and gave a weak hiss.

The Queen's voice was a whisper, so that only Kyra could hear. "I see you have retained your utter stupidity, in being that a cat has nine lives, and you have only one." Callista said this as if she couldn't quite believe the low intelligence of her stepdaughter. Kyra remembered the day after she had flunked out of the kingdom's finishing school. *You cannot afford to be both ugly and a dunce,* the Queen had said with a sneer. *Choose one.* Callista murmured, "Juniper is alive as well, I take it. Is she...did she show signs of anything strange? Did you?"

Kyra didn't say anything.

A villager cried out, "Are you the real Princess Kyra?"

Kyra turned to the crowd, saying, "No. I'm a ghost." The villagers shrunk back, faces pale and wary. "Boo," Kyra wiggled her fingers. She looked out over the crowd and saw that this didn't strike them as funny as she thought it would. Kyra thought it was hilarious. She caught a glimpse of midnight-colored hair and raised eyebrows.

Cal. He was frozen in place, realization mixed with awe on his sharp features. She wondered what he thought of her, standing in front of them all, declaring herself the dead princess. She wondered if he even cared. Why would he? *Stupid,* she thought, *focus.* Juniper, Julian, and now Luca were standing beside him. They all looked at her like she was crazy. She slowly lowered her fingers from their jazz hands, rethinking her past few words. "Just kidding," she hastily added. "I'm Kyra, don't worry. No ghosts here."

The villagers all looked worried. Juniper looked like she was going to pass out.

Callista also turned to face the crowd, blood-red lips curled in a look of distaste. "Do not be alarmed," she said. "This girl before you is no more our beloved Princess than I. It is a faerie. One of the Dark Ones, trying to trick us all."

Whispers flew through the crowd like a harsh breeze. Kyra caught the words, 'dark one,' 'creature,' and 'fae.' *No.*

"I'm not a faerie!" Kyra exclaimed.

"She's lying," Callista said smoothly. "Of course a faerie would say that."

"You have got to be kidding me! If I was fae, would I do this?" Kyra said, her tone going high-pitched as she desperately tried to think of something to convince them.

Once, she had heard someone say that faeries were not flexible. Without thinking, she cartwheeled across the stage, her skirts flying around her. She almost knocked into the Queen before falling onto the floor in a heap. The Queen looked down on her in disdain and a little pity, as if wondering how her stepdaughter had been cursed with the intelligence of a walnut. Maybe she was a little smarter than a walnut. A cashew, perhaps?

The square was quiet for a few long moments, as if no one really knew what to say. One villager awkwardly clapped.

"Did you just...cartwheel?" Callista asked, genuinely sounding shocked. Her supposedly dead daughter showing up on the stage did nothing, but Kyra cartwheeling was the thing that had finally shaken her.

"I guess I did," Kyra said, as confused as her stepmother. Why the heck did she think that would prove she wasn't a faerie? It was an impulse, and Kyra finally understood what Juniper had been saying about recklessness all these years. She still wasn't very sure what the word meant. Juni had told her to look it up in the library, and Kyra had replied with a heated exclamation of the things she would rather do than read, like gouging out her eyeballs and homework.

"People of Aazagonia," Callista continued, looking once again unshaken, "This faerie is trying to win your trust...by acting like a fool, it seems. The late princess was quite a simple-minded imbecile at times...but this faerie is making a mockery of her memory." *Ouch,* Kyra thought with a grimace. The Queen said, "I shall have the King dispose of her quickly."

A shuffle of a lumbering mass made Kyra finally notice that someone else was on the stage with them.

Her father.

He looked disheveled, like the world was singing a song that he didn't know the words to—a melody off-tune. A sharp needle of pain sliced through Kyra's heart. This was the same man who had loved her fiercely her entire life. The same man who was now going to 'dispose of her quickly.'

He rushed to her, pulling a gleaming silver object from his side.

A sword. He was going to kill her. Her father was going to kill her, as Luca should have.

Kyra looked around quickly for something to defend herself,

barely able to rip her eyes from her father. Nothing presented itself. She was unarmed.

Willing herself not to be afraid, she stood tall. That was the last thing she wanted to be as she died. Afraid. She would be brave, so Juniper could go on.

Her dad's glazed, distant eyes met hers, and she saw something in him falter. They crinkled in the way that Kyra's did when she was met with a challenge that she could not beat. Though those were few and far between.

He spoke, and it drove the splinter in her heart further. He said it low, so that only she could hear, "You...you are not a faerie. You're my daughter. I would know my daughter anywhere. You have your mother's...your true mother's eyes." His voice broke, and with it, Kyra's heart. "Kyra."

"Father," she said, trying to cover up the quiver in her voice.

"Run," He said, face paling. He raised the sword up, and—

Kyra stumbled backward, running and leaping off the stage, and hitting the ground with a hard thump. She fell over onto the cobblestone floor, knees scraping it. She couldn't feel the hurt. It was all in her head, pounding and screaming at her to *run*. She picked herself up, taking off and sprinting across the square, not daring to look back.

"No!" She heard the Queen cry out, a strangled and despairing sound.

It only made Kyra run faster.

A new plan was forming in her mind, a plan even crazier than her. It came to her in a haze of shouts and sprinting, as if the very world around her dulled so this idea could form.

She had to stop her stepmother from taking control over Aazag-onia. The coronation was going to be held in the Winter Palace...

Then she would do everything in her power to stop it.

Callista's voice paused, and then was yelling, "Arrest the King! Arrest the traitor who would not kill a faerie!"

Her father. The Queen was arresting...her father.

No time to think about that, just *run*.

But Kyra gave a quick glance back at her father. That was all the Queen needed to pounce—to use her weakness against her. A wicked smile broke out across her face as the Queen realized what she must do to get Kyra to stay.

Callista shouted, "The King is charged with treason against the monarch, in consortium with the Fae! With a heavy heart, I hereby charge him with an execution at dawn!"

Kyra stopped, frozen in place at the words. Her feet skidded across the floor, sending plumes of dust swirling around her ankles.

Locking eyes with him across the square, her father shook his head in silence. Guards had already seized his arms, tying them behind his back and beginning to bind his ankles. For an arrest; an execution.

His kind eyes were filled with a terrible fear, a look that held the all-too-familiar trace of defeat. Kyra was steeling herself to race back to him when his eyes hardened in silent sorrow. He mouthed:

"*Go.*"

With reluctance, Kyra spun on her heels, sprinting through the crowd and shoving past people to get to the horses and the others. Her father's advice had not failed her yet. It would not fail her now. She had to have faith that he would be alright, and would find some way to escape. But faith had never been her strong suit, and it was not consoling her now. No, her source of comfort came from the fact that one day, she would stop her stepmother. Revenge was her comfort. One day, she could snip the binding string in her heart and be free once and for all.

She felt tickling at the base of her heels as she ran and looked down to see dark purple shadows of something trying to grab her ankles. She blinked and it was gone. Dismissing it as the delusions of a wandering mind, she hurried onwards through the crowd.

She saw Juniper, Cal, Luca, and Jules tear themselves away from the villagers, joining her in her sprinting. She felt careless and light, as she always did when she was running, but now, she felt as if a string still connected her to the stage, a string that begged her aching heart to turn around and run back into her father's arms. She wanted to be a little girl again, who could run and be safe and warm in his hug. Who could afford to believe in things like happy endings. The girl she was now was not convinced.

She flung herself up on a honey-golden horse that she had bought in the square, its head rearing back in a loud neighing sound. She was vaguely aware that Julian had mounted his horse, pulling Juniper up behind him, and Cal and Luca had done the same on Cal's horse.

Kyra turned the horse to face the crowd once again, to face the stepmother who had turned her back on her and Juniper.

The Queen's eyes flashed with something dark and cold as their eyes met across the square. Her parting words echoed in Kyra's ears. *I am sure we will meet again soon. Perhaps we will both be changed for the better.* Now Kyra knew resolutely they would meet at least once more, when the Queen's coronation would fall to pieces. Kyra would have her revenge.

"See you at the coronation, stepmother," Kyra said, reigning in her horse. Then she echoed what the Queen had said to her that morning, but now the meaning was different. "I hope we'll both be changed for the better."

She turned her horse and galloped out into the night.

* * *

"How could you not tell us that you guys are the princesses that are supposed to be *dead*?" Cal was saying, shaking his head. As if Kyra and Juniper had done something atrocious, like plot to kill their mother and not the other way around.

They were making their way through the Southern Forest, still pitch-black with night. Kyra was thankful for the darkness, as she was not in the mood for the joyous warmth of day.

"Would you have liked me to have said, 'Hi, I'm Kyra, we're the not-quite-dead princesses! Want to buy us horses so we can escape the country?'" Kyra crossed her arms. "I'm sure that would have gone over well."

"I knew you guys looked familiar!" Jules said triumphantly.

"And you knew about this?" Cal asked Luca.

Luca nodded his head. "Yep. I'm the one who was supposed to kill them."

"That's how the best friendships begin."

Kyra suddenly locked eyes with Juniper, a million unspoken words passing between them. They both knew what was coming next, and they seemed in agreement that there was nothing to do but stop the Queen's coronation in a week. The look on Juniper's face told Kyra enough. They were both resolved to do the right thing and save their kingdom. Honestly, though, Kyra was already tired of doing the right thing. It was so much less fun than the wrong thing, and often required a lot more work. But this was bigger than cheating on an exam or pranking someone. This had the lives of innocent people hanging in the balance, and gosh darn if Kyra wasn't going to save innocent people like the revered angel she most definitely was not!

"So," said Kyra finally, "are you going to help us or what?"

"Help you how?" Cal asked, at the same time that Julian energetically said, "Yeah!"

"It's simple, really," Kyra said, then realized it wasn't actually that simple, not in the slightest. As she launched into the story, Cal and Julian's jaws lowered and lowered. Finally, Kyra finished with, "Then, the Queen reveals at the funeral that she's taking the title of ruler all to herself! She's gonna have total power over Aazagonia if we don't stop her! That's why we have to travel to the Winter Palace, stop the coronation, and punch my stupid stepmother in the face!"

Everyone stared at her with blank looks, as if she had inhaled pixie powder and was now rapping a sonnet about trolls disguised as broomsticks.

"Let me think." Cal stood with his hands in his pockets, relaxed. "Alright. I've thought. Absolutely not."

"What? Why?" Julian complained, resembling a whimpering puppy, his eyes large and pleading. "This seems like a hero-ey thing. I'm a hero!"

"What if they *are* fae?" Cal narrowed his eyes in suspicion.

"We're not! Did you see Kyra's cartwheel?" Luca said sarcastically.

Julian looked torn. "He has a point."

"Cartwheeling doesn't prove anything! A faerie can raise the dead in some stories, so they most definitely can cartwheel!" Cal shook his head in exasperation.

"Please," Juniper's soft voice came as a surprise. "Help us. We have no idea how to get to the Winter Palace on our own. And I know Aazagonia is not your kingdom, but it is ours. We do not wish to see it fall. There was a time when tyrants controlled the world, bred in hatred and fury, and it bled out to the people. Excuse me for being so frank—but I will not let this be one of those times."

Kyra gaped at her sister. Since when did she speak like a siren, all dramatic and convincing?

Cal and Julian shared a look. "Okay," they both said in sync.

Kyra huffed. "You're telling me I could have just said that boring speech to convince you? Tough crowd." But she grinned despite herself.

A smile broke out across her sister's face that could only be compared to the sun cresting over a hilltop. Juniper squeezed Kyra's hand before the smile found its end.

When they let go, she saw Cal watching her. She suddenly felt hyper-aware of the fact that she hadn't showered that day. She chanted in her head, *Please don't let me smell like horse droppings, please don't let me smell like horse droppings—*

"We can make a stop by your kingdom so you can go to that ball that your mother wants you to go to," Juniper said to Julian with an awkward smile. It might have been a trick of the light, but it seemed as if a slight flush was spreading across the tip of Juni's nose. Oh no. Of course the girl had already gone and fallen in love with the first prince they met in the forest. "Maiike is on the way to the Winter Palace."

Julian's smile faltered for a moment—but only a moment. To the untrained eye, his brief sign of uncomfortableness would only mean indigestion. Kyra, however, recognized it as the smile of someone hiding something. A secret was an Achilles heel; it was a locked box of weakness that could be opened with the right gilded key. And Kyra was a master of lock picking. She thought about what she knew of Julian's father, the king of Maiike. She remembered a kind smile, a laugh like a bear, and piano music. Their visits were brief and rare, but Kyra had always cherished the way the king had played piano for her, as she twirled and danced along the marble tiles in their floor. Jules and his family hadn't visited in years though, due to Aazagonia's wealth. Or, more accurately, the lack of it.

Julian's smile came back twice as bright. "Perfect! See, Cal, not everything's so doom and gloom. We're doing some good, and my mother will be happy with us." He suddenly frowned. "The only issue is that I'm starved. Have you got a pastry in your bag? Preferably a jelly-filled one?"

"We're out of food, Jules." Cal took his satchel off his back and opened it, showing empty leather inside. "That's why we were stopping in Aazagonia. We were supposed to get more food and water, but...we got a little distracted." He flashed a small smile at Kyra. Though it couldn't really be described as a smile, so much as a twitch of his mouth. Kyra was taking anything she could get.

"Hold up. Where were you guys headed anyways? Don't suppose you were on your way to take back your kingdom from your evil stepmother?" Kyra asked. "'Cause if so, twinsies!"

"You know what, I think you're alone on that one, princess," Cal said.

"We were on our way back from a certain slaying of a certain dragon killed by a certain heroic and brave prince," said Julian. "It was me." He tapped his sword, grinning dashingly with jittery excitement. "I slayed the dragon."

"That is very brave indeed," Juniper said, avoiding all eye contact like she was playing an intense game of the floor is lava—but the lava was Julian and safety was anywhere else.

"Now's not the time for flirting," Kyra said to the group. "We've got bigger giants to crush."

The food thing was a major problem. Kyra couldn't go too long without food, or she would be a lot more grouchy. Her stomach rumbled in agreement, basically saying, *Yeah, she sucks when she wants food.* "I'm starving."

"That is worrisome," Juniper shot a knowing look at Kyra. It got ugly when Kyra was hungry, and Juniper knew all too well. Kyra grit her mouth in a line, silently shooting a death glare at Juni for exposing her to everyone. Not that she cared what Cal—what any of them thought.

"Yeah, we're gonna need food," Kyra added quickly, hoping that no one would ask any follow-up questions. Kyra's stomach rumbled quietly again like the traitor it was.

"There's a food cart a ways ahead in the forest," Luca said, dark eyes focused on the trees. "They sell beans and cheese and lettuce. The lettuce kinda tastes like dirt, but it'll do."

Kyra said, "I'm allergic to green things."

"Well, I shall eat the lettuce," Juni nodded, saying seriously, "even if it does taste of dirt. Luca, guide us to the food stall, please."

And they went on their way, Cal and Luca's horse in the front. Kyra's eyes bored into the back of Cal, unable to take her eyes off of his bobbing head. *It was right in front of her; what was she supposed to do, look at the ground? And wind up having neck issues? No thank you.*

Tearing her gaze off Cal, she turned her thoughts to more pressing matters, more logical matters. *What the heck she was supposed to be doing about all this?* It hadn't even been twenty-four hours since the world came crashing down.

She shot an annoyed look up at the heavens, wondering what she had done to incur their wrath. Okay, nevermind. She had done a lot. Maybe she deserved some heavenly wrath. But this had to be overkill.

The forest looked calmer, happier than it had in the twilight hours. The trunks of the trees were an ivory color, the hue of vanilla pudding or cream. Dark patches dotted the trees like splashes of ink. Canvas' marred by spilled paint. The complete dark of night was welcoming, as if it was the forest's natural state. There was a myth that the whole world had been shrouded in night until the first Faerie King generously poked holes in the sky for the stars—and a large one for the sun and moon. Kyra often imagined the world like that; always night and never day. It would be a wild world indeed.

The horses trotted through the trees in silence, and Kyra tried to take in the beauty of nature. Though all she could really think about was the beauty of getting to punch her stepmother in the face at the coronation. She day-dreamed for a few minutes, not noticing that they had entered a small clearing full of moss. A circle of trees ringed the clearing. It looked like a place that faeries from Juniper's books would dance in, twirling for minutes and eternities all at once. They would sway and spin until their feet fell off; and until their hair grew long and reached the mossy floor. Enticing humans to join the dance and be caught up in it for lifetimes, the faeries would giggle while leading mortals to their doom. It was a famous story in a picture book, and probably the last book Kyra had ever read, if she was being honest.

A small wooden cart sat in the center of the clearing, with woven baskets full of...beans. Just beans. Nothing but beans. Red beans, brown beans, yellow beans, and green beans. Kyra let out a sigh. She had been looking forward to some cheese, no matter how lactose-intolerant she was. Cheese would have made her strife worth it. Not beans.

A small, squat old woman sat on a stool positioned next to the cart, smiling a warm, welcoming smile, the kind of smile that grandmothers toted. Her hair was silvery-white, lying in tangled, braided knots to her feet. It looked like the kind of hair that people who danced for a million years would have, almost a piece of the thorny brambles of the forest itself. The woman had an odd look on her face, looking at Kyra but not quite *at* her. Through her. It made Kyra uneasy. It felt as if the sky was not the *precise* shade of blue it always had been. She brought her horse to a stop.

"This is it," Luca said, jumping off the horse. It was a long way down for him.

Kyra slid off, too, joining Luca though making sure to keep a measured distance between herself and the cart.

"Come to buy beans?" The old woman flashed a toothy smile, showing crooked, jagged teeth. Kyra involuntarily took a step back.

To her discomfort, the teeth reminded her of fangs. She chalked it up to lousy dentistry and schooled her features into neutrality.

"Beans? Do you have anything else?" Kyra decided on saying. She was going to say something less kind about beans, but once she saw her sharp teeth she decided against it. Some days, she just didn't have a death wish. Only some.

The old woman said, "I'm afraid not." She held a bean in her hand. Kyra blinked. She was sure that hadn't been there a second ago.

"Nothing? Not even lettuce that tastes like dirt?"

"I can only offer you a bean," The old woman said, eyes flashing. She locked her distant, not-really-there gaze on Luca. "Young hunter," she said. "Why have you brought such an odd group to me today?"

Luca shifted nervously. "They're not that odd. Kyra's a little weird, but everyone else is pretty normal." Kyra elected to ignore that statement in favor of the bargain. When this was done, she would give him a serious talking to. Sunbeam above, she sounded like her father. The pang of guilt that was becoming synonymous with thoughts of her father made itself known. Kyra pushed that away. *He's going to be alright. He has to be alright.*

"'Tis a mismatched group indeed," said the old woman. Her pale eyes clouded over, and she froze in place eerily. Several seconds passed, and the woman still did not budge an inch. It was as if she was a painting, frozen in time and pastels.

"Is this a bad time?" Cal asked.

Jules added, "Luca, Luca, Luca. Is this lady crazy? Are you crazy, too?"

"No," Luca retorted in a huff, "you are."

"Hey! Take it back! Cal, make him take it back!"

Cal looked amused. "Don't think I will. I'm enjoying this."

"What's the use of having a servant boy if he doesn't even serve?"

Julian scowled. "I'm positive I'm the sanest of you all—looking at you, princesses—but by all means, Luca, call me the crazy one."

"Okay," Luca said. "You're crazy."

"Do you understand sarcasm, my cute little chipmunk?" Kyra smirked.

Juniper diverted the conversation with, "I am sure this old woman is not crazy. She is old; don't old people act like this?" Juniper had never known her grandparents. A faint memory of cold stares and brief hugs flickered before Kyra's eyelids. Her memory of her own grandparents had never been too warm.

Luca said, "She does this sometimes. In a few seconds she'll either be alright or start spouting nonsense. Sometimes she raps or recites poetry. It could be anything." He shrugged as if this was normal.

"Raps? So this is like my dad's mid-life crisis a couple years ago, only now it's a woman, and she has crazy shark teeth." Kyra crossed her arms. She was going to launch into one of her dad's old songs about diplomatic meetings, but luckily for everyone else the old woman jolted out of her stupor.

Hunching over her stool, the old woman's bent hands gnarled into wrinkled claws, and she let out a guttural growl. Luca cried out and bent to help her, but before he could, the old woman sat straight up in an uncannily perfect posture, every ounce of pain gone in a flash.

The woman turned and locked eyes with Kyra. She felt her entire body tense as all eyes fell to her. Normally she would welcome the attention with open arms, but then it just felt like a billion people were watching her through the old woman's eyes. A billion whispers and stares locked on her all at once. She did her best to stand tall and proud as the old woman began speaking to her. Her best was all she could do. *No. Do better*, her father would say. *She cannot*, her stepmother would reply. *Shut up, voices*, Kyra thought now.

"You, Moon's Child, shall be held prisoner in your own mind," the old woman said, and Kyra swallowed hard. That meant nothing. The ramblings of a deranged old lady. *Prisoner of your own mind?* Kyra knew she would never be anyone's prisoner, let alone her own.

"I asked for beans, not therapy," Kyra said dryly, but the old woman ignored her.

The old woman turned to Juniper, a smile curling over her face like a leaf reaching towards rain. Kyra took a protective step in front of her sister at once. But Juniper slowly edged Kyra away, to stare directly into the old woman's bat-crazy eyes.

The old woman said, "Sun's Child, yours is a different story. One of cold beauty and loss. You will learn to harness the light and use it for your own. You and your sister are strands of cloth, moon and sun, woven together. Do not forget this."

Juniper nodded curtly, though she swallowed hard. Come on, it looked like she was believing this mumbo-jumbo!

Then, as if breaking from a trance, Juniper took Kyra's hand in her own, giving a tight squeeze. Kyra squeezed back, as if letting her know that they shouldn't listen to any of the words this woman was saying. Nonsense and wishes, that's all it was. Nonsense and wishes. She considered the weird word choice of the woman: light and dark. Sun and Moon. *Juniper and Kyra.* She felt Juniper's hand shiver in hers, though not from the cold. It was as though the light breeze sweeping through the forest had suddenly turned sinister, sweeping the hem of Kyra's dress and raising goosebumps on her arms. It taunted her, the wind, mocking her for all she did not know. But what did she not know? Kyra clenched her jaw, frustrated. What didn't she know? She let go of her sister's hand to wrap her arms around herself. It didn't do anything to help the bone-chilling cold that had swept over the clearing.

"And you," The old woman said to Luca. "Not yet. Soon is your time to howl." The lady grinned, feverish and full of shadows. Luca's almond eyes widened in panic. The old woman turned to Jules next, who looked resigned. She said, "The prince with blood who reeks of death. Soon to take your dying breath," The old woman sounded mocking, almost, her voice lilting in taunt. Kyra wanted to slap her after seeing the look on Julian's face. "And now for the—"

"You know nothing about me," Cal said, voice harsh and eyes blazing.

"Oh," The old woman smiled, "but I know everything, halbling."

Halbling. Kyra knew nothing about that word save for the fact that she didn't know anything about it. It was a word that made her stomach twist into a tightly wound knot. Maybe it meant an annoying person. If so, it was suitable.

"Who are you?" Kyra asked the woman, surprised to find that her voice was hoarse.

"I am neither friend nor foe, but I know the things you hope to know." The old lady cackled and held out her palm. In it was a single bean.

It was shriveled and green, with little roots barely visible. Beans weren't supposed to have roots, were they? For the first and last time in her life, Kyra wished she knew more about the history of bean farming.

"You're offering a bean? A single bean?" Kyra asked, her voice a low whisper. It was so still in the clearing that she knew everyone could hear her. No one moved. No one spoke. No one took their eyes off the bean that lay so still in the woman's palm.

"Take it or leave it," The old lady said. "But I reckon you'll take it." Those words alone made Kyra want to walk away and never come back. To abandon this hopeless cause and give herself up to the Queen. To do that would mean she was a coward. To do that would mean she was not the warrior she knew she was.

Kyra stayed.

But it was not her hand that darted out to grab the bean; no, it was the Sun's Child. Juniper quickly snatched the bean, holding it in between her index finger and thumb. She stared at it as if it were a star she had plucked from the heavens. Not some worthless bean. Stars were bright and cast out shadows; this bean looked as if it brought them.

That snapped Kyra from her trance, and she turned to say something to the old woman.

But when she looked back, she was gone.

"That," Kyra breathed, "was the creepiest thing I've ever seen. Was that not the creepiest thing you've ever seen?"

"It was rather disturbing," Juniper agreed, nodding her head in a frenzied enthusiasm.

Kyra turned to Cal. "Halbling? Care to explain?"

Cal shook his head once, his gaze full of daggers. "I don't know what that means. It's definitely faerie, though."

"I wasn't aware we had a language expert among us."

"I know my stuff."

"It is a faerie word," Luca said, face scrunched up like he was trying to remember something. "I'm not sure what it means, though. Bling could mean something like north. Then again, it could also mean hamster."

"Two language experts!" Kyra exclaimed, smirking.

"Was that woman faerie?" Juniper asked. Her voice made the others fall silent, the word *faerie* echoing out over the dark forest. That word seemed to hold more power than any empire or ruler.

"I think so," Cal said. He did not elaborate.

"Then those were prophecies!" exclaimed Luca, face white with fear. "Did you hear her? 'Soon is your time to howl!' And the rest were all horrible things, too, things that sounded really bad, like—"

"Lies," dismissed Kyra. "Faeries can lie just as easily as they can't cartwheel. I wouldn't worry about it. The old woman must have been bonkers." Kyra wasn't so sure anyone believed her, as they silently shifted from toe to toe. Kyra wasn't even sure if she believed it herself.

"But why was she here?"

"Maybe she knows we bring the party and wanted in." Kyra shrugged.

Juniper said, "Are you serious? The Fae live nowhere near here. Why would she come all this way to depart our fates? Unless they are real and important!"

"It could've been a prank," offered Cal. "Someone trying to scare us."

"Or," Juniper said, "we have just been given our destinies, and you are too blind to see it! Julian, she said you would die! What do you have to say about this?"

"Dunno. It was probably a prank," said Julian, his words rushed and uneven. "Enough about the boring fae." The flash of anxiety that had been there a moment before was now gone. "Let's talk about what we're supposed to do with a bean. One bean, might I add. Who gets it?"

Kyra's stomach rumbled noisily. *Ugh, everything in her life was betraying her these days.* The rumble sounded as if a giant was playing hopscotch on the floor around her. If she hadn't known that it was her internal organs begging for food, she would have thought the rumbling was a multitude of volcanoes erupting. All eyes turned to her.

"I don't think the bean's for eating," Kyra said, plucking it from Juniper's hands. She ignored her sister's shocked outcry. "What's it for, then, I'm wondering? Who was that lady? You've got some weird friends, little huntsman. Then again, I doubted your choice of companionship ever since you decided to keep me alive." She flashed a smile.

Luca grumbled something under his breath, then said, "What do we do with it? The bean, I mean? If we're not gonna eat it—"

"We're gonna toss it, that's what." Cal cut off Luca, calmly grabbing the weird-looking bean from Kyra's hand.

"Hey!" Kyra fumed. "What if I do want to eat it?" She didn't. But for some reason, she did want to argue with Cal.

"That lady was definitely fae, and this bean is definitely magic."

Kyra perked up. *Magic*. She unconsciously leaned in. Her hair flung forward from her shoulders and tickled her arm as she considered the little bean. Magic might be in it. Magic that could shake the sky and carve mountains; that could part seas and lived in the very ground she walked on. She swore it. Something in her knew that magic was everywhere she went, and she could feel it everywhere around her. Images of a frozen throne room and towering, shaded trees, a crown made of icicles, and faeries dancing in candlelight. Images of desert dunes and a kingdom formed from the sand of a ticking hourglass. The haunting melody of a violin echoed in her ears as if from great caverns below, sad and sweet and lonely as the moon. She could feel snow chilling her to her core, could taste a mix of starlight and fire and sand in her veins. The thought of magic did this to her—it made her dream of places beyond everything she knew.

It made her see a world of endless possibilities, a world she knew was waiting for her, somewhere in the great unknown.

"Magic?" Kyra asked, making her tone seem bored. She was anything but, and her eyes never left the bean. "Like I'll-turn-you-into-a-frog magic?"

Cal said very seriously, "Why don't you test it out?"

Kyra made a face. "I'll pass. But me being a toad would definitely surprise the Queen."

"Now you're talking." Cal grinned. A small success. "So we all agree to toss it?"

Everyone nodded in agreement, except Luca. He looked like he was going to throw up as he said, "I don't know."

"What about?" Juniper asked.

"I just...I just don't know." Luca eyed the bean warily. Kyra watched as his hands restlessly gripped and ungripped the edge of his green shirt. She felt like they should look into his suspicions further, but before she knew it, Cal was already talking, so she snapped her head up to listen.

"Convincing argument, Luca. Am I tossing this or what?" Cal asked. Hearing no response, he gave a final nod and threw the bean over his shoulder.

It skidded across the floor, bouncing once, then settling into the blanketed moss and grey rock. It seemed to stare up at Kyra, as if saying, *Huh. You're just gonna let me sit here? Go figure. I taste really good...*

Kyra wrenched her gaze away from the hypnotic stare of the bean, as a wave of hunger and sleep-deprivation washed over her in a jolting shock. She collapsed dramatically on the floor. "I haven't slept in ages. I say we take a nap break, then reconvene in the morning."

"I don't see why not. If the Queen's coronation is in a week, and we travel by horse, we'll have more than enough time," said Julian amiably. He sat down next to her, pulling his long legs up against his chest. He looked at Cal. "Mind taking first watch?"

Cal nodded once, then went to the edge of the clearing, sitting up against one of the ashy white trees. He leaned his head back and stared off into the forest. Kyra wondered what he was thinking and if it had anything to do with her.

Kyra nestled down in the comforting arms of the moss. Jules, Juniper, and Luca did the same while Cal just pondered the trees with a look resembling sorrow. Sorrow that reached a thousand years, long and deep and immortal. Sorrow that should not have been in the look of a seventeen-year-old boy.

That didn't stop Kyra from drifting into a restless sleep. She dreamed of flames consuming a funeral stage. Flames that consumed her from the inside out...flames that ran within her veins, taunting: *Moon's Child....*

7

Prisoner of Fire and Fear

Kyra opened her eyes after a few hours of pointless sleep. She was exhausted, but that would have to wait. There was no way she was going to sleep after so much had happened. She was surprised she was even able to sleep for a few minutes.

Standing and crossing the clearing, her leather boots padded softly through the moss. She looked down and back at Juniper, who was sleeping soundly, curled up in a ball. Her curly hair sprawled around her face, jet-black rivers snaking their way across the green floor. It reminded Kyra of something; something with golden tendrils reaching across a stone wall. Kyra shook it off and crossed over the mossy stone to where Cal sat amidst the dark night.

The moon hung high, creeping towards the other side of the sky in a show of pale white light. Tomorrow it would be red—a blood moon. Kyra wondered what blood moons prophesied. The name didn't sound too promising.

Kyra took a seat across from Cal, leaning up against a tree. He didn't notice her arrival. She had always felt like a cat; she could walk across the floor and not be heard. *Nine lives,* she thought suddenly. An image of Luca holding the knife high above Juniper's scared face flashed before her eyelids. *Nine lives.* If only that were true.

Cal jumped as he noticed that she was there. "You scared me."

"Thought I was a wolf out to get you?"

Cal regarded her as one would regard a star, something unnamable and unknown. He said, "You like that, don't you? That people fear you. Not *fear* you, fear you, but that they know you're something different from the rest."

Kyra was taken aback. She swallowed and mustered up a small, mocking grin, saying, "If I was like everybody else, I'd die from the dullness."

"I know what it is," Cal said. "You're like your stepmother."

She stared.

Her hands rested on the ground, clenched up and clinging onto fistfuls of dirt and grass, hanging on for dear life. She felt dizzy, like the world was being pulled out from under her, and her hands in the earth were the only thing keeping her from flying away. She was nothing like the Queen. She would never be anything like the Queen. Cal saying that hurt deeper than any cut. A hand cracking across a face, harsh words from a red-lipped mouth, and words stinging more than blows. Those were the things she associated with her stepmother. Those were the things she never wanted to be compared to.

"You are a liar," Kyra said, her voice a low whisper, "and know nothing about me." She turned to stand, but she felt a cold hand on hers. She looked down and saw that Cal had locked his pale fingers around her wrist, made more white in the moonlight. She froze, not daring to meet his eyes.

Then the moment passed, and she wrenched her hand away from him, feeling hot anger rise. She often thought of her temper like a hearth, embers always dwelling deep within, and one gust of wind could light up the entire tempest.

She moved to start walking away but Cal said, "I didn't mean it like that. Not in a bad way. Not what you're thinking. Sorry."

She wondered how he could say he was sorry so easily. Kyra never could find the words she really meant. In her head, she always knew exactly what she was thinking. It was when she tried to say those words out loud that there was a problem.

Kyra slowly sat back down, begrudgingly wanting to hear what he had to say. "Like what, then?"

"You're not like her because she's a heartless murderer who wants to take over the world."

"You really know the way to a girl's heart."

He laughed, and Kyra felt her heart stop all at once. It was lilting and musical, like piano notes drifting in the wind. His laugh was the rustling of windchimes and the floating of petals down a forgotten stream. Heart fluttering, Kyra had no idea what the emotion she was feeling was. Kyra could name every type of anger and joy and grief and happiness under the sun, but not for the life of her could she figure out why her heart was fluttering like the beating of a butterfly's wings.

Cal, once his laughter ended, looked at her seriously. "I mean you're only like her because you can hide what you feel. I saw it on the stage at the funeral. Imagine seeing your 'dead' daughter next to you; what would you feel? A normal person would react differently than the Queen did. And you, you do the same thing. What I want to know is...why?"

Kyra shuffled, putting her hands in her lap to warm them from the sudden cold that had enveloped her. She whispered, "I'm not like her."

"I know."

Kyra, desperately wanting to change the subject, said, "How do you have such a high position in court, the servant of a prince, when you're so young?"

He shrugged, saying, "Guess Jules' father thought I'd be a good influence. He was wrong, of course, but that's a well-kept secret."

"Jules' father. The king. Do you know—does he still play the piano?"

The same sorrowful look from earlier came over Cal's face, and he turned to look out at the quiet night. "He passed away four years ago."

"That..." Kyra started, "...is very sad," she ended up saying lamely. That did nothing to encompass the grief she felt in that moment. Those kind brown eyes and beautiful melodies he would play would only exist in her memories now. She knew he was a good king, a good man, too. And Julian...Kyra only cast her gaze down, knowing her face was still a mask of somber neutrality. "My mom died, too, when I was young." She didn't know why she said it. All she knew was that she missed her real mother every day; her mother who dreamed of the stars and adventure and who had taught Kyra what it meant to be brave. When her mother had gotten sick, Kyra's whole world had fallen apart. Now she was left with a handful of bittersweet memories. Delightful stories that were all tainted with the same rotten ending. "It was from Godfather Sorrow's disease. The pandemic all those years ago."

Cal paused for a moment, as if weighing his next words. "It took my mother, too."

"Twinsies."

"We should start a club."

"That would be the saddest club ever," said Kyra with a shaking of her head.

"Only eligible if you have a dead mother." Cal half-chuckled, and Kyra's heart half-stopped. His nose wrinkled when he laughed, she noticed, tucking that information away.

"Bonus points if your stepmother plotted to have you killed."
Kyra grinned back.

"I think you'll have everyone beat on that one."

Silence ensued. It wasn't an uncomfortable silence, though. Just peaceful.

Kyra jolted once she met his eyes again. They were a pale blue, with flecks of silver that were streaked through them. Bright and angelic. She didn't know how she hadn't noticed them before. But now that she had, she found she couldn't look away.

She heard a rustle from the moss where the others slept. Juniper was asking where her sister was, but then yawned and fell back asleep.

"I'm gonna go to sleep." Kyra leaned her head against the bark, her head angled towards the lonely stars. So distant from each other, lightyears from the nearest planet. They must've envied how close Kyra was to Cal at that moment. "Unless you want me to keep watch?"

Cal said something, but by the end of his sentence, Kyra had already fallen asleep at the base of the tree, her shoulder slumped next to his.

This time, the sleep was peaceful, unhindered by dreams. The last thing she pictured before she fell asleep was a winter prince with sad eyes the color of the sky.

* * *

Juniper woke to an orange world.

Fire.

Flames encircled the sky, like a roof.

Like a cage of heat and fury.

She scrambled from the floor, terror paralyzing her every move.

She felt the warmth of the flames wrapping around her, twisted lines of heat that swiped at her arms and legs.

Her memories of fire were tainted with memories of her mother—the two of them sitting by the fireplace, reading books or playing instruments in the early hours of night. She had never gotten close to it for fear of the white-hot flames catching her hair or her dress. But now there was no escape.

The fear and fire both made her their prisoner.

Kyra was nowhere to be seen, but Julian and Luca were waking beside her.

"What's going on?" Luca asked, blearily rubbing his eyes. His face drained of color once he saw, his voice squeaking. "Nevermind! Sunbeam above, can't we catch a break? "

"Kyra!" Juniper screamed. "Kyra, where are you?"

The fire ignored her calls, spinning closer.

There was no sign of her or Cal anywhere, but she didn't care where Cal was. She wanted to know if her *sister* was okay. She frantically scanned the treeline for any sign of golden hair or a pink dress. Nothing. Dread clawed its way through her, making her heart pound in her ears.

What if Kyra was...what if Kyra was...what if the fire...

Luca jumped to his feet. Julian followed a few moments later, eyes wide and alert.

"What's happening?" Julian yelled over the roar of the flames.

Juniper looked up to the sky, where the source of the fire was. It almost looked like...like a hand. A giant, fire ringed hand. It was the size of the clearing itself, huge and orange and bright. She saw the hand—or whatever it was—swinging down, then retreating. As soon as it did, the fire was extinguished. The cool night air returned briefly, and Juniper took the time to search the trees again. She stormed forward, tears building up in her eyes.

"Juniper, wait!" She heard Julian call. She ignored him, desperately searching for any sign of Kyra. He would understand, she thought, if he had any siblings. You hated them like no other, but you loved them more than anything imaginable, too. One time, Kyra had ignored Juniper for a week after the latter had eaten her chocolate sundae without asking. To be fair, it was an extremely good sundae. Sure, she and Kyra bickered and fought, but if Juniper knew anything it was that she couldn't imagine a life without her sister.

And then she saw her.

Kyra was standing at the edge of the clearing near a large tree, Cal by her side. Juniper barely had time to wonder what she had been doing over there, when the huge hand full of fire came crashing back down, as if reaching out for her.

"Look out!" Kyra cried, as the hand swung nearer, the flames waltzing across its fingers.

Juniper jumped backward at the last second as the hand plunged into the earth.

She became vaguely aware of something tall and green rising from the ground at the other end of the clearing, something wider and bigger than the hand itself. A huge tree? But no, none of the trees had been quite so wide...and quite so tall...

The hand aimed its pointer finger at Juniper, and fire was sent in a straight line towards her. Almost crying, she realized that she had never finished reading her most recent book, a daring tale about a well at the edge of the world. Why that came into her mind at the moment, she didn't know, but all she did know was that she wanted to live to read the ending.

Hot, dry air rippled off the fire in waves. She was going to die, and here she was blubbering and crying like a baby about a stupid book. The fire raced towards her, racing its way across the moss. It was about to consume her and burn her to death, when—

Julian was suddenly in front of her, a shield separating the fire from the girl.

He scooped her up in his arms and bolted with her from the fire.

She flung her arms around him and buried her head in his shoulder, heat from the flames still clinging to her. Her tears were lost in the fabric of his shirt.

The flames cast orange light on his face. He looked like a warrior of the sun. As he gently lowered her to the ground, Juniper found herself in awe that he truly was every inch the hero.

If Juniper could have been able to fall in love twice, she would have in that instant. In fact, she was becoming more and more certain that she would fall in love with Julian every second of every day, over and over like a carousel spinning in joyous glee. No wonder everyone talked so much of love; no wonder endless ballads and books were written about this. If she had never heard of magic before, this was what she thought it would be.

He winced as he let her go, shaking his hands. "You're hot."

Juniper froze. "You are very handsome as well," she said sheepishly, relishing in the coolness of the forest floor and wondering if this truly was the time for compliments.

"Obviously. But I meant you're literally hot. Your skin was burning up like a s'more," Jules said. "Are you good?"

"Yes, I am good. Not embarrassed at all," muttered Juniper, even more heat rushing to her cheeks.

Meanwhile, the huge hand pulled back up into the sky, the light from the flames momentarily drawing back, the dark of night returning. Juniper welcomed it, her head falling back into the grass in relief. She didn't dare think that it could come back.

What was that thing? A hand? But that was a colossal-sized hand, if so. Hands like that did not belong to humans, or any animal, or even the fae-folk. As she realized with terror, her blood ran cold despite the heat still lingering on her skin.

A *giant*.

She sat up to voice her opinions to the others, but she saw that

Kyra and Cal were running over. She wanted to call out, to tell them to get away, that the hand was coming down again, but her voice wouldn't come.

Because there, on the other edge of the clearing, was a towering, tall, behemoth of a beanstalk.

She barely had time to take in the details of it, but she could see flames at the edge of her vision, and flames meant that the hand of the giant was near.

"Giant." She released a shaky breath.

Julian's face twisted in understanding. He grabbed her arm and hoisted her to her feet as the hand scooped down one last time.

The flames were doused though, and the hand was just a hand. Albeit, a hand the size of a house, but still a hand that was thankfully not on fire.

It made its way towards her, and she numbly tried to run, Julian's own hand ever-present on her arm. Something in her knew it would be no use. The hand got closer and closer; fingers outstretched like it was going to pluck her up off the floor.

She supposed she shouldn't have been surprised when it actually did.

The last thing she remembered before the world went dark was the giant's hand as it scooped her up.

8

The Beanstalk and the Boy

Cal shouted through the din, through the roaring in Kyra's ears. "No!"

Kyra stood still in the clearing, watching helplessly as the giant carried her sister, Julian, and Luca up and away into the sky.

It felt like her heart was being ripped from her chest as the hand disappeared behind the clouds. She had failed. All she could picture was her sister being picked up by the fire giant with that scared look on her face. And Kyra hadn't been able to help her in time to save her, and now Juniper could be injured or terrified or maybe even—no. To think about that would kill Kyra herself. She needed her sister to be okay. If she couldn't save her dad, or her mom, she could save Juniper.

"I'll kill it," Kyra said. She felt a burning hatred. It was pulsing through her, burning her lungs. She imagined she was a dragon, with fire rising in her. She refused to watch her sister be torn away from her before her very eyes.

She unfroze and ran forward as the long hand disappeared in the heavens, high beyond the clouds. Not really having a plan to run anywhere in particular, her feet hammered against the rocky floor.

The beanstalk was in front of her in an instant. Kyra angled her head to look up at it. It stretched high, beyond the point where air turned into sky, up into the clouds like a sword piercing through snow. It was green, with little leaves poking out all over it. Good. Those would provide sturdy hand and footholds. Kyra tied her hair back into a ponytail and jumped up to one of the leaves.

But where, exactly, had this beanstalk come from?

The answer glared her in the face. Bean. Stalk. Stalk. Bean. Was it possible this ginormous weed had come from that small bean that the old woman of the wood had given them?

Then she felt someone tap her on the leg, a quick poke. Cal. She tried to be annoyed at him, but instead found that she was looking forward to talking to him, even though she had much, much bigger things to worry about. Literally. Like climbing a ten-thousand-foot beanstalk. Which was honestly the last thing she wanted to do at the moment. At least it would be a cool conversation starter. *Hey, have you ever climbed a beanstalk? Oh, you haven't?*

Kyra jumped back down and found herself face to face with Cal. He was only a few inches taller than her, and yet she despised every single one of those inches.

"What?" Kyra asked, irritated.

He crossed his arms, the picture of order. "Exactly what are you planning on doing?"

"I plan on climbing up this beanstalk and rescuing my sister and company from a giant." The words sounded fake coming out of her mouth, like they belonged to someone else.

"Solid plan," Cal said. "Lacking any actual planning. But solid."

Kyra rolled her eyes. "And what do you propose we do? Wait around? Hate to break it to you, smart guy, but I don't think the giant's gonna come back and hand over the others with a flowery apology note."

"We should discuss our options," said Cal.

"That's the most boring thing you've said," Kyra responded. "And you say a lot of boring things." She was lying, of course, but antagonizing him grew more fun each minute she knew him. "Besides, we don't have time to discuss!"

He ignored her, saying, "Let's start with why the giant took them in the first place."

"For a tea party, of course." Kyra threw her arms in the air, exasperated. "How am I supposed to know?"

Kyra looked back at the beanstalk, curling into the sky. She tried to focus on the facts behind this whole situation, tried not to think of Juniper roasting on an open fire or being force-fed giant marshmallows.

Okay, facts. What were the facts? A giant had just stolen her sister and friends; that was a fact. The giant was the fire kind. The bean that the old woman had given them must have created this otherworldly beanstalk. She didn't know how that was possible, yet then again, she wasn't a very good judge.

Juniper was gone. She closed her eyes and tried to remember the books in the castle library, the only ones that could keep her interest for more than two seconds. They were the ones about magic. And giants...the giants were earth, air, water, and fire types...so what was a fire giant doing in the sky...? What else...what else...oh!

"Giants are attracted to magic!" Kyra said suddenly. Her eyes flit open with the revelation.

"I've read something about that, too. Giants are said to steal people that have close contact with magic. He was coming for our group because of that old woman. She must have definitely been a faerie, normal beans don't make—" He indicated the huge beanstalk "—this."

"You're right." Kyra thought of the whispers she had heard when she was little, whispers that said the Queen dabbled in magic. She thought of the place below the castle where dark things lurked. She had always thought that that place in the deep was the closest she had ever been to magic. And not the light kind.

"The giant probably sensed the magic from the old woman after the beanstalk rose up. But what does he want with them?"

Kyra shrugged. "Food? Guests? Friends? Hopefully friends. If so, he'll get sick of ours soon."

"He couldn't have picked a more annoying group to mess with."

"It's good that we agree. This would be a long climb." Kyra laughed and tucked a lock of hair behind her ear.

Cal reached out and put his hand on Kyra's shoulder. She tensed, trying to ignore a wave of electricity that spiked through her. He said, "This will be a long climb no matter what. It's going to be extraneous and extremely dangerous. One slip, you're dead."

"If you don't want to come with me," Kyra said, "I won't judge."

"I was going to ask if *you* didn't want to go."

"Right. The day I don't go is the day we're attacked by a fire giant...Oh, wait." Kyra grinned. "That already happened. I'm going, and there's nothing anyone or anything can do to stop me. My sister's up there." Her mind instantly raced to thoughts of Juniper, and to quiet those worried thoughts, Kyra began climbing. She grabbed a fistful of stalk and yanked herself up. Slipping immediately, she fell to the floor in a heap, her tailbone taking a tremendous beating.

Cal did not look too excited about her slip-up. "As long as you don't do that a hundred feet up, you'll be fine."

"That was just a practice round. And hey! Good thing you didn't eat the bean, huh? Imagine this bad boy bursting out of your stomach while you slept." Kyra patted the beanstalk and laughed.

Cal's eyes creased with a smile, and together, they began climbing the beanstalk.

* * *

Juniper slowly blinked her eyes open and saw a room gilded in gold.

A huge, ginormous, off-the-scale, gold room. It looked like a kitchen, but if a kitchen was scaled up a thousand times and painted a cheap-looking yellow by a designer who needed better training. Gigantic chairs that looked like mountains, a sink with running water like a waterfall, and a table that looked like it stretched a mile were set in the room. She thought she could even see a huge, stitched blanket that read: *Family is Forever*, across the table. Picturing a man-eating giant with a needle and thread did not sit well with her.

It was all gold. Only two things were silver.

One was a harp. The harp was sitting on the massive chair across the room and was one of the only things in the room that looked fit for a human, with delicate silver strings and shining silver handles. It put her in a trance for a moment, as if she would die if she could not have it. The only reason she broke from the trance was because of her loyalty to her violin and the fact that the harp sat next to the *Family is Forever* blanket. It was just so weird.

The other silver object was the cage she was in. The cage was decidedly less pretty. One, because she was trapped in it, and two, *because she was trapped in it.* It sat upon the kitchen table, in the middle of the room. A centerpiece of humans. It shined like the silver of her mother's necklaces, the ones with the ravens that flew across her collar. Like the necklace, the cage was somehow beautiful while being entirely claustrophobic. Juniper always thought the necklace would strangle her mother; it was so heavy and tight. The thought of it made Juni feel lightheaded, so she turned her attention away from the confinement of the cage, and towards the two boys on the floor next to her, also trapped.

Julian and Luca were sitting on the floor—well, table, really—inside the cage with her, and looking up at her with matching stony expressions.

"You still are as dazzling as a ray of sunlight, even covered in dirt and smelling like burnt bread," Julian said with his signature charming smile.

With a start, she noticed that his hands were burned, with red gashes across his palms as if he had stuck his hands into fire. Once his skin had been tan and smooth, when he had first offered his hand to her upon their meeting in the forest; now they were charred and bleeding.

"Your hands!" Juniper exclaimed, and she dropped to her knees to take them in her own. "Sunbeam above! What has happened? Does it pain you?"

Jules gently set her hands down, and said, "I'm okay, trust me. It barely even stings." He sat up a little straighter as if proving it.

"What happened?"

Luca said, his eyes bright with wonder, "You're what happened."

Eyes flitting from Luca to Julian, she was unable to comprehend what she just heard. Juniper had done that to Julian's hands? But how? She remembered the fire giant...the flames, all around her. Julian carrying her out of the fire, her own knight in shining armor...but that wasn't the point. The point was, she didn't remember *burning* Julian. "I don't understand."

"It was awesome," Luca said. "Not exactly awesome for Julian, but you got really close to the giant's hand when he had the fire all over it."

Juniper turned to Julian. "So how did you get burned? I feel as if I have asked that a billion times but no one has given me a real answer."

Julian hesitated before saying, "That's 'cause we don't really know. One second, I had picked you up, and the next, my hands felt like they were on fire. I set you down, and my hands were burned."

"My skin *burned* you?"

"That's what we've been trying to tell you this whole time, yes," Luca said, a hint of sarcasm in his normally sweet voice. Juniper shot a glare at him.

Julian elbowed Luca, then winced and cradled his arm. "What he's trying to say is, yeah, your skin got so hot that it somehow turned my hands into matching flame-thrower chew toys." He held out his hands for emphasis, and Juniper tried not to gag at the sight of the burned skin. "No hard feelings, though."

"That should not be possible..." Juniper said, thinking hard about what could've happened. She had never heard of someone getting so hot from a fire that they burned another person's skin like that.

"What we need to think about are Cal, Kyra, and the fact that we're trapped," Julian said.

Luca helpfully pointed out, "And the fact that the giant is going to eat us."

"He's not gonna eat us," Julian said, though he didn't sound so sure.

"He's definitely gonna eat us."

Juniper pulled off Julian's silver ring and slipped it on her own finger, saying, "You are not supposed to have tight things on when you have burns." Then she pulled off her black cloak, wrapping it carefully around Julian's hands and tying it in a knot. "There you go. They shall heal soon enough. You might have some nasty scars, however."

From what she knew about burns, those scars might never heal. Some scars never did, she thought, and her mother's face flashed before her eyes, her lips curled in a blindingly stunning sneer.

"What happened to focusing on the gigantic problem we have?" Luca indicated their surroundings. "And I mean literally gigantic."

"We hope for rescue from our friends below," said Juniper, "and trust in each other with the patience of a thousand burning deserts." She knew rescue would come, as it always had, if only she waited enough and prayed enough. That's how all the myths were told; help from outside powers always saved the day.

Luca frowned. "That sounds good and all, but I dunno that I have the patience of a thousand burning deserts. Or even one burning desert."

"I'm with the huntsman on that one. I say we try our best to shove Juniper through the bars of the cage and have her find a key," said Julian with a scarily serious look. Juniper nervously eyed the slim cage bars.

If she had to squeeze through, her head might very well burst open and scatter Juniper-brains all over the gold floors. As that did not sound very fun, Juniper shot down the idea as quickly as possible. "That is a good back-up idea, but I believe that help will come."

"Sometimes we gotta help ourselves," said Julian, moss green eyes filled with determination. "We can't just rely on others to save us, like some damsels in distress."

"I am a damsel. And surely we are in distress." Juniper frowned.

Julian said, "Trust me, I know. But sometimes help doesn't come, and we're all we have."

"Sometimes the situation calls for shoving Juniper through tiny cell bars," said Luca solemnly.

"Absolutely not." Juniper crossed her arms and settled to the floor, her dress poofing out around her in the way she always liked. "You two nincompoops may shove whoever you like, but it will not be me. I am waiting."

"Then it's you, huntsman." Julian grinned wickedly. "Hope you ate a light lunch."

"Just kidding. I'm with Juniper. No shoving. Waiting. Waiting is good." Luca shot off the words like a rocket, edging away from the tight bars with a nervous gulp.

Julian looked at Juniper for a long moment, then looked down at his hands. He nodded, then set the bundle of cloth and his hands on his lap. Juniper pressed her back against the silver metal of the cage. The cool metal felt good against her still warm skin. She hadn't even had time to think about what had just happened, about the burn marks on Julian's hands. As if she had carried the heat inside her...as if...as if...but no. That was silly, she was too easily convinced, and her mind was too ready *to* convince.

The cage began to rattle.

The fire giant. She knew that there were earth, water, air, and fire giants that roamed the world. The ones on solid ground were earth, water, and fire, all residing in the mountains to the east. Those that dwelled on the ground were said to be the cause of earthquakes and avalanches. Every time an earthquake would shake the world, Juniper's mind raced with images of horrible giants running down from the mountains to kidnap and eat her. The only ones she never thought to fear were air giants...they lived in the sky. Of course, the house she was in was obviously an air giant's, as it was perched in the sky. She would have laughed at her situation if not for the fear that laughing would instigate throw up. But maybe the giant was friendly...she tossed a glance at the odd *Family is Forever* blanket. Maybe the giant valued warm hugs and bingo. Something told her that wasn't it.

Then she remembered the hand that had taken her...the fire...

Only air giants lived above the clouds. So what was a fire giant doing up here?

Booming steps echoed down the hall, and Juniper looked up worriedly at the boys. They both scrambled to their feet, and Juniper did the same, nearly falling flat on her face with the rush she was in.

She crossed her arms over her chest and tried to stand in an intimidating way. Though, she was pretty short and about as intimidating as a lamppost. She put on her mean face, snarling and narrowing her eyes. It was tiring to frown; she thought for a second if this was how Kyra always felt.

"You look constipated." Luca laughed.

"I do not!" Juniper shot back, then let the mean face fall and settled for a stern look instead.

The giant rounded the corner, and for the first time, Juniper got a good look at him. He was tall, the tallest thing Juniper had ever seen. Limbs like tree trunks and hair like braided, dangling ropes, he towered over everything in the room. The giant's skin looked like orange, yellow, and red marble, swirls decorating his entire body like candle wax. His hair was a rusty red color, like dried blood seeping from a wound. It looked like it was moving—Juniper took a second look and realized that it was, in fact, moving, because it wasn't hair at all. It was flames that were licking his scalp, a huge blaze atop his head the size of a bonfire. His eyes were sparkling like crystals, fiery yellow stars. Burning bright embers amidst a sea of infernos. He was horrible and beautiful all at once in the way things far away were beautiful. How supernovas looked dazzling, but if you were up close, they would destroy you.

That was how the giant looked, and Juniper was terrifyingly amazed.

She felt incredibly small as the fear melted away and was replaced by awe. In all her sixteen years, she had never seen something so wonderfully strange. She had never seen a being whose very blood pulsed with magic, who lived and breathed fire and bone.

And deep down within her, no matter how hard she tried to ignore it, it called her.

The fire giant lumbered into the kitchen, eyes blinking slowly. Every time he blinked, Juniper waited for his eyes to open again so she could see their yellow flame. His hypnotic gaze rested on her in the cage as he knelt down and came eye level with the table.

"Hello," The fire giant said, voice smooth and silky like dripping honey. "I am Cormoran. Who might you be?"

Whatever Juniper had expected, it was not this. She had thought the giant—Cormoran—would snatch her up and eat her right away, not make small talk. She tried not to think about the fact that he could pick her up with his pinky and swallow her in one bite. Tilting her chin and trying earnestly to keep her stern look steady, she said, "I-I am Princess Juniper of Aazagonia. These are my, they are my companions, the...oh! The Dragon Warrior and...uh...Luca."

Julian struck a dramatic pose while Luca gave a small wave, face white with fear.

Cormoran laughed, a great rumbling sound like a volcano spewing lava. "Your titles do not matter to me. I do not care, girl, if you are a princess of mortal lands. It is your blood that will fuel me, not your rank or wealth."

"My...blood?"

"It's funny, isn't it? Pesky mortals spend their short time upon the soil aiming for greatness. Yet all humans are equal when set upon my dinner plate."

His words were oddly reasonable. A living legend of old was in front of her, telling her that she was going to be eaten, and yet the only thing crossing her otherwise blank mind was the thought that Cormoran's musings would look fine on a motivational t-shirt. She said, "You are going to eat us."

Cormoran laughed again, long and hearty. "Yes, girl. Unless there is something wrong with your blood." The giant snapped his fingers, and flames ran up and down his palm, casting flickering reflections over the cage.

Juniper heard Julian intake a sharp breath. *A prince with the blood of silver and of death.* Only now did she consider that that line of his prophecy meant more than jumbled together words. Julian cast his eyes to the floor and clenched his burned hands into fists. The pain of his wound didn't seem to matter at the moment.

Raising his eyes to the giant, Julian said, "My blood is tainted." He didn't go on.

A spike of worry for him launched into Juniper's heart. What did he mean by that? His blood was tainted? She didn't understand. Everything in her life had spiraled out of control, like she was in the center of a tornado and everything that made sense was whirling around her in frenzied pirouettes. The world felt so big; Juniper felt small. Everything was slipping from her fingers, just out of reach. She wished more than anything that she had Kyra by her side. She would know what to do. She would know how to save them.

The giant's lips twisted into a cruel scowl as he said, "Then I shall cast you from the clouds...not before I eat the other two. A pity that you must watch your friends be gobbled. Though perhaps you will enjoy it if you have qualms with them."

"Bet you're wishing you let me shove you through the bars," Julian hissed at Luca and Juniper.

Luca's dark eyes widened as the giant began reaching for him. He clambered backward, trying desperately to evade the giant's red fingers as Cormoran picked him up and pulled him outside the cage. Juniper watched in horror as Luca was raised to the giant's lips. Before she even knew what she was going to say, Juniper shouted out.

"Wait!" she called, and Cormoran froze. He lowered Luca from his jaws momentarily. Juniper tried not to let her relief show too evidently. Luca was not going to be eaten. At least not for another couple seconds.

"What is it, girl?" Cormoran was clearly irritated that his meal was being interrupted.

Juniper squeezed her eyes shut and racked her brain for something, anything, that would save them for a moment. Sadly, the only things that seemed to be in her brain at the moment was a lullaby her mother used to sing to her, and Julian's charming grin.

Unless there is something wrong with your blood, the fire giant had said. She had to think, but there was no time, and—

She blurted out, "Our blood is all tainted! Very tainted!"

"Is it?" Cormoran's dandelion-colored eyes glittered like little suns in their own solar system.

"Yes," Juniper said quickly—too quickly—then, "We all contracted a disease. It's a thing you can get from, from...beans!" Gears whirred in her head, drawing together something. Whether that something would save their skin was yet to be decided. "If you eat too many beans, you contract this terrible blood virus that makes your blood turn poisonous and...yes, it turns your blood so poisonous and deadly, definitely deadly to anyone who tried to eat us!"

Cormoran cocked his head and set Luca down on the table. Luca stared at Juniper, wide-eyed with shock. He didn't dare look up at the giant again.

"Oh, it's so deadly," Julian chimed in, dramatically throwing his cloak-wrapped hands over his forehead. "It's corroding us inside out. I can feel my insides burning with the fervor of a thousand deserts." He tossed a wink at Juniper as he said the last part.

"It burns!" howled Luca, clutching at his side in fake pain. He looked like a fish flopping out of water, the way he was moaning and clawing at his side. It looked odd, and after a few seconds of everyone staring at him with confused looks on their faces (even Cormoran looked concerned). Juniper moved to act as if she were in pain as well, but she remembered that she was quite terrible at acting.

It was her words that would convince the giant, not her actions. Her words were her power, and she was going to use them.

Juniper said, a little too enthusiastically, pointing to Julian, "Look at his hands! His hands have already started to corrode from

the blood disease! This is what is going to happen to the rest of us!"
She ran over to Julian and unwrapped his hands, showing off the
deep burns there.

If the giant looked skeptical before, he now looked convinced
as soon as Julian's hands were shown. Cormoran wrinkled his nose
in disgust, then said, "There is nothing worse than poisoned human
blood. Tastes like insect spray."

Luca was shoved back through the cage door and he collapsed in
a faceplant on the floor.

"Does that mean you're letting us go?" Juniper said, the hope evident in her voice. It looked like the giant would return them safely
to the clearing where they had left Kyra and Cal. She dared to hope.
Hope was her beacon; hope was her guide.

The giant smiled then, and all her hope fled like schoolchildren
from a test. His lips were strung tight against his jagged, diamond-
looking teeth. Cormoran got close to the cage and breathed slowly,
his breath hot and smelling of embers.

Cormoran said, "No, little mortals, I will not let you go. You still
will die. The only difference now is...I shall burn your blood out of
you first."

9

Above the World

Kyra climbed. One hand in front of the other, limbs aching as she repeatedly pulled herself up the beanstalk. Her whole body hurt like never before, her arms were sore, and her legs begged to rest. She kept going, though, because Juniper was somewhere above her. That was all it took to make her forget about the pain.

They were about halfway up the stalk, and the world stretched out below her.

She could see the forest at the edge of her vision, green and lush and going on for miles and miles. To the left of it was Aazagonia, her kingdom. The place that Callista was going to have kneel before her cruel feet. Beyond the forest was the kingdom of Maiike, which was where Julian's mother, and before his death, father, ruled. Where Cal came from, too. Further east, past Maiike, was the glittering desert of Bayuma and the towering city of Yen-Sing. North...north was where they were headed, to the Winter Palace. To the snowy forests of the fae.

Kyra didn't dare look at Cal. She was scared that if she looked, he wouldn't even be there anymore. Maybe he had fallen when she couldn't see. The wind up there was loud and roaring; maybe she couldn't hear Cal as he screamed her name and fell to the hard ground down below. She focused on the extraneous cycle of pulling herself up, planting her feet, then pulling up again. Kyra concentrated on the pain ringing through her lungs, her hands, her core. The pain kept her from falling. It pushed her on, like it always had.

"Princess," Cal's voice came over the roar of the wind, and Kyra felt her heart relax a little. He was alive and right next to her, and that alone helped her climb even faster. "I need to rest."

"There's a big branch up ahead, just a few more minutes. Once we get there, we can sit without worrying about falling," Kyra fought to make her voice heard over the wind. It snarled at her dress and tried to tear her from the beanstalk. The small enclave was a few feet up. It looked safe and guarded from the monstrous and ever-present wind.

They had almost reached the haven up above, so Kyra let her mind wander. She thought of how happy the others would be once she, Kyra, had saved them. She pictured Juniper beaming, Luca bowing, and Julian saying something along the lines of 'Please take my place as the Dragon Warrior. You are the coolest and awesomest person alive!' In this fantasy, Cal was there, too, and he was standing off to the side and shaking his head at her like she was the best thing since chocolate cake. Which was silly; because nothing was better than chocolate cake and to say otherwise was pure blasphemy.

Thinking so far ahead, she didn't realize when her hand, reaching up for a fistful of leaf, missed its grab.

Kyra fell.

There was a moment when she wasn't falling freely yet, when the wind went silent as she watched her hand slip. She hung in the air as if suspended by a chord, the world around her perfectly still. Cal's eyes widened. That image of Cal was burned in her mind as the moment ended, and she was falling.

Falling. The clouds stretched out above her. Her hair flew upwards, gold strands mixing with the blue of the sky. So this was what it was like, she thought, to fall from something that was taller than any tree. She thought she should close her eyes or scream. But her mouth was just parted in silent shock. Her hands clawed out in front of her, desperately grabbing for something to hold on to, to stop her fall, to save her.

She had to live. She had to save Juniper.

You and your sister are strands of cloth woven together, moon and sun. Do not forget it. Something dark inside her stirred, responding to this thought. Something cold like snow echoed deep within...telling her to reach out...

She flung her hands up above her head to grab the beanstalk.

That was her last action before a hand was gripping hers, and she was no longer falling. She felt herself being hauled up, suspended in the air by the hand, and the hand alone. Her legs dangled with the sway of the wind.

Kyra looked up and saw Cal, grimacing from the pain of holding her up. He was the only thing keeping her from falling to the floor far below. Cal was sitting in the divot of the stalk, braced against it and using all his strength to hold her there. He slowly started to pull her up. Kyra dully tried to help him, but she was so full of shock that she could no longer move.

Then she was in the haven that was the extra-large branch, and she was sitting against the hard material of the stalk, breathing heavily and almost shaking. Almost.

She desperately wanted to look at Cal, to find comfort in him, but she couldn't wrench her gaze away from the forest below. So many miles and miles below. The green calmed her breathing. The sun was high in the sky now and shone down hot and heavy.

"Cal..." She drifted off. *Thank you*, she wanted to say. *Thank you for saving my life*. But for some reason, she couldn't get the words out. They came choked and heavy, like she had a mouthful of molasses. As if saying those words would make what had just happened real. If she said thank you to Cal, she knew that the dam she had been holding up all these years would break, and she would fall to pieces. So she didn't thank him, or smile, or hug him. Instead, Kyra breathed, "Wow."

She pressed her back up against the beanstalk, trying to get as far from the edge of the branch as possible, and realized that she was still holding on tight to Cal's hand. Holding it like a lifeline, their fingers were interlocked and almost white from the pressure. Cal was squeezing back, just as tight.

Kyra didn't let go. She felt a flutter in her stomach like the beating of a dragon's wings, if the dragon was small and if there were a million of them. Butterflies in her stomach would be a better way to describe it. She had heard people use that word: butterflies. But that was used when someone was nervous around another person...So no, Kyra decided she didn't have butterflies and would never have them, because that would mean nervousness, and Kyra was never nervous. She brushed the odd feeling aside as something that might happen when you almost just fell to your death. The fluttering didn't mean anything save for that Cal had rescued her, and she was thankful. Nothing more, nothing less. At least, she tried to convince herself that was true.

"Wow," Cal echoed. Kyra still couldn't get the courage to look at him. All her life, she had been courageous. Brave. So why wasn't she brave enough to just *look* at Cal? "You almost fell."

"I almost fell," Kyra agreed. "But you caught me." It was the closest she would get to gratitude.

"You're welcome," said Cal. Kyra then, finally, turned to look at him. She felt her heart catch. His eyes were wide and he looked flustered. He was panting from the climb, his hair damp with sweat, making it look even blacker than before. Little tendrils of it clung to his cheekbones like strokes of paint from the night sky. She gripped his hand, no longer caring if it was too tight. "Are you okay?" Cal finally asked after a few moments of silence.

Kyra said hesitantly, "Don't worry about me."

"You almost fell to your death. *Are you okay?*"

Kyra looked up and down the beanstalk. "This is exactly how I envisioned my week to go. How 'bout you?"

"Precisely how I want to be spending my time," Cal said, then shut his eyes tight. Kyra watched as his breathing slowed, and his grip relaxed on her hand.

They looked out over the world below, at the sun piercing through the clouds and shining on the beanstalk. The wind had dulled to a gentle breeze, ruffling the leaves of the trees far below like bird feathers.

"You snore, by the way," he said.

Kyra whipped her head to him. He was grinning, his ears perking up in their annoyingly endearing way. She said, "I do not!"

"Uh-huh. You snored last night in the clearing. Really loud." Cal looked like he was trying not to laugh. "It was obnoxious, honestly."

Kyra's mouth fell open in shock. "I'm a princess! How dare you say that! I could have, like, ten people get you fired." Kyra wasn't sure that was necessarily true, as he did work for an entirely different kingdom, but maybe she could. If she was even considered a princess, anymore. It didn't matter, she decided, if her kingdom thought she was dead or a traitor or something. Kyra thought of her father suddenly, holding the gleaming sword over her, about to drive it down. It was easy to understand how the Queen had been able to want to kill her and Juniper; it was infinitely harder to try and understand where Kyra's dad was coming from in all this. Kyra had always known her stepmother was a cold-hearted, evil witch. Ever since the day Callista had forced her to go to a boring castle meeting, Kyra had known the Queen was rotten to the core. No kind and good mother would want their child to suffer through the torture that was responsibility. Kyra unlocked her and Cal's hands to shove him, and he just let out a laugh. "Listening to my snores is even creepier."

"You were snoring so loud, it was impossible not to hear it," he said, then after seeing the look on her face, said, "Kidding."

"Why weren't you sleeping, then?"

Cal shifted uncomfortably. "Just couldn't. Too busy thinking about stopping the coronation, I guess. That's all."

"No, no, no," said Kyra, "I didn't grow up with a sister who sucks at lying to not be able to recognize bad lying when I see it. Tell me what's wrong, or I'll shove you off this beanstalk."

"Something tells me you're joking." Cal rolled his eyes, then said, "Fine. But you can't tell anyone. Not even Juniper."

"Not even Juniper."

"Not Luca, either."

"Why would I—fine, not Luca, either. Now tell me, I'm already losing interest." She had begun to fiddle with an abnormally large leaf, folding it in half then unfolding it, over and over.

"I was thinking last night. About...well, about you." Cal met her eyes.

Kyra shoved down the jolt in her heart at his words. What was that supposed to mean? Better to joke than unpack that sentence. She swallowed hard and smirked. "Is this a love confession? Listen, Cal, I like you a lot, but I only date guys who write me love ballads and buy me kingdoms. No more, no less."

"You really are full of yourself, huh?" Cal said quickly. "I meant about you and your sister." Kyra couldn't ignore the twinge of disappointment she felt.

Cal continued, "I've met you both before, back when Jules' father was still alive. We visited your castle once, and I got to tag along, back when I was first promoted to be Julian's main servant. We got to your castle, and I was sent to fetch the king—something for Julian. A medicine. But, I couldn't find your palace's medic room. In Maiike, our medic is stationed in an infirmary below the castle, in the dungeons. I was eleven; I thought yours would be below the castle, too. I found a staircase in the library that led to the chambers below the castle." A haunted look had appeared in Cal's eyes, like he was remembering something he had tried hard to forget. Like he had seen a ghost.

She tried to remember him in her castle, but as an eleven year old. Maybe he had lighter hair or was shorter. Maybe they had talked before, and she never had realized. Kyra was suddenly sure she would have remembered him if they had.

"What did you find?" Kyra was surprised to find that her voice was tight, her words choppy. She didn't want to know what he had found in the deepest corners of the castle, but she knew that whatever it was, it had made Cal's smile disappear.

"I found a room," Cal answered. "A room that looked like a dungeon. The walls were stone, and it was cold and dark in a way that no cold or dark place had ever felt. Like...like something very old resided there." His next words hung over the sky itself. "In the room was a golden mirror."

Kyra felt goosebumps on her arms. She had felt the same way when she passed those chambers. That something dreadful lived down there. Her stepmother had always told her to never, ever go down there, or else. It was the one rule Kyra had obeyed.

"A mirror?"

"Yes," Cal said. "A mirror. The Queen sat before it. She asked it a question; I can't remember exactly what she asked. I know it was odd. Something about wanting to know who was the most fair in her land. I don't know why she'd want to know that, though."

"Fair means other things than honorable. Fair can mean looks, too." The word caught in her throat. "Fair can mean beauty."

Cal said, "That makes more sense. I've heard Callista is obsessed with her looks." It did make more sense; the Queen had always been crazy about looking the best. Vain little woman. One time, Kyra had called her that to her face and was grounded for ten weeks. Totally worth it. But why would Callista ask a mirror? Something to do with her reflection, maybe?

"So my stepmother talks to inanimate objects. She's delusional. We already knew this."

"Well...she didn't just talk to the mirror. The mirror...it talked back."

"So you're crazy, too? Of course Juniper gets to be kidnapped by a giant while I get stuck with the crazy person," Kyra said, trying to hide the jitters rising in her. She had a feeling that Cal was telling the truth. If only he *was* crazy. That would've made this a lot easier.

Cal frowned, frustrated. "I'm serious. A voice came from the mirror and told her that the 'Sun's Child' was fairer than her," He said, then looked up the beanstalk, towards the shining sun. Kyra followed his gaze, but the light hurt her eyes. She brought up a hand to shield it from her, casting a dark, cool shadow over her face.

"Gotta hand it to you. You're a good storyteller. Your realism could use some work, but other than that, I almost believed you."

"I'm not lying. I know what I saw."

"I don't know what you think you saw," Kyra said, "but it wasn't Callista talking to a magic mirror about who's the hottest of all the land. My stepmother forces the servants to tell her that as they tuck her into bed each night."

"Trying to tell me everything happening right now is normal?" Cal indicated the giant beanstalk, the chaos in the sky, and the peaceful, unbothered ground. Realization struck his features like lighting rolling over the desert. "Oh, I get you. You're a deflector."

"No, you're a deflector!" Kyra bit the inside of her cheek. That sentence had sounded an awful lot like a deflection. "You can't just tell me that my stepmother used magic! Based on something you saw when you were eleven! You sound insane! It doesn't make sense, and we're wasting time. Every second is another second that I could be using to save Juniper."

Kyra stood up, her blood boiling. However much she wanted to believe Cal, she just couldn't. Her stepmother could never use magic! She was a human! Kyra would know if she did. The woman was evil, but not that evil. Okay, maybe she was that evil, but still. The Queen's morality wasn't in question. A human wielding magic was impossible.

Cal's face crumpled, and he looked down at his feet, dejected. Kyra realized her words might have been a bit too harsh. But she couldn't go back now. She didn't know how to go back.

"Sun's Child. That's Juniper," said Kyra suddenly.

Cal hesitated for a moment, then said, "It made your stepmother flip out, hearing that her daughter was fairer than her. I was just thinking that maybe that has something to do with why your mom wanted to get her out of the picture."

"What about me, then? Why did she want me gone?" She feigned nonchalance, but even Kyra couldn't deny the eagerness for answers that burned in her.

"I don't know." Cal shook his head. "Maybe she was jealous of you, too."

Obviously Cal wasn't so smart after all. She was just...Kyra. The girl who the Queen had told so many times that she was nothing. That she would never be anything because she wasn't pretty. Kyra didn't care. There were a billion other things she would rather be before pretty. And Juniper! Juniper was *smart* and *kind* and *brave* and *weird* and *those* were the things that made her beautiful. Those were the things that made her 'fairer' than the Queen.

Kyra scoffed. "Wrong sister, pal."

"Maybe," Cal said, in a tone that suggested otherwise. "Or maybe she just thought you were annoying, Crazypants." That made them both smile. "Or maybe she's just a terrible mother. Some people are just plain wicked. The Queen's actions can't be justified. I have met a lot of people, and not all are good. Some are really, really evil just for the sake of it. Not everyone is so great and moral like you and me."

"Don't get all preachy on me now." Her voice sounded incredibly small against the roar of the wind. "I already know that in this world, good never stands a chance. And that's just a fact."

"You must not read, then." Cal had a slight, knowing smile. "Cause sure, there's a lot of terribleness and wickedness in the world, but I know for a fact that there's a lot more good. For every giant beanstalk, there are at least two people trying to climb it."

"I didn't peg you as a sap."

"And I didn't peg you as someone who doesn't see the truth in fairytales."

"Then you've got me all wrong." Kyra scowled. "They're called tales for a reason."

"Says the princess about to save her sister from a giant above the world."

Cal reached out and patted her lightly on the shoulder, smiling in that knowing way. Kyra was able to choke out a barely intelligible, *"I'msorry."*

"I couldn't hear that." Cal stood up beside her. "Mind saying it louder?" The look on his face made it seem like he did, in fact, hear every word she had said.

"I said, I'm sorry. And thank you. For saving me from falling to my doom. You may have ensured my horrible existence will go on longer. But thank you."

"Apology accepted." Cal grinned, then began climbing up the beanstalk. "See? That wasn't so hard."

Kyra rolled her eyes, then began climbing up after him. She took one last look at the world below, at the bright green of the forest, and all the kingdoms and people who couldn't care less about what she was doing right now.

"You have no idea."

10

The Giant Slayer

"What do you think that harp's for?" Julian asked. "Obviously not the giant, because he's too big for it, so who?"

"Maybe Cormoran likes it," Luca said, looking quite pleased with that. "Like a toy."

"That is cute! An itty-bitty harp in the giant's hands." Juniper giggled.

"Okay, that is pretty adorable," said Julian. He was staring at the silver harp that sat across the room on a chair, the light from the ceiling shining down on it as if to say, *Look at me, I'm an awesome magical harp.*

Luca nodded vigorously. "I second that." His eyes gleamed brown in the dark like sunlight on oak wood. Juniper wanted to paint them, if only she knew how to paint well. That was something she'd like to learn, you know, if she ever made it out of that cage alive and not eaten.

As if on cue, the fire giant walked into the kitchen, hands poised on his hips. His hair was blazing extra wildly then, and he looked ready for a fight.

Beside him was an air giant.

The first thought that went through Juni's mind was that she was about a second away from passing out from fear for the billionth time that day. The second thought was that it now made sense as to why the house was in the sky; an air giant lived there and must have invited the fire giant up. The air giant was just as terrifying and awful as Cormoran, but with inverted colors. Her skin was cold, whites and purples and blues. Hair like the wind itself, long and cascading and somehow ethereal, with a face twisted in a scowl. The air giant stood tall and imposing, even larger than Cormoran and therefore double the level of scariness. Juniper wanted to scream, but she bit it back. That would not be a very good first impression.

Her mother had always stressed the importance of first impressions, that they had to be graceful and mysterious and unique. Juniper's were always bumbling and awkward, while Kyra's were often...rude, to say the least. The Queen always excelled at first impressions, however, and it got Juniper thinking about how some evil people were blessed with great social skills. What she would give to always know what to say and how to say it.

In light of knowing this, somehow, she still chose to say, "You are very tall. I am Juniper. I am short."

The air giant scoffed, then crossed over to the cage. Cormoran said, "I told you these humans are odd."

Shooing him away, the air giant lowered her white-blue eyes to be level with Juniper. She spoke with the force of every wind that swept across the skies. "I am Blunderbore of the Air Giants. Welcome to my abode of the sky."

Juniper swallowed, wishing her introduction had sounded as cool as that. She heard her words over and over again in her head and pictured a thousand better things she could have said, like, that

she was a princess, or that people called her Sun's Child. But no, instead, she said, *I am Juniper. I am short.* Fantastic.

Then she realized that was not what she should have been thinking at that moment, because she was going to be burned alive by two
giants in about fifty seconds if she didn't start talking.

"The sky...how does that work, exactly?" Juniper asked, her voice
annoyingly bright and squeaky. It got like that sometimes when she
was nervous.

"You are asking how the sky works?" Blunderbore's massive eyebrows shot up. "I have forgotten the extent of the stupidity that humans possess."

"We are very stupid, yes." Julian nodded excessively, saying anything to get the giant's mind off of their next meal. "Humanity is
stupid beyond comparison."

Luca muttered, "Though I'm beginning to think it's just us."

Blunderbore continued, "Small human, of what were you asking?
If you wish for me to explain the atomic structure of the sky, I
shall—"

Juniper hurriedly said, "Uh, no. No thank you. I meant, um, how
does your home float above the clouds? It does not seem scientifically feasible."

Blunderbore said, cocking her head, "It is magic, small human."
Of course it was magic. Magic was infuriating in that it defied every
law of science and theory that Juniper knew; it defied and yet it
won.

"Get on with the killings, Blunderbore!" Cormoran roared, his
eyes blazing. Both literally and metaphorically. "I am impatient with
hunger for the humanlings!"

"Killings?" Julian piped in, cradling his burned hands against his
midriff. "I thought our blood was tainted. Meaning you can't kill us?
That would be so cool of you."

"You have thought wrong, wavy-haired human," Blunderbore

said. "I have been called by the good Cormoran of Fire to inspect your blood to see if it is indeed tainted by curses or poison. He believes you three to be slippery-tongued liars."

"Um, wait," Juniper said desperately, trying to think of any way to stall. "What's a fire giant doing with an air giant in the sky?"

"Yes, Blunderbore, what indeed?" Cormoran asked, crossing his arms.

Blunderbore was suddenly silent, biting her monstrously huge lip. Was the air giant almost acting...awkward?

"Well, answer the girl," said Cormoran, growing impatient. "What are we? It's beginning to feel like you don't want to date me after all."

"Can we talk about this after the humanlings have been burned and eaten?"

"No, I think we'd *all* like to know."

Juniper nodded excessively. "Yes, do tell. For as long as you'd like."

"They're stalling, can't you see, you idiot?" Blunderbore said, rubbing her temples in irritation. "And I'm hungry! I just want to eat human flesh, is that too much to ask for?"

"Oh, it's always about hunger!" Cormoran shouted. "Killing humans this, maiming them that. You'll just go on to find another giant to eat people with. Is that what you want? Because I'll climb down the beanstalk right now."

This wasn't quite what Juniper had expected when she asked that question, but it was working out nicely indeed.

"Enough!" Blunderbore said. "Let's discuss this on our own time, Cormoran. First we need to test these humanlings' blood."

"Are you sure you don't want to keep debating the nature of your relationship?" Julian asked innocently. "This seems like an important subject. Maybe you should spend a day or two in couples therapy."

Blunderbore sent him a withering look. "Human to be tested, step forward. Out of the cage."

"The cage is locked." Luca pointed out, as if that would stop the impending doom.

"I think not," said Blunderbore, and she flicked the cage door. It fell open with a clang, leaving nothing in between the two over-joyed, bloodthirsty giants and the three admittedly not-as-over-joyed-or-bloodthirsty kids.

So, the whole time, the cage door had been unlocked? Sunbeam above, the giants were right. Humans could be incredibly stupid. Looking around the room, she saw that there was about a hundred-foot drop from the edge of the table to the floor. The cage had never been keeping them captive. She tossed a nervous glance at the floor.

Juniper froze, then looked quickly at Jules and Luca. *What do we do?*

No plans or last-minute ideas popped into her head; no quick sparks of something to save them came. She had thought that she could save them with her words, but she had failed. Silence echoed out among the three teenagers, as no one offered up anything. They had been defeated at last. For the first time in her life, Juniper knew what it was to be truly afraid.

Finally, Julian stepped forward, chin raised in determination. "I will be the human to be tested."

"No—" Juniper started, but he just looked at her and shook his head quickly, as if saying, *Trust me.* Juniper decided, for whatever reason, to do just that. Saying a quick prayer in her head, she put all her faith in him in that moment and stepped back as he walked out of the cage and into the den of giants and fire.

"Go ahead," said Blunderbore.

Cormoran smiled darkly, then plucked Julian up by the back of his shirt and raised him up to his mouth. He said, "Courage is com-mendable, wavy-haired humanling. I would sit with you for tea in honor of your bravery if I was not about to eat you. Now, stick out your arm."

As if in a trance, Juniper watched in horror as Julian stuck out his arm. It dangled into Cormoran's gaping jaw. It looked incredibly small and tiny against the giant, and Juniper felt her feet freeze beneath her. She wanted to cry and scream and throw herself at the giant because although Julian seemed like he had a plan, it was looking like he was going to die no matter what.

Juniper felt Luca grab her hand, and she squeezed it reassuringly. Even though she was the furthest from being reassured herself, and she was sure she was toting yet another constipated look.

Cormoran opened his mouth, then bit down on Julian's arm with a sickening crunch.

Juniper heard someone scream high-pitched—oh wait, that was her—and she fell to her knees in agony. "Julian!"

His face was twisted in pain, but other than that, he looked alright. Well, he looked not-dead, so as alright as the situation allowed. Cormoran opened his mouth and dropped Julian down on the table. He landed in a roll, then crumpled on the floor, his arm bleeding profusely.

Juniper let out a little shriek, then ran to him. The silver of the cage and gold of well, everything else, blurred in her vision. Through the haziness of her terror she could feel Luca being dragged beside her, still holding on tight to her hand. Up close, Julian didn't look too hurt. His arm had a huge tooth mark from the giant's sharp canine, and a deep gash had been cut where he had been bit. Scarlet blood had begun seeping from the wound. Although Juniper was freaking out beyond her known limits, she breathed a sigh of relief as she saw that the cut wasn't deep.

"Can't say I've ever been bitten before," Julian grunted, tiny beads of sweat forming on his forehead.

"There's a first for everything," Luca mumbled. "Does it hurt?"

"Ask me after you've been bit," Jules said with a wry smirk, still clutching at his arm.

Juniper laughed sharply, and the boys gave her a weird look. The laugh was loud and bitter and made her sound faintly like a crazy person, but she didn't care. She was just happy Julian was okay and that she was, too.

Blunderbore watched the scene below with an amused look, like one who was reading an odd scene in a book or pondering something very far away. The blue and white swirls decorating her skin moved as if with wind. Roaring fields and clouds morphing into shapes, forced by wind, seemed to swirl in her eyes. It was a look that made Juniper startled, and she matched that look with another crazy-person laugh.

"I think the small human is...how do they say..." Blunderbore asked, "...losing it?"

"Losing it," Juniper affirmed without skipping a beat, and then, "So? Did you find that his blood was tainted?" Her voice showed that she was as much scared of not hearing the answer as of hearing it.

Cormoran licked his lips, which made Juniper gag and want to pass out all at once. He looked confused for a moment, as if tasting something that didn't sit well with him.

And then, the fire giant fell over and died.

The giant fell like a great tree trunk, the flames of his hair flickering out and extinguishing. His amber-colored eyes rolled to the whites as his knees buckled beneath him, and he crashed to the floor. The whole room shook upon his collision, and Juniper noticed absent-mindedly that the silver harp was knocked off the chair, and tumbled to the floor, lost amidst the chaos.

Blunderbore roared, but it was more of a wail of something being ripped from her very soul than a battlecry. "Cormoran!" she cried, then fell to her knees and gripped the fire giant's head in her hands. Cormoran made no move to stop her. He lay limp on the floor. A candle snuffed out.

Lass den Tod des Paten gütig sein, Juniper thought. *Let Godfather Death be kind*. It was an old faerie saying of mourning and death, and she found herself repeating it when someone passed away. Juniper said it first when her father died when she was young, and she thought it again now as she watched a legend of old fall. To watch a fire giant die was something very legendary, indeed. Something awful and wonderful like the giant itself.

Juniper took the opportunity to wrench Luca from the floor, and help Julian up, too. They ran to the edge of the table and looked down at the massive drop to the floor.

"Mortal foes! Do not think I am finished with you, yet, you poisoned abominations!" Blunderbore raged from the floor, where she was still crouched in a mournful stance next to Cormoran's still body.

Poisoned abominations. So...Julian's blood was poisonous. It had killed Cormoran. Juniper's racing mind was going so haywire that she barely had time to register the fact. How did one have poisonous blood? Shoving her thoughts away, she remembered that they were running out of time.

"Do we jump?" Julian asked. His looked out over the edge of the table in apprehension.

"We cannot jump," Juniper said, voice rising in panic, "we would die, would we not?" She tried not to picture the three of them splattering to their deaths on the hard stone floor below.

"We'd definitely die," Luca half-shrieked, his hands fiddling at the hem of his shirt.

Juniper closed her eyes and desperately tried to think of what to do.

Nothing seemed to be working in her mind, save for images of the weird *Family is Forever* blanket that clashed with the atmosphere of the room so greatly it felt as if she were going to explode. That stupid, odd blanket was taking up precious space in her mind, and—

The *Family is Forever* blanket. That was it! She still was undecided if it was cute or weird, but for now, it was helpful. She ran across the table towards it, flying like the wind. A solid, insane plan was forming fast now, and she didn't even pause to wonder if maybe she really was losing it.

"There is nowhere you can run in this house that I will not find you," Juniper could hear Blunderbore call from her kneeling position on the floor. "It is useless to even try."

Grabbing onto the blanket and tugging it behind her, Juniper ran back to the edge of the table. It was heavy. Then again, she was about as weak as a baby duckling. She yanked it over to Luca and Julian, who were staring at her in confusion.

"Family is Forever? Cute saying, but is now the time for motivational phrases?" Julian asked, skeptically grabbing an edge from her.

"We parachute," Juniper said simply, handing another edge to a wincing Luca.

"Our wrists would one-hundred percent snap off if we did that," Luca said in rising panic, inching closer to the edge of the table and peering down at the steep drop below. "Parachuting would be a death sentence." He tightened his grip on the blanket.

"Yet I see you are still preparing to jump," Juniper said, lifting her chin a little.

Luca looked at his feet, then back at her. "If my wrists snap, you're paying for my medical bills."

"If this goes wrong, we're gonna have a lot worse injuries than snapped wrists." Julian shrugged. He said, not looking at all like he was ready, "And with that, is everyone ready? We'll jump on the count of three."

Juniper nodded, though she was pretty sure it was more of a shaking her head no.

"Three..." Julian began.

"Two..." Luca continued.

"One," Juniper finished.

The world went silent for a moment as they took a few running steps, then soared off the edge of the table.

The blanket flew out behind them, billowing into the air. For a moment, there was nothing stopping their fall, and the three of them were dropping freely.

Then the blanket caught, and Juniper felt her arms jerk up, as she barely could hold on. Her wrist cracked and her legs flailed in the air aimlessly, like she was kicking an invisible enemy. She saw Luca struggling to hold on to his edge, and Jules was only using his uninjured arm.

The makeshift parachute was working surprisingly well; it had swelled out and resembled a hot air balloon, with the one edge that nobody was holding flapping in the air.

They were getting close to the ground now. Juniper knew; she just didn't want to look. But the ground had to be at least a dozen seconds away, and she knew she had time before impact.

That was why she was so surprised when her feet hit the ground after only a few seconds in the air. Her knees buckled beneath her, accompanied by a jarring electric shock spiking through her legs. "Ow," Juniper muttered.

The floor began to shake.

Blunderbore was rising from Cormoran's limp body like an avenging angel, eyes alight with fury. The air giant looked even taller now that Juniper was on the floor, and she looked *mad*.

There was only one thing worse than a giant, Juniper thought, and that was an angry giant.

"You have slayed Cormoran of Fire," Blunderbore said, her voice calm and still. "For his honor, I shall slay you."

"Wasn't she already planning on slaying us?" Luca anxiously whispered.

"I do not think she cares," Juniper replied.

"Either way we end up dead," Jules said. "So it doesn't really matter."

Blunderbore started forward, a look of malice burned into her features. She held out her hand. The air around it turned warped and twisted, like heat floating above pavement. Churning and morphing into a ball, the air rested in the giant's hand. It floated there for a second, a will-o-wisp amid chaos, then was sent hurling at Juniper and the others.

Luca and Juniper screamed in sync, clutching at each other in terror, as Julian unsheathed his sword that had, apparently, been hanging at his side the entire time. Juniper dizzily thought that he could have used it earlier, but the thought was dashed from her mind as the air-ball hit her square in the chest, and she was sent hurtling backward.

The ball of air picked her up with a huge gust, slamming her into the door behind her. It knocked the wind out of her, and she gasped for breath. Julian raised his sword as another air-ball was sent at him and Luca, but the sword was no use against wind. He and Luca were sent catapulting through the air.

"Not sure what you expected." Juniper gritted her teeth as she hauled herself to her feet. "Did you think the sword would chop up *air*?"

Blunderbore grinned and started towards them, about to scoop them up once again. Juniper groaned as the hand reached towards her, Blunderbore cackled, and—

"Stop!" A voice cried, a familiar voice, a voice belonging to...

Kyra.

And Cal was right next to her. They stood in the doorway, looking worn and weary, barely holding themselves up. Did they...did they climb the beanstalk? Juniper was so overwhelmed with happiness at seeing them, that only a second later did she realize that they would be killed by the giant, too. Now no one would be able to stop the Queen from taking over Aazagonia. And they would all be dead, too, so that wasn't great, either.

Kyra met Juniper's eyes, and nodded at her, looking her over to make sure she was alright. Juniper sent her a thumbs up as if to say, *I am alive, but boy do I have a lot to tell you.*

"Who dares interrupt the awful and powerful Blunderbore of the Air?" The air giant said, and Juniper noticed that her hand had frozen mid-air, and she was no longer about to snatch Juniper up off the floor.

"I do," Kyra said. "And Cal does, too, I guess. Do you?" Kyra looked at Cal in question.

"I don't see why not," Cal said, shrugging.

"Fantastic," said Kyra. "Now let's get to the interrupting."

* * *

Kyra ran to Juniper.

She ran across the gigantic kitchen, feet burning from the arduous climb up the stalk. The second this was over, she was going to sleep for a hundred years. And eat for another hundred. Eating was a major priority. Her stomach gave a rather loud rumble of agreement.

Juniper was lying on the floor, though why, Kyra didn't question. She grabbed Juniper's hand and hauled her to her feet, yanking the light girl into the air momentarily. Cal was helping Luca and Jules to their feet, too, though Julian was grimacing. A quick look at him and one could conclude that he was hurt; his arm had a long red cut. Was that a—was it a tooth mark? What had been going on up here?

"Are you okay?" Juni asked, even though she was the one being rescued from a giant, not the other way around.

"Better. Still awful," admitted Kyra. "Almost fell off the beanstalk. But I'm shaking it off."

"Sunbeam above, what—"

"Just laugh. No time for questions."

"Oh no! Blunderbore!" Juniper pointed at the huge, angry giant coming their way.

"Bless you."

This got a smile from Juniper, and together, they ran for the door. The wacky giant lady (who seemed to have the unfortunate name of Blunderbore) swiped at them, but Kyra yanked Juniper out of the way, sending the giant's hand grasping at thin air.

Luca was right on their heels. Since there was nothing for him to trip over, he was moving surprisingly fast. They were almost out the door. Once they made it there, they would just need to climb all the way down the beanstalk, then think from there how to get the giant off their backs. Kyra was a little more than peeved that she had just climbed up the gigantic beanstalk only to go right back down it. She admitted to herself that she was hoping for an awesome battle against Blunderbore, one where she would fight courageously and ultimately defeat the evil giant and rescue her friends. Though she had no idea exactly how to fight in a battle, she expected that she would be able to pick up on it easily enough. How hard could it be? Instead, the trio of Juniper, Jules, and Luca had managed to escape, kill one of two giants, and not die all on their own, which was a nice surprise. The only casualties looked to be Julian's weird tooth mark on his arm and Juniper's crumbling sanity.

A fire giant lay dead on the floor; his flames extinguished for good. She felt a prickle of pride for Juniper, wondering if her sister was not as helpless as she looked. Maybe Juniper had even been the one to slay the giant! That would be awesome!

Though, killing was against the law and very, very bad. Of course, don't kill anyone unless it is a giant who kidnapped you. And it is further acceptable if that giant was planning on killing you first.

The massive door was nearing now, and Kyra shoved it open with incredible force.

"Little huntsman!" Kyra called, as Luca ran up next to her, the others not far behind.

"Yeah?" asked Luca, looking relieved to see her—no one ever looked relieved to see her, save for Juniper, so that was odd enough in itself.

"How did you let yourself be captured by a giant, you clumsy baby deer?"

Luca rolled his eyes, and widened them as he looked a little bit past Kyra's shoulder. Kyra started as she realized that he was looking at the place Juniper should've been. She whirled around quickly.

Juniper was no longer there. *Ugh,* Kyra thought, *that girl is going to be the death of me.* Kyra scanned the room and saw that her sister was running right towards the giant.

The thought recalculated itself in her head; of course Juniper wasn't running *towards* the giant. But no, Juniper was indeed sprinting towards the giant's feet with a look of determination on her face. Kyra exasperatedly looked to the doorway, towards freedom, then back at her sister. The giant had just noticed that Juniper was darting between her feet and had begun to readjust herself to grab at her.

Cal and Julian had already made it to the door and were standing in the doorway. They looked like little dolls set in a too-big house, the door stretching up and away like the tallest of trees. Cal's jaw was working. He was worried. For who? Her? Then his worry was wasted, as she would be alright. Jules was slumped up against him, looking pale and his gangly features drawn taut like a string. His arm did not look good. That was worth Cal's worry.

"Cal! Start going down the beanstalk! I need to get Juniper!"

Cal hesitated, then gave a quick nod. He turned and half-dragged Julian out. Luca looked worriedly at Kyra, then disappeared behind the door. His expression melted her stone-cold heart. She made sure to smother him with endearing insults later. If there was a later...

Kyra spun on her heels, re-focusing on the plan as she began running back into the den of the giant. The exact opposite of where she wished to be running to.

The boys would be at the beanstalk in about five minutes, and down it in about twenty. Going down would be a lot easier than going up, unless Julian lagged because of his arm. If Kyra and Juniper couldn't make it, at least Cal and the others could stop the Queen. At least there was that.

Never in her life would she imagine that she would be running right at an air giant that wanted her dead. Then again, she never imagined any of this. She especially never thought the giant's lair would be so *gold*. Seriously, the giants had a huge gold obsession. Everything was painted in gaudy and fake-looking paint, as if a golden glitter factory had exploded, and the giants had gone, *Yes, we'll take it all! Everything gold!*

Kyra noticed that Juni wasn't at Blunderbore's feet anymore, and instead had made it to the dead fire giant's hand, darting in between the giant's meaty fingers. She was peeling back the large fingers to see that nestled in there was a tiny, silver harp. Not conventionally tiny—regular size, actually—but it looked small and delicate in the hands of the giant.

The harp made Kyra falter. Pausing for a moment, she saw the harp as a fallen star, shining and shimmering in silver. It was almost glowing, mesmerizing and everything the gold-painted things in the room aspired to be. Bright and pure and compelling like a kind smile.

In her hesitation, Blunderbore had reached down and swiped Kyra off her feet. She tumbled into the giant's hand and felt Blunderbore's fingers wrap around her. Kyra's rib cage contracted as the giant's grip tightened around her. After a moment, she was gasping for breath as if drowning on land, her vision going blurry. Blunt pain sparked behind her eyes, red and gold shapes swimming before her.

Squeezed to death. That was how she was going to die. Being squeezed to death in an ugly gold kitchen. The gold was almost worse than the dying.

Blunderbore raised Kyra up to her face, an evil grin upon her face that could rival the Queen's.

"Golden-haired girl..." Blunderbore said, her voice echoing out as if from across a cliff. Her eyes squinted in recognition, though Kyra was pretty sure she would remember meeting a hundred-foot-tall giant that smelled like animal dung. "By all the elements...the Moon's Child is before me. You shall be the first of your friends to die."

Kyra gasped, then managed to muster, "Sounds fun, but perhaps another time."

Kyra grinned as she bit down on the giant's thumb.

Blunderbore let out a shriek louder than thunder. "Horrible humanling!"

"You bite my friend, I'll bite you!" Kyra bit down again, harder this time. Blunderbore shrieked again, louder and louder, loosening her grip on Kyra with each rising octave of the scream.

Kyra congratulated herself for escaping the death-grip of the giant before realizing that the giant had let go of her, and she was now tumbling to the hard floor below.

"Catch me!" she screamed at the top of her lungs, desperately hoping Juniper's hearing wasn't as bad as it was when their father asked them to clean up their rooms. She caught a glimpse of her feet, then her arm, then the floor, as she did somersaults and flips through the air, seconds away from smooshing on the floor.

Then the ground rushed up, and so did Juniper's terrified face.

"Eek!" Juniper yelled. Kyra hit something, then felt the cool stone floor against her cheek. She propped herself up and saw that Juniper hadn't caught her, but had used her body as a human cushion. Juniper was sprawled beneath her, looked out of breath and scared but still smiling somehow.

Kyra grabbed her sister's face in her hands, pressing their foreheads together. "You make a glorious landing pad."

"You make a terrible lander," Juniper replied. The harp flashed silver in her arms.

They launched to their feet, then took off running towards the door.

Blunderbore was too busy attending to her bite wound to pay attention to the escaping girls. Kyra had suspicions that the giant didn't really care to kill them and instead viewed them as minor annoyances. Her suspicions were proved correct when the giant crossed the kitchen to get a bandage instead of chasing them.

Kyra and Juniper ran out the door and were met with a vast plain of sky.

The horizon stretched out forever, a sea of endless, snow-white clouds. It looked like a desert, full of beautiful arrays of pinks and oranges and reds, white sand dunes tinged with sunset. Bubbly and inviting, the clouds grinned up at the girls, wind pulling at their dresses as if enticing them to join. Maybe they could finally lay down their heads to sleep on the infinite fluffy pillows.

"We have to jump," said Kyra, breathless from the beauty of the sky.

"I think I shall favor my chances with the giant." Juniper turned to walk back inside.

Kyra said, "The beanstalk is right below. Trust me."

"No."

"You don't trust me?"

Juniper's dark eyes were pools of midnight water. "I do. To the end of the world, I trust you. I guess that counts when we are above the world, too." She took a deep breath. "Let us jump."

In sync, they kicked off from the door stoop and jumped into the sky, the ground thousands of miles below. Uncaring if they fell or flew.

As they jumped, Kyra felt like they would strike the clouds then bounce right off them. Bounding off into the sky like skipping stones, they would chase the sinking sun. It felt infinite and magical, that sea of clouds. It felt like flying over the world and not caring if you fell. It felt like soaring.

And then the clouds were whirring past her, cold and decidedly not bouncy.

Green patches began appearing at the edge of her vision, and the beanstalk rose up in her view.

The flying feeling had been a second of peace. Soaring over the clouds as the sky turned pink would be a memory she would not soon forget—a lovely moment of escape. There was no escaping the Queen once they set foot on land.

The moment was altogether peaceful, save for Juniper screaming bloody murder the entire way down.

They landed on the top of the beanstalk with a thud. Falling onto her hands and knees, Kyra panted heavily. Juniper's cheeks were flushed with excitement amidst the screaming.

"It seems," Juniper said finally, panting, "that we will not be attending our lessons today."

"Like I was planning on going anyways," Kyra said, then began climbing down the stalk, making quick work of the leaves and stems. Juniper went a little more cautiously, digging her nails into the stems and only letting go once she had sure footing.

Kyra looked down at the stalk below and saw three distant figures outlined in light from the setting sun. She breathed a sigh of relief. Cal, Jules, and Luca had made it to the beanstalk and were almost at the ground. She was going to be so glad when she could be done with this beanstalk forever. Never again would she eat a bean in penance for her suffering. Her stomach rumbled in protest. Okay, so that was a lie; she would eat a bean again, but she would never climb another beanstalk and that was *final*.

"Hurry up!" Kyra called.

Juniper was moving agonizingly slow, the harp strung on her back, and it showed that Juniper spent all her time in the library and not out climbing trees and running from annoyed shopkeepers like Kyra did. For once, Kyra could boast the merit of hating reading. "You're acting like you've never climbed down a beanstalk before!"

"I suppose that is due to the fact that I have never climbed down a beanstalk before!"

Kyra grinned, then began moving faster as she saw a huge shadow fall above the clouds.

Blunderbore had begun her descent. "My harp! Small Juniper has my bewitching harp!"

Juniper winced slightly, but she made no move to shake the harp off.

The entire beanstalk shook with an intense ferocity, shuddering and groaning as it supported Blunderbore's first tentative step down.

"Come on!" Kyra screamed to Juni through the roaring wind. "Can't you go any faster?"

They scrambled down, moving frantically as the giant closed in on them. Blunderbore was outlined in the gold of the sunset, her translucent hair turning orange, the wind whipping it about. The sky was her background, the beanstalk a strip of green against the clouds. The giant looked terrible and glorious as she wailed into the world, wailed in heartbreak and from a loss so profound it shook the forest, lit up in the color of burning candlelight. It was an image seared into Kyra's brain, an image that belonged in a storybook with a caption, 'Happy Ever After.' This was no storybook, Kyra thought, and there would be no happy ever after.

The others waited anxiously below, but Kyra and Juniper were still about thirty feet up the stalk. Taking a deep breath, she jumped the remaining distance.

She landed on the hard ground with a sickening crash and rolled a few feet like she had practiced jumping from trees. Cal was there in an instant, helping her to her feet.

Juniper was still around twenty feet up, clinging to the beanstalk. The giant was about halfway down now, and it would be a matter of minutes before Blunderbore's feet touched the ground, where she could wreak havoc on them all.

The wind swept Juniper's hair in the air, tangled curls flying all about. Tinted in the pink of the sky, Kyra's sister clung even tighter to the leaves. She shook her head slightly, though it didn't seem as if she was shaking her head at anyone but herself.

Juniper curled her fingers around the harp, closed her eyes, then pushed off from the beanstalk. Soaring through the air, the girl resembled a bird flying down from the sky in its first turn jumping from the nest. She crashed to the floor, bruised up but unhurt. Her eyes danced with exhilaration. It occurred to Kyra that that look dominated Kyra's own face all the time. Danger was gorgeous because with it came the thrill of reminding herself that she was alive.

"Now what?" asked Luca.

"Now, we chop down this freaking beanstalk," Julian said, pulling his sword from its sheath. It had an ebony hilt and gleamed silver in the same way that the harp did. He raised it above his head, then swung down at the bottom of the beanstalk with astounding force.

The blade connected, but Jules collapsed as soon as it did. He crumpled to the floor, sword clattering against the moss of the clearing. Kyra's eyes widened as she saw his arm was not bleeding anymore, but still, the gash ran long.

"Prince Julian! Jules, are you alright?" Cal said worriedly. Jules' eyes had fluttered and closed, fatigue getting the best of him. Juniper threw herself to the floor next to him, forehead creasing in anxiety. She took his burned hand and held it against her.

Luca bent down to pick up the sword, his brown hair rippling in the wind. He took one swing at the beanstalk, and it did nothing. He tried again, but to no avail.

"Very cute, you brave kitten, but we both know you can't cut down this beanstalk." Kyra took the sword from Luca and held it high above her head, preparing to strike.

"Moon's Child!" Blunderbore screamed from above. The giant had called her the nickname earlier, too. Wait—how did she know that was what she was called? Kyra—no matter how much she wished it were true—wasn't famous. There was no reason an air giant would know it. It was a regional nickname. "Put the sword down! I will tell you the origin of your gifts! Your gifts!"

Her origin? Simple; her mom and her dad loved each other very much...easy as that. Kyra snorted.

Besides, her gifts lied in the area of bad jokes and scowling. Who was the giant to stop her? Kyra was about to bring the sword to the base of the beanstalk, when—

"You wonder why you are drawn to magic?" Blunderbore shouted over the roaring of the wind. "Two girls, moon and sun, woven strands of the same cloth!" It sounded weirdly similar to what the old woman from the clearing had said before...did all the magical creatures get together every Monday for book club? Did they exchange magical prophecies and weird sayings there? If so, people were going to have to get more creative.

"You're going to have to try harder!" Kyra shouted back. "I've heard it all before!"

Blunderbore smiled darkly. "Oh, my girl, you will wish you have."

Kyra let the sword fly.

Part Two: Moon

"'If I can't order the moon and sun to rise, and have to look on and see the sun and moon rising, I can't bear it. I shall not know what it is to have another happy hour, unless I can make them rise myself.'
Then she looked at him so terribly that a shudder ran over him, and said, 'Go at once; I wish to be like unto God.'"

—*Brother's Grimm*

11

Wolf's Claw

The sword swung straight through the beanstalk, sending it crashing down.

The beanstalk fell, taking the old air giant down with it. Juniper could hear Blunderbore cry out against the wind as she collided with the ground, then was still forevermore.

Another giant dead, gone. *Lass den Tod des Paten gütig sein*, Let Godfather Death be kind. Juni knew she should be rejoicing; the monster was defeated and they were safe. But all she felt was tired and hungry and lonely. She had people around her, but watching that giant fall and die made her feel incredibly alone.

Kyra let the sword clatter to the ground, and she drew a hand to her dress, scrunching it up in the fabric, hiding her shaking hand away from everyone's view. But Juniper could see.

Night was falling rapidly, the sun a sliver against a faraway horizon line. It was a spot of red against the black outlines of the trees, like an ever-watching eye staring out over the forest. Lighting the treetops on fire, the sun watched them all in crimson calm.

Birds were chirping, composing their last songs of the day.

"Juniper!" Kyra called to her. "The birds are singing for you."

It was a joke they had had their whole lives, that animals flocked to Juniper wherever she went because she was so good and pure. It was something that always made the two of them smile, and they sure needed it. Now, Juniper just ducked her head down after a weak grin. Her heart just wasn't in the mood. Kyra frowned.

Cal's curiosity was prevalent. He said, "The birds are singing for her?"

"Yeah," Kyra said, the wisp of a smile on her face. "They always do."

"The giant slaying," Cal said to Kyra, "was not terrible."

"You expected less?" Kyra grinned, but her voice was stiff. Maybe her mind was still on the giant's words. *You wonder why you are so drawn to magic.* Juniper wasn't sure what she thought it meant. Maybe another trick or something that the Queen was playing. Kyra turned to Julian, lying on the floor. "Jules? You alive?"

Julian nodded weakly. "Never better." He collapsed immediately after.

"So, anyone wanna talk about what just happened?" Cal asked. They all shook their heads 'no' in sync. Cal said, "Didn't think so."

"We need food. Luca, you're a huntsman." Kyra shooed him off. "Go hunt."

Luca sighed, then wandered off into the forest, knife in hand. Juniper silently wished him good luck. The knife hung awkwardly at his side, as if he barely knew how to grip it. Not that Juniper was an expert in anything like that; no, she just knew that Luca was no good at it either, which made it weird that the Queen had enlisted him to kill her and Kyra. Wouldn't Callista want someone who would get the job done?

An awful thought struck her. What if the Queen had given Luca the job of killing them because he was just an apprentice on purpose? What if the Queen had planned on killing Luca right after he got the job done? Luca would have gone back to the castle, only to be murdered by his very employer. He would never have even seen it coming. It was too dreadful even to consider, and that was how she knew it was right.

It was becoming easier and easier to associate her mother with evil things like that. Juniper couldn't decide if she was alright with that or not.

All she knew was with every passing second, she was changing from the girl she used to be. And that didn't seem so scary.

Amidst the chatter and excitement of the others, Juniper was able to easily slip away. Often, she had found that she needed time for herself, to think and to dream and to comprehend what was happening around her. This was one of those much needed times.

She wandered off into the woods, feet slinking over rock and singed grass. Her legs carried her through the peaceful forest. She didn't stop walking until she found a place where the grass was no longer charred from the previous night.

Juniper sank to the ground, happy to take in the calm of twilight, the still of the forest. Each creature that wandered like her was fast asleep by now, dreaming of the day. The only difference between Juniper and a nearby squirrel was that the squirrel had delights to dream of. Juniper only had ghosts.

A group of flowers near her had settled in for the night, their pink and blue petals drooping downwards in sleep. Flowers always served to remind her of her father. His sweet singing voice and lovely smile, a smile that could light up any room quicker than a candle. A smile that chased away darkness in droves.

Her father's name, Jakob, was a scar in her heart that had never fully healed. Each time someone mentioned it in passing or in a conversation, that name twisted in her soul, piercing her heart like a sword. She missed him more than she could even know, and she knew that he would know the right thing to say right then. He always knew how to tilt the world back on its axis with his wisdom and well-thought-out words. Or maybe even Jakob couldn't help her now, what with how crazy her world had turned in a matter of days.

Across the dense thicket of trees, a small bluebird hopped forward.

"Hello little friend," Juniper said, fluttering her fingers in greeting. "I do not suppose you can cheer me up?"

The bird hopped closer, almost close enough to touch now. Its little clawed feet grazed the grass lightly as it stopped right in front of Juniper, amber eyes angled upwards in what she assumed was hello.

"Let us channel my father's spirit, then, hm?" Juniper scrunched up her face, deepening her voice and crossing her arms. "Juniper, dear, chin up: hope is like a tree; steadfast and always...branchy." She frowned, letting her crossed arms fall to the moss. "That was quite awful."

The bird dropped its beak, looking at the floor as if bashful. If even a bird thought her speech was disastrous, she had big problems on her hands.

"Shall I channel my mother, then?" Juniper sat up straighter and pursed her lips, pretending to be her mother. "Juniper, dear, crying is for losers and peasants. Princesses, and future rulers, at that, do not make blubbering mockeries of themselves. Leave the dim-wittedness to your sister and wipe the tears off your face. We don't need puffy eyes for the banquet tomorrow."

The bird hopped around, giggling in tandem with her in the soft silence of the night. It had been many hours since Juniper had giggled like that, and she wondered at the ways of the world; how one moment everything could be alright and the next the world could tilt off its axis.

"Hmm...how about Kyra? She would say to 'shake it off.' Unhelpful. Though I should know better at this point than to ask her for any type of wise words. We are alike in that."

Inching closer, the bird nestled up in the crook of her crossed legs. Its huge eyes looked up at her in knowing.

"What *I* would say? Now, that's the most absurd thing you have said, little one. I have no great speeches or wisdom to impart. One would be a fool to go to me for advice on any matter. I know nothing to say of heartbreak or sorrow. The only thing that I understand is that giving up is not an option for me."

The bird cocked its head, flapping its wings in an earnest agreement.

"Very right, my winged friend. Very right, indeed. I shall not give up quite yet. That would be a great folly of mine." Juniper stood at once, feeling that the stars shone a little brighter than they had before. "Just because it is night does not mean the sun no longer exists. It will rise again tomorrow, as it always does. With that light comes the hope of a new beginning."

She reached down and gave the bird a quick pat on the head, saying, "Thank you for your help. I shall not forget your kindness soon."

Then she skipped back to the camp, nestling in against the newborn warmth of the fire.

About thirty minutes later, Luca arrived with food, and the group feasted happily.

"That was so awesome when the giant shot air-balls at us," Julian said, gesturing with his hands excitedly.

Luca affirmed, "Totally. And the parachute part was cool, too." Nice to see someone had come around on the parachute idea.

They were sitting around a campfire, scarfing down fish that Luca had managed to capture. Somehow. He had come back soaking wet, his hair dripping everywhere, and a sour expression on his face. She guessed the journey had not been pleasant. Juniper had tried not to laugh as he tied up the fish over a fire, watching as it slipped from his grasp.

Now, they were all crowded around the flames, shoving food into their mouths like their lives depended on it. Normally, Juniper was a vegetarian, but right then it couldn't have mattered less.

The flames swayed before her. She thought of Julian's burnt hands, how she had somehow carried the heat inside her...she didn't want to think about it. Juniper grumbled, "It was something. Not awesome, but something."

"Juniper, you are so ungrateful. I would pay to have air-balls shot at me," Kyra said with a huge bite of fish in her mouth.

"Excuse me for not thinking things that almost killed us are cool," Juniper replied, the hint of a smile on her face.

"So what's next?" Luca leaned forward from his place on the ground, his brown eyes sparkling like the wood of the small violin Juniper used to own.

"What do you mean, what's next?" Jules narrowed his eyes. "We cross the forest and head into Maiike, the best kingdom ever, for the ball!"

Juniper had forgotten about the ball. Some coming-of-age celebration for Jules where he would find a wealthy princess to get engaged to. Big whoop. Juniper only viewed balls as places where she would be judged for her bad dancing. She found it best to stand in a corner and chat with someone else who looked as out of place as her. What if she had attended that ball and Jules had gotten engaged to her, if things were normal? That didn't seem so bad...

"A ball?" Kyra wrinkled her nose in disgust. "I'll pass."

"Me too?" Juniper asked hopefully. She did not need to go to a huge gathering when she had so much on her plate. She could barely stand to go to events like that when she had nothing going on. Let alone a plot to stop her mother from taking over the kingdom.

"It'll be fun!" Cal mockingly nudged Kyra, who gave an annoyed snort.

"I've never been to a ball." Luca looked small then, with his wide-eyed wonder. Childlike, even.

"Then you're in for a treat, little huntsman! It might be the worst thing you ever have to do in your adorable little life." Kyra tapped his nose.

"Balls are fun! I don't see the issue. You get to dress up, dance, and talk to people!" said Jules incredulously.

The other four stared at him blankly.

"That is exactly the issue." Juniper chomped down on her fish.

Cal said, listing things out his fingers as he went, "So we stop in Maiike. Then we can get more horses—we can each get one, so I don't need to share with Luca anymore—then we go to the Queen's Winter palace and stop the coronation. By the way, how exactly do we plan on doing that?" He nudged a falling wood piece with his foot, pushing it back into the fire and sending showering embers cascading down.

Kyra threw a scrap of fish into the fire, watching it burn in glee. "Easy. We walk in and say, 'Hey, Callista! You're evil! And you suck! Punching time!'"

"The scariest thing about that is you look completely serious," Cal said.

Luca looked majorly concerned. "You're joking, Kyra...right?"

"I wish she was," Juniper answered, wincing slightly at the murderous rage in her sister's eyes.

"Sounds like a plan!" Julian happily reached for yet another fish to eat.

"We aren't thinking about this right. What's the best way to stop someone who's seemingly unbeatable?" Cal asked.

"Punching," Kyra answered.

"Diplomacy," offered Juniper.

"Pizazz." Julian did flashy jazz hands.

"Ask them nicely." Luca flushed when he saw everyone was staring at him. "What? I thought we were just throwing ideas out."

"You're all wrong," Cal said. "It's going in right under the person's nose. We'll sneak in."

"The Queen will have the palace guarded heavily," said Luca. "We need to get past them. That will be the big challenge. Once we've made it through the guards, it should be pretty easy to get to the courtyard of the Winter Palace. Then we can figure out a way to come to a peaceful agreement with the Queen."

"Or I could just punch her in the face," Kyra muttered. "Punching seems easier."

"We could try and find a way up the walls of the castle," said Luca, looking at the fire in concentration. "Or through the moat."

"The moat could work," Cal said, nodding appreciatively. He had a look on his face that looked like, *At least one of them isn't an idiot.* Juniper wished she could contribute to the planning, but she knew nothing about storming castles and fighting queens. The only thing she contributed was screaming when something scary happened.

"That's enough planning for tonight." Julian yawned. "My brain hurts." He stood up and brushed his pants off, the fire making his green eyes orange. Shadows from the flames danced across his face like waves rolling to shore. Juniper jolted as he turned and walked a little ways from the fire, settling down in the dirt to sleep. How long had she been staring at him for? Shoot. It could've been hours for all she knew.

She suddenly remembered Cormoran the giant biting down on him and dying from his blood. *A boy with the blood of poison and death.* She needed to ask him what that meant, and how he had known his blood was tainted. Her mind was already whirring, thinking of different theories and stories she had heard that had people with poison blood.

"I'm not tired," Luca said, bouncing his knee up and down. "I'm wide awake. This was the most exciting day of my life."

"Oh?" Cal asked, raising his eyebrows. "I was going to say terrifying, but exciting works, too."

Kyra stretched out her long legs. "Someone talk about something interesting, or I'm gonna fall asleep."

"Want to hear about my favorite book series?" Juniper asked. By the time she said the word, 'book,' Kyra had pretended to fall asleep, her head lolling backward and fake snores coming from her mouth.

"Sure!" Luca put his chin in his hands.

"I'd rather rip off my fingernails," said Kyra. "But by all means, go on." Her head drooped back, her eyes flicking shut as she pretended to be asleep again. Luca prodded her cheek to check if she was really asleep. Kyra snapped her mouth open like a crocodile, feigning a bite at Luca's finger. Luca wrenched his finger away, jumped back with panic, and fell. Kyra snickered then closed her eyes again as Luca scrambled back to his place around the fire.

"How about I tell you all about how I saved Kyra's life on the beanstalk?" Cal asked, eyes dancing with mischief. Kyra sat up at this, her eyes snapping open with alarm.

"Nonono, we really don't need to share—"

Cal ignored her and said, "We were climbing up the stalk, when I saw Kyra slip..."

Juniper nestled forward as Kyra slung back.

* * *

"Juni, can we talk?" Kyra asked a while later, already walking a few feet away from the fire.

The boys were all asleep. Even with Luca's self-proclaimed energy, he was passed out next to the dying fire. The embers slowly flickered out, the warm light winking out of existence.

"Of course." Juniper stood up. Her doe-eyes were wide with confusion.

Kyra gave a quick look at Cal, who was sleeping soundly on the floor. He had his arms tucked beneath his head, his knees drawn up into a little ball. She immediately looked away, her eyes darting up a tree.

They walked into the forest, meandering aimlessly. Kyra trailed her fingers among the tree trunks, fingers running along the leaves. The night was cold and unforgiving, the moon barely a red fingernail in the sky.

"So. Wanna tell me why you risked your life to go get that harp? Sure it's nice and all, but you don't even know how to play it. Am I missing something here? Is that a world-class instrument? 'Cause it seems pretty dumb of you to put yourself in danger over a harp." Kyra hadn't even realized how angry she was about it until this moment. Juniper could've died, and all over a measly harp. Juniper could have *died* over nothing.

And though the harp was beautiful...there was something else about it. Something sinister and entrancing all at once. Already, Kyra had felt herself drawn to it in an inexplicable way. She had seen the others cast longing glances at it, too, and she wondered what it really was.

Juniper bit her lip. "It was indeed foolish."

"There has to be a reason you did it."

"Perhaps..."

"Sunbeam above, Juniper, just tell me!"

"I...I felt like I needed to get it. As if it were calling me," Juniper said, winding her hair into a braid. "Nevermind."

"I think...I think I understand. I've felt that before, too. Do you think the harp is...magic or something?" Kyra asked. The harp could be magic—faerie—that would explain why they were drawn to it. Maybe it had a spell or something put on it that made it irresistible to humans. That would make sense. If there was any other reason, Kyra didn't want to think of it. *You wonder why you are drawn to magic—*

"I know not what I think," Juniper said sharply. The girl had tensed since the word magic had rolled from Kyra's lips. "I know that you did not need to go after me."

Kyra jolted. "Of course I did! Do you really think you would have been able to get yourself out of there? You couldn't even climb down the beanstalk without my help!"

"I am not helpless."

"I didn't say that!"

"Words have layers beyond the surface of speech," said Juniper, her gaze riveted on Kyra's. Kyra wanted nothing more than to look away, to not be staring into her sister's innocent eyes. She focused her attention on holding her gaze. She had fought monsters and conquered beanstalks. She could meet someone's eyes.

Just tell the truth. Kyra hesitated, then said, "Sometimes you can be a little naïve—"

"And you can be an ice queen. It is hard having a sister who never even acts like one," Juniper said. The Queen's face flashed in Kyra's mind, a perfectly blank canvas with no emotion slipping through the cracks.

"I don't act like a—fine, I'll just cry all the time and make big dramatic scenes everywhere I go. That will show you I love you better than saving you!"

"Stop that," Juni said, her shoulders drooping. "Stop deflecting."

Kyra crossed her arms over her chest. "Why do people keep telling me that?"

"We should not have to!" Juniper said, voice dropping suddenly.

"And you should understand that the world doesn't revolve

around you! I'm sorry, Juniper, but the sun and stars and gravity aren't all pulled to you!" Kyra fumed. "Giants can still kill you, and queens can still hate you! You may think that just because the king-dom adores you means that everyone does, but it doesn't!"

"I have never thought that." Juniper's voice fell. "And I never will."

Kyra stumbled, taken aback by her sister's words. "Juni, I didn't mean it like that."

"Do not speak to me as if I am a child," said Juniper. "When you are my elder in age alone."

Kyra said quietly, "I didn't know this would happen."

Juniper's hair shielded her face, a curtain of black curls. "Neither did I."

"If it weren't for me, you would never be in this mess," realized Kyra. "The Queen wanted to kill me, not you. You would be at home. Safe." *I'm so sorry.*

"I suppose it matters not, does it? We are here now."

"Suppose not."

Kyra and Juniper walked silently. Kyra's head was turned up to-wards the sky, towards the stars above. They were barely visible through the trees, but Kyra could still make out the familiar constel-lations, the steady trails of light that would always be there. She felt terrible for what she had said. She felt awful, actually, and needed to find the words to communicate that. How? This was so frustrating.

"Juniper, I—"

Kyra was cut off by a scream.

It was an earth-shattering, terrifying-sounding scream of fear that shook Kyra to the core.

The scream itself did not shake her. The thing that shook her was that the scream was *familiar.*

Luca.

Kyra and Juniper looked worriedly at each other, then took off sprinting through the forest. Towards the sound of it. The scream. Twigs and branches slapped Kyra in the face as she ran. They scratched at her arms and legs and tore at her dress. She didn't care. She was only thinking that the boys were the ones screaming. She realized that she and Juniper were running right for the danger, but none of it mattered in the face of that scream.

Her feet flew on the ground, pounding as quick as her heartbeat. No sound was heard save for her feet hitting the floor. The twigs scraped and clawed at her as if holding her back. As if trying to stop her from going forward. As if anything could stop her from going forward.

She burst into the clearing and saw nothing but a nightmare come true.

Cal was standing in front of Luca and Julian, his arms in front of them as if to ward off an attack. Luca's face was twisted in terror, and Kyra finally saw the source of his scream.

Across the way, hidden amongst trees and shadows, were three people. They were dressed in black, with shaggy hair and glittering purple eyes. Beautiful eyes, if not for what they represented. That was not the issue.

The issue was, they had the eyes of the feared Dämonenwölfe.

The Dämonenwölfe were humans that could morph into wolves whenever they so chose. They were people that were bitten by other Dämonenwölfe, contracting the disease of being half-wolf, half-man. Kyra had been told stories by the kitchen staff when she was small.

When monsters under the bed still were myths, and not standing before her.

The staff had told her stories of humans who transformed into wolves and could rip out the throat of anyone who crossed them. Stronger and faster than anyone who walked the earth, they howled with the moon while they fed on little children. *They will eat you up,*

Moon's Child, eat you up for dinner. Kyra shuddered as she beheld the three people, tall and framed in moonlight like black sketches on silver paper.

Cal met Kyra's eyes, goosebumps raising along her arms. He mouthed, "*Run.*"

Kyra gave a slight shake of the head, then walked across the clearing to join him. She didn't even need to wonder what the Dämonenwölfe wanted.

She knew well enough that they were out for a midnight snack.

The Dämonenwölfe originated from faerie magic as all dark things did. Once upon a time, a faerie boy was harmed by a man and his pet wolf. The faerie cursed the man to forever be fused with his wolf as a wanderer. A rogue of the night and the hunt. Since then, their population grew to be shunned and feared. True wanderers. Lost souls howling at twilight.

Their trademark was their eyes. Lilting ranges of lilac and lavender, glimmering and sparkling with old magic of the fae. A mark to ensure they never found a home.

The leader of the pack, a tall woman with freckles and beady violet eyes, stepped forward from the shadow of a tree. The other two people lingered in the treeline, concealed by shadows. Their glowing purple eyes were the only thing visible in the night.

The freckled woman walked forward, intentionally slow. Her expression was one of a predator viewing its prey, a cold smile written across her lips. It made Kyra shiver.

"Greetings, travelers," The Dämonenwölfe spoke. "You may call me...Emma. I would say I don't bite but...we all know that would be a lie. What do I call you?"

Kyra was about to give her name when Cal spat, "I know better than to give my name to someone with fae blood. Especially when it's clear you are a hunter of the moon." Dang, that was good. Kyra needed to remember to think before she spoke. She had almost given her name to a fae creature. That was the number one rule in the book; even one-year-olds knew that. Names were power to the fae. If someone had your name, they had you.

Emma said, "R-i-ght. Probably smart."

"What do you want, demon-wolf?" Kyra said, making her voice sound confident and sure. She schooled her features into their impassable wall, her face a fortress. Nothing allowed in, nothing allowed out.

"My friends and I are just looking for a way through," said Emma. "You kids look nice enough. Wanna help a girl out?" She smiled with her teeth, and Kyra wasn't sure she imagined the flash of fangs she saw.

"Of course," Juniper said, ever the goody-goody. "Where are you headed?"

"A nearby kingdom. I think it's called Maiike?"

Julian tensed, his hands closing into fists. *His kingdom.* "It's not open for the fae. It's not open at all, actually. Sorry." Kyra wondered how she would feel if the three Dämonenwölfe had been heading for Aazagonia instead. She had no claim on their fates anymore, no way to protect them from so many miles away.

"That's a shame. We're starved," said Emma casually. She picked at her chipped black nail polish as she spoke, flicking little bits everywhere. Gross.

"What would you eat?" Luca asked warily.

"Oh, you know." Emma cocked her head. "Whatever we happen upon."

Kyra scowled. "That's rich, real funny—"

Cal slung an arm around Kyra's shoulder, cutting her off. It seemed light and airy, but Kyra knew it was a warning not to aggravate the Dämonenwölfe. His touch also made her knees feel weak and her heart contract, enough to make her feel like she was lacking oxygen. "My friend here means that you're talking about eating...not regular food. Is that right?"

"That's right." Emma winked. "We eat people! No need to beat around the bush."

"You won't be entering my kingdom. Ever. Half-wolves who eat people would raise a couple complaints." Jules raised his chin.

"We'll see about that."

Kyra started forward, about to kick some serious wolf butt, but Juniper shoved her back, stepping forward herself. Kyra wanted nothing else than to launch forward and kick Emma down, then karate chop that stupid smirk off her face.

Juniper took a different approach than karate-chopping. "We have a great huntsman among us. He could get you something to eat."

Luca nodded along with her, a queasy smile on his face as he feigned calm. "We have leftover fish."

For some reason unknown to Kyra, he looked even smaller in the red moonlight. As if his skin was made from blood, his hair from the darkest shade of crimson roses. His brown eyes swam with anxiety. No; that wasn't quite the right word. They shone with terror, red and daunting.

"Fish is good," Emma relented. "But what we're looking for is a little different. We just need one bite of something, and then we'll be fine. One bite of this something sustains my pack for a few days. I think you know what that something is." Humans. She wanted one bite of a human.

Why did every person they had met so far want to eat them? It was getting old fast.

"No way," Kyra said, half-shouting into the night. One bite, and they'd be a Dämonenwölfe, too. One bite and their lives would be changed in a particularly fangy and hairy way.

Emma pouted. She said, "You can help us, it'll be fun! Like a deal.

Honestly, this would be so easy if you just let me take one measly bite. It probably wouldn't even hurt." She reconsidered her words. "Probably."

"No," Cal said firmly.

"How 'bout you, handsome? Just one little nibble?" Emma indicated Julian, who gulped.

Kyra instinctively looked to Julian, fury clouding her vision. No way would Kyra let Emma hurt them. If it had to be anyone, it would be her. She had solved that quicker than any math equation.

"I won't let you hurt any of them." Kyra bristled, stanced for a fight.

"Are you sure you want it to happen this way? One of you could volunteer."

"Why would we ever do that?"

"Because," replied Emma, "it would make all our lives a lot easier. In about one minute, you'll all be running away. I'll be chasing. And whoever's last will be my unwilling volunteer." Her teeth glittered in the red moonlight as she bared them in a smile. "Like a game."

"You aren't hurting any of them," Kyra repeated, her heart not really in it.

"Bor-i-ng." Emma stopped picking her nails, looking back up at the group. "I swear, I didn't want it to happen this way. I really don't like hurting people if I don't have to, but," she said, shrugging nonchalantly, "sometimes even my kind heart isn't enough to stop the hunt. Jackson, Wilhelm, get them." She waved her hand in the air, and the two figures in the trees stepped forward.

Jackson and Wilhelm were huge, monstrously beefy men that looked like they worked out at least thirty times a minute. They advanced, padding quietly across the forest floor.

"Wait," Juniper said, stricken. "We can figure this out."

Emma guffawed sharply. It sounded off, deranged, more shriek-like than laugh. "Oh, it's far too late for peace. I gave you a chance. Now, hold the screams for a minute. Let me have my spotlight."

Emma began to morph, warping into something beastly and strange. Her arms stretched out, growing dark fur and turning animalistic. A glint of silver was visible in the moonlight as her nails sharpened into claws. Her nose, ligaments visible as it twisted, turned into a snout. Teeth stretched into sharp fangs, her bones snapping and sticking out to rearrange. Her tendons and muscles were visible as they shifted and grew grotesquely.

The only thing that was remotely similar to the freckled girl Emma had been a few moments ago were the eyes. Glaringly bright purple eyes amidst the dark night sky that was her fur.

"You can scream in horror now," the wolf who had been Emma snarled.

Kyra felt bile rise in her throat as Juniper let out a shriek. The other two men began their own transformations. Splotches rose in her vision, and she could hear Cal screaming at her, but his voice came from far away, as if she had sunk below water and his voice came from the shore. He shook her, but she couldn't rip her eyes from the disgusting morphing of the Dämonenwölfe.

"Kyra!" Cal was screaming, his voice cracking. "Run!"

That was what she finally heard. She spun, stumbled, then ran. She and Cal sprinted away from the transforming Dämonenwölfe. Juniper and Luca bolted ahead, Jules lagging a little behind. His hurt arm hung limp at his side.

Kyra heard a bone-chilling howl echo out from somewhere behind her, and it made her legs move faster. She looked back to see if the wolves had begun chasing them yet, but the night was pitch black, and she couldn't see a thing. Curse her bad vision. She wished she had got the glasses she needed from her suitcase before she had been taken off into the woods to be murdered.

"Just keep running, Kyra. Don't look back," Cal breathed, noticing her quick look behind her. "Just keep going."

"I. Can't. Talk. When. I. Run," Kyra said back, panting heavily. "Try. To. Keep. Up."

He grinned. Another howl came from behind, and the grin dropped from Cal's face as quickly as it came. Kyra looked back. A flash of purple came from somewhere far in the trees, and the sound of claws scraping against dirt and stone.

They picked up the pace and caught up to Julian, Luca, and Juniper. Juniper was breathing heavily, her motions labored and slow from exertion. Luca looked like he was running based on pure adrenaline and terror, like a toddler hyped up on coffee. So he was doing surprisingly fine. Naturally slower than the others, he fell behind with Juniper. Kyra's heart sank.

There was nothing she could do about it except pick them both up and carry them over her shoulder like a sack of potatoes. That would just slow all three of them down, however, and she was sure it would not be enjoyable for any of them. So she bit her tongue and kept going, trying her best not to think about the two of them back there.

And the wolves howling and snarling behind them.

They ran aimlessly through the forest, vaulting over tree stumps and dodging huge bushes. They couldn't outrun the wolves. That was a grim fact. Eventually, the Dämonenwölfe pack would catch up to them. They were being chased by the best hunters in the world. What could they do? Her brain couldn't work. She couldn't think; all she could do was *run* as fast as her legs could carry her.

They ran like that for several minutes, calling back to each other when there was a large rock or tall root, shoving branches out of the way, and having everything inside them screaming in terror for what lay behind them.

Kyra looked back once to check on Juniper and Luca.

Juniper was helping a fallen Luca. His leg was stuck under a root, and Juniper struggled to pull it out.

His red cape flashed like the red of sunset, spilled out around him as he desperately tried to pull his leg out from the root. Red like burning incense, like the purest apples, like the fiercest shade of a rose.

The cape was red like the blood moon above.

A howl echoed across the forest.

The wolves were dark shapes darting amongst shadows.

Juniper was crouched directly in their path.

Kyra froze. Stopped running. Her heartbeat pounded in her ears like a roaring ocean as she watched Juniper unsuccessfully try to pull Luca's trapped leg out. Juni tried again. Nothing. She shoved the toe of her boot in the dirt to keep from screaming at them to *Move, oh please, just get up.* But they were making no progress, and the wolves were nearing.

"What are you doing?" Cal began, but Kyra was already running to them before she could answer.

She took off towards Luca, throwing herself on the floor next to him. She grabbed his leg and wrenched it out with tremendous force, cracking the root in two in the process.

"Can you stand?" Kyra asked, urgency unmistakable.

Luca tried, but his leg buckled beneath him. "No." He said the word quietly—not as a negative but as a terrible, unmistakable death sentence. People didn't escape wolves on the hunt. There were never stories of fortunate survivors of Dämonenwölfe attacks—only sickening tales of those lost to the hunters of the night. Kyra didn't know whether she would rather become one of them or die. To live and be a half-human, half-wolf wasn't really living at all, was it? A small part of her felt bad for Emma and her friends, that they were condemned to a life of wander and ruin.

Juniper paled. "We can carry you, or fight. We will think of something."

"Guys," Luca said, eyes widened in pure, unfiltered terror. "Look."

The Dämonenwölfe were a few feet away, but they had stopped running. They snarled and growled, grim beasts with awful grins.

"Go! Leave me!" Luca shouted at the girls.

"Can't get rid of us that easily, little huntsman," Kyra's voice wobbled as she shook her head sadly.

"Get out of here! Go!" Luca tried again, weaker.

The sisters stayed.

Emma paced, baring her teeth. Her wolf claws dug into the ground, dirt flying everywhere with each step. It splattered across a nearby tree like blood. Her fangs were sharp and huge, poking out from her lip. Moonlight hit them and glared in Kyra's eyes. She said the first thing that came to mind.

"I didn't think," Kyra said, her voice hitched, "that you would have such big fangs."

"I'd say that's a compliment, but I don't think that's what you meant. And besides..." Emma giggled, or whatever a wolf could do that sounded like a giggle. The wolf-girl said before she pounced:

"The better to eat you with, my dear."

12

Lavender

Juniper registered two things as the wolf flew through the air, claws out and mouth yawning open wide.

One was that the wolf really did have big teeth, and two: The wolf was flying right at her.

The Dämonenwölfe soared right at her, its claws poised to strike her in the heart.

The next part seemed to happen in slow motion. Juniper almost didn't understand what was going on. One moment, the wolf was about to lock onto her, and the next, arms were wrapped around her, shoving her out of the way.

Someone had knocked Juniper out of the path of the oncoming Dämonenwölfe, because she didn't feel sharp claws digging into her skin, but warm, human hands encircling her shoulders. She closed her eyes as she hit the dirt, her knee scraping a rock as she fell.

Kyra. Of course, Kyra had to save her. Juniper really had to get a handle on that; she didn't want to be a damsel in distress all the time. Admittedly, if Kyra hadn't shoved her out of the way, she would be wolf food. She shoved Kyra's hands off her, (maybe a tad too hostilely), about to thank her, when she saw the wolf landing.

The wolf was still on its track, headed for the person who had been standing behind her.

Luca.

Juniper's mouth went slack in horror as she saw the wolf land on a terrified Luca. Her blood ran cold as the wolf reared back, then sank its jaws into Luca's leg, a sickening crunch ringing in Juniper's ears. The sound played over and over again in her mind as she struggled to stand.

The scream of agony he uttered would live in her mind forever.

Luca. *No.*

That would have been her. That should have been her. If Kyra hadn't knocked Juniper out of the way, it would be her being bitten instead of Luca. It was too heart-wrenching to even grasp; she felt her heart swell up and her throat close on unshed tears. "Luca!" She chokingly cried out.

The wolf sank its teeth into Luca's leg, then pulled away. Her purple eyes flashed delightedly. Juniper thought the awful Dämonenwölfe would go for another bite, but it slunk backward, leaving Luca to whimper and grab his leg in agony.

Kyra was at his side in an instant, but Juniper backed away, slipping over stones and raising a shaking hand to her mouth.

The Dämonenwölfe grinned, scarlet-red blood dripping from her fangs. Emma said, "That's all I asked."

"You monster!" Kyra screamed.

"I asked for one bite. You could have given it to me easily. Tell your friend to find my pack when he can no longer resist the pull of the hunt. We will be looking for him," Emma said, then stalked off into the night. The other two wolves followed her. Juniper watched as they melted in with the darkness of the forest.

Cal had run over, hoisting Luca up in his arms. Luca was wincing, looking anywhere but his leg. The leg was ripped apart as if slashed with a knife. Huge fang marks were imprinted in his flesh. It was her fault. It was Juniper's fault. That should have been her. *That should have been her.*

"What happened?" Julian's voice. He jogged over to them. His face went slack with horror when he saw Luca. He looked to Juniper to explain, but she couldn't find her voice to speak.

Kyra answered instead. "The wolves caught up to us. One jumped at Juniper and I shoved her out of the way. Luca was standing right behind her, so the wolf got him instead." She caught Luca's gaze, then looked away quickly. "It was my fault. I didn't realize that if I moved Juniper, the wolf would bite him." Something told Juniper that wasn't true. That Kyra would do anything for Juniper, no matter the cost.

Nonetheless, the weight lifted off of Juniper's shoulders. Yes, it should have been her, but she didn't tell Kyra to push her out of the way.

"We need to get him help. We need to do something!"

"Maiike is a couple miles in that direction," Cal said, swinging Luca in his arms as he pointed. "Can you make it, Luca?"

Luca gritted his teeth, then nodded. But then something amazing happened.

The injury on Luca's leg began...closing up.

It was healing, the skin closing up over the wound, the blood flowing back into his body as if traveling back in time. Suddenly, his leg looked like it had before the wolf had bit him, as if nothing had ever happened.

"Your leg," Juniper said, amazed. She looked up at him to see if he looked better, but his eyes had snapped shut, as if the wound closing was even more painful than the wound itself. Then he was still. Very still. Cal set him gently on the ground, eyes roving over Luca's miraculously healed leg.

Luca's eyes were still closed. He looked as peaceful as if he were asleep.

"He's okay," Jules said, raking his hand through his hair.

Cal let a smile show through, rubbing his eyes in joy.

Juniper realized she had been wringing her hands out. She stopped and knelt down next to Luca. "Is he sleeping?"

Cal shrugged. "The shock must be taking a huge toll."

Juniper looked up to Kyra to celebrate but went rigid. Kyra looked as if she had seen a ghost.

Juniper said, "What is it?"

Kyra met her eyes. Juniper jolted. Kyra's eyes were bloodshot, little red lines winding their way across the whites of her eyes like tendrils. It reminded Juniper of something she had seen in the castle long ago, snaking tendrils of the frame of a mirror...

Kyra said, her voice slow and steady, "You guys are idiots."

"Hey!" Julian protested. "You really wanna go there?"

"Yeah, I do." Her bloodshot eyes roved over the forest, never resting on one thing.

Cal said tiredly, "Kyra, stop this."

"You're idiots!"

"Stop it. Stop it now," Jules snarled. "This isn't the time for name-calling! Luca's hurt!"

"Everyone, calm down! We must stand together or not at all!" Juniper cried, overcome with emotions that she didn't understand. Somehow, she felt as if she knew what was coming, had known all along, but her mind had not caught up. Her very bones understood what was happening, but she still did not.

"You're all idiots if you think Luca's just hurt."

"What do you mean?"

"I mean that this is worse. So much worse than if he had just died."

Juniper stared at her sister in shock, as if Kyra had slapped her. She couldn't think of anything to say. What could she possibly mean? Maybe Kyra was just in shock. Maybe they all were.

Cal was the one who spoke. "You don't mean...?"

Kyra nodded. "I mean it." Her gaze was riveted on Luca's leg.

Cal put his head in his hands.

"What?" Jules asked the question for her, his eyes flitting back and forth between Cal and Kyra. His voice picked up shrilly. "Tell me what's happening!"

"We're going to have a Dämonenwölfe huntsman," Kyra said finally, slumping to her knees.

Juniper looked down at Luca, understanding dawning. Luca had been bitten by one of the Dämonenwölfe. He was transforming into one of them. He would live as a human but have the ability to turn into a wolf at any given time. He would be a wanderer, an outcast, someone who fed on humans when real food wasn't enough. The thought made her sick. Poor, little Luca. He didn't deserve it. *That would've been her.*

"How long?" Juniper asked, palms sweating.

"A minute. Maybe longer." Cal's voice was grim.

"What can we do?"

"There's nothing to do," Cal said. "We just have to let him transform."

Juniper nodded, watching Luca's still face.

Suddenly, he stirred, taking a heavy breath, and Juniper almost threw herself on him in happiness. He was alive; that was enough. He could still live almost normally, and that was enough.

Something stopped her from hugging him, however. No matter how much she knew he was still the same old Luca, the sweet boy who tripped over nothing and laughed at everyone's jokes, she couldn't stop herself from flinching back from him. He was dangerous now, and she didn't know how he would react to a hug from her.

Then, he stirred again.

Luca's eyes flicked open. They were a deep, dark lavender.

* * *

"Luca?" Juniper asked. "How do you feel?"

Kyra was standing a few feet away from everyone else, her arms crossed across her chest and her gaze locked somewhere deep in the forest. She pictured the wolves running with the wind far from there, laughing and thinking of their next victim. Of their next life to ruin. Kyra bit the inside of her mouth, trying to quell her distress.

She had knocked Juniper out of the way of the wolf, but in doing so, she had doomed Luca. It had been a split-second decision, a do-or-die. It was either have Juniper be cursed to live as a Dämonenwölfe, or Luca. Kyra had just thought: *Not Juniper.* So she had flung herself onto her sister, knocking her out of the way and saving her life. And dooming Luca in the process.

Kyra had known. She had known that Luca would be bit if she knocked Juni out of the way. She had known, and she had still done it. For her family, for her sister. No matter how much she wanted to deny it, she would do it again in a heartbeat.

It sounded like something her stepmother would try and say to rationalize her actions.

"I feel..." He blinked slowly, as if trying to acclimate to a bright area. Every time his lashes closed over his eyes, he looked like himself. Then they opened, and the deep violet irises shone.

Jules swallowed, his voice gentle. "Do you know what happened to you?" No one spoke the word Dämonenwölfe. It was as if the word had been banned, locked away forever in an unspeakable box that could not be touched.

"Yes."

"Do you want to talk about it?" Juniper asked, reaching a tentative hand out to his shoulder.

In a flash he jerked away from her touch as if it were poison, his purple eyes flashing with something equal parts hurt and rage filled. It was gone as quickly as it came.

"No," said Luca, and there was something in his voice that was final.

Kyra uncrossed her arms and joined the others. "Do you still want to come with us to stop the coronation?" Magic ran through his veins now. Kyra reflexively looked at her own arm, the twisting veins of blue.

Luca's mouth was a thin line. "Yes. I'll still come."

Juniper squeaked and hugged him tightly, throwing her arms around his torso. Luca didn't hug her back.

"Maiike's a few miles away," said Cal, breaking the heavy silence.

"Then let's get going. The coronation is in a couple days. We still need to go to Jules' stupid bachelor ball. Then we leave for the Winter Palace," Kyra said.

Luca rose to his feet, his foot about to catch on a rock. Kyra already had her insults ready. Miraculously, Luca's foot missed the rock. He didn't fall, or even stumble. He just stood up like a normal human being. Kyra gasped, looking at him in astonishment.

"What?" Luca asked, looking worried. "What's wrong?"

"You didn't trip when you stood!" Kyra grinned easily, and the worry melted from Luca's face. It was replaced by a look of pride, his shoulders puffing out.

"Guess you can't call me little huntsman anymore." Luca held his chin high.

"Nice try. You're never getting out of that," said Kyra.

And with that, she began walking eastward towards Maiike. The others followed in her wake.

Luca sighed, but he had a broken smile on his face. He closed his eyes, and for a moment he was the boy he had been before he entered the forest. When his eyes opened, that boy was gone for good.

13

The Kingdom by the Sea

They walked on in silence, the birds tweeting and signaling the coming of morning. Kyra let out a sigh of relief when she heard the first bird's song, thankful the long night was ending at last. A nearby mockingbird tweeted, weaving a beautiful melody, notes floating sweetly.

"The birds are singing for you, Juniper!" Cal called up. Juniper turned back around and smiled at him, a beaming ray of light brighter than the sun itself. *The birds sang for her.* The birds signaled the coming of the sun. Juniper was the Sun's Child; it only made sense that the birds sang her arrival, too.

The forest was slowly disappearing around them, clumps of green trees giving way to clearings and patches of grass. The flat dirt-and-moss covered ground turned into rolling hills, and the leaves gave way to clear skies. A gentle breeze rolled in as the sun became visible, casting warm, golden light on the hilltops.

The hills dipped forming cliffs that jutted out over the coastline, giving way to sparkling blue ocean and salty air. The water stretched out for forever, extending along the side of the grassy hills like a blue desert. The breeze became tinged with a sort of far away cold, like the wind itself brought whispers and greetings from the waves themselves. Kyra imagined countries far beyond the horizon line, the wind having traveled them all.

Kyra found herself walking in step with Cal, their shoulders brushing every couple of steps. Every time their shoulders brushed, Kyra's lungs compacted like boulders crushing them; she forgot how to breathe. She would have spent all day being acutely aware of their shoulders and how they touched, but she broke the silence, words slipping out her mouth before she could even fully think them through.

"What's your favorite color?" Kyra blurted. It sounded so childish; she wanted to slap herself.

"What?"

"Your favorite color," Kyra repeated. She focused on each step. One, two, brush Cal's shoulder, one, two, brush Cal's shoulder. "Everyone has one. If they say they don't, they're lying."

"Grey," he said simply, smiling like there was a joke only he was in on. Kyra longed to be in on the joke, too. "And you?"

"It used to be red." Aazagonian red, the symbol of the blood shed that had decided the dusty land's fate. Founded in war and bred in fury, her kingdom had been her world. That world had changed ever so slightly now, growing larger and more wonderful with each passing day. Now, her favorite color was a robin's egg blue, the color of the sky and of frost, ice-covered lakes, of almost transparent river water, and of pale hydrangeas. The color of a certain person's eyes. But she couldn't say that. She would throw herself off the cliff before she would ever subject herself to that kind of humiliation.

"What is it now?" Cal asked.

"I'm figuring it out. Holding interviews and having each color submit a resume."

"Rightly so." He nodded like she had said something intelligent instead of terribly stupid, like she thought.

"Picking a favorite color is not for the faint of heart."

"Agreed." Cal said, humoring her, "People can't just choose a new favorite color every day. It's serious business."

"If you didn't agree, I'm not sure we could be friends anymore," Kyra said matter-of-factly. She didn't mean it. Not for a second.

Cal said, with a mischievous grin, "In that case, nevermind."

"Hey!" Kyra exclaimed, unable to keep the smile off her face now as she punched him in the shoulder.

"Ouch! Fine, fine, I'll take it back!" Cal said, nose scrunching up with a smile. He shoved her hand off him as she reared back for another punch.

"Not until you say sorry!"

"In your dreams."

With that, Cal raced down the hill, and Kyra chased after him. She laughed the whole way down, side hitching as she let her laughter ring out loud and clear. The sun was rising high over the ocean, making the water sparkle.

Then, towards the bottom of the hill, Cal tripped, rolling over and over until he collapsed in a heap at the bottom of the hill, panting and cheeks rosy. Kyra slowed as she neared him, standing over him and gloating. She wanted to remember him forever in this way, smiling with the wind ruffling his shirt.

"Wanna say sorry yet?" she asked, cocking her head.

"Nope." He stood up and took off running.

Eventually, they both got tired of running and both didn't want to give in, so they drafted up a quick truce and walked on.

After a while, she remembered what he had said on the beanstalk about magic and crazy stepmothers and a talking mirror.

"Wait up a moment," Kyra said.

Cal stopped walking, letting the others clamber ahead, joking amongst themselves and taking in the smell of the ocean with large breaths. Juniper was zig-zagging in between Jules and Luca, playing a game of some sort.

"What's up?" he asked.

"The mirror you saw when you were a kid," said Kyra slowly. "What did the voice sound like?"

Cal's expression darkened, his eyes becoming clouded over. He looked as if he remembered that moment, that night, when he had stumbled upon the Queen entranced in some dark magic. "The voice in the mirror? A man's voice. It was deep. Almost...musical. It sounded like someone very old but very young at the same time was speaking. And I thought about that voice for a long time after that. Because it felt like I knew the person speaking. Nevermind. Why do you want to know?"

"I just wondered if you ever heard the voice again. Maybe you've met the person before."

Cal shook his head slightly. "I would recognize the voice if I heard it. I know that for sure. It's not something I'd soon forget."

"And Callista...you're sure the mirror said that the 'Sun's Child' was more fair? That the mirror didn't mean that the Queen was?" Kyra asked.

"I'm sure of it. Your stepmother was definitely angry about it. She wouldn't be angry if the mirror had said *she* was the fairest. I know she was mad, because when she got up to leave, her palm was dripping with blood. I think she had dug her nails into her palm out of spite."

Kyra shivered, picturing drops of blood falling from her stepmother's palm like water falling from a melting icicle.

"Why do they call you those nicknames?" asked Cal. The breeze had picked up a bit, ruffling the hem of his shirt. Standing atop the hill, the wind tussling him, he looked like a hero straight out of Juniper's books. But better, because he was real, imperfect, and wonderful. "I've thought about it a lot and I can't figure it out."

"Even your great mind has its faults, it seems, because this mystery is easy. I'm terrible and Juniper's amazing," Kyra said like it was obvious, which it was, "Duh. Everyone in my kingdom loves Juni because she's, well, her, and they don't like me because of a rather embarrassing incident with laundry day and an accidental riding of a wild boar. Stress on the 'accidental' part."

Cal laughed, a lilting sound with ups and downs like the hills themselves. Kyra's stomach followed, doing flips and flops along with it. Her heart did an entire month's worth of acrobatics classes. "Whatever happened with that laundry day, I don't think I want to know."

"Good call."

"Not sure it's wise of me to want to be friends with you, after all," said Cal.

"You'd be right. A goody-goody like you would shiver at my long list of misconduct. In fact, I'm banned from several sections of the kingdom."

"We are very different people." The corner of his mouth tilted up. "But whatever did happen that day, I don't think that's it. I don't think that's why you're called Moon's Child."

They began walking again, trailing lines along the coast. Kyra didn't ever answer him. She couldn't find the words, and she didn't know if she agreed with him or not. Moon's Child had always been her second name, the thing most people referred to her as. She had never thought to question it. Sun and Moon. Day and night. Light and dark. Juniper and Kyra. *Two strands of the same cloth, woven together.*

Soon, the kingdom of Maiike was visible.

"There it is!" Julian cried out, pointing at his home. "Maiike!"

Maiike was nestled in between two large hills, the entire kingdom fitting in a large valley as if being hugged on both sides by grass. On the left of the kingdom were the cliffs dropping off to the coast, to the ocean. The right had the rolling hills that hosted miles of farmland. The castle, which sat in the center of the valley, was large and imperial, white stone clashing with blue banners that swayed in the wind. Homes were splattered on the hillsides, dotting the hills. Large farms extended out towards them, with little people far away that looked as small as ants, with their simple straw hats and rakes. Kyra could see the bottom of the valley; that looked to be the least rural. It was very different from Aazagonia, with cobblestone streets and houses built very close together. Most of the houses had spires reaching up into the air, red roofs meeting to make sharp points. For some reason, Kyra thought it would hurt very much indeed if someone were to fall on that point, and if she had grown up in Maiike instead of Aazagonia, she was sure that theory would be tested.

The kingdom was livelier than Aazagonia. Significantly less dusty, too, which was a plus. People bustled around, flitting this way and that like busy bees. As they neared the kingdom, she saw women carrying huge bundles of fabric and men holding pitchforks and baskets of colorful, strange-looking fruits. Banners were being hung all around with the emblem of Maiike; a blue rake crossed with a yellow and white sword. Preparation for the ball, it seemed. Kyra couldn't remember the last time they had had a ball in her kingdom. Not since her mother died. Not since the Queen had come. Come to think of it, most of the kingdom's money was syphoned to the Queen...she thought of the hungry-looking citizens in the streets, the dirt and filth lining the town. Why had Aazagonia fallen from glory once the Queen arrived? And what did she use the money for?

Kyra suddenly remembered the Queen disappearing for hours or days on end, on trips to a magical 'spa' trip. But the Queen never came back rejuvenated or relaxed. She always came back more anxious and more easy to anger. What sort of spa did that?

As they descended the hill that led into the kingdom, a dirt path showing itself, Cal and Jules raced to the front of their little group, drinking in the sight of their kingdom with pleased smiles.

"Do I look okay?" Julian asked, turning to Cal and standing up straight. Jules' blond waves were mussed, his red jacket askew. The arm of his shirt had been torn through when the giant had decided he would be the afternoon snack. Despite all that, he looked like a prince. Somehow, his eyes still gleamed with riches. Kyra looked herself up and down, noticing that she most certainly did not look like a princess. Even when she *wasn't* dirty and dinged up, she was pretty sure she still didn't look like royalty.

"Okay enough," Cal said, fixing Julian's collar and dusting dirt off his jacket. Kyra remembered with a jolt that in this world of kingdoms and balls, Cal was Julian's servant.

"Really? Don't lie to me Calais or I swear—"

"Yes," said Cal. "Ready to break all the kingdom's hearts."

"Just how I like it." Julian grinned deviously. "See you at the ball, party people!"

Then he took off towards his kingdom, his jacket flying out behind him as he ran down the hill and into the town. Julian loved his kingdom with his heart and soul. Kyra couldn't even imagine loving something so much. She watched him greet citizens with smiles, hugging people and being hugged like they all knew each other well. Like they were family. Kyra had a weird feeling in her chest, a feeling that she had never felt before. It was a mix of joy and a pang of longing.

Cal turned. "You guys ready to meet the Queen of Maiike?"

* * *

The throne room was beautiful. Juniper stared in awe at the circular dome. It had five entryways leading into it, each with sky blue curtains draped above it. The ceiling was a marble color, with gold and blue banners hanging from it. There were seashells and sea glass embedded in the floor, and paintings of mermaids and sea monsters lined the halls. Hugging the thrones were two entryways, making the whole room feel large even though it was quite small.

On the left side, the room devolved into a balcony, looking out over the rolling hilltops of the kingdom and the cliff-lined ocean. Juniper could even see a sliver of the sandy beach below.

The king's throne was empty, silent. The queen's throne, however, was not empty.

Queen Ingrith sat regally on the white and blue checkered throne, gazing out at the sea as they entered the room. A golden crown sat atop her wavy blonde-grey locks. She was tall and wiry, like Julian.

The five of them had been escorted by armed guards who peeled off as soon as they made it safely to the thrones. The guards hadn't said a word the whole way up. It had been quite awkward, as the group was used to unfiltered chatter up until that point. Weird, Juniper thought, that the noise now comforted her instead of scared her.

The moment her son came in, Ingrith sprung from her chair, racing across the room to envelop him in a tight hug. She squeezed him tight, her long hair spilling over Julian's shoulder as she did. Juniper knew that in Maiike, the regent's length of hair symbolized how long they had gone without war. Since Ingrith's hair was past her knees, this meant Maiike had been at peace for a long time.

"My son." Ingrith beamed. "I'm glad you're back in time for the ball. And Calais, good to see you. I trust you've been taking good care of my boy?"

Cal nodded, for once looking awkward and out of place as the mother and son hugged. "Doing my best. He's quite the handful."

Julian threw his head back and let out a guffaw, crossing over to Cal to give a quick slap to the back of his head. Cal opened his mouth in protest, about to retaliate before Ingrith was speaking again. "Boys, boys. Very rude to scuffle when we have guests. Almost as rude as not introducing me to our lovely newcomers."

Juniper realized Ingrith was looking directly at her. All eyes turned to her expectantly. Juniper felt heat rise to her cheeks. She tried to remember her name as she said, "M-my name is, uh...Juniper." At least it wasn't as bad as: *I am Juniper. I am short.*

"Godmother Luck smiles down on us," Ingrith said, pleased. She bowed her head graciously. Juniper remembered reading a book on the customs of Maiike after they had visited so long ago. The saying meant 'it is lucky to meet you.'

For a moment, it looked as if Ingrith would recognize the two girls that she had met so long ago in the castle in Aazagonia. But she must have heard the news of their 'deaths' because she didn't ask. Or she didn't care to.

But for a moment, her eyes had flashed, *I know you.*

"Kyra," Kyra said, giving a small wave of her hand. She schooled her face into a fake-looking grin. Their mother's voice rang in Juniper's head. *Stand up straight, girls. Have you ever seen a hunchbacked princess? Juniper, darling, try not to look like you're going to hurl when you introduce yourself.* Oddly enough, instead of making her more anxious, the voice helped. She felt herself stand up straighter and mustered up a (hopefully) nice-looking smile. A smile that said she wasn't going to throw up. Not this time.

"I'm Luca," Luca said. The group had thought up the excuse that his purple eyes were a rare genetic mutation. Who would believe innocent-looking Luca was part wolf?

"I didn't expect Julian to bring home friends," Ingrith said, giving a confused look at the group's condition. They all looked beat up and dirty, most of their clothing with rips in it and their arms smudged with dirt. Juniper didn't even *want* to know what her hair looked like. It was crazy enough as it was; she knew it now would look like something had died in it.

"Neither did we," Cal muttered under his breath.

Julian said, "We met in the forest. I saved them from...trolls." He indicated his hurt arm. "My friends live by the North Mountains." That was where the Winter Palace was located. "I thought I'd guide them there tomorrow."

"That's very kind of you," Ingrith said, clearly satisfied with her son. She almost looked as proud as Julian, no matter how fake the excuse was.

Cal began hesitantly, looking at the floor, "Your Majesty...is it alright if I go say hello to my grandmother...I know she's down in the village, and it would only take a moment."

Queen Ingrith nodded. "Of course, Cal. You can spend as long as you wish with her. I'm sure she'll be pleased to see you. In fact, take the rest of the day off, if you are back in time for the ball."

"Thank you, Your Majesty, I—" Cal was cut off by a whoop of joy. Oh, no.

Kyra was no longer standing beside her. Juniper resisted the urge to facepalm.

"Guys!" Kyra was standing on the balcony, on the railing of it, at least. She was leaning out, pointing at something in the ocean. "Come look!"

Juniper offered up an apologetic half-smile at Ingrith, who was staring at Kyra with a blank look as if she were an eight-legged fire giant wearing a pink tiara. Juni ran out to the balcony.

"Get down from there!" Juniper hissed, tugging her sister's dress pleadingly. "You're being rude!"

Kyra looked down at Juniper, upturned eyes alight with exhilaration. The wind whipped her pink dress around her ankles, her hair flapping, the humidity curling it like strands of sunlight or molten gold. She was smiling, beaming with a childlike awe. "Mermaids!"

Juniper's face went slack. She stared up at her sister, gaping in dumbfounded shock. "What?" *Mermaids.* She had never seen one in real life, couldn't even imagine what it would be like in person. Mermaids, unlike Dämonenwölfe, were made of light magic. They were birthed from the sun, good and wonderful and strange.

Kyra held out a hand to her, and Juniper took it without hesitation. Juniper was hauled up to the edge of the railing and met with miles and miles of sea. The ocean stretched out so far that Juniper felt like crying.

The daylight seemed as if it were holding its breath in anticipation of her and let go as she set her eyes on the sea and hills below.

How could the world be so strange and full of wondrous things? How large was the ocean, and how far could leaves ride on the backs of the winds into the sky? The horizon line was the stopping point for her line of sight, but she knew that it was no end. Juniper wondered if she ran fast enough, would she glide over to the edge of the world and fly off of it into the cloudless sky? Some might say her wondrous ideas were silly. Juniper herself knew that nothing was impossible until you tried it. And if the world boasted such beautiful things as endless seas and countless stars above, then why should dreams of flying be deemed foolish?

Kyra pointed to a spot next to a jutting cliff.

There, amazingly, were little spots of color amongst the blue of the ocean. Jumping mermaids, splashing and playing in the water, their tails vibrant pinks and blues and yellows. One had green skin, another had orange, yet another had red hair. They disappeared under water for a second, before breaking the surface with a splash and soaring into the air, jumping high like colorful raindrops that fell upside-down. When they fell back down, hitting the water gracefully and nearly splashless, they were swimming underwater, their hands out in front of them as if guiding the way.

They were swimming away, Juniper realized, quicker than lighting, and gone in a flash. But she had seen them. Real live mermaids. She was leaning forward, her feet curling around the railing of the balcony. It felt like the only thing holding her back from soaring into the sky and joining the mermaids in the water. The wind teased her, pulling her to follow. The familiar tug in her heart was present—the call to magic.

The Queen's coronation was in three days. They would stop it, and they would save their kingdom from her. They would not let Aazagonia fall to tyranny.

Juniper squeezed Kyra's hand as the two sisters stared out over the world they had never thought to know.

The world they would soon know as well as they knew the very sun and moon itself.

14

Slippers of Glass

"I have got to say, that dress is...quite...something."

"Shut up."

Juniper giggled from where she sat on the bed, watching Kyra try on several dresses some servants had brought to them. Kyra twirled in front of the mirror, wearing a blue plaid dress with incredibly puffy sleeves.

"It's not that bad," Juniper lied, biting her lip to keep from laughing.

"You're right. It's awful."

Juniper had already found the dress she was going to wear to the ball that night, mostly because she didn't want to ask for another one. Hers was a golden, strapless dress that poofed out around her. She had always loved dresses that poofed; she loved twirling and seeing the hem fly out around her until she was dizzy. A lady in waiting had done up her hair in an elegant bun and traced little strands of gold through it. She had never felt so regal. And *clean*. Showering and scrubbing her from head to foot in preparation for the night's festivities, the servants had done their job.

Julian had been whisked away almost immediately after they had met with his mother. He was getting dressed up all fancy. Luca had gone off with him, probably not knowing where else to go with Cal off visiting his grandmother.

The girls had been given two elaborate suites that looked out over the ocean. Juniper looked out at the sea with fond eyes, glad to not be far from it. She was used to the dusty flats of Aazagonia and the forest that bordered it. The ocean was a welcome change.

Anything, really, was a welcome change from the dust and trees that reminded her of home. And of her mother.

The gold of her dress made her think suddenly of a similar golden mirror. But she had never seen a mirror like that before, so why did she remember one so vividly? Her step-father had always told her that her imagination could go wild when she wanted it to. But this mirror didn't seem like something she had dreamed up. No, it felt more like a memory.

Queen Ingrith's flashing eyes flit through her brain. The lady couldn't remember that she had met the two girls when they were little, as if partaking in a walking dream where things seemed just a little too fuzzy. A little too far out of reach. Ingrith's eyes held a forgotten memory from long ago, and sang a haunting melody.

She broke from her thoughts as Kyra whirled in front of the mirror, having changed into a new dress. This one had tight long sleeves that yawned at the edges. The dress reached down to her ankles (it was a little short, but most dresses were short on Kyra). To top it off, it had no plaid anywhere in sight, so that was already a step up.

"Doesn't this one just scream, 'Hi, I'm supposed to be dead so please don't recognize me?'" Kyra asked jokingly, but the pleased look on her face said enough.

At the ball that night, they were expected to dance and chitchat with nobles. That was not Juniper's favorite thing in the world, and she wondered how the others felt about it. She thought about that morning, when she had seen Kyra and Cal goofing around on the hills. Hmm...

Juniper looked hesitant at her sister. She said, "I am going to ask you something, and you are going to give me an honest answer."

"Should I be scared?" Kyra plopped down next to her on the bed, the dress spilling out around her like flower petals. Her hair had been pulled back into a ponytail, with two strands pulled out the front.

"Depends on your definition."

Kyra countered, "You know as well as me that I don't peruse dictionaries in my free time. Maybe it's best if you don't ask."

"I thought you were never scared..."

"Ask away."

"Is there something going on with you and Cal?" The question tumbled out of Juniper's mouth, words mushing like jelly.

Kyra's face flushed red for a moment—for one moment, but it still happened, so it counted—and then returned to nonchalance. "Why, does he wanna know? This isn't grade school. I'm not looking for him to write me a love letter and give it to me at recess."

Juniper said carefully, "No. I was just curious. Do you care if he wants to?" She felt a little mischievous asking this as she watched Kyra's face give away a flash of disappointment. She didn't enjoy the rush that scheming brought for too long because she immediately felt bad for trying to coax information out of her sister like that. "Hah! So you do care!"

"What?" Kyra said, caught off-guard. She sat up quickly, looking flustered. "I don't care!"

"You do! You fancy Cal!"

"You speak like a grandmother."

Juniper grinned devilishly. "Changing the topic, I see."

Kyra let out a fuming breath. "I do *not* like Cal!"

"Do too!" Juniper couldn't shake a goofy grin off her face. She instantly wished she could take it back, as Kyra had grabbed a diamond-encrusted pillow from the bed and was chucking it at Juniper. "Nonono—"

The pillow hit Juniper square in the jaw, sending her careening backward and falling on the bed with a thud.

Kyra stood over her, relishing the triumph with a pleased look on her face. She held the diamond pillow in hand, raising it over her head as if going to bring it down again. "Repeat after me."

Juniper nodded her head, fearful of another pillow assault. Those diamonds could *really* hurt.

"Kyra does not," Kyra began, eyeing her suspiciously.

"Kyra does not," Juniper repeated.

"Like Cal and will not like Cal ever. Repeat. Go."

"Like Cal..." Juniper bit her lip, already expecting a huge smack in the face. "And will like Cal forever!"

The pillow came raining down, but Juniper didn't even register it, she was laughing so hard. Her giggles came in hitches as the sequins smacking her windpipe made sure no laugh lasted too long.

Juniper tried to shove Kyra off her, to no avail. "Ahaha! Hahaha—Ow! Stop! No, seriously, I mean it, Kyra, stop this at once—"

Juniper was cut off by the door slamming open. They sat up and looked at the intruder standing in the doorway.

Luca stood uncomfortably, leaning against the doorframe. He was wearing a white button-up shirt underneath a grey vest, with little frills popping out of the vest at the collar. Standing as stiff as a board, he looked like the vest would rip in two if he even breathed.

"Aw, don't you look cute," Kyra smirked, running over to him and yanking at the puffy nonsense poking from his shirt.

"Quit it!" Luca complained, swatting at her hand. "I didn't choose it!"

"Simply dashing!" Juniper gushed, actually meaning it. His brown hair was combed for once, his tan skin clean. Juniper had been sure all this time that the freckles on his nose were specks of dirt, so this was a pleasant surprise.

"So so cute," agreed Kyra.

Inspecting himself in the mirror, Luca relented, "I guess I look a little cute."

"And you all look as gorgeous as a sky full of stars!" Julian boomed, sliding into the room with a flourish. He looked, well...like a prince. A very, *very* nice looking prince. He was wearing a white long sleeve with gold embroidery and a blue cape, matching his blue pants. His curls had been slicked back to fit under a golden crown. He was every inch the handsome prince; the hero to save the day. Juniper felt like she was falling down a gaping rabbit hole when he met her eyes.

Julian bent to one knee, holding out a hand to Juniper with a serious look. She took it, still feeling a bit like she was rocking on a boat, as he said, "My lady, you especially look stunning."

"Thank you," Juniper said, trying not to squeal. Squealing would ruin the moment, for sure. "I am charmed." Was that what you were supposed to say? She didn't know what she was supposed to say. Oh, no, that was definitely the wrong thing to say.

"And I think *I'm* gonna be sick," Kyra said, pantomiming throwing up onto Luca, who wrinkled his nose at her.

Heat rose up her cheeks. She was being silly. Besides, the point of the ball that night was for Julian to find a wealthy princess to get engaged to! There was no room for Juniper to be all ga-ga over him, especially not then. She quickly wrenched her hand back, suddenly self-conscious in the way it hung by her side.

Julian coughed, then stood. "You look lovely too, Kyra. Don't hit me for saying that."

"Where's Cal?" Kyra asked easily enough, but Juniper raised an eyebrow at the eager undertones of her voice.

"Cal's meeting you three down at the ball. He's setting up some last-minute buffet tables. Shrimp ones, if you're wondering. They're a Maiikan delicacy. To die for!"

As they walked down the hall, they passed huge portraits of a bunch of old men and women, most wearing the same crown that Julian had on his head. Juniper stared at the winding pattern of the carpet, the blue and yellow lines meeting then dividing over and over again as Julian explained what was going to happen at the ball and how he would dance with every eligible woman in the kingdom, as well as several visiting princesses. And servant girls. *Splendid.*

Eventually, they made it to the large double doors of the ballroom.

Julian stopped short. "I can't enter with you guys, 'cause I have to go down some huge stairs once the ball begins. It'll be really awesome. They're gonna announce my name in a really deep voice and blow trumpets. The whole shebang."

"I will make sure to be watching," Juniper said.

"Your shoes," Jules said suddenly, looking down at her feet. "They're glass."

Juniper looked down at her shoes as if seeing them for the first time. They were a golden shade of glass. "They are quite hard to walk in. One must make sacrifices for beauty."

Julian seemed to find it hilarious, though he found most things funny. "My mom made me wear a corset. Don't tell anyone, though. It's an insult to my six-pack." The thought of Julian's six-pack made Juniper's brain short circuit for a moment.

Juniper giggled, shaking her head. "You are too full of yourself."

"You're not full of yourself enough."

"Perhaps we both have lessons to learn."

"Perhaps indeed." Julian looked at her for a long moment, as if realizing something he had forgotten, or if he was discovering something new. He coughed, then said, "Now stop distracting me, Sun's Child, or I'll be late to my grand entrance."

"Julian..." but she drifted off, unable to finish whatever it was she was going to say.

"I have to go," Julian said quickly, his voice oddly fluctuating. "Things to do, places to be, shrimp to eat!" and with that, he scurried off up a flight of stairs.

Juniper stared after him, baffled, waiting until she could no longer see him before she turned and entered the ballroom with Luca.

She felt helpless watching Julian go, wanting to run after him like they did in books. She wanted him to throw his arms around her and dance with her all night, and in this fantasy she was graceful and sure and confident, and people complimented her for things other than her beauty. People came up to her, awed at her dancing and intellect, how she held herself with the grace of a queen. No one whispered about the girl who was *just so pretty*, then gawked as she stumbled or made a fool of herself.

She wanted people to see her as someone who was worth more than the curl of her hair or the slope of her nose. She wanted people to look at her and think, *There goes a brave and good person.*

The fantasy dissolved as the doors slammed shut behind her, a reminder that some things were not meant to be.

"Do you wish Julian was your date tonight?" Luca asked as they walked in.

She shook her head. "He is going to be engaged by the end of the evening." The excuse sounded lame, even to her. Though she did like the idea that they were star-crossed lovers—even if he didn't quite love her back.

"Don't be upset. I'll be your date," Luca offered up, taking her arm. "Then we'll have each other to talk to all night."

Juniper smiled happily, blinking back tears that she hadn't even realized were forming.

Taking his hand, they entered the ball, her glass shoes clacking omens both good and bad.

* * *

Kyra scowled at the dancing people, pressing herself into a corner. She had successfully avoided small talk all night.

The ball was unlike anything she had ever seen and admittedly pretty spectacular.

The magnificent ballroom had huge marble columns reaching up the ceiling, which was covered in paintings; greens and faint pinks and yellows caught her eye. A line of tables sat in a connecting room, filled with piling tables of food and desserts that Kyra had already ransacked like a starving vulture that had never seen cake. People were milling about in groups around a glass dance floor.

Women in poofing dresses danced with men in elegant suits—most had the fluffy white collars that Luca had, so she couldn't busy herself with taunting him about it anymore—twirling and whirling around the glossy floor. They pirouetted and lifted each other in the air, all somehow knowing the exact same dance at the exact same time. It was almost creepy how in sync they all danced.

Did most people spend their time learning those dances? How did everyone know what to do, unless they'd been practicing? Kyra had so many questions, like, would she have to start learning those dances some day? If so, she was packing her bags and running away to go live with the muskrats, for real.

Ducking away from some guy as he walked up, she held her glass of water up in front of her face. He turned, looking disappointed, as he walked up to another girl and asked her to dance. They waltzed off to the dance floor, laughing obnoxiously.

Suddenly, she felt a tap on her shoulder. Cal. He wore a white shirt with a black suit jacket, his shirt decidedly not frilly. Kyra's pulse began to race like she was in a battle.

"I was kinda hoping you'd have to wear epaulets." Kyra dusted off his shoulder where the epaulets would be. "Then I could die happy."

"Has anyone told you how funny you are?" Cal said mockingly.

"Two times a minute."

"Must be a mistake." He looked at her as if noticing she was dressed up for the first time. "You look nice." His voice had gone soft, a change from the sharp edges it usually toted.

"Lying is a sin, Calais."

"Well, you're not covered in blood and dirt. So that's a step up from the usual," said Cal, his regular voice returning.

Kyra rolled her eyes, resisting the urge to smile. Then, he was grabbing her arm and pulling her out to the dance floor. She yanked her arm back in alarm.

"Woah, woah, woah, what are you doing?" Kyra said, maybe-sort-of-slightly panicking. If there was anything she and Juniper bonded over, it was the fact that they both hated to dance.

"We're dancing. We have to. If I'm not looking busy, someone will order me to set up another shrimp table."

"Absolutely not," Kyra said, but she was already letting his gravity pull her to the flurry of dancers. "I don't know how."

"The great and infallible Kyra doesn't know how to dance? I'm shocked."

"I never learned." She tucked a lock of hair back into her ponytail, nervous for some reason. Her real mother had never thought dancing was important, and her father refused. Of course, her stepmother would never teach her; that was far too beneath Her Royal Hoity-Toity Ness.

"It's easy," Cal said, putting his hand on her waist, and guiding her hand to his shoulder. "You'll be fine. You've fought giants and wolves and evil queens. You can dance for a minute."

"One minute. No more, no less," Kyra said, looking around at the other dancers. The band had begun playing a new song, a sweet piano tune rising high above the other instruments. Dancers had slowed, stopping the quick twists and flips, instead swaying easily next to each other. Kyra had never felt more out of place.

But when she met Cal's gaze, she felt something click into place.

* * *

Julian was finished dancing with the seven millionth girl when he ran over to Kyra, pulling her on to the dance floor. She didn't even try to protest as she took in all the glares and glances she was getting from people all over the room.

"Don't you have more important girls to be dancing with?" Kyra asked, feeling like she was gonna get jumped after the ball by a mob of angry townsfolk.

"I have to dance with every eligible girl," Julian replied, swinging her around. "You're a girl, and you're eligible, so sorry."

"Ugh, for how long?"

"About thirty seconds. The Trial by Fire's beginning."

"Trial by Fire? What's that?" Kyra asked, intrigued. It sounded exciting and definitely had to do with flames, which would spice up the ball a bit more. Flames always did. She knew from personal experience.

"This lame tradition Maiike does at every prince's engagement ball. My dad used to say it's a way to convince the haters that we're royal. So lame. Basically you walk through flames and it gives a symbol of who you are. For princes, it's supposed to reaffirm their super royal blood," Julian explained, looking uncomfortable for a moment. He tugged at his collar as if it constricted him, then guided her over to where a small crowd had been gathering. "It's time!"

The crowd formed a circle around a patch of ground where a silver pot sat, the glow of small silver embers visible deep inside.

Queen Ingrith stood before the pot, a warm smile on her face. "I'd like to start out by saying I'm so honored to have you all here tonight. I am overjoyed seeing all of you in the palace and having a good time, as well as all our visiting royal families and noblemen. The stars shine down on us here tonight. Now, if my son Julian would please come here."

Departing Kyra's side, Julian broke into the circle with a regal nod of his head. His goofy smile was gone, replaced with a serious, no-nonsense look. He stepped beside his mother. "It's a pleasure to have you all here."

Kyra heard a snicker beside her and saw that Luca and Cal had walked up to stand next to her at the edge of the circle. Luca had put on a pair of shaded reading glasses to hide his eyes. She wondered where Juniper had run off to. Instantly Kyra wondered if she was in trouble, if she needed help. Calm circled her as she realized that Juni was probably hiding out in the bathroom not wanting to talk to people. Kyra would join her after the fire thing and see if she was alright.

"The Trial by Fire is a generations-old celebration of who we are," Ingrith said, extending her arms towards the small bucket on the floor. At Ingrith's words, the embers began to heat up, small flames dancing in the bottom of the bowl. Incredibly, the flames began to rise, floating higher and higher with her every word. "We were graced with this revealing pot by a faerie a thousand years ago. It used to be a ward against unnatural threats, a way to uncover spies in our midst. Since our foes have long gone, the pot may be used for more entertaining measures. Now, we use it to celebrate the upcoming king and prove his worthiness for the throne. Julian, please step into the flames."

The fire inside the bucket had gotten so large, it roared almost as tall as the ceiling, extending straight up into the air like one of the tall columns encircling the ballroom. It flickered, and the crowd gasped and stepped backwards as little sparks jumped off the fire. The sparks reminded Kyra of a group of sunbeam sprites she had seen in the Southern Forest when she was little, whirling in the air.

"He'll be burned," Luca said, leaning forward in worry.

Kyra just shrugged as Julian stepped into the flames. His whole body was covered in fire in seconds, however, he looked as if he was unharmed. He looked fine, actually, way too fine for someone who was in the midst of a wall of flame.

Kyra watched in awe as a picture began engraving itself above Julian's head. A picture dripping in black liquid, suspended high in the flames.

* * *

Juniper looked out from the balcony, longing to be anywhere else than the castle. She had left the ball after twenty minutes, too overwhelmed with it all. Too many people; too much noise had driven her away.

Mainly, she couldn't stand to watch as Julian danced with girl after girl, twirling them and laughing. Maybe he had already met his future bride.

A small part of her was happy for him. He seemed to be having a good time. But an even larger part of her was filled with sorrow.

I want to get to know you. He had said to her what felt like forever ago. When she had fallen in love.

It was then that she realized that she didn't even know what it was like to fall in love. She had never been in love, had never seen it before. Kyra's father and Juniper's mother didn't seem to love each other, not really, and the memory of her real parents love seemed hazy, like a passing fog. All she had to reference were books, and it felt like even those were lies. Because in books, the princess always ended up with a prince who loved her more than the distance of a thousand oceans. He loved her enough to save her from demons and witches and dragons, enough to split mountains and to fell evil. The prince loved the princess endlessly. Infinitely.

Juniper sniffled, wiping away a moonlit tear. She felt as if she would never know that kind of love. Maybe she would never have a dashing hero that would save her from villains.

Maybe she had to find the hero in herself, first.

She was interrupted from her sulking thoughts by footsteps coming from the throne room. She whirled away, using her arm to wipe away the remaining tears. Sunbeam above, she probably looked awful, all puffy-eyed and miserable. It was almost funny, she thought, how much of a pity party she had been throwing herself for a boy she had just met.

The visitor was standing in the balcony's entrance, his skin gleaming with moonlight. He stood tall as if he held up the world on his shoulders. As if the world was his. His eyes were almond-shaped, monolid and dark green. Not green like Julian's emerald, grass-colored eyes, but dark like the scales of a slithering snake. He was attractive in an offsetting way, in a way that reminded Juniper of the edge of a cliff overlooking sharp rocks below. Like if you got too close to him, you could fall and drown.

He was leaning against the railing, his dark lashes fluttering in concern. "Why are you crying?"

Juniper wanted to kick herself with her stupid glass shoes. She probably looked like a mess. "I am not."

"Prince Julian's not all that great, you know. He's kinda dumb."

"I..." The mention of Julian's name slapped her across the face, and brought her denial crashing down. "How did you know?"

He shrugged easily. "Lots of girls in there are crying over him right now. Half the party, I believe."

"He is my friend. Who he marries is none of my concern," she said indignantly, raising her chin higher as if trying to make herself believe it.

"Sure," the boy said, a knowing look in his eyes. "In the meantime, I'll keep you company. I don't get all the fuss over dances, anyway."

"Me, too."

"I'm Tora."

"Juniper," she said, wondering if she should shake his hand. Weirdly, that was the best introduction she had ever made for herself. Her voice was wobbly and her eyes were shining from tears, but she still felt louder and more sure of herself than she had ever been.

"Juniper," Tora said, mulling the name over. "I think I know of someone named Juniper. Isn't there a princess with that name from Aazagonia? I heard she was the fairest in all the land. Or something."

Juniper froze. *Play dumb*, she thought. "Aazagonia? Never heard of that. Is that a flower?" *Too dumb.*

And who still said 'fairest in all the land?'

"Hm." He sidled closer, crossing over to where she stood on the balcony, trailing his fingers along the railing. They were long and slender, good violin playing fingers. Maybe she should say something about that? She racked her brain for something to say, anything at all, anything—

"Do you hail from around here?" She immediately wanted to slap herself in the forehead. She really did talk like a grandmother.

"No." He shook his head. "I'm from Yen-Sing." A kingdom further west, many, many miles away. She thought of sandy dunes and desert, of hot summer days and cold winter nights, sand becoming purple in the evening. She had visited there, once, with her stepfather on a diplomatic trip, but had never been back since.

"Why are you all the way in Maiike?"

He looked out over the ocean as if somewhere very far away. "I got a job out here."

Juniper wanted to ask what kind of job and what 'out here' meant, but before she could, he was staring at her in an odd way, like one would look at a jewelry box they admired, or at a flower they wanted to paint. Not like someone would look at a girl they liked talking to.

She was about to find an excuse to leave, when suddenly he leaned forward.

Juniper thought he might be attacking her, so she took a quick step back.

"Relax." Tora's snakeskin eyes glittered. "Princess."

And then he kissed her.

* * *

The flames were forming an image. A crown dripping with black ink, as if corrupted by acid.

Julian was looking up at it, wide-eyed, the shock clearly written across his face. But wasn't this supposed to happen? The Trial by Fire was a way of proving his royal blood, right? A crown looked pretty darn royal to Kyra. But then why did Jules look so surprised? In fact, the entire crowd watched the image with looks of apprehension and awe.

Ingrith reached her hand into the flames. Pulling Julian out of them, she held him firmly by the shoulders. Her knuckles were white with pressure. She whispered something to him, and he nodded, a grave expression returning to his face. Tilting his crown back into place, he straightened out his cape.

"What happened?" Kyra whispered.

Cal was watching the spectacle with a hard-set jaw. "The Trial by Fire revealed more than we thought it would."

Kyra flung her gaze back to Julian, wondering what that could possibly mean but feeling like she shouldn't ask. So, she kept quiet for once, exchanging a worried look with Luca.

And where *was* Juniper? It's not like she had any pals at the ball to hang out with. The endless suitors trailing in her wake all night probably hadn't soothed her sister's nerves, either. Maybe she had gotten lost or something. They'd find her soon enough, wandering through the halls or huddled in the bathroom. Yeah, that was what would happen.

Ingrith spoke finally, addressing the hushed murmurs of the crowd. "The crown is the image we knew would show. The signifier of royal blood; Julian is the heir to the throne. Now, I know you must be wondering about..." she hesitated, eyes flicking quickly to Julian then back on the crowd, "...The other component of the symbol. The black liquid dripping off of it. An emblem of the fae."

This sent more whispers throughout the crowd, some even sending hateful glances towards Ingrith and Julian. The fae were hated all around. Hated for what, though? She knew they were tricksters and evildoers, but a faerie hadn't been seen in ages. They walked among men and giants, before disappearing into their lands up North. And yet, humans still despised them.

They must have left a mark one would not soon forget.

Ingrith continued, "The emblem of the fae in my son's image means nothing save for a simple taint in his blood. Have no fear; the taint is not anything to worry about; my son does not belong to the fae. It was a curse put on him long ago that will not interfere with his rule of Maiike one day. 'A prince with the blood of silver and death will be the one to bring Cemeflient's dying breath.' Trust in that prophecy. Trust in your Dragon Warrior."

The crowd began to clap awkwardly, slowly, still eyeing the image burned in fire warily.

A taint in his blood. Julian had...a curse put on him? She had to grill him about that later, once the crowd was gone and it was just the five of them again. That sounded cooler than cool.

But the look on Jules' face at that moment made Kyra rethink if it was as cool as it sounded. He looked like he was going to be sick, underneath an expertly crafted poker face. Kyra didn't know when she had started being able to see past this facade, but she did.

Julian swallowed hard, saying, "I will make my decision in an hour. In the meantime, feel free to walk into the flames and be tried by the fire."

A girl next to Kyra said, "He's so dreamy. I hope he chooses me!"

"No way, your laugh is far too annoying. He'll choose me for sure!" Another girl said.

"Our love will triumph over all!"

Luca put a restraining hand on Kyra's shoulder, which was good because Kyra was about to vomit.

Julian spoke again, a new kind of light in his eyes. An idea. Oh no. This would be interesting. "Wait! Let my honored guests go through the fire, first! Luca, Cal, Juniper, Kyra! Come up here!" He waved excitedly at them.

The entire crowd turned to them, eyes alight with mixed jealousy and curiosity.

Kyra got ready to say a hard no, but the look on his face was too happy to ignore. It was the least she could do. She shrugged at Luca and Cal, who looked like they'd rather be anywhere else, and walked into the center of the circle. Luca's mouth was open in a scared look. There was nothing to be scared of except for a few eyes on them and a harmless fire. Cal followed Kyra, calm and collected.

A delighted look had come over Julian's face. The look faltered as he noticed that Juniper was not among their ranks. His eyes flashed with hurt, but for what, Kyra didn't know.

"I'll go first," Kyra said, eyeing the fire. She stepped into it, and she saw her arms and legs, then her hair, her torso, become alight with flames. Orange light burned around her, though it didn't hurt. It felt like a light tapping, or a warm prickling. The flames consumed her entire body.

She looked up, ready to see an image that would tell her 'who she was.' Please. Like that was real. The only thing stupider than this was...well, her stepmother.

An image was forming, a crescent shape outlined in black.

A moon.

She wanted to laugh at the absurdity of it all. Of course it would be a moon; that stupid image would haunt her forever. She would never escape the nickname, 'Moon's Child.' She was sure people would cry out to her on the streets when she was ninety years old, calling her that name. It would probably make an appearance on her grave, with her luck. So of course her symbol was a moon, like some cruel joke someone was playing on her from afar.

It finished emblazoning itself in the flames, and Kyra watched as the black outline of the moon began dripping black, liquid oozing and falling into nothing.

Faerie.

That meant—that meant faerie.

The black liquid was a symbol of the fae, Kyra had heard Ingrith say. As soon as she saw it, she launched herself out of the fire, and the image disappeared as quickly as it came.

In its spot was just the gently rising flames, the red and gold fire climbing to the ceiling.

She looked around, flustered, whirling and spinning to look at the faces of the crowd, to see if anyone had seen what she had just seen.

Thudding in her ears like the ticking of a clock, her pulse raced.

Her heart pounded. *Buh-bump. Buh-bump.* She searched the crowd, horrified that someone else might have seen the symbol of the faerie in her own image. An image that was supposed to tell her who she was. Who she was...who was she?

The flames flickered dauntingly, mocking her, as if saying, *We know you more than you know yourself. You wonder why you've always been drawn to magic—*

Buh-bump. Her hand shook as she saw that no one else had seen. If they had, they would all be reacting as they had to Julian's, with fear and loathing. But it wasn't true. It couldn't be true. Why would her image have the faerie symbol? *Buh-bump.*

Kyra took her spot next to the others, gaze locked on a spot on the floor. Cal had his eyebrows raised in question. She wanted to tell him, to spit out the words and do away with them forever, but a ringing voice in her ears told her not to give it away. Not to tell that what she saw was a sign of the fae. The voice in her head was her stepmother's, urging her to keep it a secret. It, oddly, was good advice, and she never thought she would admit any incarnation of Callista's words would help her. She shouldn't tell the crowd; they would have questions that she couldn't answer. Don't give it away, don't—*Buh-bump.*

"What did you see?" Cal asked quietly, so that only she could hear.

"Nothing." The lie rolled off her tongue easily enough. She didn't meet his eyes.

He looked at her for a long time, though Kyra didn't care. She was too busy clenching and unclenching her fists around her dress, trying desperately to think of a joke or force up a fake smile. It wouldn't come. All she could focus on was the booming of her own heart and the image that marked her burned into her mind.

You, Moon's Child, shall be held prisoner in your own mind. The old lady had said that in the clearing, and there it was again, that stupid, *stupid* nickname that somehow everyone knew. Is this what the crazy old lady had meant? That Kyra would go insane? Because she had to be insane if she thought she saw a faerie symbol in the Trial by Fire. Yes, that was it, Kyra decided. She was just going insane. She had dreamt it all up, and was so sleep-deprived that her mind was playing a trick on her.

"My friend here knows I love pranks. She must have been trying to make a joke." Julian coughed, then smiled at Kyra with tightness. "Well then. Cal, do you wanna go?"

Cal shook his head wordlessly. Good choice. It would probably show him a lie, too.

Logic. Think about the facts. Facts.

The facts were, she needed the attention off her. People would start asking questions...so...Luca. He was an adorable little turd. Surely the crowd would love to see him go through the Trial by Fire.

"Right, then, Luca." Kyra shoved him forward like an offering.

Luca sent her a helpless look as he stepped into the flames. He must've been mad that she made him stand up in front of everyone. He'd thank her later. Besides, the kid needed more experience in front of crowds.

Cal murmured, voice laced with alarm, "What do you think you're doing?"

Kyra didn't answer. She just watched the image burn over Luca's head. The crowd was all watching him, and even Cal had averted his gaze from Kyra and onto the wall of flame.

Luca had his arms clasped in front of him, his head turned upwards as if gazing at the stars at night. As if sending out a prayer, eyes upturned and wide with mixed shock and horror. But why...?

A terrible thought dawned on Kyra. Far too late.

Luca was not an ordinary huntsman or even a kid. He was a hunter of the night.

A Dämonenwölfe. The full reality of what she had just done sunk in. She had shoved Luca forward, into the Trial, without even remembering that he was one of the wolves. How could she be so stupid? She had forgotten the biggest detail of all in her hectic plan to get the attention off her. She dug a nail into her palm, trying to think of a way where Luca's identity wouldn't be revealed in front of a whole crowd of fae-hating townsfolk.

"Luca! Get out of there!" she yelled, waving her arms to get Luca's attention.

It was too little, too late. The image had already taken its full form above his head.

A crisp image of a wolf's head stood in the fire, its eyes glowing a luminescent purple. Black liquid dripped from its mouth—the black blood of the fae.

"Dämonenwölfe!" Someone in the audience cried. People had begun pointing, snarling at him. The crowd looked more fearsome than the wolves could be, and certainly more fearsome than Luca could be.

"Monster!"

"Demon-wolf!"

Luca looked around fearfully before bolting out of the fire, shoving past Kyra and bumping her shoulder with a force so strong it knocked her back into Cal. She watched him go, then ran after him, ignoring the shouts that came from Cal and Julian.

Fleeing the ballroom, Kyra followed Luca through a door he had slammed open.

"Wait!" Kyra called out to him as he took a turn down a left hallway, then down a flight of stairs. Kyra took in the staircase hurriedly, trying to keep up with Luca. It shouldn't have been a hard thing to do, (he had little legs), but she couldn't run in the stupid high heel shoes she was wearing.

Luca wasn't tripping or falling all over himself, too, so that didn't help. Maybe becoming a Dämonenwölfe made you unable to trip. She thought of Emma and her delirious laugh, hoping it didn't make people crazy, too.

Kyra had to stop him from running from this. Running from your problems, she thought, was the biggest lie of all. Luca needed her, and gosh-darn-it, she would be there for him.

Kyra slipped off her shoe and chucked it at Luca.

It hit him aggressively in the back, and he turned to face her with pure confusion, the high heel clattering to the ground.

"What is wrong with you?" Luca asked, incredulous.

"Many things." Kyra shrugged, then grew serious. "Luca. I-I-I'm sorry." The words did not come easy, and that was something Kyra was saying more and more lately. Forgiveness seemed to be her enemy, forcing its way into her life. Or maybe it was more like a shadow, following her around and creeping in where she least expected it. Kyra didn't want to forgive. Not her real mother for dying; for leaving her. Not her step-mother for hurting her. And especially not herself for being weak enough to let it all happen.

Luca whirled around to pick up her shoe, but Kyra was already there, picking it up rather aggressively. Hyped up on adrenaline, she was not prone to being gentle.

She supposed they looked picturesque, her in her blue ball gown and him in his suit, standing on the steps of a grand palace. Save for her holding one shoe like an idiot.

"Someone should write a story about that," said Kyra, slipping the shoe back on.

"It'd be pretty lame. A girl throwing her shoe at a guy like a crazy person? It would need something to spice it up."

"I wouldn't know." Kyra grinned. "I don't read." She sat down on the steps, putting her chin in her hands. "I'm such an idiot. And a bad friend to you."

"That you are." Luca chuckled, then sniffled, using his sleeve to wipe away at his eyes. Kyra realized with a start that he was crying. She tried to think of something to say to comfort him, some wise words about everything would be okay, and he'd be alright. Nothing came.

Luca broke the silence first. "It seems so silly to be crying right now. Selfish."

"Sometimes you just need a good cry." Kyra had never had one.

Luca fiddled with his sleeve, damp from tears. He said, "It just, it never really hit me, you know? That I'm actually,"—He swallowed hard—"That I'm actually a Dämonenwölfe. It's weird. I never thought I would be this...this thing with faerie magic inside me. That I'll always be this, forever and ever, until the day I die. I don't want to be a wolf. I want to be a normal kid. I want a life where I won't be feared. Everywhere I go, people will see my eyes and know that I'm a Dämonenwölfe. That's terrifying."

Kyra nodded, looking out past the steps and out the window, at the sky full of stars and the moon, with its ever-present eye, watching her, waiting for her, almost. Luca's words reminded her of herself as a child, waiting, wide-eyed for her stepmother to love her and care for her like a mother was supposed to. To cherish her and hold her and sing to her like the other mothers did. But the Queen never did those things. Instead, she ridiculed and hated Kyra from the start. At first, Kyra had been hurt and even cried over it, wallowing in her sorrow that she would never have a kind mother who made her peanut butter and jelly sandwiches with the crusts cut off, or tucked her into bed every night with a kiss. She had cried over everything she was missing out on. But soon, she had learned to accept the lot she was given in life. She had hardened and adapted like a snake shedding its skin.

Now, she never cried. That was a hurt from a long time ago, from when she had been a different person. A person who understood that it took more strength to forgive than want revenge. Now, Kyra was overcome with her inability to understand this simple thing. "The hurt will pass," is all she said in that moment. It felt like nothing compared to what she felt in her heart, but she kept spewing out the words she had kept close, locked down inside the depths of her soul. "The hurt will come, first. It will hurt and hurt and hurt until you feel like you can't hurt anymore. Then, it will pass. Most things do, with time."

Luca looked up at her, eyes shining. "It doesn't feel like it."

"It will."

"I don't think I'm strong enough for this."

"You're stronger than you think. This wolf business will show you just how much. I know it. Everyone else knows it. Now you will, too."

He smiled then, his lopsided grin that looked like a half-moon. "Someone should write a story about that instead of your shoe idea."

"Let's do it, then. It can be called, *Kyra and Luca's Guide to Having Sucky Lives*: in stores near you," Kyra said. "You'll write it. I'll pose for the cover."

"Somehow, that doesn't seem fair." He wiped away the remaining tears from his eyes, now giggling.

They sat like that for a while, staring out the window at the sky, echoes of laughter and chatter coming from the ball, the faint tune of the piano murmuring in their ears, and the red carpet of the staircase contrasting against the black marble floor.

"You are a cutie-pie, even when you're crying," said Kyra, putting her arm around him and squeezing him tight.

"You know, you've told me that so many times I'm starting to believe it."

He squeezed back.

15

The Sun's Child

Juniper wrenched away from Tora as soon as his lips touched hers. Sunbeamabovesunbeamabove*sunbeamabove*. He was a stranger with a creepy smile, and he was kissing her, and Sunbeam above, what had her life turned into? Since when was she making out with boys she just met?

"Excuse me!" she half-shrieked, her face flaming, spluttering, "You walked in on me crying, you can't just—you can't just kiss me!" A part of her wanted to keep kissing him, to forget about Julian and the ball. But another part, a larger part, still felt something weird about Tora. Something strange and off-putting.

Tora quirked an eyebrow up. "You seemed like you wanted to."

"I seemed like I—butyoucannotjustkisssomeoneyoujustmet—"

"Slow down," he said. "Anybody would be lucky to kiss me."

Juniper said, "I was not! I am going back to the ball! Leave me alone!" She spun, her golden dress swirling out around her, poofing out in the way she loved. But she didn't love it now. Now, the dress just reminded her of her own naivety.

As she began walking away, Tora snatched his hand out, grabbing her by the shoulders.

"What are you doing?" Juniper said, her voice sounding wobbly and weak in her own ears. She stared up at him, squirming to get away. His grip held strong.

Wait a moment.

He had called her 'Princess' before he kissed her.

He wasn't supposed to know who she was. How did he know who she was? How did he—

"You thought I came here to get away from the ball?" Tora sneered.

"That is what you said," Juniper pointed out, unable to help herself.

"I came here," said Tora, "because your mother wanted me to find you and your sister. She said *you* would be easily found, because you're naive. Stupid, pretty girl, easily found and easily tricked. Seems like she was right."

Juniper was shaking now. Tora worked for the Queen. Her mother had duped her again. Her mother was going to capture her and Kyra. And, to make matters worse, the Queen thought she was stupid. Not the most important thing to take away from that, but this was shaping up to be the worst week of her life. Her priorities were off. "I am not..." Juniper paused. "How did you find us here?"

"The Queen saw your little friend Prince Julian when you stormed the funeral. It was easy enough for me to track you all here. Easier to find you alone."

"Why in the world would you kiss me if you were sent here to capture me?" Her voice rose as she spoke, wobbly and high-pitched.

"For fun." Tora's green eyes gleamed, his mouth curving into an unsettling smile. "You are the fairest in the land."

Juniper wrinkled her nose and spat, "No one says that anymore!"

"And you're going to tell me where your sister is. Then we're going to go to the Queen. She misses her horrible little daughters." He tugged her off the balcony and into the throne room, throwing her down on the floor. She skidded, her beautiful dress tearing at the hem. Her bun had completely fallen out now. Desperately scrambling across the floor, she tried to get away from him.

"You can't run, Sun's Child," Tora said, sticking out his tongue. His tongue was forked, slithering like a worm.

"Who—what are you?"

"My name is Tora," he said. "But you may know me as the Snake Prince."

The Snake Prince. Where had she heard that before? An image flashed in her mind's eyes, a book cover of a snake with green eyes. A story originating a thousand years ago, when the fae walked the earth. A tale of a boy who was enchanted, turned into a serpent by a faerie woman whose harvest the boy had tainted.

But that was it, just a story. A story. She said, "That is impossible."

"You have no idea what's possible." Tora's serpentine tongue flicked out, then retreated as if catching a bug. He cocked his head at her on the floor. "Now tell me where Kyra is. If you do, maybe we can strike a deal. I'll only kill your sister, not you. Maybe we can—"

Juniper sprang from the floor, howling like a banshee. Crumpling her fist and swinging at him, she punched him in the face. *CRACK.*

Tora stumbled backward, clutching at the spot where her fist had connected with his face. He pulled his hand away from his cheek, and Juniper gagged as she saw that his skin was flaking off where she had punched him. It peeled away to show dark green scales.

"You stupid brat! Get back here!" Tora growled angrily.

"Do not dare threaten my sister or me again!" Juniper yelled back at him as she ducked out of the throne room. "Or I will punch you somewhere that will hurt a *lot* more!"

She heard Tora snarl from behind her. The sound of footsteps.

But, weirdly, the footsteps weren't even coming towards her. It sounded as if Tora had turned around and walked back out to the balcony. Juniper hesitated in the doorway where he couldn't see her. Maybe he was giving up, and she could take him out right here and now. But who was she kidding? She could never beat him if it came down to a fight.

"My Queen," Tora said, and Juniper felt every cell, every fiber of her being, freeze. She put a hand over her mouth to stop herself from shouting. *No.*

"Tora," said a voice in reply, a silky, musical voice that was dripping with venom. The Queen. Callista was there, somehow, she was there, and she was going to find Juniper if she didn't get out of there *now.* "Where are my daughters?"

But Juniper's feet were stuck to the floor, unable to move, as if caught in quicksand. She slowly peeked her head around the corner.

Tora stood, alone, staring out at the sea. The Queen was nowhere to be found. In his hand was a small, hand-held mirror, the kind that Juniper often saw strewn about in the Queen's chambers. He was speaking to the mirror. As if it would respond. Unless... "I was unable to capture Princess Juniper. She...made things a lot harder than I would have liked them to be. But your daughters are still within the castle walls. There is still time."

"Good," Callista replied, though her voice was clipped and short. "I can't believe you couldn't manage to capture one measly sixteen-year-old. Especially Juniper. No matter. I suppose I'll have to fix it myself."

"When will you arrive?"

Juniper could almost hear the cruel smile on her mother's face as she said, "I'm already on my way."

* * *

Kyra and Luca were walking back into the ball when Juniper ran up to them, cheeks flushed. Her knuckles were red and raw. Dress torn in one place; curly hair dropping from its bun—she looked like a mess.

Kyra arched an eyebrow in question. "Do I even wanna know?"

"Why is your hand bleeding?" Luca asked.

Kyra grabbed at Juniper's hand, inspecting it thoroughly while Juniper yelped in surprise.

"You punched someone!" Kyra preened, dropping her hand. She crossed her arms. "I don't know whether to be proud or worried."

"Who was the unlucky victim?" Luca tilted his head quizzically.

"A guy. He—It does not matter. He works for the Queen," Juniper said, her voice racing as fast as lightning.

The Queen. No way. Kyra said, "Very funny. Hah-hah. Julian's about to announce who he's gonna marry. Let's go support him. Though I appreciate the effort you put into this charade, now's not the time for jokes. "

Luca gave Kyra a look like, *Says you.*

"This is no joke." Juniper looked frantic. Something in her voice told Kyra to believe her, to believe her sister, because what reason did she have to lie about this? And if it was a joke, a chance to try and dupe her, well, then Kyra could just hold it over her later. Win-win. Or was that really a win-win? Sounded more like a lose-lose, actually, if one option was the Queen and the other was getting tricked by Juniper.

"Okay, I believe you," said Kyra, sighing. "Tell me what happened."

Juniper launched into her story, ending it with, "And so now the Queen is coming to the ball, and she is going to kill us!"

Luca's eyes were as big as saucers. "And probably eat us!"

"She's not gonna eat us," Kyra said. Albeit a little doubtful.

"How do you know that? People are always trying to eat us lately!" Luca exclaimed.

"If what you're saying is true," said Kyra, "we need to get the others and get out of here. Now."

"We might not have time to get the others," Juniper said, casting a nervous glance at the door, as if expecting Callista to storm in any second with a bedazzled fork and knife, saying, *Ready to eat you alll-lll!*

Kyra did a double-take at her words. Was she saying they were going to leave the others behind? She thought of Cal, never saying goodbye to him, or worse, never seeing him again at all. "We can't just leave Cal and Jules. What if Callista takes them? And tortures them for information or something?"

"Good point," said Luca. His nervous eyes never left the doorway. "Let's get them, and then get out of here. And then never go to another ball for the rest of our lives."

"Agreed," Kyra and Juniper said in sync.

Spotting Cal immediately, Kyra saw him struggling to carry a huge bowl of shrimp over to one of the buffet tables.

"Hey," said Kyra, jogging over to him. "Drop the shrimp. We're leaving. It's urgent."

Cal set down the shrimp on the table with a heave, the shrimp bouncing around disgustingly. He wiped a sheen of sweat off his forehead, then said, "We're leaving?"

"Yes, Juniper got attacked by some snake guy. Punches were thrown. Juniper basically is the next greatest boxer of our generation, and the Queen's coming so *we have to go*," Kyra said, already walking away.

"I have so many questions about that sentence."

"I'd love to answer them but what about 'it's urgent' do you not understand?"

Cal sighed and followed her over to Julian, who was in the middle of a large group of giggling girls.

"And then, the giant actually bit me..." Julian was saying, but he stopped when he saw Kyra. "Hey, guys! What's up?"

"We're leaving. *Now*." Kyra glared at him so he would get the point.

The girl from earlier with the pink dress sneered, her eyes narrowing, "And who are you? The girl from the Trial who ran out like a baby."

Kyra was immediately pulled back into the Trial by Fire, the image of the fae burning bright above her as she desperately tried to escape it. It wasn't real, anyway, so it shouldn't matter if anyone saw it. And if they did, who cared? She knew it wasn't real...

Despite all that, it still mattered to her. That was the terrifying part.

"Okay, no, we're not doing this," Cal said lightly.

"What?" The girl in pink looked shocked.

"Kyra's not a wimp," Cal said. "She's braver than anyone I've ever met, and a million times braver than you, I bet, if you're content to sit here and insult people who infringe on your insecurities. Now would you please move out of the way?"

Kyra stared at him, mouth hanging open. The...bravest...person he had ever met?

"Well, she's interrupting. She's being rude." The girl rolled her eyes, her friend high-fiving her in the process. She had never wanted to slap someone, then stuff her face in a shrimp bowl more in her entire life. *We don't slap people, then stuff their faces in shrimp bowls, Kyra.* The girl in pink looked Cal up and down with disgust. "And who even are you? A servant?"

"Yeah. So what?" Cal replied.

The phrase was so simple, it almost made Kyra burst out in laughter. He was so calm, so true to himself, that it was hard to argue with him. The girl in pink seemed to think so, too, because she stood there, spluttering for a response, her face growing bright red.

Kyra tried to think of a comeback to both shame the girl and address what Cal had said, but Julian was already speaking, his eyes ablaze with anger.

Julian said to the girl, "I think you're being mean."

The girl in pink replied, a frenzied look on her face, "I'm so sorry, Prince Julian."

"Save it for someone who cares," Jules announced, looking rather pleased with that comeback. He pushed past the group of girls, who were now all gaping at him. They scurried off, probably gossiping or something. That would've been her, she thought, if Aazagonia had remained wealthy. She would have been at this ball, flirting and dancing with Julian and whispering with the other girls. A pang of longing went through her again, a pang for the life she could've had if her stepmother had never entered the picture.

But that meant Juniper wouldn't be in her life, either. So none of it mattered in the face of that. A million times over, Kyra would choose it. It was as simple as that.

"Uh, thanks, you guys," said Kyra, looking the two boys in the eyes as they walked away.

"No thanks needed! If anyone messes with my friends, they get a nice slice of comeback pie!" Julian pumped his fist in the air in excitement.

"Couldn't have said it better myself," Cal said as he and Kyra shared a smile.

The three of them joined up with Luca and Juniper, and they walked towards the door.

"So we're just leaving? Not getting supplies?" Cal asked as they made their way to the doorway. Eyes watched as they went, mostly on Julian.

"Not saying goodbye?" Julian said, throwing his cape behind him as he looked across the room where his mother sat, talking and laughing with a group of commoners.

"I don't think we have time," Kyra tried to say as gently as possible.

Juniper ushered them forward, eyes frantic and hands fluttering around her. "We have to hurry! Tora is coming! He is coming and we will all be gobbled up! Come on!"

They made it to the door, just as Julian said, "Did I forget one of our enemies or is this Tora guy a new one?"

Suddenly, the door slammed open, a cold ocean breeze sweeping in as Kyra got a glimpse of outside, of the steps leading down into a wide, moonlit courtyard with tall trees saluting the stars. Kyra could see that the moon hung high in the sky, almost exactly in the middle of it. Midnight, then. Or close to it.

The moon was suddenly blocked off. Someone had stepped into the doorway after strutting up the steps, their head cutting off the light from the moon, a stopgate of all things light, as per usual.

The Queen stood there, her raven necklace gleaming around her neck. Shockingly red, her lips were twisted into a pursed line as she beheld her daughters. Her silver, spiked crown sliced upward, knife-blades slicing through the air.

Kyra stared at her stepmother, shell-shocked, for once at a loss for words. All she could see was that terrible, beautiful face staring down at her, the face that had haunted her. She was standing right in front of them, so close she could reach out and touch her. So close she could reach out and scream at her for all she had done.

"Hello, daughters," Callista said, waving a hand. "Surprised to see me, I presume? Kyra, stop trying to kill me with your eyes. Juniper, close your mouth. Don't betray your surprise at seeing me. Have I taught you nothing?"

Kyra saw Juniper close her mouth, then open it again, then clamp it shut, her doe-eyes wide with panic.

"Queen Callista," Cal said, his eyes hard-set. "Why are you here?"

"I was invited. Don't look so surprised. I'm quite popular in the royal circles."

"And I don't hate your guts," said Kyra dryly. "We can both lie, see?"

Cal repeated, "Why are you here?"

"I won't speak to you, boy. I want to speak to my daughters. Will they come with me somewhere a little...quieter?" She tilted her head, her necklace dangling to the side as she did.

"No," Juniper said, surprising Kyra. "No, we will not come. We will not!"

Juniper shoved past the Queen, stepping out onto the palace steps. Kyra and the others followed, and Kyra felt Callista's gaze burning into the back of her head. Daggers of fire searing into her brain.

The door to the ball slammed shut behind them, blocking out the stream of music and voices that wafted from inside.

Callista just watched them edge down into the courtyard, the stones clacking beneath Kyra's high-heels. Was she just going to let them go like that? Kyra knew it wasn't true, that the Queen would be one step ahead, plotting ways to ruin them all.

Run, she wanted to scream to the others, *run and never look back.*

A moment later, a dark figure stepped out from behind the trees, a boy with nightmare black hair, slitted serpentine eyes, and pointed ears. Juniper froze beside Kyra, goosebumps visible on her arms.

That must've been Tora. He opened his mouth, leering at Juniper with a forked tongue. He was giving Kyra major heebie-jeebies. The snake tongue wasn't even the worst part. It was the eyes...his eyes creeped her out. She shook it off, her tongue heavy in her mouth as she searched for words.

Kyra sneered. "The Snake Prince, huh? Don't suppose you shed?"

Tora just smirked, his serpent tongue flicking back into his jaws, standing tall and poised, almost laid-back.

"Tsk, tsk," Callista said, pointing her finger at the boy. She still stood on the steps, in the middle of the stairs as if they were her throne. "If you five try to run, I'll have Tora kill you where you stand. Ugh, you all look so serious. Lighten up, please? If you look so scared all the time, you'll get wrinkles. Moon's Child, come here. I won't ask again."

Kyra moved to walk forward to the bottom of the steps. Juniper whispered in her ear before she went, "Do not let her." Don't let her what? Normally, she might have been able to understand her sister, but all she could see was Callista on the steps, Callista bandaging the bruises that she herself had put there, and always, always, the sorrowful tune of a violin that seemed to follow Kyra wherever she went, as if she could never escape. It was the first instrument Kyra ever heard out of a symphony, the first thing she heard when she closed her eyes at night, and the sound that seemed to accompany her to her nightmares as well as in life.

Kyra stopped at the bottom of the steps, Callista a few steps up, towering over her with the extra height. She was taller than Kyra nonetheless, but now, she looked monstrous, like the beanstalk had looked in the glare of fire in the clearing. She was wearing a black dress that flowed straight down, with tight sleeves and her hair hanging loose around her shoulders—a figure intimidating and calculated and everything Kyra didn't want to be.

"What do you want." She didn't ask it so much as a question. It was more of a still, hanging statement.

"I want my daughter to look me in the eyes." Callista raised her chin.

"Don't call me that."

"What?"

"Your daughter."

The Queen laughed. "I will call you whatever I want. It's hilarious the way it makes you squirm," Callista said, looking down at her to see her reaction. Kyra didn't budge. She had heard it all before. "I will call you whatever I want, because you have brought nothing but annoyance to my life. But you knew that. I'll give you credit where credit is due: one thing you aren't is dense."

Kyra sucked in a breath, saying half-heartedly, "Gee, at least I'm not dense."

"Don't joke or pretend with me. I'm the only one who doesn't buy it." Callista said, her voice dropping low. "Now tell me: does your sister despise me?"

"Hates you like no one else." Kyra's voice dripped with venom.

The Queen's carefully constructed mask didn't falter, but her smirk did. Then, Callista was shrugging, tucking a dark curl back into place. "That's alright. It's only natural, I suppose. I'm the competition."

"You actually see this as a competition? Just because Juniper is prettier than you doesn't mean you should be pitted against her!" Kyra struggled to not let her voice break.

"She," The Queen said, her musical voice turning dark for a moment, "is not prettier than me." For a moment, Kyra saw the deranged woman behind the mask, the lady who craved attention to feed her vanity more than anything.

"She is. Even your magic mirror said so—"

Kyra was cut off by a hand meeting her face, a slap cracking across it with a ring that bit into her face. It stung for a moment before fading away, a dull throbbing in her cheek where the ring had connected.

Callista snarled. "Brat. You think you know everything, huh? Think it's a magic mirror, do you? It's cute, you and your little boys that you and Juniper have as pets now. Which one of them stole your cold, ugly heart? Which one of those boys gets you as their prize for helping?"

"I am mine," said Kyra, "before I am anyone else's."

Callista regarded her as one would regard an alien species. "Puh-lease," Callista said, "Whatever. I could honestly care less. I won't kill you where you stand for one reason: I need you. Then I'll kill you, and you'll scream so loud it'll echo for miles. It will be so fun! For me, at least. Not so much for you."

Kyra tried to ignore that last part. "Need me? For what, someone to follow you around and tell you how pretty you are?"

"Funny. Oh, that's right...you don't know. Kyra, love, we are going to have so much fun!" Callista clapped her hands together giddily. She called out to Juniper, who was standing across the courtyard with the others, "Juni-tree, come up here please!"

No. But Juniper had already begun walking across the courtyard, her head hung low, her gaze locked on the floor. Her curls hung over her face, concealing what Kyra knew was a torn expression.

Juniper came up next to Kyra and took her hand in hers.

"You, my Queen, are fair, it's true," The Queen said in a sing-song voice, something akin to jealousy lighting her eyes. She walked down the steps as she said this, putting her finger under Juniper's chin and raising it to look her in the eyes. "But the *Sun's Child* is a thousand times fairer than you."

"Hello, mother," said Juniper softly.

"You look so much like your father, dear," The Queen said in an equally soft voice. Something akin to grief flashed across her face for the barest moment. "He would be so proud of all I have accomplished."

"You're insane." Kyra wanted to rip her stepmother's hand away from Juniper.

"Rude. In time, you girls will see my aims. I'm a simple woman. I don't care for the power of Aazagonia, don't you understand? My goals are much more important than a measly little kingdom." The queen's eyes glittered like black emeralds. "My goal is for love." So the Queen wanted more than Aazagonia? The love of more kingdoms? The world?

"No one will love you," said Kyra.

"There will be no other choice."

"That's not love." Juniper finally spoke, her lip quivering.

The Queen laughed, a harsh, dark sound. "You don't know what love is, Juni-tree. *I* know what it is. I know what it is to love and be loved. Will you come willingly, or not? It might be more fun if you don't come willingly. Once again—for me, at least."

Kyra stepped back, crumpling her hands in fists. She could take down the Queen easily if she tried. But Tora...he was a wild card. Maybe if Luca transformed into a wolf...but she couldn't ask him to do that. And yet...

"We will fight you for as long as we can," Juniper said simply. Her eyes still didn't meet the Queen's. "Until we cannot fight you any longer."

Kyra brought her fist back, readying herself. "Aazagonia doesn't deserve to have a crazy lady as their monarch."

"Yay! This is going to be so entertaining. Because, you still don't know, do you?" Callista clapped her hands giddily. "Oh, you don't!"

Kyra and Juniper exchanged an uneasy look, hairs rising on the back of Kyra's neck.

Every echo of words spoken to her whispered in her mind. *You wonder why you are drawn to magic...woven together...Sun and*

Moon....You, my Queen, are fair...You and your sister are strands of cloth, moon and sun, woven together. Do not forget this. Do not forget this.

The Queen threw her head back and laughed, echoing off the palace steps, her raven necklace bobbing as if laughing with her, both of them in on a joke that Kyra wasn't.

"I have magic," she said, her hands glowing purple, "and you're not gonna like it."

She flashed her hands forward, purple light exploding into the sky like drops of fallen starlight.

* * *

A purple burst of energy streamed from the Queen's hands.

Twisting, winding, crackling like electricity, the magic struck Kyra in the chest and sent her careening backward through the air.

Juniper watched in horror as Kyra struck the marble fountain, crumpling to the floor. She heard Cal cry out as Kyra lay still, very still. Too still. Juniper's head ached, and her vision became dizzy.

"She's not dead. Calm down, Juniper, you dramatic fool." Callista inspected one of her nails, her face radiating pure glee. Her palms still glowed a faint purple, the veins in her wrist flowing violet.

Callista was a *human*, no matter how much Juniper doubted. How was this possible? No one had magic that was human. The only people who could wield magic like that were the fae.

The Queen said, "I'm not going to kill you."

"What did you do to her?" Juniper asked, feeling helpless and small.

"I wanted to show you what I'm capable of."

"But how? How do you have magic?"

"Don't you want to know why I'm not going to kill you?"

"Why?" Juniper asked. "You tried to have us killed before! Why not now?"

"Oh, poor, sweet, unassuming Juni-tree." The Queen raised an eyebrow as if gauging her reaction to her words.

Juniper felt tears prick the corners of her eyes. "Do not call me that. Please..." *My parents always called me that. You don't get to anymore.*

Her mother tsked. "I'm not going to hurt you. I never will, darling. We're family. Soon you'll thank me for all of this. Because, my dear, magic shows itself in times of need. I needed you to have your magic show. You were never in real danger. If anything, I thought the huntsman's apprentice would be killed, not you. So...has anything interesting happened to you? When the knife came at you, did anything happen?"

"You put me in danger to see if I had magic?" Juniper asked incredulously. "Well, good news! I do not! Humans cannot have magic!"

The Queen waved her hand lazily. "Tora! Attack those boys!" she shouted, pointing at Cal, Jules, and Luca, who were inspecting Kyra.

Tora edged out of the shadows, and Juniper jolted upon seeing him. The side of his face that Juniper had punched had peeled away entirely. His serpentine scales were shining in the moonlight, slimy and pallid and oozing with wretched-looking pus. He launched himself at the boys, baring his hands like claws.

Juniper didn't have time to even cry out, or scream at the Queen for him to stop because by the time she was facing the Queen again, her hands were glowing purple.

"If your magic hasn't shown," The Queen said calmly, "I guess I'll have to continue to force it."

Light ruptured forth as the Queen thrust her hands forward. Juniper saw it up close now and could see that the purple looked like flames; lilac fire exploding from what looked to be the Queen's very veins.

Also, another important fact besides what the purple flames looked like was the fact that they were coming right towards *her*. She yelped and ducked out of the way, throwing herself to the floor and rolling across the cobblestones, barely avoiding getting hit with a wall of purple light.

From her vantage point on the floor, she was directly in line with Kyra across the courtyard, still lying motionless, eyes closed. Kyra was the one who was supposed to fight, not her. Juniper would never be able to stop the Queen on her own.

Not by fighting, at least. Her cheek was cold against the floor as she pushed herself to her feet, despite everything in her screaming at her to stay down, to lie on the floor and give in.

"I thought you said you wouldn't hurt me," Juniper said. "That you need us."

Callista's purple hands died down, glowing faintly now. "I do need you—more than anything. But I need your magic, first. Now come on, Juniper, put up a fight!"

Her mother shot out another burst of flame, and this time, it connected to its mark.

It hit Juniper in the heart, electrifying her like a light-bulb. It picked her up and sent her flipping through the air, sky tumbling over ground as she collapsed in a heap on the floor. Groaning, she tried to prop herself up but saw swimming stars.

"Come on, love, prove you aren't completely useless! Fight me!" Callista cackled, sending a burst of light into the sky. It lit up the dark night with flashing color. Now all her veins were lined with dark lavender, crisscrossing her body like lightning bolts. Her eyes were especially dark. They had turned violet down to the whites, her entire socket filled with purple. She began singing, "*Mother Sky flies* *high above...*you know this song. Sing with me! Sing like your father did! *And all the birds sing her praise...*"

"I..." Juniper couldn't think how to finish the sentence, her entire body buzzed with jolting electricity.

And then a hand was pulling her to her feet, standing her up. "Juniper?"

"Kyra...?" Juniper asked, then realized that Kyra didn't have a gentle voice or crow-colored hair. Her sister was lying at the base of the fountain, still, alone and asleep.

"Thankfully, I'm not Kyra," Cal said, grinning, but there was a hint of worry. "I'd be a lot less conscious."

Juniper asked, "Where is he?" She didn't need to say Tora's name for Cal to know who she meant.

A flash of darkness crossed Cal's face as he said, "Jules and Luca are handling it."

Juniper felt her stomach lurch in fear. "Are they alright?"

Cal never got to answer her question. A stream of purple lighting lit up the night sky, cutting just over her head and then slamming into the fountain with incredible strength. The fountain shattered, little shards of marble cascading everywhere, the water rushing out into the floor. The shattering was beautiful, in a way. A billion little marble teardrops soared through the air and then scattered; a flood of water followed.

"Get down!" Cal shouted, dropping to his hands and knees as another burst of fiery purple flame came at them.

Juniper grew very angry. It was one thing to hurt her; quite another to go after her friends.

"You want a fight," Juniper said slowly, "then you are going to get one."

Cal gave her a weird look. "Who are you talking to?"

"It was supposed to sound poetic!" Launching to her feet, Juniper ran over to the Queen, determined like never before.

She could hear Cal spluttering and calling out her name, but she ignored him, running—then pausing to kick off her intensely tall high-heels—and then running again, skidding to a stop at the bottom of the steps.

"There you are," Callista said, sounding bored, her entire eyes glowing purple. "I was beginning to think you were going to lay down and give up."

Juniper said meekly, "Appreciate the confidence in me, mother." Actually, Juniper had believed the same thing about herself. It would have been so much easier to just roll over, surrender, give up.

But she had people counting on her now, her friends, her kingdom, her sister.

Herself.

Juniper had always been drawn to the magic of the world, the bright light that shone through every person. Even the magic of the fae called out to her, begging for her to hear its voice. She had always heard the call within her, longed to run to it. Whenever the sun rose over the treetops or the ocean waves crashed, Juniper felt a small tug at her heart saying, *Come home.*

Her home was counting on her. That was why she had to fight the Queen. Give it her all to save the only home she remembered. People—her people—were counting on *her*. No one else could bear the burden she had now. Not her father. Not Kyra. Not Julian. This was her battle alone to fight.

You will learn to harness the light and use it for your own, child. Remember it.

Juniper wanted to be the hero of her own story, for once, and unlock whatever was hiding deep within her, something old and so very *bright*. The light deep within her blinded like sparkling diamonds in her soul. There was so much in Juniper that she wanted to let free, so much good and wonder and beauty beyond the surface of what others saw. In her core, she felt that light trapped away, begging to be let loose and unleashed on every star in the sky.

She had to give it her all and try to fight the Queen with whatever she had, no matter what happened. If she didn't try, her kingdom would fall into the hands of a tyrant. Her people, the people that she was supposed to rule one day, would pay for her surrender.

Every moment of her life had felt like a surrender. Every time she ducked her head to hide, every time she gave in to her mother's wishes, every time she let others decide her fate had been small surrenders, small wavings of a white flag.

Juniper pictured that white flag in her mind, as Callista began glowing again, her hands glowing with flames underneath her skin.

She pictured herself, racing down a field full of sunflowers in the daylight, laughing and having her hair stream out long and curly and *free* behind her. She pictured the ray of sunshine that cut through the library floor, illuminating dust particles and sending them dancing around like tiny pixies. She thought of sand and flowers and dancing, of letting herself go without care. She pictured tall trees that stretched up towards the sky, of the mermaids jumping through the air, sending droplets of water spraying everywhere. She thought of golden dresses swirling around her, and of Kyra's face when she tried to hide a smile. She pictured Julian smiling and saying her name like it was the most beautiful word he'd ever heard. She pictured throwing herself into the arms of someone who she loved fiercely and who loved her even more.

But most of all, she pictured the sun.

She thought of the sun locked away in her heart, of white light pouring from it, seeping from her veins and into the world, flooding out like the breaking of a dam.

And as she pictured this, blinding light burst from her hands. Her veins glowed a brilliant white, and Juniper felt magic coursing through them.

The magic exploded out of her like the shattering of the sun.

* * *

There it is, The Queen thought at long last. *There is my Sun's Child.*

16

At the Stroke of Midnight

The next thing Juniper felt was falling.

It was as if she was plummeting from some great distance, flipping like an acrobat through the darkness that surrounded her—some great void of nothing. Her mouth was open to scream, but she had nothing left to give. Her mind was, for the first time ever, completely blank. No worries pecked away at her, no wandering thoughts or questions about the world.

Just falling. It was almost peaceful.

Was this death? Falling forever and ever through a bottomless pit of absolutely nothing? It felt like years had passed since the moment her hands glowed white, but it also felt like milliseconds. Was it possible that it had been both? Was any of this possible?

It shouldn't have been. The Queen shouldn't have had magic, and neither should Juniper. But Juniper didn't have magic, did she?

She swept all those thoughts out of her mind and focused on the feel of the fall. Like living and dying a million times over, with every flip and turn, she breathed then stalled, lived then died, wondered and then *blank*.

And then she was falling to the floor, and her hands scraped the stones as she put them out to catch her, alive and in the real world. Her breath came in ragged gasps, and she looked up through the curtain of dark hair that had fallen over her face.

The Queen had fallen back on the steps, her dress splayed around her as she sat up, amusement written across her face.

Cal was a few feet away; eyes widened in shock. Jules was across the courtyard, scrambled on the floor in surprise. His gangly limbs were sprawled out around him. Luca and Tora were nowhere to be seen. Cal was staring at Juniper blankly. And Kyra...Kyra was still unmoving, the water from the fountain soaking her dress. The water spread as if it had all the time in the world. Slow and deliberate. Juniper's head pounded, and for some reason she couldn't focus on anything except the blue of her sister's dress turning darker. Darker than midnight.

Far away, the clock was striking midnight, but the night was just beginning.

Juniper looked at her hands, her heart beating out of her chest.

Her fingers looked normal, as if nothing had ever happened. As if a current of light hadn't just blown everyone off their feet. As if that wasn't *magic* that had burst out of her.

Callista stood, righting the spiked silver crown on her head.

"Now you see," the Queen said. "Now you know."

Juniper just stared, unsure and terrified of what she would say next.

Callista continued, "And don't think you've won this battle, Juniper." She gestured around, at Kyra so very still on the floor, at Luca nowhere to be seen, at Julian, his fancy clothes shredded, and at Cal, who looked like he had seen a ghost. But finally, her gaze rested on Juniper. "It doesn't look like a win at all."

"You.." Juniper croaked out, her voice hoarse and raw, "do not..." she broke off in a fit of coughs.

Her mother laughed. "I'll see you at the coronation, darling. Next time, I'll expect a real fight. Soon, this will all make sense, I promise. All my hard work will show you what these years have been leading to."

What? Make sense? Next time...? Hard work...?

The Queen pulled out a small hand-held mirror from the fold of her dress, and then, in an instant, she was gone. Vanished into thin air like a sliver of sun slipping past the horizon line.

Cal immediately ran over to Kyra, but Juniper just stared wordlessly at the little cracks in the cobblestone below her where bits of rock and dust had gathered. Forming their own little world in the split of stone, they didn't care about anything at all. How she wished she could join them in their tiny world of no worries.

She wanted to run to her sister, but she was frozen, unable to lift her head for fear of what she might see.

Jules was beside her now, looking down at her with wonder. "You have magic."

"No. No, I do not." Juniper said firmly, too afraid that if she tried to stand, she would fall again. Her vision swam, colorful mermaids blotting out the night sky as she tried to stand, and then wobbled and collapsed.

"Hey, hey, here," Julian said, helping her up. His face was cautious. Scared. Of her?

Juniper let his hand fall as soon as she could stand without doubling over. She turned and hurried over to the remains of the fountain, where Kyra was blinking her eyes open.

"What happened?" Kyra asked, then winced, grabbing at her back. "I just remember being shot at with magic—though that can't be—and then nothing. Where's Callista? Did I punch her?" She asked weakly. "Oh, please say I got one or two punches in."

"We'll fill you in later," Cal said, shooting a glance at Juniper, who felt like her face was on fire. "Just rest for a moment."

Kyra nodded, and shut her eyes tightly. Her wet hair clung to her cheeks, strings of a violin clinging to its wood.

"What was that?" Cal whirled to Juniper. "Why didn't you tell us you have magic?"

"I did not know," Juniper said pleadingly. She thought again. "And I do not have magic."

"Don't lie. I saw you, glowing white and then that beam of light ricocheting everywhere. I saw what you did." Cal said, his jaw working.

"Are you fae?" Julian asked at last. She knew the question would come.

"No!"

"She can't be fae," said Cal. "She would know."

Juniper swallowed hard. "Then what...what am I?"

Cal sighed, ever the logical. "We'll have to figure it out later. For now, we have to find Luca and make sure we're all unharmed, then form a new plan around this. Juniper, you're good? Okay. Jules? Good. Kyra should be fine. She hit that fountain pretty hard, though, and Luca—"

"I'm here," Luca's voice came from behind.

He was in wolf form, his fur grey and his eyes shining purple. He stood tall and large, framed against the silver moon, but he looked incredibly weary.

Juniper's breath caught, and she realized that he would be craving meat. She had to go back into the ball and steal some shrimp or something because as soon as he turned back, he would be hungry. She didn't want to be the only thing in front of him when that happened.

"No hello?" Luca asked, his nervous voice incongruent against his wolf body. It was weird to see an animal talking, especially when the voice was Luca's. His fangs were ivory knives, dripping with—was that green *blood*?

"Where's Tora?" Julian asked quietly.

Wolf-Luca shook his head. "He won't be an issue anymore."

"I am sorry you had to turn," Juniper said quietly.

"It was going to happen sometime." Luca bowed his head, gaze locked on Kyra. "Time for me to accept it. Use this new power instead of cowering from it."

Cal nodded, looking off somewhere far in the distance, as if pondering some great mystery. "Tora's not human. That's for sure."

She hadn't even thought of that. Juniper suddenly felt Tora's slimy hands on her shoulder a few hours ago and felt his serpentine eyes gaze into hers. He had called her names. She shook it off. Names may have meant something to the fae. Not to her. Not anymore.

"I'm turning back," said Luca, and Juniper quickly looked away. After seeing the Dämonenwolfe turn before, she had no desire of ever seeing it again. She heard the sound of bones crunching and tendons re-forming before she turned back around to see regular Luca standing there sheepishly, his hand behind his neck.

"I'm starving," was all he said, gripping his stomach.

"I shall get you some shrimp," Juniper said quickly, trying to get as far from the others as possible. She still felt drained and not-all there as she hurried up the palace steps.

Julian began, "Juniper, wait—"

Ignoring him as she opened the door to the ball, her golden dress dirty and ripped in some places, she stared at her hands like they were inhuman.

Maybe they were.

* * *

Kyra watched as Julian sulked to the front of the ballroom, where a small stage had been constructed. He looked tattered and weak, his crown half-falling off his head. Own back hurting, Kyra stood up against a wall so that no one could see the large rip in her dress where she had hit the fountain.

The other four hadn't told her what had happened in the fight against the Queen. Despite her endless begging, she wasn't sure she wanted to know, what with the dreary looks on all their faces. Juniper especially looked sick, giving darting glances to her hands. Did the girl have to destroy a rainbow or something? Make a baby cry?

"So Julian's picking someone to marry? That seems...weird. What with him being sixteen and all." Luca looked skeptical.

Juniper scowled. "It is ridiculous. This tradition should be abolished." Kyra guessed her sister's annoyance came from a different place.

All Kyra wanted was to just get some sleep, but the others had nagged about how important this was to Julian and how they should just be *oh-so supportive of him.* If only they were so supportive of her need for a nap. Julian raised his head, and Kyra was surprised at how he held the whole room's attention. She could almost see the king he would be one day, a stern but kind ruler. She saw the making of a warrior, could imagine a long beard that meant peace had lasted for years.

She even imagined Cal standing off to the side, and maybe herself visiting them, too.

For diplomatic reasons, of course. She was all about diplomacy.

Juniper was pressed up against the wall next to her, face scrunched in a scowl. She wouldn't look at Julian.

"I have resolved to make my decision," Julian said, "as to who I am going to marry."

Giggles and whispers echoed across the ballroom in a wave,

each girl nervously bumping the other one, crossing their fingers in prayer. Kyra wasn't sure to gag or laugh or a weird mix of both.

"Who do you think he's gonna choose?" Cal elbowed her in the side.

"Her." Kyra pointed to a kind-looking, dark-skinned Sihiri girl. She must have traveled a long way to be here tonight. Kyra had seen her talking with Julian a lot that night, making him snort with laughter for several minutes.

"My money's on that girl." Cal nodded his chin at a girl wearing a yellow dress. "I overheard them talking about how many dragons the two of them have slain. Julian was very impressed."

"What'll I win? 'Cause I will win."

"Whoever wins gets bragging rights for eternity."

Kyra said, "Eternity? Looks like it's going on your grave, Calais."

He smiled, then they turned their attention back to Julian. He was saying, "And that is why I have come to a...very...difficult decision. Kyra, if you would please come up here?"

"*What?*" Kyra half-shouted, half-laughed. Juniper let out a choked sound next to her.

Kyra chuckled nervously as all eyes turned to her. Hilarious. He did not just say *her* name. There was no freaking way she was going to marry Julian. Of all people, she was sure they were each other's last choices.

"Kyra?" Julian asked, an urgent tone laced underneath his words. "You coming?"

"Right," Kyra said slowly, only because the guards were giving her dirty looks, and she was worried what would happen if she said no to the future king in front of his entire kingdom. "Why not?" She added, murmuring it just so that Cal could hear.

He spluttered, obviously taken aback, but he didn't say anything. She didn't know why she thought he would say something. He just watched as she walked through the parted crowd. Too aware of every eye on her. She held her chin high and made her gait long and what she thought looked regal. It was more akin to a toddler learning to walk.

She heard someone whisper, "Her? But she's so...ugly."

Kyra whirled on the voice—an old geezer with overalls—and said, eyes flashing, "Did your mother ever teach you to hold your tongue? Listen, old man, I have a horrible maternal figure and even I know better." Kyra was practically spitting at this point. "There is more to a girl than beauty. You are nothing more than a fly beneath my boot who is unsatisfied with his life. If you didn't hear Julian, I'm your future queen, so say goodbye to your friends—if you have any—'cause I can get you banished with the flick of my finger."

She continued on, balling her fists in her dress, glad to hear that the murmurs had stopped, and people were just staring at her silently. They were probably thinking, *So this lunatic is gonna be our future queen? Lovely. I'm moving.*

Kyra stepped up onto the stage, and she stood next to Julian. He grabbed her hand and held it high in the air. A mix of cheers and boos cascaded from the crowd. Luca was the only one clapping awkwardly across the room.

Kyra leaned over to Julian to hug him, whispering through gritted teeth, "Care to explain?"

Jules said, "Try to look a little less murderous right now, and I'll explain later."

They waved at the crowd as they slowly filed out and Kyra realized with a pang that neither her nor Cal had won the bet. No one could have ever guessed that it would be her. Surely she could say no, right? Cal stared at her blankly, pale blue eyes standing out in the crowd. Kyra's gaze sought Juniper's, but she was still looking at the floor.

Once the rest of the crowd had filtered out, and the servants were beginning to clean up, Kyra whirled on Julian.

"Okay, *betrothed*, what the heck?" Kyra asked, yanking her hand from Julian's and crossing her arms.

"You're a placeholder."

"Every girl's dream."

Julian gave her a look. "We're not actually getting married. I couldn't decide between everyone! Have you ever had a room full of people all wanting to kill each other over you?"

"Can't say I have," said Kyra. "I've had a room full of people wanting to kill *me*, though."

"Rhetorical question. Listen, there's another ball in a year, and I'll invite you back and we'll break up. I'll choose a new bride once I can actually decide."

"Good. I was worried for a second that you had fallen in love with me," said Kyra, smirking. "Wouldn't be surprised. Happens a lot."

"You stole my line!" complained Julian.

"And your heart."

"Dude!" Julian exclaimed, "That was a great comeback! Now let's go explain to our friends that we aren't engaged. But I'm gonna add that you actually love me to see the looks on their faces." He grinned deviously, then jumped down from the pedestal, making a beeline for the others and running like a madman.

Kyra shouted after him, "Then I'm telling them *you* love *me*!"

"Whatever you say, my betrothed!"

Kyra rolled her eyes and ran after him.

* * *

"Juniper, can we talk for a second?"

"Of course." Juniper hesitated slightly as she turned to meet the owner of the voice. She already knew who it was. Who else would it be?

Julian raked one hand through his hair, his crown long forgotten somewhere in the ballroom. "You know that I'm not actually in love with Kyra, right?"

Juniper froze, knowing a blush had already risen in her cheeks, betraying her. She had been standing at the edge of the ballroom, watching all the sulking girls slowly filter out of the ball once Julian had announced his choice of future bride. They dragged their feet, wearing pouty expressions and casting scathing looks at the unbothered Kyra. Juniper had been doing her best to avoid Julian, but here he was, forcing her to confront her own jealousy that had sprouted in her heart like a weed.

Deciding on a vague answer, Juniper said, "If you were, I would have several questions."

That made him laugh, but something in it sounded hollow. "That, and the fact that Cal's head would explode if I was."

Juniper's jaw dropped. "Does Cal...?"

Grinning wickedly, Julian said, "What kind of friend would I be if I told you that?"

"If you are so loyal to him," said Juniper, finding the ceiling very interesting, "then why did you pick Kyra as your bride at all?" She rushed her next words, trying to sound light and airy, "You could have picked me to be your stand in. I would have happily complied." *Because I'm a little bit madly in love with you.* "Because you are my friend."

"That's what friends do. Pretend to be each other's fiancés." Julian did that funny little cough thing again. "You're right, though. I guess I could have chosen you."

Her heart sank. Would it really be so horrible to be engaged to her? Even if it was fake? She wanted to ask him why he didn't. She wanted to ask him why he was acting so weird and what was wrong with his blood. But most of all, she wanted to ask him if he truly was wearing a corset.

Instead of any of that, she said, "I see."

"I chose Kyra because...well because—" Julian fumbled for words, for the first time that she had known him. "—she's just...you know. She's my friend."

"And I am not?"

Julian did not respond. His face was strained, but he said nothing.

Juniper's heart sank. That was all she needed to see. As she began walking away, she said, her voice a quiet mix of soft and sharp, "Goodnight, Julian. You will make a wonderful husband one day."

* * *

"Are we going to talk about this?" Kyra asked, flinging off her shoes and watching them slide across the floor once she and Juniper made it back to their room.

They had said goodnight to the boys a few minutes ago and had all gone off to their rooms to get a good night's sleep for tomorrow's journey.

Wincing from where she was standing, Juniper raked a brush through her knotted curls, her back to her sister. She slowly pivoted on her heels, turning to face her. A part of her wanted to vent to Kyra about it all, but another part, a larger part, thought it might be better to just forget that it had happened. "What is there to talk about?"

"Apparently white light burst out of you like a holy pinata." Kyra raised an eyebrow. "But if you think there's nothing to talk about, then by all means, keep braiding."

Juniper set the brush down. "I am not even sure what happened."

"Start with what you do know."

"Nothing!"

Kyra warned, "Juniper."

"Fine." She begrudgingly sat down on the bed, wrapping her arms around herself. She remembered the way her veins had glowed, how she had pictured the sun shining down. "Is there any way the sun could actually be my parent?"

"I'm not sure how to answer that without delving into the birds and bees," Kyra said, leaning back amusedly. "Unless you need the talk—"

"No," Juniper said hurriedly. "It is just...I was thinking about my nickname. 'The Sun's Child.' All light magic comes from the Sunbeam at the edge of the world, right? And the magic that came from me was white. Light magic is white, while dark magic is black. I think there's some type of light magic in me. Possibly. I am not sure, and I do not even know how that would be remotely possible. It should not be. I am not faerie, and I have never made a deal with one, so if there is light magic within me...it just...it just should not be there. It goes against all odds."

Kyra nodded, taking this information in. "And you're sure you don't have any faerie heritage?"

"Beyond sure."

"Then you're right. It doesn't make sense. At all. Humans *don't* wield magic, especially not light magic. I've heard of people that made deals with the fae, and as a result they were able to use dark magic. But never light," said Kyra, her hand absentmindedly rising to her mouth to bite her nails.

"Kindly cease biting your nails," Juniper chided. Kyra had that bad habit since they were little, when she was thinking hard about something. Juniper's step-father, the King, had always scolded her for it.

A flash of surprise crossed Kyra's expression, her eyes widening for a moment before she schooled it back into an easy grin. The expression of surprise came few and far between on Kyra, and it reminded Juniper of when they were kids. Though when she thought of them as kids, memories surfaced. Memories of rushing water and violin...

Kyra pulled her nail away from her mouth. "Why shouldn't I?"

"Bacteria. Teeth shifting. Infection. Shall I go on?"

"Please no." Kyra waved her hand, then muttered, "Know-it-all."

"You say it like an insult."

"Oh, it is."

"I'd rather be knowledgeable than an infection-rife nail biter with shifting teeth."

"Riveting, but off topic." Kyra rolled her eyes, but she was grinning. "The Queen had magic, too. That's what she used to knock me off my feet and destroy the fountain. That's another impossible thing that's pretty possible because, well, it literally happened. So either we're all slowly falling victim to hallucinations from the shrimp, or Callista actually has magic."

"I saw it. And I had no shrimp. The boys said they saw it, too. The magic was purple. Not white, not black. It could not be light or dark magic."

"Do you think it's even faerie magic?"

"I have never read about purple magic." Juniper shook her head. "It does not exist."

Kyra sat up, and Juniper could practically see the gears turning in her sister's head. "But it's possible that it *could* have existed a thousand years ago, when the fae were still out and about, partying among us humans. There could be another type of magic, besides light and dark. A magic that *humans* can use."

"So you are saying our mother learned an old type of magic? To do that, she would have had to learn it from a faerie."

"When you say it, it makes less sense."

224 - BROOKE FISCHBECK

"Like you said, I exploded like a holy pinata tonight. I am past trying to make sense of any of this."

"Except," Kyra said, "your pinata explosion wasn't as fun, because there was no candy."

Juniper said, crossing her arms, "Next time I shall try and explode with candy instead of magic to satisfy you."

"Now you're talking."

Juniper turned off the dimly lit lantern lighting up the room, suddenly very afraid of the dark and what lurked in the shadows. Racing back to her bed in fear of whatever monster could lie beneath it, she pulled the covers around her in her scared routine she had done since she was a child. Since her father had died, and every monster seemed to be lurking nearby.

"Goodnight, Kyra," Juniper said, the fluffy, soft covers muffling her voice. The bed was like a cloud, or at least what she expected sleeping in a cloud would feel like. The fact that she had actually jumped through a cloud the other day didn't help. "May Mother Goose be kind as you slumber."

Kyra stood in the doorway, her gangly silhouette outlined by the light from the hallway. For a moment, she just stood there, unmoving. Then, she closed the door after her, saying softly, "Sweet dreams."

* * *

After putting one foot in the horse stirrup, Kyra slung her leg over the saddle. It was morning, the day after the ball and the night's events, and her head *hurt* from all the information she'd been told. The crisp air served a cold reminder of the task ahead. Defeating the Queen. Saving her kingdom. Running off and fighting jungle monkeys. It was the kind of morning that bit into you, resembling drinking cold water after shoveling down mint leaves.

She didn't quite know what to make of any of it, and she didn't really feel like trying. Her back was aching from hitting that fountain last night, and...she was sounding like her father again.

Kyra steered her horse away from the steps, wanting to get away from all the goodbyes. Julian was on the palace steps, hugging his mother tight and possibly crying. Kyra imagined him tearful at least, a child who loved his mother more than anything in the world. Imagine that. Cal was shaking hands with several of the castle servants, having said goodbye to his grandmother when it was still dark. Luca and Juniper were mounting their horses. Kyra once again felt that pang of longing she had felt upon first arriving in Maiike. As she looked around the group, however, the pang was...duller.

The last stretch of their journey to the Winter Palace was upon them. The Palace was further north than Maiike, and they still had more forest to go through. The Northern Forest, this time.

Her newfound engagement was going swimmingly. She and Julian had fist-bumped on the way out. Juniper was taking it surprisingly well, only looking like she was hanging on by a thread fifty percent of the time instead of one-hundred, so that was a win. Luca didn't seem to care much, and Cal...well, Cal seemed happy enough.

Happy for his two friends being fake-engaged. He didn't say much about it, only grunting and making weird facial expressions whenever it was brought up, which Kyra chalked up to a gastrointestinal issue. Her mind couldn't comprehend it as anything else.

And now they were riding up the valleys of Maiike, cutting across the beautiful green fields on their horses. It was so much nicer than traveling by foot; she always had complaints when she had to run or walk anywhere.

Nothing but blue sky was ahead of them. Well, blue sky and the ever-impending threat of doom and death brought by the Queen.

But mostly blue sky.

She couldn't even let her mind think about last night. The Queen showing up to crash the party—insane. The Queen having magic—insaner. Juniper exploding with white light like some faerie-goddess-princess-volcano: the most insane thing ever. And she didn't let her mind wander to the symbol that was in her Trial by Fire, the dripping ink of faerie. She just wanted to let her horse run into the wind, pretending she was a regular girl out for a regular ride, and that she didn't have the fate of an entire kingdom resting on her shoulders.

Soon enough, the rolling hills had flattened out to grassy plains, letting Kyra and the others know that the cold north would soon be upon them. They had packed bags of food and clothes, and all were wearing coats and pants that would keep them warm. Kyra herself was wearing brown pants with her trusty leather boots, then a black long sleeve tunic, and a pale pink cloak that fell to her knees. Her hair fell loose around her shoulders to keep her neck warm, with one small strand woven into a braid. Juniper was wearing something similar, and Kyra had seen her secretly swishing the cloak around like she was a knight on a quest.

As the plains gave way to dirt, and tall, dark trees, Kyra fell back with the others, drawing her horse to fall in line with them as they stared out at the Northern Forest, drastically different from the light and airy Southern Forest.

The trees here were crooked and thin, each a bent hand clawing at the ground and sky. The ground was covered in thin dirt, but Kyra could see that as the elevation rose, so did the snow that blanketed in thin sheets of powder. Eventually it would turn into ankle-deep terror.

Kyra was about to voice her complaints, but the words died on her tongue.

Because a small, homely-looking house sat at the edge of the forest, smoke from a chimney tracing swirls in the air.

That wasn't the weird thing; in fact, lots of people lived on the edge of the Northern Forest.

The weird thing was the entire house was made from candy.

17

The Candy House

"I really, really want to eat it." Julian's gaze was fixated on the little candy house.

"We cannot just eat someone's house!" Juniper said.

Kyra said, cocking her head, "I've never heard that rule before."

"That's because it shouldn't have to be a rule!" Cal said, eyes wide in disbelief. "You don't eat other people's homes!"

"Who builds a candy house and expects people not to eat it?" Luca asked, shaking his head. He jumped once he saw Juniper and Cal's gazes boring into him. He added on quickly, "But we really shouldn't eat it."

"Pushover," muttered Kyra.

The house had a path made of chocolate bars, stark and brown against the white snow. Its walls were made of gingerbread. The roof looked to be covered in swirling buttermilk frosting, all different colors mixing together like rainbow cream. Stones deep-set in the walls were, on a second look, gumdrops and cake and icing and so much *chocolate*. Candy-canes formed a neat little arch over the walkway, cheery and bright and smelling of peppermint. Peanut butter and chocolate were whipped together to make a delectable array of trim around the windows.

Though surely not practical, it was the most beautiful sight Kyra had ever seen. She almost thought she would have to wipe a tear from her cheek. If she ever wanted a house, she was totally going to have her contractor build her a mansion made from pure chocolate. Even if it would eventually melt...it would be awesome while it lasted.

"I have an idea," Julian said, jumping down from his horse with a flourish. "What if we each just take a little nibble. The tiniest little bite. That wouldn't be so bad, right?"

Cal looked at him like he was crazy. "Someone could be home! Do you want whoever lives here to walk outside and find you *nibbling their house?*"

Julian and Kyra shared a look like they were considering it. Which Kyra definitely was. It wouldn't be that bad, right? She played the conversation out in her head. *Hey, I'm just gonna take a bite out of your windowsill, then scram. Is that cool with you? Perfect, thanks.*

Juniper jumped from her horse, walking over to Julian with crossed arms. "There could be a billion different diseases and germs on that thing!"

"She's right. It could be unclean," said Cal.

"Unclean? I'm Cal, and I hate fun and everything good in the world. Waah-waah." Kyra mimicked Cal by strutting around, standing tall and wagging her finger at everyone. She crossed her arms and stood toe to toe with him, as if challenging him. "I'll take my chances."

Cal worked his jaw. Then, he relaxed his posture and crumpled his hand into a fist, impersonating Kyra. "I'm Kyra, and I don't know when to stop."

"I'm Cal, and I care more about germs than my friends." Her voice rose more than she would have liked it to.

"I'm Kyra, and I care more about candy than stopping my evil stepmother from taking over my kingdom, which I should care about but apparently I'm more invested in a stupid piece of chocolate!"

Kyra narrowed her eyes at him. "We just fought the Queen. We can take a rest for a moment. And the coronation is tonight. We have more than enough time to stop for five minutes."

"Oh, really? A break? Come on, Kyra, there are people counting on us right now! Every break we take is a waste of time! Even this fight is wasting time!" Cal said.

A waste of time. Against her will, she thought of dancing with him at the ball, and the way he had laughed infectiously, how he had spun her and her heart had flip-flopped, doing somersaults to the tune of the piano. *A waste of time.* "So it's all a waste of time, then? Us—" She gestured to everyone, catching herself, "—All of us getting to know each other, it's all for nothing?"

"You know I didn't mean it like that."

"I don't know what you meant," Kyra said cooly. "But I do know that I want chocolate." And with that, she turned on him, her boots sending chunks of snow skirting as she stomped over to the house.

She heard Luca say timidly, "You guys both did pretty good impressions."

Julian muttered, "Read the room."

As soon as Kyra began making her way over to the house, Julian was bolting to the side of the house. Gleefully ripping off an icing decoration, he shoved it into his mouth in handfuls.

Kyra walked over to the house and tossed hair over her shoulder, saying to no one in particular, "I haven't had chocolate in ages." It wasn't exactly true; she had taken some chocolate from the chocolate fountain at the ball. But it wasn't exactly a lie, either, because she had only gotten one bite in before her murderous stepmother showed up to crash the party, seeking destruction. Parents really were the worst, weren't they?

She shoved down her rising anger as she ripped off a piece of chocolate peanut butter from the windowsill of the house, munching on it in silent irritation. She was mad at Cal for whatever reason, but mostly, she was mad at herself. Why couldn't she keep her wrath in check? And he was right, too; that was the worst part. They shouldn't have wasted any time getting to the Winter Palace. And yet, she just had to go and ruin things, like she always did.

Like she always did. An image of a vial full of dark liquid set to the tune of a bittersweet violin melody passed through her mind. *Why?*

It was a memory that she could barely grasp at, just out of reach. She felt like she had lots of those memories locked away where she would never find them.

"This bubblegum is really good," Luca said, blowing a bubble the size of his head.

"Let me try!" Julian beelined over to where Luca was standing near the door of the house, shoved him out of the way, and crammed more handfuls of sweets into his mouth. An uneasy feeling laced itself in Kyra's stomach as he inched closer to the door. "You've gotta try this!" Julian waved Kyra over.

"One second," said Kyra, swallowing hard as the uneasiness grew.

She glanced over quickly at Juniper and Cal and saw that they were holding the reins of the horses and staring at them with glares that were eerily identical.

Kyra took a few steps towards the door, her gaze latched onto it.

As she neared it, it swung open, revealing a dark entryway shrouded in shadows. And candy. Still lots of candy.

A wad of peanut brittle fell out of her mouth as she saw that no one was there. The door was opened by itself. Who was inside? Or, maybe more appropriately, what?

Juniper shouted out from where she was standing, warning, "Don't you dare go in there!"

Kyra locked eyes with Cal, who had his head tilted towards her, his eyebrows doing that funny little furrowing thing that they did when he was concerned. Plopping another piece of candy in her mouth, Kyra smirked.

"Watch me."

* * *

Juniper groaned as Kyra entered the candy house, the door creaking open wider as she went.

"Do we go after her?" Cal asked, his voice feigning nonchalance but his stance betraying him. He was standing on the balls of his feet like he wanted to run forward.

Juniper shook her head, pulling a thin yellow ribbon around her braid to hold it in place. "She is trying to make a point. It is best if we do not give in."

Cal gave the barest shrug, but he didn't disagree.

Julian and Luca, however, followed her into the house, pieces of swirled chocolate and gummies falling from their fingers as they went. Juniper's heart winced when she saw Julian, like it had since the ball. *Get over it*, she thought with a pang. *He could care less about you.* And it was true, she knew it, but she couldn't get her heart to understand. Especially since he had gotten engaged to her sister the night before. Juniper may not have been an expert on romance, but she was pretty sure that was a bad sign. It was enough to help her start moving along. But not quite enough, she realized sadly, as he disappeared from her sight and into the house.

"What's wrong?" Cal asked.

Juniper braced herself and met his eyes. "Um. Nothing." She mustered up a weak, unconvincing smile.

"You really are bad at acting." The ghost of a grin was on his face. "You can tell me what's up."

"Fine. But you must pinky-promise not to tell anyone, alright? *Anyone*."

"Pinky-promise?"

"Yes," Juniper said, her tone going dark. "It is sacred." She let go of one of the horses' reins, then stuck out her pinky.

Cal considered her for a second before lacing his pinky with hers. He said, "Now tell me."

Juniper was about to launch into the whole story about her crush on Julian, every single gory detail, hot, humiliating tears already rising in her eyes, when she heard someone cry out from inside the house.

Julian.

She exchanged a quick look of panic with Cal, before they both were racing towards the house, their boots pounding against the packed-tight snow, arms swinging quickly against their sides. Juniper dropped the horse's reins that she held, and she heard them whiny after her. Cal had already made in through the door, but Juniper was a few feet behind, her short legs not nearly as fast as his.

The door had begun screeching shut on its own accord, scraping against the gingerbread floor as Juniper hurriedly pumped her legs faster.

If she stopped or slowed, she wouldn't make it. Did she want to make it? She could potentially be safe, cut off from the horrors that the house might have within.

But if she didn't, the others might need her.

"Juniper!" Cal yelled from inside the house. "You don't need to!"

But she did. No matter how scared and weak she felt, she needed to help her friends when they were in danger. That was courage, right? Bravery in the face of fear?

She pushed herself forward, and barely made it through the door as it closed, locking behind her like a tomb. A pillow of dust billowed out around the hinges, as her eyes slowly adjusted to the darkness.

Cal was standing next to her in the entryway, one hand waving away the grime floating through the air. Juniper coughed, feeling like her lungs were being coated with soot. She started as she saw Kyra, Julian, and Luca, standing in what looked to be an entire kitchen made out of pure candy and cake.

She saw what Julian had been screaming about, and her blood ran cold.

A wall was rising up from the floor, dividing the entryway from the kitchen, blocking Juniper and Cal off from the others, a black mass of steel that was rising up steadily. The floor shook as the wall rose, the very framework of the house trembling.

The wall was now at Luca's height, rising higher with every passing second.

"Jump over it!" Cal was shouting, his hands cupped over his mouth. A quiver went through the house, and it threatened to knock Juniper off her feet.

Kyra was trying to hoist herself over it, but the wall was steadily meeting the ceiling, too tall for her to climb it.

Julian tried and failed. His blond waves had fallen in his eyes, coated with dirt falling from the rafters. "We can't!"

"Try!"

Kyra leaped at the top of the wall, desperately flinging herself at it, to no avail. Juniper watched in sinking dread as she jumped, then missed, then jumped again, then missed again, her eyes alight with animalistic anger.

"We can't!" Julian repeated, then hastily grabbed at Kyra, pulling her down from the wall as it almost met the ceiling. "It's too high!"

Juniper finally found her voice. "It is too high," she said quietly, gentle like the dust settling around her. The wall almost met the roof. There was a thin sliver left, and she could no longer see the top of Kyra's head.

"We'll get out of here! We will!" Kyra's voice came, muffled, as the sliver disappeared and the wall met the ceiling, cutting the kitchen off from the entryway with a thick sounding boom.

And then it was silent, the house stopped shaking, and the grime finally settled. Juniper stared at the wall silently, the spot where Kyra's head had just been. She closed her eyes and shook her head, bringing her fingers to her forehead.

Cal cursed and spun to the door, jiggling the doorknob. It didn't budge. The door was locked. They were trapped in the tiny entryway, the darkness stifling and reminding her of a grave.

She tried not to freak out in the company of a near stranger, steadying her breathing. She opened her eyes. "So," she said, and to her surprise her voice did not wobble or shake, "How do we get out of here?"

"I don't know if there's a way out. I already scanned the area for windows or openings. Nothing. The windows were a facade. This was a trap," Cal backed up against the far wall, sliding to the floor. He clasped his hands together, almost as if he was trying to calm himself, too.

"Do you think..." Juniper said softly. "Do you think we are going to die?" Her brain was shrieking, *We're going to die we're going to die we're going to die.*

"No," said Cal, and she believed him. "The house is magic, obviously. So it's trapping us for a reason. We just have to see what it wants."

"What could it want?"

"I'm not sure. Why don't you ask it?" Cal suggested.

Juniper looked away, face flushing. She must've been annoying him, so she just sat down gingerly and pulled her knees to her chest, determined to keep silent forever and ever until she died.

She felt Cal's soul-seeing stare on her again, and she shifted uncomfortably, letting her hair fall in her face to cover up her mortification. What was he thinking? Probably about how awkward she looked.

"Sorry," Cal said.

Juniper looked up, startled. "For what?"

He gave her a look, his eyebrows shooting up. "For being sarcastic with you. I forgot you don't like that sort of thing."

"Oh." Juniper blinked. "I accept your apology."

He regarded her with a keen look, as Juniper fiddled with her cloak hem, filling the silence with the humming of a song her father had sang to her when she was little, before he had passed away.

The other lyrics were a little fuzzy in her mind, but she knew that the chorus went,

> *Mother Sky flies high above,*
> *And all the birds sing her praise,*
> *Beneath the Juniper tree,*
> *Tweet, tweet, the birds sing her praise,*
> *Down by the Juniper tree...*

She remembered being small, her father tucking her into bed after a long day of playing and pretending, back when she lived in a small cottage in the outskirts of Aazagonia. It was before her mother had married Kyra's father, before they had moved to the castle, and before the Queen had changed, turned meaner and vainer. In those days, Juniper could almost picture the woman she had been, a woman who laughed often and sang her daughter to sleep. Her mother had worn flowers in her hair back then, a different color each day, lilies and roses and geraniums. Her lilting voice from those times still haunted her in her sleep. *One day, little Juni-tree, you can wear flowers like this, and you will be fair, as long as you find people who love you. They will always find you beautiful.* She and her father had danced into the night, the petals falling to the stained, carpeted floor. Juniper had scraped the flowers off the floor late that night, draping them in her hair and dancing around.

"That's a lovely melody," Cal said once she had finished her humming.

Juniper smiled. "Thank you. My parents named me after that song. For the Juniper tree, they told me."

Silence fell upon the two like a blanket of snow. They sat for a moment, the sound of nothing making uneasy thoughts creep in. Juniper mused on the lyrics of the song, not quite remembering the voice of her father. The thought filled her with panic. Was it scratchier? Deeper? She could have sworn he pronounced his l's with a sharp lilt...

To distract herself from her catapulting thoughts, Juniper inquired quickly, "Your name—Calais. What does it mean? I can hear traces of Maiiken in the syllables, but I haven't been able to put them together."

Cal looked away quickly, a shadow passing over his sharp features, before saying, "It means, 'Son of the North.'"

Son of the North. Like the Northern Forest. Interesting...maybe his parents had been into faerie stories, like Juniper was. Maybe his mother had stayed up all night to read them, getting lost in the world of magic and wonder as she hid under her covers. Maybe his father had loved to tell tales of the fae, spinning magical stories of fright to his son as a roaring fire blazed behind him. "Do your parents like the faerie stories?"

Cal swallowed hard. "I guess they did."

"Oh. I am very sorry for your loss. Losing a parent...I am sorry."

"It's okay."

"How so?"

"My grandmother once told me that it doesn't matter where you come from, if you know who you are," said Cal, and he pulled his legs tight against his chest as if giving himself a hug. Juniper wanted to hug him, too, but she was sure he wasn't in that kind of mood.

If you know who you are. "I do not know if I will ever know who I am." She thought of her mother holding up a mirror, of her father singing her to sleep, and of Kyra climbing a tree. Everyone else seemed to know, so why didn't she? She looked down at her hands reflexively, remembering the coarse white lines that had filled her veins, the burst of light that had rippled from every spot of her body. It felt like a faraway dream that had happened to someone else, not to her. How did she have magic?

"One day, you will," Cal said. "There was a time when I was unsure of myself, too. But then I realized that your past doesn't define you so much as what you do with your present."

"I wish I understood your wisdom, but you lost me."

His mouth quirked up at that. "Let me know when you're found."

Juniper nodded slowly, then let herself relax against the wall, sticking her legs out in front of her. She began humming again, but louder this time.

Tweet, tweet, the birds sing her praise,
Down by the Juniper tree...

* * *

Kyra slammed her fist against the wall as it hit the ceiling, her knuckles cracking against the hard, tacky material. She cradled her fist, then tried again, accomplishing nothing except bruising her hand. Now there was nothing to do but wait for a way out. Or for whatever had wanted them trapped. Kyra slammed her hand against the wall one last time.

"It might be difficult to believe, but punching isn't always the answer," Luca said from his spot on the floor. His arms were wrapped around himself, his breath visible in the cold air.

"It's rude that this place has no fireplace." Kyra gave in, sinking down to the floor and rubbing her hands against each other to warm them up.

The kitchen that they were trapped in had a table made of a sweet looking cream cake with chairs made of licorice, but none of them sat at it for whatever reason. There was a dull oven, unreasonably large. What kind of food was the inhabitant of this house cooking? Northern Forest turkeys must've been the size of a horse if the oven was that big.

Julian piped in, perking up, "Do you guys want to play a game?"

"That idea sucks." Kyra smirked up at the ceiling.

"That's no way to speak to your future husband and king," Luca taunted, wagging his finger in the air mockingly. "But that idea does suck."

Julian whined, "I thought you were on my side—"

"You aren't *my* future husband and king," Luca said.

Kyra said, "Then again, I'm not marrying you for real either. I'm living in the jungle in a candy mansion with a hot guy who is decidedly not you."

"Fighting ninja monkeys?" Luca asked.

"Fighting ninja monkeys." Kyra gave a quick nod of her head in agreement.

Julian frowned, saying, "Fighting ninja monkeys seems cool."

"Well, what are you gonna do when this is all over?" Luca said, his almond eyes glassy as if picturing the three of them swinging through the trees and shooting flaming arrows at monkeys garbed in

240 - BROOKE FISCHBECK

karate uniforms. It was a vivid image in Kyra's own mind, one that would probably never come true. Her stepmother was strong. There was a chance that they wouldn't succeed at stopping the coronation. If they ever got out of the candy house, that is.

"Oh, my adorable little huntsman," said Kyra. "Julian won't have time. He's going to be attending to his princely duties, isn't that right?"

"Yeah." Julian picked at a gingerbread floorboard. "That's right." *A prince with blood of silver and death.* Kyra studied him, scanning over his face and his scabbed hands from the burn that Juniper had given him.

"What did your mom mean when she said that your blood was tainted? Are you a traitor or something? Did you put an old lady's cat in a tree? Part your princely hair on the side rather than the middle?" Kyra asked lightly, but her voice was deflated. "I'm assuming it doesn't mean you secretly collect toenails or something earth-shattering like that, so what is it?"

Julian didn't look up at her taunts. "It means nothing. Stop asking, okay?"

"Julian..."

Luca said, reaching out a comforting hand, "Julian, we—"

"I said stop!" Julian swatted Luca's hand away, scrambling to his feet in an instant. "I don't need to tell you anything."

"There's no need for that," Kyra said, quelling the fire within her at his brash slapping of Luca's hand. Her stepmother's hand flashed before her, cracking across her face to the music of an echoing melody. Luca pulled away, hurt written across his features, as he settled back into his corner. Kyra swallowed. "Just sit down. We won't ask any more questions."

Julian begrudgingly began to sit back down. Suddenly, his eyes became wide with fear, his face frozen in horror like one of those marble masks from ancient plays.

Kyra snorted. "Sunbeam above, Jules, you look like you just heard one of my father's rap songs for the first time. They're not that bad, but the one about the Sultan of Yen-Sing is a terrible diss track—"

"The walls," Julian said, cutting her off abruptly. "They're moving."

It was true. The walls on all sides of them began inching slowly forward, moving slowly across the floor, screeching and sliding closer and closer.

The walls. They were closing in on them. Literally.

They moved achingly slow, almost taunting them. Kyra almost wished the walls had moved fast, squishing them in one second like people-pancakes. Not this. Slowly being crushed to death was infinitely worse than if it was over in an instant. Kyra felt her lungs contract as she thought about it.

Luca's face drained of color, making him look ghostly pale in the dark. "We're going to be squeezed to death!"

Kyra launched to her feet, putting her hands against the wall, cool to the touch.

It kept moving forward as she tried to push it back. She shoved against it, throwing her whole weight at it, her shoulder clanging against it brutally. Julian and Luca were doing the same, shoving the other walls with all their might. It didn't stop the walls from moving inward. She threw herself at it again, ignoring the jolting pain rippling through her.

Juniper and Cal were on the other side of that wall. Were the walls closing in on them, too?

Kyra slammed herself against the wall again to shove that out of her mind. They would be okay. Kyra had promised them that she would get out of there, so she would. Her back ached for her to stop, but she pushed through it, relishing the pain because it took her mind off the world around her. The stinging of her shoulder reminded her to keep fighting, to *stay alive*.

242 - BROOKE FISCHBECK

She surveyed the room, looking for something, anything, that could help her. Her gaze stopped on the tall rafter beams above that held the ceiling together. The roof of the house curved into a triangle, with the walls stopping directly below that.

The rafters would be untouched by the walls closing in.

"The roof!" she exclaimed, jumping up on the small table in the center of the kitchen. It wobbled beneath her as she grasped at the rafters but missed.

Then Luca was beside her on the table, jumping up at the ceiling, too, but missing it by inches. Kyra flung him up and hauled him to stand on her shoulders. He stumbled before standing upright and reaching the rafters. His hand gripped a beam, and he pulled himself up with a grunt, sitting with one leg slung over the rafter beam.

The walls were getting closer now, shoving all the furniture in the room closer together, smushing the large oven until it ripped in two. A hissing sound brought Kyra's attention, and she saw that the unnaturally large oven had been ripped in two as it was shoved across the room by the wall it had resided on, cutting deep marks in the floorboards. It rested for a moment, before the oven was savagely punched forward by a different wall, it's metal splitting with a sound like the falling of a tree. Why was that oven so large? It looked like it was big enough to fit a...

Person.

Humans, she realized with a sickening jolt. *That oven was used for humans.*

Kyra was removed from her trance on the oven as she saw the walls had covered more ground. They were about to touch the edge of the square table. About to crush her into tiny Kyra-bits.

"It's the house!" Luca cried out at the same time she thought this. His voice was echoing from the rafters, looking like a small dove sitting in a nest.

Kyra screamed up at him, "You're right! The house is trying to kill us!"

"Never expected you to say those words!" Luca yelled back.

"What, 'the house is trying to kill us?'"

"No!" cried Luca. "You said I was right!"

Julian climbed up onto the table easily, then with one fluid motion, was up in the rafters with a sprightly jump. He stuck out a hand to her.

She seized it, grasping his wrist with all her might as he pulled her up beside him in the rafters.

The house shook and groaned as the walls closed in on each other, the chimney whistling and whining like it was upset. More dust fell everywhere, as bubblegum balls and pieces of colored chocolate bits fell around them, raining down like tears. The walls met each other with a ringing sound, at last closing the distance. Kyra closed her eyes and thanked the heavens for letting her not be down there.

Teetering a little on the thin rafter beam, Kyra stood up and reared her fist back. She punched a hole through the gingerbread ceiling. Light filtered in as crumbs rained down, a glimpse of the sky now visible. She pushed her head through the hole, making room for the rest of her body as she tumbled out onto the roof and then collapsed in a pile.

The sky stretched out blue above her, with a few dense storm clouds to the east. Snow would be coming soon. Snow white as the heavens. Sky as blue as Cal's eyes.

Julian pulled himself through the hole, gingerbread crumbling around him as he shoved his shoulders through. Kyra stood to her feet as they pulled a heavily breathing Luca through the hole.

The three of them stood atop the roof, about fifteen feet up. Easy; that was the equivalent of some of the *shortest* trees Kyra had jumped from when she was done climbing.

Luca latched on to Kyra's gaze, following it to where she was staring at the edge of the roof. He groaned. "Don't tell me we have to—"

"We have to," lamented Kyra, and she took a couple of running steps before jumping off the edge of the house. Pain reverberated up her spine as she hit the ground, snow seeping into her hair. It hung in limp, wet strands around her face, cold enough to make her shiver.

She could almost hear Luca's whimper as he and Julian followed suit, tucking and rolling once their feet hit the ground, face planting in a snow pile. In other circumstances, it would have been funny. Admittedly, it was still funny, and she let out a chuckle at the bewildered looks on their faces.

The house behind them creaked, shuddering in its framework.

Juniper and Cal. She looked around, hoping to see the edge of curly hair or the flash of bright blue eyes. But nothing. She couldn't see them anywhere.

"Are they—are they still...?" Luca brushed the snow off his pants in a repeated, slow motion.

Julian bit his lip. "I don't see them anywhere. Where are they? Guys! I don't see them!"

Come on, you guys, Kyra urged. *Stay alive.*

18

The Fiercest Storm

Juniper launched herself up from the floor once she noticed that the walls were closing in, her dark purple cloak swinging around her.

"Cal," Juniper said, her voice rising in panic, "tell me the walls are not closing in on us."

Cal scrambled to his feet in alarm. "We need to think of a way out."

"I thought there was no way out!" Juniper cried, eyes wide.

Cal responded with a reluctant, "I did say that."

"How are you so calm all the time? Please, just freak out for once!" Juniper wanted to cry and scream all at once. She felt the tears rise in her eyes. If she blinked, they would surely fall. The walls inched forward slowly in taunting. They would be crushed within minutes.

"Don't cry," Cal said. Like saying that would make it stop.

His easy tone of voice only made her cry harder. She felt the tears rolling down her cheeks and could taste the salty tang of them as they trailed down their path. Sunbeam above, could she humiliate herself more in one day? She hadn't even thought it was possible to be so embarrassed. At least she was continually proving herself wrong.

She buried her face in her hands. "I am a mess."

"Everyone cries. Our tear ducts are scientifically proven to be unstable."

"Mine seem to be the most." Juniper hiccupped, and the tears fell faster, blotting out her vision. "My mother says it's unladylike to cry."

"Your mother! That's it!" Cal said, eyes alight. "Use your magic to get us out of here! The glowy-hand thing!"

That made her sobs falter. She raised her eyebrows. He actually looked *serious* about that. "I cannot just call it up—even if it is magic—whenever I want! I do not know how to control the glowy hands, they just happened!"

"You have to try," Cal said. No pleading. No encouraging words. Just Cal being Cal.

She nodded. Closing her eyes, she placed her hands out with the palms facing up. Just how she had envisioned the fae using magic in books. She tried to picture her veins glowing white, like the night of the ball.

Come on, Juniper, she chided herself, *think.*

Juniper tried and tried to call up whatever deep well was locked inside her, to let all that light free like she had the night before. She remembered thinking of happy things, of good things, but all she could think of right now was that they were going to be squished to death.

Cal's back was pressed up against the wall now, and it inched him forward with every passing second. Juniper realized with a jolt that the wall behind her was also shoving her forward.

Cal said, "I take it it's not working."

"No." Juniper scowled. "It's not."

She pressed her palms against the gingerbread wall, feeling it nudge her inward slightly.

"Try again?" Cal asked, the wall shoving him forward another inch. The entryway was infinitely smaller, now, about a quarter of the size it had been. Soon, there would be no space left.

Juniper tried to call up the magic, but she felt nothing but a void inside her. Terror and fright ate away at her, the most corrosive acid, making her unable to concentrate. She clenched her eyes shut and pictured the sun. Nothing. It was as if all the magic had picked itself up and moved out, leaving her behind to be crushed.

"I am so sorry, Cal. It is not working."

Cal took a shuddering breath, then gave a curt nod. "Well. I'm glad that I got to meet you. You and Kyra are one of a kind." His breath hitched on Kyra's name, and Juniper wondered if maybe he did feel something towards her sister.

Juniper offered up a weak smile. "I am glad I met you, too."

The walls were closing in quicker now, and almost covering the entire room. With one last shove, she was side by side with Cal, walls on either side of her, pressing against her skin lightly. She knew it would not feel so light in a moment.

"I have taken a fancy to Julian!" Juniper blurted out, the dark making her brave. "Well, I am...getting over it," she lied.

"Why are you telling me this now?" Cal asked, but he didn't look surprised.

"In novels, people confess things when they are about to die."

"True," Cal said. "Well, I suppose I'll confess that I organize my clothes alphabetically and by color." Juniper noticed that he was wheezing slightly from the pressure of the walls. "My grandmother calls me her clean little sprite."

The walls had pressed them further, squeezing them tight. It cracked on Juniper's rib cage, cutting off her air. "What," she heaved, her breaths coming in ragged gasps as her lungs squeezed tighter, "is your grandmother like?"

"Messy," Cal struggled to readjust himself as the walls shoved them together. Juniper's head barely reaching his shoulder, her knees pressed up against his calves. "She's the messiest person I know." He took a sharp breath and did not go on.

"She sounds lovely."

Silence stretched as the walls squeezed tighter, slowly pressing the life out of them. Sweat broke out across Juniper's brow as the cold wall reached her head. Every square inch of her body was now touching a wall, and every curl of hair on her head was being smushed. The pain came next, the pain after the silence, like a slow pressing at her temple.

"No," Cal breathed. "Don't be silent. It can't—it can't be silent."

Juniper closed her eyes in the dark, thinking of something to say. What did she want her last words to be? No one would ever know them, anyway, so it shouldn't have mattered. But it did.

And then it struck her.

"Mother Sky flies high above.." she choked out, her voice raw and quiet as the walls pressed harder, "And all the birds sing her praise..." She thought of her father, smiling down at her and singing this same song to her, tucking a lock of hair behind her ear in a gentle gesture. He never told people he loved them, she suddenly remembered. He never said those words. But Juniper had known, in those small moments, the moments when he would tuck her hair behind her ear like that. She had known and she had loved him so fiercely, as much as he had loved her. He had loved her so much and he had died. She never remembered him on his deathbed, though, sick and with bags under his eyes that resembled sunken pits. She remembered him like this—singing and smiling down at her like she held every star in the sky in her eyes. "Beneath—" she coughed, unable to go on.

"Beneath the Juniper tree," Cal finished her lyric softly, his voice barely a whisper, his usual rasp soft. "Tweet, tweet, the birds sing her praise."

Their voices joined in a sad, sweet harmony, "Down by the Juniper tree."

At that moment, Juniper felt a different sort of light. She felt broken and scared and so very tired, but she felt something stirring within her. Love for her father, her family, her new friends.

She felt the magic of the sun, light magic. It flowed through her veins in uncontrolled joy, and it burst out from her in waves of white light.

Tearing down the walls and sending her catapulting to the floor, the magic ran rampant in huge bursts of energy. Her eyesight blotted with dark spots.

Her legs gave out from under her. She was tired and afraid yet happier than she had been in a long time. Because she had saved them.

As her vision went dark, she could only see Cal's wide blue eyes above her, and hear the melody of their voices mixing together,

Down by the Juniper tree.

* * *

Kyra watched in a trance as the house exploded in a burst of white light.

Ears ringing, her vision erupting with the flash of brightness from all around, she fell to the snow. Not even registering the cold biting into her skin. Her arms wheeled out in front of her, catching at the ground and holding her up.

She was vaguely aware of someone yelling in her ear, but Kyra just heard an intense ringing, the yeller's muffled voice echoing from what felt like through layers of moss.

Kyra looked up from the snow, the wet powder clinging to her face and dripping as she looked up at the wreckage that was the candy house.

Shambles. Ruins of the gingerbread and sweets were strewn about.

And there she was.

Juniper.

She was standing amidst the ruins; her fists crumpled at her sides. Kyra's mouth gaped open as she saw her eyelids flick open, revealing not the familiar brown eyes that Kyra was so used to looking into, but milky white sockets like gaping holes of pure snow.

Juniper's veins looked like white spiderwebs, creeping up her body and draped in white, glowing faintly against her skin. Her hair was sticking out everywhere, the little springs jutting out, dark and contrasting with the white snow behind her. Her arms hung high at her sides now, her hands gleaming white and clear, unfiltered magic pulsing from them. The only word that Kyra knew to describe it was *radiant*.

She looked like an avenging angel, a figure in white like a faerie queen of ballads. Like a faerie herself. Kyra could only watch in amazement as her sister conducted light magic as bright as the sun's rays on a clear day.

And then Juniper returned to herself, her glowing veins disappearing, her eyes and skin returning back to their usual dark brown. Her lithe body hit the floor in a heap.

Kyra was up and running to her in an instant, ignoring the ringing in her ears and the throbbing of her skull. Kyra threw her arms around her, hugging her tight. Juniper was unresponsive on her knees, chin hanging on her chest. The only clue that she was even still alive was the slight trembling of her heartbeat, pounding against Kyra's own.

"You did good, Juni, you did good," Kyra repeated, over and over into her sister's ear. "I'm almost proud of you." She had never said anything like that to her sister in all her years.

"Have you replaced my sister with someone kind?" Juniper looked up at her, and every fear and vulnerability that was lodged in Kyra's chest was gone because Juniper was smiling goofily like she always did. That stupid, wonderful smile. "But I know."

"Don't get all vain now, just because you have magic." Kyra squeezed Juniper's shoulders, then let go of the hug.

"And to think, I was just about to go off on a rant about how great I am."

Kyra stood and was suddenly aware that Cal was standing there, too, his arm slung around Juniper, his eyes hollow with something that Kyra couldn't understand. He had almost died a few seconds ago.

Before she knew what she was doing, she flung her arms around him, throwing herself into a hug. She felt him stiffen with surprise, then his arms were around her, and he held onto her tightly.

"You almost died, you jerk," said Kyra softly, her voice muffled against his chest.

She felt him grin against her hair. "I'm glad you're okay, too."

"Sunbeam above," Julian was calling out, sprinting over with his hands cupped around his mouth. His cheeks were ruddy with cold, his lashes specked with little dots of snow. "That was the craziest thing I've ever seen."

Kyra hastily let go of Cal, not wanting anyone to see that she was capable of hugs. She inspected her nail as if it were the most interesting thing in the world.

Julian knelt down and pulled Juniper into a tight hug, not letting go for a solid ten seconds. Juniper looked like she might die of happiness on the spot. Maybe she would get into life-threatening situations more often if Julian would hug her more. Kyra noticed that Cal gave Juni a secretive thumbs up when Julian finally let go, and

Kyra raised her eyebrow in amusement. Juniper just beamed in response.

"Let's get this straight," Kyra said, "I'm not taking any of the blame."

"The blame for all of us almost being killed by a house, simply because you wanted chocolate?" Cal asked innocently.

"No, I was thinking of a *different* time when we were almost killed by a candy house just because I wanted chocolate."

Luca said, running up to join them, "Juniper, that was awesome."

Juniper stood, smoothing her hair back. Her cheeks reddened as she admitted, "It did feel pretty fantastic."

"It looked cool, too," Julian said eagerly, exaggerating with his hands. "Like you were on fire. But with light. A magic-blazing-awesome-human-marshmallow."

The corner of Juniper's mouth lifted up. "That is very kind, though I am not sure what it means."

"Hey!" Kyra half-shouted excitedly, elbowing Juniper, "This time, you *did* explode like a candy pinata!"

Juniper looked bewildered, then grinned wickedly. "I said I would, did I not?"

Luca asked, "How did you do it? Use the magic?" His purple eyes were so wide, Kyra imagined little violet swimming pools within them. A sinking feeling filled Kyra's chest as she realized why he would be so eager. He was a Dämonenwolfe; he now had faerie magic within his veins. Maybe he thought Juniper did, too.

And maybe Juniper *did*. Kyra remembered Luca's pale face looking up at her the night of the ball when they had sat on the stairs, his lip trembling, moonlight casting long shadows. *I never wanted this.* Did Juniper?

"I do not know," Juniper said, shrugging heavily, her words weighted. "It just happened again. How to control it is beyond me."

Julian said, "What does your magic even do? So far, it's just been flashes of light that knock everything down."

"When she learns to control it, it will be more concentrated. More like the Queen's magic, how she was able to send it out in short bursts or spells," Cal offered. "Or maybe it can't be controlled."

Kyra watched Juniper, trying to gauge her reaction to that. But Juniper was silent, staring at a space beyond Kyra's shoulder in concentration. Kyra could practically see the gears whirring in her head.

"What's that?" Juniper asked, then pointed to the spot she had been staring at.

They all turned to see what she was looking at and looked down in surprise.

It was a scarlet piece of parchment, with loopy scrawls written across it, half hidden by the thin snow. Kyra was sure that that hadn't been there before. The writing was cursive and had fancy curls, twirling and crossing over the parchment like the dancers had spun at the ball.

"That's the Queen's writing." Kyra peered closer, reaching to pick it up.

"Are you sure?" asked Luca, eyeing it nervously.

Kyra grinned. "The cursive 'm's' are evil and pretentious. Sort of the Queen's trademark qualities."

"Can 'm's' be evil?"

"Let's find out," said Kyra, and she went to open the envelope.

"No!" Cal swatted at Kyra's hand. "If it's Callista's writing, it could be a trap."

"It could also not be a trap."

"Up to you. But if you get turned into a toad, don't come crying to me."

Kyra reached down and snatched the piece of parchment from the floor, waiting expectantly to start sprouting antennae or have a watermelon grow inside her.

Nothing happened.

Unfurling the letter, Kyra smirked triumphantly, "The letter is addressed to me and Juniper, anyways, and I didn't even turn into a toad. Win-win."

Trying to conceal a smug grin, Juniper muttered, "If you were a toad, you would be a lot quieter."

"Just read the letter!" Luca said anxiously, peering over Kyra's shoulder to get a better look. Callista's handwriting was so cursive-y, it was almost hard to translate, as if it were written in another language.

"*Darling daughters,*" Kyra began, making her voice high-pitched and nasally to imitate the Queen, even throwing in a few hair flips and struts, "*I hope you enjoyed the fun candy house I placed for you. If you're reading this letter, I suppose you survived it. I can't say I'd be surprised; I made it so even a toddler could escape.*"

"You're right!" Julian exclaimed, staring at the ruins of the candy house. "That cursive does sound evil!"

"Told you." Kyra picked up her nasally impersonation of Callista again, "*I thought I would write to you and let you know that it was me who placed the house there, as a trap. Tora begged me not to send this, but what's the point of accomplishing something if no one knows you did it? Anyways, see you soon. Cheers to more memories! Can't wait to make more!—Queen Callista of Aazagonia, Soon to be Prime Ruler.*"

"Tora? I thought Luca handled him with his Dämonenwölfe craziness," Julian brought his hands to his face and baring them like claws. "I saw it with my own eyes. Tora was done for."

Luca said, "I wouldn't say done for."

Kyra said, while pinching his cheeks as he squirmed out of her grasp. "I bet your little wolfy claws did a number on him."

Juniper had paled, fidgeting with her braid as soon as Tora's name had been mentioned. She finally spoke. "I think if Tora is still on the Queen's side..." she hesitated, then continued, backtracking,

"I think we need to get moving. We still need to cross a section of the Northern Forest before we make it to the Winter Palace. We need all the time we can get to stop my mother."

Kyra took the reins of her horse and laced herself into the saddle, solemnly facing the Northern forest as if they were in a staring contest. Kyra did not blink. Then again, neither did the forest, as it didn't have eyes. Looking out at the sky as if it held answers was never the right move. The sky had yet to respond all her seventeen years.

The others wordlessly mounted their own horses. She clutched the letter tight to her chest. A gust of wind came up, signaling that a snowstorm was approaching. Clouds becoming dark and heavy, they roiled in the sky like a sea of grey snow.

As they set off into the forest, Kyra let go of the scarlet-colored letter, watching wordlessly as it drifted off with the wind. A stain of blood against the blanket of white.

19

Sunk to These Depths

Snow fell swiftly, covering the already bleak landscape with a layer of powder. The forest transformed into a wonderland of cold. The sky was grey and dark, the sun hidden from the world, and blackened trees twisted upward as if clawing at the clouds. It did not make for a welcoming image. The snow had thickened, making it harder for the horses to trudge through, but a snow-shoveled path soon revealed itself, leading to the Winter Palace like a winding river. One thing about rivers was they always flowed on. No matter if the destination was cursed or if the traveler was, too. Rivers were reliable. Rivers did not care if Juniper was terrified of the night ahead.

The snow dusted everyone's scalp, little flecks of white that chilled them to their core. Juniper imagined she was a dragon, puffing out smoke and flames as her breaths became visible in the cold air.

Uneasiness crept in, an unwelcome visitor, as they neared the edge of the forest. Knowing that this was where the fae had resided before hiding away in the mountains did not help. She became convinced with each passing moment that the fae were still out there somewhere, waiting to be found. Watching her. Juniper shifted her cloak tighter against her shoulders, casting wary glances around the forest as the horses trekked onward.

They reached the Winter Palace by nightfall.

The tall, dark spires were the first things visible, stark black stone against a grey sky. Next came the tower, where Juniper knew nothing resided save for an old mattress. The tower was a thin, black spike, the tallest part of the castle. It was a toothpick compared to the bulking monstrosity that was the rest of the palace. An ornate drawbridge had been let down, yawning over the frosty moat as if expecting company. Guards were stationed at the drawbridge, draped in red and gold, standing immobile in place like toy soldiers. The coronation would take place in the courtyard of the palace, and the Queen might have thought Aazagonians would trek across the world to see her be crowned. No citizens or people filtered in, though. No one was coming to see their Queen take sovereignty. Save for Juniper and the others.

The forest did not yield for the Winter Palace. Crooked trees dotted the landscape, protecting the walls of the castle like guards. Snow blanketed the tops of the spires and buildings, giving the palace a haunting aura. Juniper had never liked spending her winters there; it had always felt so dreary and icy. She much preferred the airy lightness of the Summer Palace, tucked in by the seaside. At least in the Summer Palace, there were people always around, games to always be played. But for the winters, Juniper had been stuck inside, feeling lonely and always so *cold*.

The group's horses stopped behind a large black locust tree. Its leaves were dead and gone, remembered ghosts of a time without snow. Juniper wondered if the Northern Forest even knew what the sun looked like.

Julian let out a low whistle. "That is a *nice* palace."

"I was going to say the opposite," said a shivering Luca. "It looks so sad."

"Cheer up, huntsman. I'm sure the evil palace where we might die is lovely in the daylight," said Julian.

The Winter Palace did have a sorrowful look about it, as if it had seen the world burn before it and was unable to move, locked in its framework amidst a sea of snow. Despair was wound around it like a snake.

"I found my stepmother out here one winter," said Kyra, grey eyes clouded as if years of pent-up storms were gathered inside. "She was standing in the snow without any jacket, crying and holding a flower. I asked her what she was doing, all cold and wet, and she looked up at me and said, 'Why? Are you afraid?' I wasn't. But looking out over the castle, thinking about what we're about to do...I'm...I'm still not afraid. But I never figured out what it was she was doing, knee-deep in the powder..." Kyra trailed off, not finishing the sentence, as if forgetting what she was talking about. Her eyebrows furrowed, her face becoming hooded in thought. Lost to the eerie, impatient traveler that was memory.

"Is everyone familiar with the plan?" Juniper asked suddenly, successfully taking the attention off her sister.

Everyone nodded. Except Kyra.

"I might be just a tad hazy on it," Kyra said sheepishly. "Just a tad."

Juniper rolled her eyes, then said to the boys, "You three go ahead. I will explain the plan to Kyra. We will meet you by the moat."

They nodded and jumped down from their horses, tying them to a tree. Then, they set their packs full of food and supplies at the base of the tree. They headed down to the moat, pulling up their hoods so as not to be spotted.

"You really do not understand?" Juniper asked dubiously.

"You say that as if you expected me to know it. But no, I've surprisingly got the plan down," said Kyra, hopping from her horse and bringing it over to tie it to a tree. She slowly looped one end of the rope around another. "We sneak in through the moat, go through the grate, and then hide out in a storage closet till the coronation, when we burst out and stop the Queen, punching her in the face and saving the day!"

"That is...actually the right plan. So why act like you did not know it?"

Kyra popped her hood over her head, her grey eyes stormy. She hesitated again. Two hesitations in a matter of minutes. What was going on with her? "It's just...we have to go through the water to get to the grate. Um. I..."

Juniper nodded, a memory flashing before her eyes. A memory of a riverbank with roaring water running by. A summer day with a warm breeze and the strings of a violin crying out a mournful tune. She offered, after shuddering, "You should stay behind. We can find a way to get you in the castle without having to go through the moat."

Kyra didn't even consider it. "No. I'm going through the moat. I have to go with you. I wanted to—I actually don't know what I wanted by bringing this up. Let's just go." She shoved forward, hood casting long shadows on her face. Shadows like the clawed, gnarled hands of the black trees above. Shadows that said more than any whispered sentence or pleading gaze could.

"Kyra, wait." Juniper placed a light touch on her sister's shoulder, stopping her in her tracks. "It is okay that you are scared—"

Something flashed in Kyra's stormy eyes."I'm not scared."

"Do not do that with me. Do not pretend that fear is another enemy to be conquered," Juniper said, something stirring inside her. Something true. Something that she had learned in these past few days, amidst monsters and men and everything in between. "With-out fear, there would be no such thing as bravery. You are my sister, Kyra. I will always be there for you, like you are for me. No one is free of fear. Not even you. I remember what happened that day on the river. I was there."

"Yeah, you were there," Kyra spoke with daggers, face twisting into a scowl. For a moment, it reminded Juniper of the Queen. "You were there. But you didn't do anything."

The words struck Juniper like a blow. Her mouth fell open in hurt. "I was a child. A child who only knew to obey her mother, because her father had been her guiding light. And that light was something she knew was never coming back, no matter how much she hoped." The words spilled out of her mouth like a waterfall, tumbling over each other as if they couldn't get out fast enough. Guilt spiked up in her like a paintbrush dipped in water, the tendrils of dried paint drifting among the clear blue glass. Guilt that was fren-zied and panicked, guilt that belonged to no one else but her. "I know I should have done something. You would have, for me. I was just a child," she finished lamely.

"All we have is each other. We have to be each other's light. I'm trying to be better than Callista every day. Every day. I want to be better." Kyra's voice came quiet, scarily quiet. "But I was just a kid, too." A quick vulnerable look passed over her sharp features as she said this. Kyra let that look fall in fury, before trudging forward to the moat where the others waited, her footsteps clamping hard on the tightly packed snow as she trailed her way towards the palace. Her sister was a fortress stronger than the castle itself, with walls impossible to knock down. Walls that Juniper herself had helped construct.

The footsteps in the snow were the only sound penetrating the blanket of white as Juniper stood alone with her racing mind, not knowing whether to follow or flee. To atone or give up.

She pushed all of her wild thoughts out of her mind, remembering what they had come to do. Stop the Queen; then she could address the hurt between her and her sister.

The moat was wide and, frankly, disgusting. It had murky brown water that was slightly foggy over the top, with reeds reaching high. Looking more like sludge than water, it boasted dank green moss floating at the top, the smell of it nauseatingly wafting upward. The moat reached right up against the castle walls, and Juniper knew there were small grates along the rim of the wall, hidden deep under the water's surface. Kyra had found the grate a couple winters ago, when she was 'exploring.'

Kyra was already back to herself. How did she do that so easily? "Ready for a swim, everyone?"

Luca gagged. "I didn't realize it was gonna be so...gross."

"Yes, it does look rather revolting," said Juniper. She tied her hair back into a braid, her curly hair not going back without a fight. Once she had wrestled it, she turned back to face the moat. For some reason, she had thought it would look more inviting and less disgusting.

It did not.

"Did something die down there?" Julian wrinkled his nose up and waved his hand in front of it.

"Not yet," murmured Kyra, her grin eerie in the yellow-green light from the water.

Kyra shifted from one foot to the other, plainly trying to hide her discomfort with a feeble grin. She eyed the water as if it were an enemy, tracing the toe of her boot through the snow.

"Put your shirt over your faces to block out the smell." Cal pulled his long-sleeve shirt over his mouth and nose, then said something that sounded like, "Mphghh gfbp pbfh."

"Can you say that one more time, but in our language?" Luca asked.

Cal pulled down the shirt over his mouth. "Oh, right. I said; I'll go first. The grate should be right below…" He indicated a spot next to where he was standing. "Here. About fifteen feet down, if we can trust Kyra's judgement. It might be hard to see when you're diving but use your hands to feel around. Remember to always keep moving, 'cause the water will be cold. If you get stuck in the grate, I set up a system where we'll always have someone within range to help. Keep alert, and if you start seeing stars, come back up right away, understand?"

He stepped down towards the moat's edge, snow tumbling into the water as he clumsily trudged ankle deep into it. He winced as his feet became submerged, peering down into the clouded depths of the moat.

"Good luck, soldier." Kyra saluted him, her voice barely a whisper. Cal gave a salute back, before stepping off the bank and diving down into the deep. He barely made a splash with his dive, his black shoes the last to disappear underneath the surface of the water. *Godmother Luck, smile down on us,* Juniper thought. She tried not to think about drowning with nothing but the smell of rotten eggs for comfort.

"I'll go next." Jules sighed, shedding his long red cloak and burying it with snow. Tentatively, he dipped his toe in the water. He made a face. "Yeesh. This water is *cold.*"

Then he took a deep breath, and jumped in. Icy water splashed on Juniper's foot.

"Okay, I guess I will go." Juniper shivered, wiping off the droplets on her leg.

"Remember, Juniper, you have to dive straight down—straight down, got it? Reach out, and you'll feel the grate. Once you've got hold of the grate, pull yourself through, and then swim to the surface on the other side. Easy," said Luca.

"Easy," Juniper repeated unsurely, feeling as if it would be fairly not easy. Then she stepped onto the edge. Water reached her calves, drenching her black pants and making them stick to her legs, freezing cold. Her teeth chattered as she gave one final look back at Kyra and Luca, before diving down into the water.

It was as if a thousand wasps were pricking her skin. The cold stung and bit and thrashed, a living entity with a ruthless mind of its own. Her entire body was screaming at her to go back to the surface, to get wrapped in her cloak and settle down in front of a fire. But she forged on, swimming down deeper and deeper. With every downward kick, it became harder to see through the murk. Her mouth was clamped shut against the repulsive water in a protective ward. She didn't know how far down to go, or if she was even nearing the grate. Her hand felt out against the slimy castle wall, begging to find the grate. What would it even feel like? Was the grate square, circle, triangular? She had forgotten to ask. Oh, *no*, she had forgotten to ask! What if it was octagonal? Panic laced her skull as she let out the air in her mouth, watching it drift up in bubbles. The disgusting water seeped into her mouth.

Shivering, she swam forward and forward, thinking of warm fireplaces and hugs and Julian's smile—it always made her blush. Maybe it would cause heat even underwater? She wanted this swim to end. Anything but this cold that threatened to destroy her. About to turn back, she peered ahead, and then...

There—she could see through the din, a large grey something—it had to be the grate.

Juniper swam towards it and hooking one hand around it, felt barnacle-covered metal. Yes! It was the grate, barred and square.

She squirmed through it, pulling her body through a small opening and then kicking off it upwards once she reached the other side.

The cold was now a dull, throbbing pain throughout her limbs, a muffled reminder that she had a purpose beyond this terrifying endeavor. She frantically kicked upwards.

And then.

Something wrapped around her leg. Something slimy and cold.

Terror launched itself like a rocket inside her as the thing yanked her down, forcing her deeper and deeper into the water. She watched as the grate flashed by her, and she was pulled into the depths.

Her scream was silent underwater. It sounded like gurgling water, strangely peaceful. As if the scream were far-off and distant. Like it could've been someone else's. The tendril that was wrapped around her ankle slithered up to her waist, tightening its hold. Juniper struggled, trying and failing to squirm out of its grasp.

Now she could see the thing that had grabbed her was a black mass, a huge, thick tentacle. Cold fear made her struggling cease.

Could it be...was the tentacle attached to a...?

Juniper balled her hand into a fist, slamming it down hard on the tentacle with all her might. It loosened its grip for a moment—just a moment—but it was enough for Juniper to kick upward and use the momentum to swim up to the surface.

Once she reached the surface, she filled her lungs thankfully, taking gasping breaths.

Juniper found that she was in a sort of tunnel, with a low arched ceiling that let no light in. The channel of water that she was in wound around the edge of the castle, on the other side of the walls.

The castle wall was to her right. To her left was a stoop leading to a door, elevated from the water. Standing on the stoop was Julian and Cal, soaking wet and shivering.

Julian registered the look of alarm on her face. He reached out a hand to her knowingly, using that to ask what was wrong.

"Meeresfrüchte!" Juniper gasped, her voice ringing out in the silence. "*Sea faerie!*"

As soon as she had uttered the words, she reached out to grab his hand, but she already felt the slimy demon pulling her back under.

Her hand slipped from Julian's the way sand fell through an hourglass, inevitably and unstoppable.

Taking a deep breath, Juniper was wrenched back underwater.

Julian shouted, "No!" He then jumped into the water after her, making depths of the moat foamy and bubbly. *Little diamonds*, she thought. The bubbles looked like sparkling silver teardrops, the loveliest ornament on baubles and jewelry.

The tentacle of the Meeresfrüchte pulled her deeper, holding her by her wrist. It dragged her into the deep. She reached her hand up to Julian, who was frantically swimming towards her. Their fingertips grazed, the last remnant of sand slipping through an hourglass, but it was too late.

The demon had already dragged her too far.

The Meeresfrüchte were an old class of sea demons, usually residing in the ocean. Many wars had been fought between the sea faeries and merfolk. They had never been found in castle moats! When was the last time the janitor inspected the water? Surely he would have found that there were *sea monsters* living there!

The tendril pulled her down, down, down.

Kyra and Luca swam upwards, side by side, their legs and arms kicking quickly as they tried to reach the surface. No black tentacles had wrapped around them, so Juniper assumed they were doing pretty good right then. Better than Juniper, at least.

Something dark flashed in the corner of her vision. Another tendril, an arm of the sea demons that resided in the deep, ground lurkers who fed off unsuspecting sealife. All Juniper felt was fear, fear that her friends would be attacked by the same demon that held her in its grasp.

Before she knew what she was doing, Juniper was raising her arm out towards the tentacle, fingers spread wide as if to say, *Stop!*

A strand of white light burst from her fingertips like frantic rays, shooting out at the Meeresfrüchte with a bright flash of light. Magic.

She did a small victory dance that was restrained by the sea demon holding her in a death-grip.

A shrieking sound came from somewhere below, and the tendril that had been reaching out towards Kyra fell away, slithering back into the depths. Kyra kicked forward after looking down into the deep, stunned. Juniper knew that Kyra couldn't see her because of the murk, but she imagined that her sister's gaze was locked on her, telling her that everything was going to be okay. The two glimmering forms quickly kicked to the surface, not knowing that she was still down there, far from the safety of the stoop above.

The wailing, gurgling sound from the darkness below continued on, a surprisingly human sound. This scream, unlike Juniper's, did not sound as if it were far-off and distant.

It felt like it was right next to her.

The tentacle holding Juniper slackened. Juniper thought that maybe it had given up and was going to let her go. In reality, its attention had strayed to someone else.

Julian was being pulled down beside her, a black tentacle wrapped around his torso, tugging him down through the water like a plummeting anchor. He was next to Juniper in an instant, the tentacle tying them together before beginning to pull them down deeper.

Eyes wide with panic, Julian struggled to escape the grip of the Meeresfrüchte, pulling at the tendril that bound him to Juniper. If only he hadn't jumped in after her, he would still be safe above with the others. A sinking feeling filled Juniper, a feeling that this was all her fault. Again. Sunbeam above, why did she always ruin everything? She couldn't save Kyra that day at the river so long ago, and she couldn't save Julian now. She was a useless, pathetic princess who was only good for finding trouble and was no good at saving herself from it.

Juniper tried to call up the magic within her again, but she felt nothing. Nothing but emptiness. Not even the slightest stir of the light magic saying in Kyra's joking voice, *Hey, we're here, but we're taking a lunch break right now, call back in ten.* Nothing.

The tentacle pulled her and Julian down to the bottom, their boots touching down on the moat's floor. Tufts of sand spurted around her like a desert storm. They floated up, little clouds of ash and diamond, glittering as they went before they, too settled into the sandy floor beside her with delicate grace.

The huge, hulking mass of black, slimy flesh that was the Meeresfrüchte regarded them in a glare that Juniper assumed was hunger. She couldn't really tell, actually, because the monster didn't have a face. It was an undefined circle-like shape, with tentacles poking out from every surface. Its mouth was an oval, with sharp teeth ringing around it in triangles, a purple tongue roving the edges. Juniper felt like throwing up, but she knew if she threw up, it would just float around her head in the water, and that would kill her before the sea monster could.

Another tentacle snaked out, grabbing Juniper by the head and yanking her forward, towards its mouth. Julian's hand grabbed hers, quick as lightning. He dug his feet into the sandy floor, a strangled, burbling sound coming from his mouth, bubbles trickling out in little o's.

Juniper couldn't see any of this happening, as she had a tentacle wrapped around her head. Because of course she did.

Julian's hand held her firm, while the tendril pulled her in the opposite direction. One slip of Julian's hand, and she would be sent tumbling into the jaws of the sea faerie. She prayed that his grip held true. Her head felt like it was being torn in half, pain reverberating around her skull as the Meeresfrüchte clung onto her like the last cookie in the jar.

"Julian!" Juniper screamed, not knowing or caring if he could understand her. "On three!"

"Grgmph?" Julian screamed back, voice muffled by water.

So that wasn't going to work. New plan.

Without thinking or even deciding to think, Juniper dug her fingernails into the slimy skin of the tendril around her forehead, feeling her sharp nails breaking through. *Hah. Who should file their nails more often, now, mother?* A black, oozing substance drifted through the water after she did this. It seeped from the wound and trailed its way up to the surface in little wisps like dark, thick smoke escaping from a blacksmith's chimney.

The Meeresfrüchte howled, and Juniper dug her nails into it again, then karate-chopped it off her in a quick succession. Falling from around her head, the tentacle went snaking back to the blobby mass of the demon, currents of black liquid drifting from it as it went.

Keeping hold of Julian's hand, she began swimming in fevered strokes to the safety of the surface. The black, blood-like liquid that had come from the sea demon was clouding the water, making the already unclear water impossible to see through. Juniper didn't *need* to see, though. She just needed to swim upwards like her life depended on it.

Which, frankly, it did. Very much so.

She broke through the water and didn't take any time for herself to even breathe. All she wanted was to be as far from the sea demon as possible. So, she just climbed up onto the dry stoop where Cal, Luca, and now Kyra were waiting. They hurriedly pulled her and Julian up.

Juniper rolled onto her back, panting and coughing up spurts of water and demon blood. She tried not to think about how disgusting that was, but failed, gagging infinitely. Julian was taking huge breaths beside her, gasping, as if drowning on land and aching for oxygen.

"You didn't say that there would be Meeresfrüchte!" Luca said to

Kyra as they kneeled down next to Juniper, dripping onto the stone stoop.

"I didn't *know* there would be Meeresfrüchte!" Kyra retorted, looking angry as ever. "If I had, do you think I would have led us through there?"

Luca raised his eyebrows.

"You really think so little of me, little huntsman?" asked Kyra mockingly.

"Are you two alright?" Cal asked the gagging, grossed out Juniper and Julian.

Juniper shared a look with Julian. She said, "Terrified, cold, and covered in sea demon blood. But uninjured."

Julian sat up frantically, eyes dancing with adrenaline. "We almost died down there! I could feel it! We were *this* close to being fish food! I swear, I've never been in a cooler situation." He crossed his arms triumphantly, then seemed to rethink his words. "Deadly and terrible, too, of course."

"My magic...happened again. It did not feel more under control, though." Juniper looked away, thinking of how she still couldn't call it up to her when she wished. It just seemed to explode out of her when she least expected it, rather than acting as a tool for her to use whenever she wanted.

"Yen-Sing wasn't built in a day, or something like that. You'll get the hang of it eventually." Kyra waved her hand like it was no big deal. Juniper grumpily thought that it seemed like a pretty big deal. And she still didn't even know why or how she had the magic, let alone how to work it. Juniper rubbed her temples. This was giving her a headache.

"I just cannot believe there would be sea faeries in a castle moat," Juniper said, frowning. "It simply does not make sense. Meeresfrüchte live in the sea. And for the demons to have come this far inland...?"

"Another of the Queen's surprises," said Kyra as she wrung out her sopping wet hair.

Cal said, "Hopefully there are no others." He reached out to the little wooden door that led to the tunnels underneath the palace. Turning the handle, he said, "Because it's time for phase two of the plan."

* * *

It smells like feet.

That was the only thing Kyra was registering at this point; that the stupid underground tunnel was ripe with the smell of feet. Feet that hadn't been washed in centuries; feet that had been dragged through dirt and animal feed and Callista's wicked soul. That's what the tunnel smelled like.

Her hair was dripping all over the place, so she tied it up in a ponytail, trying to get the feel of water off her back. She hated water. It reminded her of something she tried hard to forget.

The group had to walk half a mile under the tunnels to get to the center of the palace. The courtyard where the coronation would take place tomorrow was located in the exact center of the Winter Palace, and Kyra knew of an empty cellar that lay directly beneath it, hidden underground. They would hide there, then, they would jump out, confront the Queen, and make her admit her crimes in front of everyone.

But first, they had to make it through the gross tunnels, sopping wet, and without a trace of food. It was going to be rough, but Kyra could do it. The food part was going to be tricky, though. She needed to get her mind off it, so...

"Cal."

"Kyra."

"What are you gonna say to the Queen at the coronation, you know, when it's your turn?"

He twisted the bottom of his shirt, water spilling out from it as he gave her a confused look. His eyebrows did that funny furrowing thing. "When it's my turn?"

"Yeah. I'm thinking that we'll all be in a line, and we'll each confront her one-by-one, saying dramatic stuff like, 'You killed my family. Now you'll pay.'" Kyra's face fell. "Except, she didn't kill any of our families—not that we know of, at least—I bet she's done something atrocious along those lines. I don't know what my cool saying is gonna be."

"How about 'You tried to kill me. Now you'll pay," Cal made his voice deeper, a serious look coming over his face.

Kyra was appalled that he was such a dork. And that she thought it was funny! Could he be turning her into a dork? "It doesn't have the same ring to it, though, does it?"

"No, it doesn't."

"How 'bout, 'You suck.' Then I punch her."

"I like that. Easy. To the point. Elegant in its simplicity, almost."

Juniper interrupted, "We have almost reached the cellar."

The group stopped walking, Luca notably slamming into Kyra's back, not noticing that she had stopped.

The tunnel had a sharp turn up ahead, cutting off to the left. Kyra knew the cellar would be a few feet around that corner, waiting for them, unguarded and ready for the taking. Hiding out there would be the easy part. Stopping the coronation would be harder.

"I'll go look around the corner to make sure it's safe," said Kyra, jogging forward. "Then we're home free, Kyranators."

Cal shook his head. Kyra couldn't see his face clearly in the dark and from where she was standing, but she did see that his nose was doing that scrunching thing again. "Kyranators? I don't remember agreeing to that name."

"I don't remember asking," Kyra said, ducking behind the corner and winking at him. "Kyranator."

Feeling unnaturally light, she didn't notice the guards until she was fully around the corner.

Two guards in red and gold were stationed in the hallway, holding longswords and wearing the Aazagonian emblem, the golden arrow of fire. They looked up when they heard her footsteps, suddenly, and locked eyes with her.

"Well," said Kyra, sighing. "I don't suppose you'd believe I'm a ghost?"

She spun on her heel, sprinting back around the corner. The guards let out a string of yelling after her, and she could hear their metal armor clanking behind her. So they were chasing her. Fantastic.

Then a thought; a terrible, *heroic* thought hit her.

She shouldn't run back to the others. That would only lead the guards to them, too, and then they would all be caught. The right thing to do would be to turn around, all alone, and turn herself in. She would say she had come here alone, that the others were nowhere to be found. That would be what was best for the kingdom, and for her friends, too, no matter how much she would hate to do it.

Kyra should've turned right back around and given herself up to the Queen. For the safety and future of everyone she loved. It would've been the good thing to do; what a hero would do.

But it had been a long time since Kyra had thought of herself as any type of hero.

Maybe now was the time to start. Maybe the girl she used to be would be selfish, would lead the guards straight to the others only so she wouldn't have to face the Queen alone. That was something the Queen would do, and Kyra had vowed to be better than her.

Kyra came to a complete stop, letting the guards run up beside her.

Maybe it didn't matter if Kyra wasn't meant to be a hero.

Because maybe, just maybe....it was never too late to try.

"Where is your sister?" A guard with a heavy Yen-Sing accent drawled.

"I'm alone," said Kyra. "I've come here alone."

And then Cal skidded around the corner, looking concerned, and that lie came crashing down faster than Kyra running towards chocolate.

"No!" Kyra shouted.

It was too late. The guards had already seen him. One of them yelled, "There's another one!"

Then Kyra felt something slam into her back, and she fell on the floor in an instant. A guard had knocked her over, and was now standing, sword at her neck, above her. Her back twinged with pain, still sore from her fight with the Queen when she had slammed into the fountain.

The guard inched the tip of the sword to her neck, eyes blazing.

Cal ran forward. "Stop!" He cried but was waylaid by the other guard. The guard slammed into him, pinning his hands behind his back with brute force.

The guard holding Kyra yanked her to her knees by her collar, forcing her up, the sword still trained on her. The other guard brought Cal over and slammed him beside her on his knees.

Hopefully Juniper and the others could take the time to escape and find somewhere to hide. But Kyra heard no footsteps or sound from the other hallway, no sound of movement at all. Maybe they had been captured, too, by some other guards. Or maybe they had escaped! She didn't save Cal, but her actions had saved the others. And that had to be enough, for now. Heroics were already tiring her out.

Kyra tried to jump up and run, but the sword bit into her shoulder blade.

"Let it go, Kyra," Cal said quietly, gaze locked on the small, flowering bloom of red where the sword had punctured her shoulder.

Kyra only nodded at him.

"Where will you take us?" Cal asked the guards, his voice resigned. They both knew the answer.

One of the guards smiled, flashing crooked teeth. "To the Queen, of course."

For the first time in a long time, Kyra remembered what it was to be truly afraid.

20

Born and Bred

The Queen laughed when Kyra and Cal were brought before her.

It was a laugh that was like a tall wave in the sea. Gorgeous and musical, all the while being awful and destructive. And it went on for what felt like years. Kyra didn't even know someone could laugh for that long without taking a breath.

"Are you done with the evil laugh? Can we skip ahead to the villainous speech?" Kyra asked, rolling her eyes.

"Hold on." Callista laughed for a couple more seconds before turning to her. "Now I am. It's funny how you didn't even last till the coronation tomorrow. You'll never hear this again, but I expected more from you."

They were in the Winter Palace's royal chambers, the Queen sitting daintily on the house-sized bed, one leg crossed over the other. Her long hair dangled to the side as she regarded them with glee. Kyra and Cal were on their knees on the floor, the guards standing behind them with their broadswords pointed at them. Daring them to move.

Kyra could see into the bathroom, could see a million different powders and creams that Callista used. Smiling from its dais, the Aazagonian crown twinkled red. The gold of the crown was glinting as if reflecting off of something, as if reflecting off of a similar mirror...

"Where is your sister? And I could have sworn there were two others. Maybe I'm wrong, though. A blond, handsome oaf and an adorably small wolf?" Callista cocked her head expectantly.

Kyra scowled. "Juniper and the others are nowhere near here." *Hopefully.*

"Hmm." The Queen didn't seem surprised as she inspected her nails. "I don't believe you."

"You don't have to," Cal said. "They're long gone by now."

Callista looked at Cal as if seeing him for the first time. She stood up and crossed over to him, inspecting him by pushing some of his black hair out of his face. Her long fingernails dug into his chin, and it made Kyra want to slap her. More than usual, that is.

"Oooh." Callista patted his cheek then stalked back over to her bed to sit once more. "You're the halbling, aren't you?"

Halbling. There was that word again, the word that the old woman had used in the forest what felt like forever ago. What was it that she had said to Cal? Kyra couldn't remember, but she did remember that word: Halbling. A faerie-sounding word, Luca had said.

"What does that mean?" Kyra asked, unable to help herself. "Halbling?"

Cal's head sunk low as she asked this, his eyes dropping to the floor. Did he know what it meant? Was it possible he knew, but didn't tell her? Hurt spiked in her. But no, that was absurd. She could trust Cal.

"I'll let him tell you," Callista said, her red lips twisting into a cruel grin. She prodded Cal. "Go on, then. I'm sure *you* know what it means."

"I don't." Cal's voice was a whisper.

Kyra knew Cal was a million things. He was kind, brave, smart; he was selfless and witty. He was confident and sarcastic and brilliant; he had eyes like crystals and a nose that scrunched up when he smiled. He had been a great friend to Kyra, that she knew. She knew his favorite color was grey and that he liked things organized. He liked to play the piano even though he was terrible, and he always knew how to say just the right thing to make Kyra smile. She knew more than she ever thought she would know about him over these past couple of days, like how he was confident in himself and in her, that his heart was huge and weird and ready to give, and that he liked to believe in good over evil any day, because there is always truth in stories.

She knew all these things and with each new thing she learned, she wanted to know more.

But she also knew one more, very important thing.

Cal was a terrible liar.

"You know what that word means. I know you do," Kyra said slowly, her heart turning to stone. She thought she would feel angry at him for keeping things from her, or despair that he didn't trust her. But all she felt was sorrow. For once the anger inside her was quiet. So quiet in the room, Kyra thought she had gone deaf.

"I don't," Cal repeated, as if he believed it himself. But his mouth was a thin line, and his eyes were fluttering slowly like the beating of a butterfly's wings. Open and shut, open and shut, open and—

"But you have to know," the Queen said, amused. "You would know."

"I don't—I...I can't," Cal had become more panicked now, his breaths coming quicker and his face flushing. This was the first time she had seen him lose his cool. It was awful. "Kyra, you would…it would…*I can't.*"

Kyra never wanted him to look like that ever again. She never wanted him to be afraid to tell her anything. "You don't need to tell me," she said finally, going against everything her brain wanted to say, "If you don't want to." *I wish you would want to.*

"Fine. Don't tell her." Callista's eyes glittered. "I know who'll tell us everything we need to know."

She stood up and walked into her bathroom, disappearing behind a stone wall.

"Kyra." Cal's voice was pleading.

"What?" She was unable to hide the hurt in her voice, and she sounded like a kicked puppy. She let her face harden into its familiar uncaring mask. Kyra made her voice sound almost bored, as if she couldn't care less about what was going on. Or how she felt so betrayed. "What is it?"

"Kyra, I—"

"Children, children!" The Queen was walking back into the room, something heavy in her arms. "It's time for a show."

Kyra watched in a trance as Callista revealed what she was holding.

It was a golden mirror like the one Cal had described from his childhood, the one he had seen when he accidentally wandered into the Queen's underground chambers back in Aazagonia. The mirror that Kyra had never seen before but had had endless dreams about that were too vivid and awful to even be called dreams. Nightmares, more like it.

"Would you like a demonstration of how this works? Actually, I don't care. I'm gonna show you anyway. It's my favorite little toy." Callista shifted the mirror in her arms and placed it on the wall above her bed.

"I suppose you're going to start talking to the mirror like a maniac?" Kyra asked, feigning boredom, but actually leaning forward on her knees to get a better look at the mirror. It drew her to it, called her forward like all magic did. She thought of Juniper and her magic hands. *Two strands of the same cloth, woven together, Sun and Moon.*

"Yes, I am," Callista replied sharply. "And it's going to be glorious. We'll see who you're calling a maniac in a few minutes."

"Still you," Kyra muttered. She angled it so only Cal could hear. Then she remembered that Cal was keeping a world-shattering secret from her or something like that, and she decided not to grace him with her side commentary anymore. Neither of them deserved it right then.

"Dark one here, on the wall, who is the fairest of them all?" the Queen said, reaching out to touch the surface of the mirror.

Those were the exact words Cal had said Callista had uttered years ago. At least he hadn't lied about that. Dark one. Old one. Those were both names for the fae. What kind of magic had Callista been dabbling in?

For a moment, nothing happened. The mirror looked like a regular old, good-for-nothing-except-staring-at-yourself mirror.

And then, it changed. The glass surface of the mirror swirled to black. Like a churning sea or a rippling storm. All trapped beneath the mirror's glass.

A voice spoke out, loud and deep. "You, my queen, are fair, it's true, but the Sun's Child shines a thousand times brighter than you."

Kyra instinctively looked at Cal. He mouthed, *The voice.* The voice he had heard forever ago, the voice he had said he would recognize anywhere.

Callista's eye twitched slightly, but that was the only thing that gave away her disappointment. And Kyra knew she would be more than disappointed; the mirror had practically told her that her daughter was hotter than her. Not that that was in any way a normal thing to get angry at. The Queen had left any semblance of normal behind when she had tried to have her daughters killed. That was for sure a party foul.

Then the mirror returned to its normal old, reflective self, all traces of weird voices and black swirls gone.

"Now you see how it works. Shall I ask it something else to show you?" the Queen locked eyes with Kyra, begging her to say yes. To give in.

Kyra knew that Callista was counting on Kyra's weakness. That the curiosity of knowing what a halbling was—what Cal was—would be too much to handle. And it *was* too much for her to handle.

But she also knew she would lose Cal forever if she asked the mirror.

"No," Kyra said, and she heard Cal let out a breath of relief. "I don't care enough."

Thank you, Cal mouthed. Kyra pretended not to notice.

"Well, I do. I want your little worlds to come crashing down around you like mine had to. I want you to hurt, Kyra, because I have known my own share of loss. And if I have to hurt every day, hour, every *second* of my life, then you should, too." The Queen was panting heavily now, as if the force of her words had drained her. "And Juniper will understand at last, what I have been striving for. Which reminds me, I need to keep the little brat here." Callista reached out a hand, purple igniting along her arm.

Her veins glowed, her eyes turning violet down to the whites.

No. The others. Kyra tried to stand, crying out, but she was forced back down by a guard's firm hand on her shoulder.

"Stop it, stop it!" Kyra shouted, to no avail.

Cal joined, "Don't hurt them!"

Callista ignored them, thrusting her hand towards the wide open window. Purple sparks rushed from her fingertips, flying out the window like mini thorn branches.

"What did you do to them?" Cal asked, eyes flaming. "What did you do?"

"I just sent your friends a little party favor." Callista waved her hand. She leaned in and whispered, "But if I'm being honest, they'll probably die."

"You can't kill them! Juniper's with them!" Kyra realized in alarm. "You said you needed us. Don't you still?"

Callista sighed, twirling a curl of ebony hair. "I need you both, Moon's Child. Juniper's safe, I promise. If those three are even a little smart, they'll be fine."

"They're screwed, aren't they?" Kyra said deadpan.

"Totally," said Cal.

"It's just a safety measure." The Queen rolled her eyes. "As long as they're still inside the castle, they'll be fine. I need Juniper to get what I want."

"And what is it that you want?" Kyra asked, wrenching her mind from worry.

"You'll see." The Queen smiled wickedly. "You'll see. Now onto the matter of our little halbling friend."

Cal took a sharp breath. Kyra thought she could practically hear his heart beating rapidly. Beating faster than raindrops on stone. "Get on with it, then."

"Dark one, here..." Callista began, locking eyes with Cal, "...holding the boy's secret. You no longer have to keep it."

"Does it always have to rhyme?" Kyra joked, swallowing hard and not taking her eyes off the mirror.

The Queen sneered. "It's for show. You wouldn't understand." Her eyes were also locked onto the mirror as it swirled into that dark night color, the color of Cal's hair and the color of ink spilled across paper—the color of the black locust trees outside the castle walls.

Kyra was about to fire a retort back, but the mirror began to speak.

The voice in the mirror said, "The boy with eyes of a forget-me-not bud, is born and bred with faerie blood."

The mirror's darkness morphed away, and all Kyra could see was her own pale expression reflected back, mouth hanging a little open and eyes widening in shock. The Queen's smug smirk hung over her, reveling in her stepdaughter's expression.

Kyra was speechless. Her mind was blank. Her fingers grasped at the floor beneath her knees.

Born and bred with faerie blood.

Cal was...

He was...Cal was...

"*Fae.*"

* * *

Juniper surfaced in the moat, gasping for breath.

Waiting for her on the bank was Julian and Luca, both sitting cross-legged in the snow. They scrambled to their feet and helped her climb out, sending piles of snow tumbling into the icy depths. Although the snow was a source of her displeasure, she had to admit it was hypnotizing in its powdery silence.

They had just fought the Meeresfrüchte...again. When Kyra and Cal had been captured, Juniper and the others had been forced to flee, diving into the moat and swimming for their lives. Luckily, Julian thought to use his sword, which apparently he had been holding on to this whole time. It really could have come in handy earlier when he and Juniper had been close to death, but she didn't really care. They were safe, so that was all that mattered.

But Kyra and Cal...Juniper couldn't stop worrying about them, wringing her shirt out frantically and shivering in the snow.

"What," Luca said, "are we gonna do now?"

Shrugging, Julian said, "Sit in the snow and cry?"

Juniper felt like crying anyway, and she was already sitting in the snow, so she shook her head eagerly. She felt hopeless. There was nothing they could do now. Their only options were to come up with a new plan to defeat the Queen, go home and give up, or, as Julian suggested...sit in the snow and cry. That was sounding like the best option to her, so she buried her head in her knees in despair.

How could she have let everything go so wrong? She had magic; she should have been able to do something! Worthless magic. Juniper couldn't even use it! It was as if she didn't have it at all.

Juniper had tried so hard to be a hero. To save herself and her friends like the great conquerors and witches in the epics she had read. All she felt like right now was a failure. A *cold* failure.

Teeth chattering, Juniper pulled her arms tighter around her like a hug. Julian saw this and picked up the dry cloak that he had left behind, draping it over her shoulders in a chivalrous gesture.

"Princess, you look as beautiful soaking wet as you do in the finest clothes," Julian said, standing tall and staring down at her with gleaming green eyes.

That was when she snapped—like really snapped. All the pain and fear and loss that had been building up inside her came crashing down as soon as a cute boy complimented her. That might've been the most absurd thing to happen yet.

As she stood, the cloak slipped off her shoulders. "It is cruel for you to say that!"

Baffled was the only word to describe Julian's expression. "What?"

Juniper was bewildered herself. She rarely lashed out like that, and to be honest, it felt pretty good. Not even considering what she was saying, she continued. "How am I supposed to get over you if you keep acting so...so...so Julianly!"

"Should I go?" Luca was glancing quickly between Juniper and Julian.

Julian ignored him, raising an eyebrow. "Get over me?"

"I did not say that..." Juniper tried to backtrack, her cheeks heating, but she knew it was no use. The look on her face was enough to give it all away. "Fine. I do—did—fancy you. I am getting over it, though." Crossing her arms, she tried acting nonchalant. Her legs wobbled, and she struggled to not fall over. So much for nonchalant.

"I really feel like I should go..." Luca hurriedly backed away.

Julian's expression was soft now, his eyes filled with remorse. "Juniper. You are beautiful." That was the worst thing he could have said, and the last thing she wanted to hear.

"Beautiful. That is the most horrid word in our language." She kicked at a pile of snow, watching as it scattered into patterns of white and blue.

"I don't think so."

"And why is that?"

"Beauty isn't just looks," Julian said slowly. "It can be a lot of things. I don't think you're pretty because of your face. You're beautiful because of your heart and everything that makes you, you."

The fireworks returned in all their glory, brightening the sky with their wonder and purity. Juniper almost did a happy dance, though that would have surely ruined the moment.

"So you love me?" Juniper asked, eyes widening in hope.

Julian hesitated, and the fireworks faded to dim little bursts of dust. "Woah, woah, woah. That's a little fast. You can't fall in love with someone in a week. It's...impossible."

Juniper repeated, "Impossible."

"Yeah." Julian crossed his arms, not looking like he believed it. "Right."

"Good," Juniper said again.

"Juniper...have you ever thought that maybe, I dunno, you don't really love me? That you just love the idea of love?" Julian swallowed hard. "It just seems to me like you keep waiting for some epic romance or amazing rescue...I just wish you could see that you don't need, I dunno. I just wish you could see yourself the way I see you."

She groaned, slapping her forehead in pure disbelief at the levels of her naivety. "Sunbeam above, I am a case."

"I just—I just can't, Juniper. Trust me," Julian said, looking miserable. "You'll find someone amazing who deserves you. That's not me. I'm not someone to love. And besides, I have so many, um, princely duties to attend to. I would never see you."

"I get it," Juniper said dejectedly. She wrapped her arms around herself, drawing back from him. She stumbled a bit. "You don't need to make up excuses." Suddenly she knew that she would always be the girl who fell in love with mist, and every other thing that could easily slip from her grasp.

"It's not. An excuse, I mean. There's some stuff I have to deal with."

Juniper narrowed her eyes. "Can you tell me?"

"No."

"Why not?"

"Can't say."

"If you would just say you do not like me, that would be a lot easier to deal with than whatever it is you are withholding." The words were coming out her mouth fast now, tumbling out like a rushing river. "Whatever it is, just say it. Then I can walk away with a high head and a slightly bruised ego. I may not know what I deserve, but it is certainly not this."

"I...I can't."

"Then I have my answer."

"Wait—"

His words were cut off by a rumbling sound coming from the castle.

On a second listen, she realized it wasn't coming from the castle...it was coming from the ground. The snow was shaking, white flakes flickering like candlelight, locked in a dance with the rumble coming from afar.

Juniper saw a flash of purple in the corner of her vision. No. It was coming from a window of the palace, a purple spark sailing through the air and landing at their feet. A firework and a fire all at once. It flashed, then disappeared in the wash of snow, burrowing like a hedgehog in the ground. The purple looked like the remains of a magic spell. And the only person Juniper knew with purple magic was the Queen. It was too much to hope that a servant girl had learned magic, right?

She swallowed hard, dreading what was coming next. A giant? Wolves? A magic house made of candy that would squeeze them to death? A billion thoughts raced her mind, yet she knew that whatever was about to happen, it was not going to be good.

"Think we have time to run?" Jules asked.

"Probably not," Luca answered.

"Why can we never have a break?" Juniper lamented.

A spike of something brown shot up into the sky like the beanstalk, something prickly and rough, sending snow scattering as it went.

A giant thorn branch.

Of course it was a giant thorn branch.

Juniper dived out of the way of the branch, elbows skidding across the cold snow. She jumped to her feet as another brown, sharp thorn burst from the floor in between her hands. Rolling to the side, she barely avoided it as it impaled the air where she had been.

A thorn rose up from the ground near Luca's feet, sending dirt, snow, and rocks flying into Juniper's face and cutting little nicks in her arms and legs. She longed for a time when this was not normal. Evading a massive bush of thorns popping up from the ground, that is.

Luca managed to jump out of the way in time, his foot catching slightly on the brown mass but otherwise okay. He clambered away on all fours, and Juniper hated thinking it, but he looked like a wolf moving through the snow.

"Juniper, look out!" Julian yelled from a few feet away, waving his arms like crazy.

That wasn't very helpful, as he had not told her which way to look. The thorn-thing could rise from anywhere, so she just beelined to him like a madwoman, her arms flailing around. She didn't dare look behind her for fear of a thorn branch chasing her.

Luckily, that didn't happen, and Juniper made it safely to where Julian stood.

Thorn branches were rising rapidly into the air now, curling and connecting and forming a huge mass. A bramble. Was that what thorn bushes were called? Okay, it was not the time for that question.

"We have to get away from here," Juniper said. "As far as we can. The thorns cannot extend into the thickened forest, right?"

"You got it, boss." Julian saluted her with two fingers.

He ran towards the forest, away from the winding wall of thorns, his footsteps the only sound amidst the creaking and groaning of the branches intertwining in the air like writhing worms.

"Come on!" Juniper called Luca. He was kneeling in the snow, doting a look known only among people who had just avoided impalement, which was probably a select few.

Together, they followed Julian into the night, zig-zagging through a forest of thorns and hulking branches. By watching the ground and seeing where it shook a little, they were able to locate the thorns before they even burst through the snow. It was risky and it was scary and it was undeniably exciting.

Suddenly, Juniper saw the snow in front of them tremble, the area where Luca was about to step on.

"No!" She screamed and threw herself at him, knocking both of them into the snow. The place where Luca had been about to step let forth a new thorn. Juniper was strewn across Luca, both of them goggling at the spot where Luca had just been. He would have been turned into a shish-kebob if not for Juniper's body-slam.

Luca blinked. "Thanks for tackling me. Though I've gotta say, I never thought it would come to this."

"Not in a million years," Juniper agreed, still wide-eyed.

"Are you scared right now?"

"Terrified."

He grinned as a response, and they jumped up, clearing the distance to Julian in a few bounds. Thankfully leaving the maze of thorns behind them, they reached the thick forest. Out of breath but alive.

Dozens of branch-like stalks had been rising from the ground, an army of thickets winding themselves together. Soon enough, it was a huge mass of prickles and branches. A new type of forest, one that was intricate and impassable. More wall than hedge.

Hedge. That was the word.

A thorn hedge. A huge, thick, terrifying thorn hedge.

It rose up into the sky, intimidatingly marking its territory. Juniper saw that it wound around the entirety of the castle in a huge circle, criss-crossed branches forming a dense and dark thicket. The castle could barely be seen, black stone a haze behind brown thorns. Fifty feet of thorns, long as swords, threatened every inch of ground.

"So," Julian said, regarding the massive thorns warily. "I don't suppose sitting in the snow and crying is still on the table?"

21

The Wicked Queen

"Fae," The Queen said gleefully, watching Kyra's reaction carefully. Kyra clamped her mouth shut in order not to show anything she was thinking.

Callista continued, "Halbling means half-faerie. Your boyfriend's mommy was a faerie *tramp* who bred this little abomination. It's so cute how you both look right now! Like you both want to murder me! If that isn't couple goals, I don't know what is."

"He," Kyra said slowly, brain not working, "is not my boyfriend." *Nice going, Kyra, really got her with that one!* It sounded futile to the insults that had just been thrown at them, but she couldn't think of anything else to say. Nothing would compensate for everything she was feeling. If only she knew how to *say* what she was feeling. Like a storm of her own making was brewing inside. Demanding to be set free and unleashed not only on the Queen, but on Kyra herself.

"My mother was not a tramp." Cal's voice was quiet, his annoying calm ever-present. "You're just jealous that my father loved her so much and your husband doesn't love you."

The Queen's eyes flashed with something unreadable. "Loved her so much that he left her? And you, too? He probably couldn't stand the sight of you both. Faeries, hiding amongst humans like rats scurrying through the floorboards. Disgusting." She wrinkled her nose and made a face.

Their conversation seemed like it was a million miles away and buried under a thousand feet of sand. Kyra felt faint, slow, sluggish and stupid. Major emphasis on stupid.

"Heritage doesn't make me disgusting. It's what's in my blood that makes me half-faerie. A halbling. But it's what's in your soul that makes you evil, " Cal said coolly. He looked off wistfully as if he was repeating something he had heard from long ago. "It doesn't matter where you come from if you know who you are."

Kyra stared at him, for once in her life rendered silent. She had told him so much about her, had let him into her life so fast. And all this time, he had never cared about her at all. Not even enough to tell her that he was fae. That was a pretty big deal, she thought. The fae were the known enemies of humans, people who tricked and tortured them for centuries. Wars and battles had been fought against the Dark Ones because every faerie had been a blight on humanity. The fae from a thousand years ago had brought nothing but horror and hurt. War. Aazagonia was born from one of those wars. For centuries, her forefathers had slaved away tirelessly under fae overlords who belittled and wrought pain on them. The Aazagonian War a thousand years ago had flipped the power balance. But even her kingdom's past showed her that faeries were evil. Fearsome.

She felt so stupid, like the universe was playing some big joke on her. Like she was an idiotic tourist who was being duped by some side-show magic act. The way the Queen was looking at her sure felt like it. But the way Cal wouldn't meet her eyes, the way he didn't even look at her, made her feel like the biggest idiot of all.

The Queen said, "Don't spit wisdom at me, halbling, when you have the blood of murderers and tricksters."

"Quit talking. Let me think." Kyra's voice was deadly low. Her head pounded as strong as a dragon's heartbeat.

For some reason, that shut both Cal and The Queen up for a few moments.

When Kyra finally sorted out a few thoughts in her head, she said, "Call him scum again. I dare you."

"And you'll what? Fight me?" The Queen asked, a cat-like smirk resting on her face. She gestured to the guards holding swords to their backs. "Go ahead and try."

Kyra bit the inside of her lip, using her entire willpower to not strike The Queen down where she stood. The guard would run her through if she tried. The Queen needed them alive, sure, but nothing was stopping her from hurting them. So she kept still, too still, still enough that she was sure the entire room would crumble in the weight of the silence that stretched for millennia. Cal was not scum, and no one should ever call him that.

Cal, who was half-fae. Who had lied to her all this time. Who she didn't even know.

Cal had pretended all this time to care about her when really he had been lying from the moment they met. All her life, people had lied to Kyra. Her father had told her that he would always keep her safe. *Lie.* Juniper always said that everything would be alright. That hope was the way to win. *Lie.* Her real mother had told her that she would never leave her. But she had; she had died. *Lie.* Kyra told herself that she wasn't scared of anything. She told herself that nothing could ever hurt her. She told herself that she was a fortress, strong and emotionless and unbreakable as the moon. *Lies.* Cal and his easygoing smile. All one big, fat *lie.*

Callista tucked one ankle behind the other. "Next on the agenda is a little trip down memory lane. Want to see something exciting?"

"Go fall in a bottomless pit." Kyra strung together a sentence somehow.

"Please," added Cal.

Her stepmother frowned. "You're supposed to say, 'Yes, mother, I would love to see something exciting.'"

Grinning without mirth, Cal said, "Yes, mother, I would love to see something exciting."

"You two are insufferable, honestly." Callista groaned, then turned back to the mirror, walking around the bed to stand in front of it. She said, "Time for a little blast into the past. Ready to understand why Juniper's been a bit glowy lately?"

Kyra's mouth went dry. "You know why she has magic?"

"Honey," Callista said, tossing her black hair over her shoulder. "I put it there."

"You *what?*"

The Queen ignored her, gazing deep into the mirror. "Dark One here, of all matters tragic, show me of my path to magic."

The mirror swirled, and then it was still. It said, "Queen of heartbreak and of glass, I will show you of your past."

Kyra suddenly felt dizzy as the world spun around her. Black spots appeared at the edge of her vision. "...Cal?" She asked, though she didn't know why she was asking. Nothing made sense. When losing consciousness, things often didn't make sense.

The last thing Kyra remembered before everything went dark was the haunting refrain of a violin, loud and clear against a roaring river.

* * *

"I love you," A woman's voice said, giggling. "I love you more than every blade of grass in the world."

"That is a lot of grass."

"Well, that's why I said it, you dolt!" Laughter trickled in. "It's a lot of love."

Kyra jolted upwards. She had been lying flat on her back. Cal was next to her, looking just as confused and bleary. She was about to ask if he was alright, but she stopped herself.

Liar. Half-faerie. Cal. *Liar.*

They were in some sort of shack, in the middle of a kitchen. Daytime light lit the area with joy and warmth. Hydrangeas petals lined the floor, sprinkled about on the stained carpet like scattered pink stars.

Kyra looked around to find where the voices were coming from. Her jaw dropped.

Standing before her, dressed in a simple, flowy frock, was Callista. But she looked younger, at least by ten years. She had her hair braided neatly, no makeup or jewels adorning her figure. She was...smiling, but not how she usually did, fake and feline. It looked like a real smile, a happy smile, a smile that Kyra had never seen her wear.

Callista was looking at someone, tall and thin. He had the same dark skin as Juniper, the same kind brown eyes and tightly-wound curls. The way he looked at Callista made Kyra feel sick. He looked at her as if she hung the moon and stars. *Juniper's father.* Were they in the past? Had the mirror transported them there somehow?

"Callista?" Kyra asked tentatively, standing up in shock.

Her stepmother didn't seem to hear her. She was just staring at the man in front of her, eyes shining, with love. *Love.* It made Kyra sick to know that the Queen was capable of such human things. It was unnatural—like pigs flying.

Cal shook his head. "They can't hear us. It's a memory. The Queen is showing us a memory." Smart-alec.

"My flower, I love you too, no matter how doltish you think me,"

The man said, his voice soft, his smile sweet and shy. He pulled her into his arms, holding her tight. "But you know we cannot do this."

"But why?" Callista asked, nuzzling into his arms. "Jakob, I know it's possible."

The man—Jakob—sighed. "Yes, it seems possible. But that does not make it right. Godfather Death decreed war many moons ago, but that did not make it right. Just as the lily blooms and dies, so must we let life pass."

"Juniper misses her pet."

"It is the way of things."

Callista looked at the floor, where Jakob couldn't see her face. But Kyra could. Callista's eyes were shining with something different now. Something eager and ambitious. Something dark and greedy, and it looked like the Queen Kyra knew. Not this stranger who giggled and told people she loved them. "I've heard rumors that the fae are still lurking in the Northern Forest. I could find them. I know it. It's as if I hear them calling...I could find a way to bring Juniper's bunny back to life."

"To do that would cheat death itself. It is wrong." Jakob's voice was stern now.

The moment passed. "You're right, like always," Callista said finally, her smile returning. "Let's go find Juniper."

The two walked out a door leading to a garden. Kyra could hear a little girl singing softly. *Down by the Juniper tree...*

Suddenly, the memory vanished, the kitchen swirling around them and the petals on the floor rushing up at her in a blur.

Kyra was now standing in a dusty field, rain falling down like tears. Cal was next to her, again, his hair looking blacker with the water.

"Where are we now?" Kyra asked. "Another memory?"

He lifted his chin at a place behind her, his expression dark as the clouds above. "I think I know." Thunder rippled through the sky as he said this. Lightning lit up the sky in all its terrible glory.

Kyra turned to see that in the center of the bare plain was a group of people dressed in green mourning colors. A rectangle hole had been dug in the ground. A grave. It was a funeral, then.

In the middle of the procession was Callista, her head hung low, her hair sticking to her cheeks. The rain mixed with the tears falling from her face, until Kyra couldn't tell which was which.

Beside her, small and delicate looking, was a young Juniper. Kyra's heart caught in her throat. Juniper looked the same, save for longer hair and wider eyes. She was shorter, too, of course, but Juniper was always short. Kyra was running to the funeral in an instant.

"Kyra, wait!" Cal ran after her. The rain fell harsher now, the lightning in the sky cracking like a whip. Rumbles echoed as if giants stepped across the field in grief.

Kyra came skidding to a stop in front of young Juniper, reaching out to wipe a tear away. Her hand passed through her as if she were a ghost.

Little Juniper looked up, tears slicking her face in heavy streams.

"It's going to be okay," Kyra said. "I promise."

The girl did nothing to acknowledge that she had heard her. Then Cal's hand was on her shoulder, pulling her away. "She can't hear you." Kyra cherished his warmth in the cold, but she shoved his hand away anyways.

"Don't," Kyra warned, surprised that her voice was shaking.

Cal didn't look away from her, lightning framing him against the dusty flats. He didn't reach out to her again, but he stayed near.

"Miss?" One of the funeral-goers was prodding Callista. "Do you have any final words for your husband?"

Kyra stared down at the grave, finally seeing who had passed away. She was greeted with the sunken face of Jakob, Juniper's father.

She shuddered, wishing she could avert Young Juniper's eyes. Lightning illuminated the sky, making Jakob look twisted and wrong. Like he should've been laughing and playing with his daughter. Not in the ground.

In his hands, clasped tight and crumpled, was a single pink lily.

Callista's voice was hard as steel. Eyes lacking sorrow. Voice calm. Mouth firmly set in a thin line. Her flowing tears betrayed her. "We will meet again one day." Then she reached down into the grave, and, with a gasp from the other mourners, she wrenched the lily from the dead man's grasp.

With that she grabbed a sobbing Juniper's hand, tearing her away from the funeral as a grave-digger piled mounds of dirt onto Jakob's still body.

Kyra didn't watch them go.

She only stared at Jakob's closed eyes as the dirt covered them, and the world around her swirled again, dirt and lightning crackling around her as a new scene took place.

Now they were in a courtyard, it looked like, but made of moss and flowers instead of stone. The walls were covered, every inch, in greenery and colorful plants. The barest hint of snow lined the ground, but Kyra didn't feel the cold. *It's a memory,* she reminded herself, Jakob's lifeless brown eyes—Juniper's eyes—still etched in her mind.

The courtyard had a man in it. He was wearing a long black cloak, draped across him humbly, as if the cloak was unworthy of gracing this man's shoulders. His back was turned to her and Cal. Pale as dawn, his hand reached out to a budding flower. A voice came from behind them.

"You look rather brooding," The voice said musically. Kyra turned.

Callista was walking into the court, wearing an elegant, ruffled dress. Silver flashed upon her brow. The Aazagonian crown. This was a memory from after she had married Kyra's father, then.

The man turned, pulling his hood down. Kyra's heart stopped. He was the most handsome man she had ever seen, snow-cold and impossibly beautiful. He had white hair, though he looked only a few years older than her. Looks could be deceiving, she reminded herself as his orange eyes glowed like fiery embers. His ears were pointed slightly, and he had twisting orange lines that covered his skin like grapevines. The marks, the eyes, the setting...the man could only be...he could only be...one of the Dark Ones.

A *faerie*. Callista was meeting with a faerie. She had never seen one in real-life, if this even counted as real life. No one had, for thousands of years. Kyra had about a million questions, none that she could properly articulate.

Instead, she said to Cal, her breath coming quickly, "He's got orange eyes."

"Observant," Cal said, gaze trained on the fairy man. "But the first thing I noticed is that he's a faerie." His voice caught on that word—faerie. Cal, the faerie liar.

"I noticed that, too."

"What's your stepmother doing with a Dark One?"

"Not having a gossip sesh, I'm sure," Kyra said, as the beautiful fae man began to speak.

The faerie said, "I am brooding. Come to grovel again, have we, Your Majesty?" That voice...it sounded so familiar. As if Kyra had heard it before. It was deep and strong like a song of sorrow, like a wretched poem detailing failed wars.

"That's the voice," Cal whispered. "The voice from the mirror."

Callista raised an eyebrow. "I suppose I have. But I prefer to call it calling in a favor, not groveling. Your Majesty."

Sunbeam above.

"He's the fae king!" Kyra half-shouted, shaking Cal mercilessly. "Cal! This guy's the king of the fae!"

Cal looked deeply disturbed, ignoring how Kyra shook him. "What does the Queen want from the faerie King?"

"Please," Callista said to the fae king, "I'm not asking a lot from you."

The Faerie King shook his head at a flower hanging over his head, sighing as if he had witnessed centuries of those same flowers bloom and die. All flowers wilted, and in their place remained nothing more than memories. Flickerings of the fallen to make way for the new. He plucked it, and Kyra saw with a jolt that his fingertips were glowing red. *Magic. The magic of the fae.* "It is a lot to ask, you understand? The spell would require years to be completed. It has many rules and ingredients."

"I'll do anything."

"Those," The King said, voice dripping with venom, "are unwise words."

Callista didn't bat an eye. "I don't care. I want him back. I want my Jakob back."

No. By this time, her husband would be dead. He would be dead and buried in the dirt, Kyra was sure of it. She had seen the memory of his funeral a few moments ago. He was gone...it wasn't possible. But the look in Callista's eyes said otherwise.

"You are married anew, are you not?"

"I am." Callista's eyes had hardened. "But we do not love each other. I married him because of you. You told me, remember? 'Marry into the royal family, and I will give you what you ask.' I have done exactly as you said. It is insufferable, living in the castle. But I wait it out in hopes that you will return the favor."

"You have helped me. So I will help you. First, you must do one more thing for me." The King let the flower in his hand fall. It traced a whirling path to the floor before finally resting in the powdery snow.

She didn't hesitate. "Yes. Anything."

"Once every ingredient is assembled and ready, you must take power of Aazagonia. The king there, since he is born with royal blood, has more say in the matters of the kingdom, no?"

"He does."

"You will imprison him when the time is right. Then you will ascend to the throne as it's sovereign ruler."

"But why do you want me to be the sole ruler of Aazagonia?" Callista asked, eyebrows furrowing in confusion. "I hardly see how that helps you."

The King's cold face was unflinching. "Once you have the rulership, you will hand it over to me."

"I see. Even the fae are lulled to power," Callista said. "Deal. Now tell me the ingredients for the spell."

So that was why, in the present, the Queen was taking power for herself so suddenly. She was going to give it over to the fae King in exchange for...something.

"The ingredients are such as these: The person who performs the spell must be the deceased's most loved. That is the most important thing. Then you shall obtain something the deceased held in his hands. Then you will need two conductors of magic, one of the light and one of dark. That is all."

Callista looked troubled. "Humans can't do magic, though."

"There are...loopholes. I shall teach you them, little queen. I will teach you the way of the Dark Ones. You are worthy. Of all people, you have found the court of the fae-folk. For that, you must be special indeed."

"I know I am." Callista smiled. "I heard the call, and I answered."

The words chilled Kyra to her core. Not because they were eerie. But because Kyra herself had thought the very same thing countless times—the call to magic. The knowledge that she was different. It was like looking in a mirror. And she did not like what she saw.

"The first thing we must accomplish is teaching you magic," continued the King. "A long-forgotten form, from when the fae and the mortals were allies instead of enemies. Magic that will be strong enough for this spell. You are lucky that I am so willing to help."

"I'm thankful."

"It will take many years. Are you prepared for this?"

"Yes." Callista's eyes shone. "More than you know."

The King looked pleased, his bare feet padding in the snow as he crossed over to where Callista stood, no longer looking away from her. His amber eyes looked like little fires concealing miniature worlds of flame. "And you have two mortals in mind to be the light and dark conductors?"

"I assumed I could use faeries for that part."

"No." The King's voice was harsh now, the light dancing in his eyes gone. "The fae cannot use the magic of the light. And if you have one conductor as a human, the other must be human as well. You see the difficulty of this spell? It will require a great deal of secrecy and effort. The humans you choose must be worthy as you are."

"And you will teach them the magic?" Callista asked.

"Light and dark magic cannot be taught. I will be teaching you a different kind of magic, an old kind that humans used to use long ago. Light and dark magic have never been known to be used by humans. So the people you choose cannot be taught. The magic must be planted in them, in their very veins like faerie newborns. I will show you how...though I must find out a way first. I will travel to the scholars of my people, high in the mountains. They alone will know a way to give humans the unknowable magic. When the time is right, and you have learned what I must teach you, the conductors will start to show their magic to the world with a little...prompting...on your part." The King's face looked long in the shadows of the flickering candles.

"And you are helping me for what gain, exactly? Why do you want to rule a mortal kingdom when you have the spoils of your own people?"

"Must I tell you? We all have our secrets."

"I'm not a fool."

"If you insist. There is war brewing amongst the fae and humans again. Ruling both a fae and mortal kingdom would lessen my worry. I could join whichever side is winning at whatever time with no hindrance to me." The King looked away once more. "Now, do you know who shall be your conductors?"

"I have two people in mind," Callista said darkly.

Then the room swirled again, in a waterfall of flowers and amber eyes.

Kyra was in a familiar place, a place with many happy memories.

"Where are we now?" Cal asked.

"My favorite place in the world." Kyra could almost smell the baking goods, taste the gorgeous piles of chicken and roasted things and cakes. "The kitchen of the castle in Aazagonia."

White walls and clean, swatched floors lined the kitchen, with servants and chefs bustling around in a fervor, hurriedly simmering and cooking different elaborate meals. Kyra could see the familiar faces of many beloved servants that had chased her from this same kitchen years ago.

And then the entire business of the kitchen stalled, servants freezing and standing at attention. They turned to face the door.

The Queen was silhouetted in the darkness from the hall, a twisted grin on her lips.

"Your Majesty," said the Head Cook. "To what do we owe this honor? Was there a problem with one of your meals?"

"On the contrary." Callista waved her hand nonchalantly. "Lunch was excellent, breakfast, too. I'm sure dinner is going to be just as extraordinary. But may I talk to you for a moment? Everyone else can get on with their work. I don't want to keep you waiting."

The kitchen returned to its hasty work, clanging and sizzling echoing around.

Callista crossed over to the head cook, clutching something in her claws, something barely shining in the dim kitchen light. Kyra couldn't see what it was. Maybe she didn't want to.

"What can I do for you, Your Majesty?" Cook asked expectantly, absent-mindedly adjusting her white-topped hat.

The Queen said, "Oh, nothing much. I was wondering where my daughter's meals are?"

Cook squinted uneasily, then led the Queen over to two shining plates of gorgeously dressed turkey that made Kyra's mouth water even at this moment when so much information was being thrown at her at once.

"Here they are. Two plates of roast, right here." Cook nodded her chin at the two meals, laid side by side.

"I'm trying to get the girls to take vitamins," The Queen said. "For their growth, of course."

"Of course."

"And...the only way they'll eat them is if they're placed in your delicious cooking," Callista said like she was sharing a secret, a secret only between her and Cook.

"Oh!" Cook beamed, looking happy that her food had been complimented. "You want to put the girls' vitamins in their meal! How clever!"

"Perfect." Callista smiled. "By all means, go on with your work. I don't want to interfere with your schedule."

"Thank you kindly, Your Majesty." Cook bowed deeply before scurrying off to pull a batch of yellow potatoes from a pot, pushing away the trails of smoke with her fingertips.

Callista, however, hadn't taken her eyes off the meals meant for Kyra and Juniper—a younger Kyra and Juniper. She pulled her hand up, the hand that was holding the glinting something.

It was two vials, light and dark. The light vial was glimmering with sparkles and sunshine. The other vial, the dark vial, was a shade of black unlike anything Kyra had ever seen. So dark, it sucked in the light around it.

Kyra held her breath as the Queen uncapped the white vial, pouring it's shimmering contents on the plate marked, *Juniper*.

The Queen poured the other vial on the plate labeled Kyra.

Kyra barely had time to process what was happening, as the scene was swirling, and the memory drifted away. It was quickly being replaced by a new scene, a terribly familiar scene.

A riverbank.

This new memory was near the Aazagonian castle, on the banks of a river that Kyra had spent her childhood playing by, swimming in, and pushing people into. The rushing river was clear blue, trickling along pleasantly. It boasted a huge oak tree, with arms that stretched wide that were good for climbing. Moss lined the thick branches. The grass was green and full. A bird could be heard tweeting in the distance, the melody sweet and becoming. Summertime in Aazagonia, a summer from long ago. A summer that should have been perfect, if not for the events of this day.

Kyra's stomach dropped to her ankles when she heard the echoes of a young girl laughing. It was a laugh that came echoing from the top of the hill leading down to the river. A laugh that was as familiar as any.

Young Juniper, about ten years old, came racing down the hill, her curly hair flying out behind her as she slipped on the grass and tumbled the rest of the way down.

"Kyra, come quick! It's lesson time!" Young Juniper called out, laughing all the while.

And then, Kyra watched in a trance, as someone came beelining down to the river. It was Kyra herself.

But it was a younger version, about eleven years old. Her hair was cropped short (after an accident with her hair getting stuck in a beehive) and her skin was tan and freckled with the summer sun.

Kyra watched in stunned silence as her younger self waded ankle-deep in the water, hiking her long dress up to her knobby knees.

"It's you." Cal was appalled. "It's you, but as a kid."

"Your mind astounds me," Kyra half-heartedly said, knowing what happened in this memory. She remembered this day by the river's edge. She remembered it and hated it, hated herself for re-membering it. Her stomach dropped and began doing loopty loops, rolling over and over in an endless pattern of dread. She said, voice a bit too high, "Obviously that's me. Do you know anyone else with such drop-dead gorgeous looks?"

"Shh, they're talking," Cal said, but he did not answer.

But she had no time to think on this more, as the younger version of herself had indeed begun talking.

"Your mom's not expecting me to play the violin, too, right?" Young Kyra said as she stomped around in the water, sending sparkling droplets flying through the air in graceful arcs. Spotting a school of grass-green fish, the young girl raced after them. A devil-ish grin lodged itself on her face as she tried to catch the green-blue splashes of color in the clear water.

Young Juniper shook her head, sitting down in the grass. Her yel-low dress poofed out around her, making her look like a flower with petals forming a halo around her. "I do not think so. We only have one violin. It belonged to my father."

"Yuck," Kyra said. "Learning is boring, don't you agree?"

"No."

"You're the only one."

Young Juniper smiled at Kyra's younger self fondly. Kyra remembered what it was like to have just gained a sister, to be unsure and unwilling, even, to get close to her. But against all odds, Kyra and Juniper had become sisters. And Kyra wouldn't have had it any other way.

"This is really weird," Cal said, looking confusedly between Young Kyra and Kyra.

Kyra didn't say anything because she knew what was about to happen. She knew that in a few moments, someone would climb over the hill and change Kyra's life for good. What once had been days of starlight and adventure shifted to fear and eventually, strength. This marked the day that any hopes of having a kind stepmother were dashed.

"Tah, tah, my girls, your mother has arrived!" Callista's voice came, and then she was there, walking down the hill in a flowy pink dress, a violin in hand. She knelt down next to Juniper, pulling her to her in a quick hug. Juniper giggled as the Queen made a mock show of bowing low to her daughters.

Callista ruffled Juniper's hair. She said, "You look so much like your father, darling."

Juniper smiled up at her shyly. "Time for my lesson?"

Callista's expression soured once she saw Kyra dancing round in the water, the hem of her dress soaking and her sharp elbows squawking like a chicken. Callista donned a smile, then said, "Come along, Kyra. You'll watch Juniper play."

Kyra shrugged and bounded out of the water, spraying it with each step. "Sure."

"Play now, Juniper." Callista handed her daughter the violin.

Juniper hesitated, then cradled the violin in her arms like it was glass, scared to break it maybe, or scared to even touch it. The last thing she had of her father. The last memory of him. Juniper began playing that haunting tune, the bow of the violin sliding over the strings in symphony, ringing out against the warm summer air. It sounded like snow and ice and glass, like a courtyard of flowers or ageless amber eyes. It sounded like all of those things, but most of all, it sounded like magic.

"Do you want to try?" Juniper asked Kyra, handing it to the girl.

Kyra nervously took it, holding it awkwardly. "No, I don't need to."

"I insist," Juniper said.

Callista was watching with a dark gaze, eyes fixated on the violin. Her lost husband's violin.

Kyra pulled the bow against the strings, and it rippled out an ear-shattering screech that made everyone wince. Kyra's fingers curled around the handle. "I can't do it." She let her hand fall into the grass, the tip of the violin scratching against a rock.

That made a sound similar to the music Kyra had been making, a loud, awful sounding SCRATCH.

"You insolent girl!" Callista shrieked, ripping the violin from Kyra's hands and shoving her to the floor. "You have ruined my husband's violin!"

"That's not my Dad's." Kyra looked confused.

"Not—not that husband," Callista said angrily, her curls falling from her bun and splaying out. "Are you even going to apologize?"

"Jeesh. I'm sorry," Kyra said, hastily deflecting. "It's just a stupid violin."

Callista's gaze turned murderous. "What did you just say?"

"I said your violin is stupid."

The Queen's hand was out and cracking across Kyra's face in a stinging slap, sending her flying backward once more. Callista did it again, and again, slapping her across her face multiple times before curling her fists and saying, "You ugly little wretch! How dare you? You disrespect the dead like this? Answer me!"

Kyra looked up at her with tear-filled eyes, clutching at her face. "I—I'm sorry, I didn't, I didn't—"

"But you did it."

"Why...why did you...?" Kyra asked miserably.

"Oh, you getting hit isn't my fault," Callista said, her voice low, "you brought this on yourself, Moon's Child."

"That doesn't make—" Kyra was cut off by another slap across the face, sending her crashing into the floor, her hands clawing at the dirt in fistfuls, holding on to anything, anything to take her mind off the pain.

Callista turned to Juniper, who was watching the encounter fearfully, eyes wide like a deer. Callista said, "Play on, Juniper. I am simply teaching your sister how to behave."

Juniper's lip trembled as she raised the violin to her chin, hesitating to play. Maybe she was wishing she could run to her sister. Maybe she was too afraid. A million what-ifs and maybes played across the girl's face in that moment. None were to be.

"Don't look at me like that, Juni-tree," Callista said softly. "I don't want to hurt Kyra. If she hadn't scratched your father's violin, none of this would have happened. It's her fault, don't you see? Not mine at all."

Juniper nodded slowly, looking like she was going to be sick. She began playing the bittersweet tune as Callista crossed over to Kyra, rearing her hand back in a hard fist.

The haunting melody echoed as the scene swirled away into black.

22

Through the Thorns

The hedge maze loomed tall over Juniper and the others, blocking out the sky with its thorns and brown branches. Luca was in full wolf form, sliding through gaps that no regular human could fit through. Contorting his slim grey body through holes in the thicket, he turned back to Juniper to let her know which way to go. Juniper would then follow him. Knife in hand, she would cleanly sever thorn from branch. Once she finished with the thorns, Julian would step forward and use his sword to part the way.

It was entrancing, watching Julian with his sword, slicing and chopping through the thick brambles. Juniper watched again and again as he raised his sword high into the air before bringing it down against a branch and splitting it cleanly in two. They made their way towards the castle at an agonizingly slow pace. So slow, she was pretty sure she saw a snail beating them.

It went on like that for a while, Luca navigating, Juniper disarming, and Julian chopping. The steady flow of sounds became a rhythm, like a beating of a drum.

On and on until Juniper couldn't take it. The cold didn't even bother her anymore, because she was dripping with sweat. Probably smelling extremely bad. Probably so bad, Julian would never even look her way again.

"We should take a rest," Juniper finally said, sitting down and drawing her legs near. Jules nodded, crumpling to the floor. His sword clattered to the ground and almost hit Juniper on the way down. "Hey, watch it with that," Juniper grumbled. Part of the scowl in her voice was due to the sword almost impaling her, but most of it was from their argument earlier. She was humiliated at what had happened, barely able to look Julian in the eyes.

"Sorry, Your Royal Grumpiness."

"I am not grumpy," Juniper said rather grumpily.

"Tell that to the look on your face."

And then Luca, no longer in wolf form, came bursting back through the brambles, his almond-shaped eyes bright. "Why are we stopping?"

"Too tired," Juniper said. "Need rest."

"Humans," Luca complained.

Juniper pointed out, "You know you are still human?"

"Half-human," Luca corrected knowingly. "And I'm really hungry."

Julian gave a wary look. "Don't get any ideas."

"I'm not gonna eat you." Luca crossed his arms. "Whatever. I can wait 'til we get to the castle." Luca sat down, cross-legged. Juniper studied him, envisioning the man he could become. A hunter of the night. Right now, it didn't seem possible that Luca could be anything other than sweet and kind. But Juniper knew that the dark magic of the wolves was in his blood, now. And it would make itself known very soon.

"My mom's gonna be so mad at me for being gone for so long.

I'm gonna be grounded for life." He looked off in the distance as if envisioning his mom lecturing him.

"You have a mom?" Juniper asked incredulously, then mentally kicked herself for sounding so stupid.

"No, I just showed up one day as a sixteen-year-old with no parents."

"I forgot we all have families beyond all this. That we have lives to go back to one day...that if we succeed, the queen will be gone forever, and we can get back to normal." Juniper tucked her hands underneath her legs. They were ever-present reminders of the magic dwelling within her. "I have forgotten what normal even feels like."

"Maybe life is never normal," Luca pondered. "Maybe we'll look back on this one day and think that this was normal."

"If I ever look back at this as normal, then my life will be at an all-time low." Julian chuckled. "Because this has been psycho. I've never been almost-killed this many times in one week. And that's coming from a guy who slays dragons on the regular."

Juniper cracked a smile at him, but it faltered once she met his eyes. Bravery spiked in her. She asked a question she had been waiting far too long to ask. "Julian...what is wrong with your blood?"

The smile on Julian's face disappeared suddenly, his face becoming clouded. "Nothing."

"Fine. Do not tell us. Keep us shut out."

Jules nodded after a long stretch of silence. "If I tell you, you can't say a word. We'll go on like nothing ever happened, okay? Like you don't know anything at all."

"Okay," Luca and Juniper said in sync.

Juniper sat forward, intrigued. She would finally find out what 'A prince with blood of silver and death' meant. This was a mystery that had eluded her for so long, and she was finally finding out.

"When I was a baby," Julian began, "a faerie dragon attacked my kingdom. It slaughtered dozens of people, burned down homes and ruined lives. There was no way to stop it. Maiike's army was too small. In order to bring peace, my father made a deal with the dragon. In exchange for that peace...the dragon put a curse on me."

"A curse?" Juniper found herself asking, scared for the answer. Hairs were standing up on the back of her neck, goosebumps having lifted on her skin even though she was still drenched with sweat from the arduous heft through the thorns. She imagined little baby Julian, with a huge curse on his shoulders from the start. She shuddered.

"That's my blood curse. It's tainted. Diseased, you might say. Remember when the giant Cormoran died from tasting my blood? It's because of that. If anything tastes my blood, it will murder them. But that's not the only thing the curse decreed. On the day I turn eighteen, my blood will kill me, too. The poison will kill me at midnight on my eighteenth birthday."

Silence echoed out among them. Juniper's throat closed up. She felt like she was choking. The silence stretched out long; it clawed at the edges of her.

"That is—"

"No." Julian's voice was rough, his eyes watering. "I said not to speak. Don't make this harder. Now you know, okay? Now you know."

"You're seventeen," Luca said quietly. He didn't need to explain for Juniper to know what he meant.

"I know that, huntsman. My birthday's at the end of summer."

"I am so sorry," Juniper said. She felt tears well up in her eyes and didn't care that they came falling down. To think that Julian would be gone from this world soon was too much to handle. His smile, his laugh, all gone by his eighteenth birthday. He would never get to be an adult. Never marry, never have a family or become king. He would never get to live the rest of his life. Juniper felt tears trickle down her cheeks, warm and salty and sad as the sea.

"Cheer up, guys. I'll find a way around it. I always do." Julian watched her sadly. "This is why I didn't want to tell you. I don't usually tell anyone, because look at you, you're both crying. Come here," he said, and extended his arms outward.

Juniper launched herself into his arms, wrapping her arms around his torso and holding him tightly, her tears dripping onto his shirt. Luca grabbed her hand and squeezed it tight. She said, anguished, "You will never have the life you are supposed to."

"I've found," Julian said, holding onto her, "that no one really does."

She felt tears falling onto her hair, and she wasn't sure if it was Luca's or Julian's or both.

Julian said, "I've made my peace with it. We all get our time here, right? That time could be up today, or tomorrow, or in seventy years. But we all get our time. It's not about when it ends, so much. It's about what we make of it that counts."

"When did you get so wise?" Juniper asked, crying still. Not knowing what to say or how to say it.

Julian squeezed her tight. "By hanging out with a pretty smart girl. Now can we stop this sob-fest? I thought we decided we weren't lying down in the snow and crying?"

She laughed, her tears mixing with giggles.

Luca said, sniffling and wiping his nose. "I think I got snot on both of you."

"Disgusting." Juniper wrinkled her nose to confirm their words.

"Well, you let out the entire ocean on me, Juni, so I wouldn't be talking," Luca replied, helping her to her feet and showing off his drenched shirt full of her tears.

"The ocean is nowhere near here."

"That's not what I—nevermind."

"Julian," Juniper said, understanding dawning in her. "We will find a way out of it. I do not care what it takes. I will do anything.

Magic is the lifeblood of this world. There must be a way. And if there is one, I shall find it."

"Once we defeat the Queen, I'll hold you to that promise. We have about twenty feet to cut through. Do you think you guys can make it?" Julian asked, brushing himself off and grabbing his sword. It gleamed in the moonlight, silver and ebony. Starlight and shadow. Was his blood curse the reason he couldn't attach himself to a relationship? Why he couldn't admit if he saw Juniper in that way or not? Why he couldn't pick a bride at the ball and instead chose Kyra...it was all coming together. But now it didn't quite matter. Because now everything was different.

Juniper nodded slowly, her fingers tightening around the hilt of her knife. Luca transformed into a wolf again, his bones snapping and anatomy reorganizing. Juniper hurriedly looked away as he did, trying to think of other things as the grotesque transformation occurred before her.

Luca, now in wolf form, padded forward and began guiding his way through the thicket, Juniper following and cutting off the thorns, then Jules following her and snapping the branches in half for them to walk through.

Eventually, after about a half an hour, they had managed to cut through the entirety of the brambles. Stumbling out of the thorn maze, the trio collapsed in the snow thankfully.

As soon as Juniper stepped foot in a thorn-free patch of snow, however:

The thorns disappeared.

Juniper watched in awe and annoyance as the entire hedge maze sunk back into the ground from which it had come, burrowing through dirt and snow. It was as if the thorns had never even been there at all.

"You have got," Juniper said, "to be kidding me." She fell back in the snow, staring up at the sky.

"We're right back where we started!" Luca said after transforming back into his human form. It was true. The moat lied to the right of them, the castle and its huge, unbreakable walls taunting them as if saying, *Hah, hah, you guys are losers!*

"There's no way I'm going through the moat again," Julian shook his head quickly, his wavy locks shaking around with it. "I've seen enough sea monsters for a lifetime."

"Then how are we supposed to get in the castle?" Luca's eyebrows furrowed.

"I have an idea that definitely won't work. But it might," Julian said. "One issue. It involves acting and pizazz. Which you two are sorely lacking in."

"I have pizazz!" Juniper argued half-heartedly, not even trying to deny the acting bit.

"You most certainly do not."

"I cannot tell if that is an insult."

Luca rolled his eyes. "Get on with the plan, pizazzer."

"Which is surely not a word," Juniper added helpfully.

"Not the point," said Julian. "We're going to waltz right through the front door. Not actually! You get the idea."

Juniper propped herself up with her elbow, cocking her head at the drawbridge that led into the castle walls. The two guards were still there. They could try and fight them, but that would cause too much attention. They would be captured, just like Cal and Kyra.

Carriages were rumbling down the path from the forest, entering the drawbridge after someone got out to talk to the guards for a moment. They rolled into the castle walls, daintily going on their way and not caring that there were three tear-covered, moat-smelling teenagers watching with dumbfounded expressions.

"I thought no one in Aazagonia would dare come watch the coronation!" Juniper exclaimed.

316 - BROOKE FISCHBECK

"Obviously you're wrong," Julian smirked, nodding at the carriages as they entered. "Those guys are getting in easy-peasy."

"Easy-peasy," Luca repeated, looking confused. Why did everyone always say that phrase? When they said it, she felt as if things weren't going to be easy-peasy, not peasy or easy at all.

"So what you are saying," Juniper said slowly, her mind wrapping around the idea, "Is for us to hide in a carriage and enter the palace that way?"

Julian groaned. "Not even close. My brilliant idea is for us to walk up and pretend we're nobles from a visiting kingdom. They'll let us in with no questions asked! We get to pretend to be different people, and it's way easier than fighting a giant sea faerie demon for the third time in one day!"

"Assuming we do not blow our cover or get recognized," Juniper said, "...that might actually work."

* * *

The tired-looking guard gave them a long, bored stare. "Name?" He drawled.

Juniper smiled cheekily, trying to look as inconspicuous as possible. She had wiped the dirt and snow off of her dress, and now she actually looked...presentable, at least. Presentable was a start. "Duchess Xoni of Jakar."

Juniper, Luca, and Jules were standing on the drawbridge at the check-in for the coronation. One guard, the guard before them, was holding a white piece of parchment in one hand, his lidded eyes drooping down at them like he hadn't slept in a hundred years. The other guard was sitting in a chair, passed out and snoring louder than a dragon with a cold. He had a little snot-bubble that dutifully expanded and contracted with each shuddered snore.

The tired guard waved them away lazily. "You aren't on the list."

"There must be some mistake," Julian edged in, flashing a charming smile. "We're very close personal friends of the Queen."

"Name?" The guard looked unamused.

"Duke Koh of Jakar," Julian winked, then acknowledged Juniper. "This is my wife."

Juniper held her too-wide smile, her cheeks hurting from the exertion. She then thought to tone it down. The guard looked slightly scared of her.

The guard looked from Juniper to Julian. "Your wife? You two look awfully young."

"Thank you!" Juniper said cheerfully, exaggerating with her hands as she talked like Julian did. "Too kind! I get that a lot, actually, people saying I look sixteen instead of, um, you know, my actual age. Which is very old. And you know I am not dishonest because my back hurts all the time which is a well-known adult hindrance."

Julian was just staring at her, open-mouthed. Juniper couldn't believe it either, and it had come out of her own mouth. Sometimes she wondered if her brain just stopped working once confronted with people. She closed her eyes and inwardly groaned, wanting to crawl into the forest and have the earth swallow her whole.

"I meant," the guard said, giving her a look that could rival death, "that it's impressive that you two are able to be members of the court at such a young age."

"It is," Luca finally piped in from where he was standing behind Juni. All eyes turned to him. Smile sinking, he quickly said, "Impressive, I mean. It's impressive."

"And you are?"

Luca froze. His face turned pink. "Their son."

"Their son," The guard repeated. He looked at Juniper's dark complexion, Luca's Xiangshian eyes, and Jules' fair hair. "Guess the family gene pool isn't very strong."

318 - BROOKE FISCHBECK

"I'm...adopted."

"We picked him up at the orphanage. He was a little scamp, he was." Juniper chuckled nervously, everyone looking at her with bewildered expressions. She rambled on, "I still remember the day he was born. Just like yesterday. Except I was not actually there, because he is adopted. But I can imagine it was a great day, when our son was brought into this world." Juniper couldn't seem to stop talking.

"It *was* such a great day, even though you weren't there, uh, Mom." Luca was pulling at his collar as if hot, but snow was beginning to fall. "I remember it like it was yesterday, too. It was so, uh—dark? When I was in the womb, it was dark, and then it was light. So great. I would totally recommend it."

The guard blinked. "You would recommend being born?"

"Uh. Yeah." Luca beamed wide, holding up ten fingers. "Ten-out-of-ten."

Julian put an easy arm around Luca, ruffling his hair—a bit too hard. "My son here is such a delight. Such a delight. My whole family is such a delight." He chuckled nervously, shooting daggers at Juni and Luca. Juniper reached out and pinched Luca on the cheek for good measure. The look he gave her after made her scared for her life. Julian continued, "Now may we please be granted access to the castle?"

"I already told you. You aren't on the list." The guard gave the list a quick tap with his finger.

"Listen, bud, how about I cut you a deal." Julian winked again, leaning towards the guard.

"Sir, bribing is prohibited."

"Would you be saying that if I had a pile of gold with me?"

"Do you have a pile of gold with you?" The guard asked dryly.

Julian's face dropped, his smile falling away. He sulked, "No. Not at the moment...?"

The guard just shook his head, scrunching his nose up. "Bye-bye, then. Pray to Godmother Luck that we never meet again."

Julian and Luca turned to go, when an idea dawned on Juniper.

"Wait!" She shouted, spinning back to the guard, too excited to care if the idea sucked. "What if I gave you a harp? Luca, run and get the harp!" Luca gave a nod before running off the drawbridge and into the section of the forest where they had left the horses and bags. Sitting in Juniper's would be the silver harp that she stole from the giant's house.

"A harp?" The guard raised an eyebrow. "Are you joking?"

"You have to see it first," Juniper said hurriedly.

"Trust her," Julian affirmed, but he stared at her, long and hard.

Juniper had been pulled to that harp, entranced by it like no other. She had had to have it, no matter what. But maybe that didn't apply to everyone else; maybe she had only been hypnotized by it because of her magic.

"I'll give it a look. Just know you're cutting into my break," the guard complained, then elbowed the sleeping guard in the gut. "Wake up, Kylan. You have to take a double shift, since I've been dealing with these lunatics."

"Hm?" The sleeping guard—Kylan—grumbled and sat up, blinking rapidly and rubbing his beard. "I'm up, I'm up."

"Did you see those thorn hedges like twenty minutes ago, Kylan? One almost impaled me on my way to this shift."

"I was asleep."

The guard said sourly, "Right. You didn't see the spiky thorn hedge that nearly made me a shish-kebab because you were *asleep*."

Kylan frowned. "It was my break."

"It was his break," Juniper echoed, shrugging.

"I need a raise." The guard rolled his eyes.

Luca came running back up the drawbridge, stumbling over his feet as he went. In his arms was the harp, shining silver in the moonlight. Juniper felt that small tug in her soul as he brought it up, coming to a halt next to her. She wanted nothing more than to bring it into her arms and hug it tight, play it even though she had no idea how to play a harp. She felt her eyes water as she looked at it. Maybe she didn't need to give it up just yet...

The guard looked interested now as he snatched the harp from Luca's hands. His eyes gleamed with a hunger only described as greed, sullen and sharp. Julian and Luca's eyes had glazed over with want. So the harp had the same effect on everyone...hmm. Faerie magic? Stories of enchanted shoes and wells danced across her mind.

The guard spoke slowly, "This harp...all you want for it is passage into the castle?"

Julian said, "Yep. Just passage in exchange for that awesome instrument."

"And you really are good friends with the Queen?" The guard asked, already clutching the harp tight to him, a vulture with his prey.

"I would even say best friends," Juniper nodded exuberantly, thinking of how many times the Queen had tried to kill her in the past week. Minor details.

"Fine. Get in there—quickly." The guard signaled over his shoulder, his eyes never leaving the harp.

The three hurried past him and headed towards the castle, high-fiving and giving silent looks of celebration.

Juniper felt adrenaline racing through her as if she had just won a race. It was because of her that they had been able to get into the castle! That had been her! Sure, she had kind of messed the first part up with her bad acting, but nevermind all that! She was elated that she had done something right, giddy with happiness at the excited looks that Julian and Luca were giving her.

They ran into the entryway of the Winter Palace, which was a dark, high-ceilinged place that always reminded Juniper of a church. Candles lined the walls, flickering and lighting up the room like tiny stars. It was almost pretty, the candles and their warm glow. If not for what they were celebrating.

Royals and nobles were mingling around the room, as well as peasants, too. In fact, it looked like most of Aazagonia had shown up to the coronation. People Juniper recognized from her childhood, who knew her when she was a peasant, and who knew her after, too.

"Now what?" Luca hissed between clenched teeth, trying not to draw attention to them.

"We just need to lie low and come up with a plan to find Kyra and Cal. Probably starting with the dungeon," Juniper said. "I know where it is. Kyra once got us locked in there when we were kids. Long story."

"Let's go." Luca shifted uncomfortably. "I'm scared someone's gonna recognize me."

Julian raised an eyebrow. "You're right; *you're* the one we need to worry about people recognizing, not the dead princess we have with us." His voice was rising despite himself. Julian was a naturally loud talker, Juniper had found. "But I'm sure people will recognize you."

People had begun turning to look at the newcomers with quizzical expressions. Juniper tried to quiet Julian hurriedly.

But someone in the crowd, a cook that used to work in the castle, she thought, had noticed them. The cook's jaw dropped a little, confusion crowding her features. "It's Princess Juniper!"

Oh no. Oh no no no.

"No! Princess Juniper is dead!" Princess Juniper said, eyes widening with panic.

"I would recognize my princess. It really is you!" Cook pointed at her, waving people over to her.

The whole crowd had turned to them now, staring at her and the others with shocked expressions.

"So lying low seems like it isn't gonna work," Luca whispered, voice laced with alarm.

"When do our plans ever work?" Julian shrugged.

Julian and Luca whirled around, booking it out of the entryway and towards a nearby hallway.

Guards lining the room began to shout.

Juniper gave an apologetic smile...

Then spun on her heels and ran.

The entire room erupted in shouts and chaos. Echoing after her were the surprised yells of her kingdom. It only served to make Juniper's smile widen.

"How was that for pizazz?" Juniper asked slyly as she caught up to the boys.

"Not bad," Julian replied. "I mean, it was basically a disaster, but it sure wasn't lacking pizazz."

Rounding the corner of the large room, Julian and Luca successfully made it out. Juniper was lagging a little behind, still trying to wrap her mind around what she had just done, an ear-splitting grin dominating her face. She felt fearless. She felt as if she could fly, taking off into the sky and spreading wings like an old dragon.

All of that melted away from her mind, her smile falling away, as soon as a voice traveled across the room to her ears like a sweeping desert wind.

"Hello, little princess."

Fear choked and strangled her, a clammy hand around her neck. Fear like the flash of snakeskin beneath a boy's skin, like the slimy tongue of a serpent. Like the shine of a slitted green eye in the moonlight and hair being ruffled by an ocean breeze. Fear like she was being preyed upon, tracked by a slithering beast that shared the body of a boy.

She turned to face Tora.

He was across the room, staring at her with a twisted smirk on his lips, his hands clasped behind his back. Juniper's stomach roiled as his forked tongue slid out, bidding her hello with a hissing sound.

Juniper spun and ran for her life. Heart pounding and breath catching, she surpassed Julian and Luca. Unfiltered terror was the strongest compeller.

"What's wrong?" Luca called up to her.

She didn't take the time to look at him, just breathlessly spoke. "The Snake Prince." They turned into another hallway, Juniper leading them to a doorway. "This leads to the dungeon." She slammed the door open and saw a set of spiral stairs that would take them down, down, down, into the dark and damp jail of the Winter Palace. It hadn't seen prisoners for so long; most were kept in the general dungeon back in Aazagonia. But she bet her life that Kyra and Cal would be down there, waiting in the dark.

Cold seemed to emanate off the stone walls. Tora's footsteps came from somewhere down the hallway. He would be upon them soon, would see where they were headed.

She let the door close behind them. It fell shut, dust flooding around them as it went. Footsteps echoed past the doorway, and Juniper held her breath, motioning to the others to keep quiet.

The footsteps passed away after a few moments. Juniper was able to breathe again.

Luca broke the silence. "He won't find us." His voice was hardened, as if he was trying to convince them all. Including himself.

"After you," Julian said, giving a gentlemanly bow to Juniper.

Taking a deep breath, she descended into the dungeon.

23

Daylight

Kyra's eyes slowly adjusted to the dark room.

She was in a cell. The dungeon, then. Kyra was lying on the metal floor, dirt and grime coating it. Huge bars were in a square around her, encasing her like a tomb.

"Kyra," Cal said. His voice was quiet, but it rang out across the silence. "I didn't know..."

She sat up and found herself face to face with him. Metal bars separated them. In the cell next to her, he clutched at the bar with one pale hand.

But she wasn't thinking about him at all. Only her stepmother's voice rang in her mind from so long ago. *You brought this on yourself, Moon's Child.*

"Did you see it?" Kyra's stomach turned. She pressed her forehead against the cool metal bar, biting her lip to keep it from quivering. Violin melodies seemed to be tracing their path around the room, laughing at her.

"I saw it," said Cal. "And I'm so sorry. Your stepmother was horrible to you."

"Don't," Kyra warned, her voice wobbling. "Don't act like you're my friend. You lied to me, Cal! You lied to me all this time. How could you not tell me you're half-fae?"

"I-I didn't want you to think less of me. I know the way the world hates the fae. If you thought of me like that...it-it would be too much."

"Then you don't know me at all. What makes me think less of you is you not telling me. You're making me hate you, Cal." Kyra's voice cracked, and she met his gaze, her words burning like acid.

Cal's face crumpled. His blue eyes filled with despair. "You...?"

"No. I hate *her*. I hate her, I hate her." Kyra's voice was foreign to her own ears. It sounded cold. It sounded like the Queen's. "She's horrible, yeah, but so what? Everyone in the world has their problems, so what? That makes me no different. None of it matters, anyway. People cry and they complain and they snivel because they think it matters. Even Callista has her baggage. At least I understand that none of it actually—" She stopped short, catching herself, too afraid to finish the sentence. Her eyes stung—an alien feeling.

He just looked at her with sorrow and understanding. "She hit you. You never said she hit you."

"It's not important."

"It is. You don't deserve it. No one deserves that," Cal said.

You don't deserve it.

For some reason, the words made Kyra falter in her anger. It made her stop and look up at him. She looked at him, and for the first time in a long time, she let the floodgates open. Kyra let out all of her anger, and sadness, and fear and hate. She let it all barrel out of her at once. Because she hated so much, and she had never even realized it. Hate that was buried within her like a gnarled tree's roots. Hate that had finally, finally, after years of slowly seeping through her, had clawed its ugly hands to the surface.

All this time, she had felt like less. Like it was her fault that her stepmother hated her. Kyra had never stopped for one moment to think that she didn't deserve it. She was ugly and stupid and unlovable; why wouldn't she deserve it?

But Cal had said four simple, sad words. *You don't deserve it.*

Kyra let all of it fall away, let all of it rush out of her like a waterfall.

Tears rolled down her cheeks for the first time since that day by the river. Huge, salty tears splashed to the ground.

Then a hand was on hers through the bars, warm amidst the cold. Cal didn't say anything. He just sat with her as she cried.

"Kyra." Cal said her name as if it were a bright star shining in the sky. "My grandma once told me a story, a long time ago. It was about a girl who rescued her seven siblings from the jaws of a sea monster, but in the end, the sea monster captured her. My grandma would say, 'the girl spent so much time saving everyone else that she didn't take the time to save herself.' Only when the girl managed to figure that out, did she fight her way out of the monster and save herself. I think of you as that girl sometimes. You are the bravest person I know. I knew that as soon as I saw you in the forest, and you looked at me with your stubborn gaze, and I knew."

Kyra's tears kept falling. Every time she blinked, more would fall. She couldn't tell anymore what they were for. Cal's other hand reached up to her face, making her look up at him. Through the cell bars, he rested his forehead against hers, and he continued, voice soft.

"I knew you could fight your way through anything. You are the Moon's Child. You always think it's something bad, like you're some unwanted rock in orbit. But you know what I think that means? It means you are a light that shines through the dark. Through anything, the moon shines on. Through anything, Kyra, you shine on because that's what you do. It's what you always do. It's why your mother hates you. Because she knows that you shine brighter than her."

"Cal...I..." Kyra couldn't find the right words. That was it, wasn't it? She never could describe what she was feeling. So she said all she could say, the closest thing to what she was feeling. "I feel like I'm falling."

"Falling? In love with me, then? Took you long enough."

"Shut up," she said through the tears, and a shaky smile disappeared from her face as soon as it had come. "I don't mean it that way...I mean it like, like, um..."

"Like the floor's fallen out from under you and everything you ever knew has been turned upside down?"

"Exactly."

Cal said quietly, "I felt the same way when I found out I was a halbling."

"You already said it better than I ever could. It doesn't matter. Not to me. I'm learning, Cal. Learning to forgive," said Kyra. "...Cal?"

"Kyra?"

"I don't hate you. Not at all."

"Good. I don't hate you, either."

And maybe Kyra believed those words for once.

Kyra hesitated, still gripping his hand like she did on the beanstalk, like she was slipping and his hand was the only thing holding her up. "I don't care that you didn't tell me you were a faerie. I don't. If I was in your place, I would have done the same thing. Just...just tell me everything, from now on."

"I will." Cal squeezed her hand like a promise. He repeated, "I will."

Something was still nagging Kyra, pawing at the back of her mind.

"Did you see...did you see the vials? In one of the memories?" Kyra asked, surprised and annoyed to find that her voice was nervous. "The dark and light ones?"

"Yeah, I did," Cal said slowly, as if treading lightly.

"The light vial was for Juniper. The dark one went in mine. Do you think—"

"Isn't this cute?" An unwelcome voice rang out through the dungeon. "Kyra and her halbling being all adorable." It was The Queen.

Kyra groaned, sitting up and turning to the front of the cell. "You really are the worst."

The Queen was standing outside the cell, leaning up against the wall with her arms crossed.

"We saw your memories. I'm sure Jakob would be very proud of all the horrible things you've accomplished," said Cal.

Callista's eyes darkened for a moment, her face unreadable. "It's all for him, anyway." She shook off the dark look and smiled again. "Though you have been extremely pleasant, the time for niceties has passed."

"Aw, and to think, I was just about to ask you how your day was. Full of terrible deeds and evil magic, I presume?" Kyra asked, unable to help herself.

"Nope. It was actually spent perfecting a certain fun spell to ruin your life. But I digress."

"By all means, continue," Kyra said in a bored tone, but it was to hide the spark of unease that had flared up within her. A spell to ruin her life? That didn't sound pleasant. Or fun.

The Queen asked, "Since when are you polite?"

She snapped her fingers, and sparks began to brew, twitching and jumping across her palm. Her veins became filled with a violet glow, rushing through her and reaching her eyes to make them an eerie purple, filled down to the whites.

The sparks forming in her hand began soaring from her fingers, cutting through the cell bars and making their way towards Kyra. Her eyes widened in surprise as the sparks met her temples, meshing in and filling her own veins with a similar glow.

Kyra's head swam with purple, voices echoing around her but none seeming like they were in the room with her. Distorted and far-off. Her lashes fluttered as she tried to regain a sense of balance, but her head just lolled forward. She felt drunk off of the air itself, legs numb and neck lolling.

"What did you do to her?" Cal's voice came from far away, cutting through the dizziness like a knife. His words were laced with threat. But somehow, Kyra knew he couldn't do anything but watch. The metal bars surrounding him made sure of it.

The Queen's muffled voice came then, a stark contrast to Cal's clear one. She said, "You'll see."

At her words, Kyra felt the urge to stand on her wobbly legs. She walked forward as if held up by puppet strings, guiding her towards the cell door. The clink of her forehead against the bars was the only sign that she had reached the cage door. The pain was dull and barely registered.

Everything around her was out of focus, seen through a window covered in rain. The only thing she could concentrate on was the Queen standing before her, with eyes dark as a sky without stars.

"Child of the Moon," Callista said. "Rise."

The Queen took out something gleaming gold. A set of keys. Callista unlocked her cell.

Kyra thought she might jump at the Queen, or scratch her red nail polish off, or something horrible like that. Instead, all she felt was that jittery calm flooding her senses. Anxious and peaceful all at once, not mad at the Queen at all. No, not mad or spiteful.

In fact, she *loved* her mother. Why had she ever hated her so? Kyra grinned at the Queen, a tight-lipped, warm smile. She loved her mother and would do whatever she asked, because that was what you did for someone you loved, right? Right. Good girl, Kyra dear, good girl.

The Queen said, "Go to the East Tower."

"I will go to the East Tower," Kyra repeated.

"Don't let anyone stop you."

"I won't let anyone stop me."

"There, you will find something very special. You will know what to do from there. And don't repeat what I'm saying anymore." Callista looked supremely irritated, and Kyra felt a surge of shame. She never wanted to make her mother feel bad!

"I won't repeat—got it," Kyra caught herself, giving a reassuring smile.

"Even under a spell and you manage to annoy me like no other," Callista smirked, then shooed her away. "Now go and do as I've asked."

Kyra began walking out of her cell, before someone yelled her name. Oh, it was Cal, wasn't it? She had forgotten about Cal. Funny how she couldn't seem to think straight. Why couldn't she think straight? Her mother had said something about a spell a moment ago...but loved ones didn't cast spells. Besides, her mother would never do that to her. The Queen was the kindest, gentlest, most compassionate person Kyra had ever met. She wouldn't hurt a fly! And she was very pretty, too, a thousand and one times more pretty than Juniper, she would even say.

Kyra ignored the panicked yells emanating from behind her, the yells that most definitely belonged to Cal, the little halbling boy. Whatever he was saying to her wasn't important. She just had to go to the East Tower, like her kind mother had told her to.

Cal didn't matter. Cal didn't matter. Cal didn't matter. Something repeated that in her head, over and over. Yet through the din and confusion in her mind, she thought, *Cal matters more than he should.* That was a silly thought indeed! The boy didn't matter; she had to keep moving and stop thinking about him. A little tug made itself known in her heart as she left the dungeon. She silenced it. Trivial.

And then she was already climbing the winding staircase to the East Tower. Wowee! Had she already crossed the entire castle? That sure was fast of her! It struck her as funny for some reason that she had run there! Kyra loved to run, didn't she? Gosh, she did love running. And her beautiful mother. She loved her beautiful, amazing mother. And reading, too! Reading, running, smiling, vegetables, and her mother were her only loves.

Higher and higher until she could see a window up above. Pinks and oranges burned across the sky like the strokes of a paintbrush tracing their way—a sunrise. The long night had finally ended, and with light came the promise of new beginnings. The coronation would be at noon, and the festivities must have begun last night.

Something bad was at the top of the stairs. Kyra knew it. Something very bad indeed.

The door inched closer and closer, each step bringing her nearer and nearer to the sinister presence at the top of the stairs. Uneasiness lodged itself in her stomach, but a voice in her head told her it was good and bright and happy, nothing bad at all. That made the anxiety leave and the calm return. She placed a hand on the door and gave it a shove. Kyra had never been this high in the East Tower, had never touched the door. Still, she knew that sometimes the door stuck and you needed to give it a shove, like that one door she and Jakob—wait. That wasn't her memory. That was someone else's.

But it didn't matter. Nothing mattered except shoving the door open and stepping into the tower almost robotically. Mechanically and odd. Her legs were lodging in the floor, her heels pressing against the stones as if her body didn't want her to take another step. Onward she pressed.

The room was dark save for one window with a small slip of light filtering through, one ray of pink splaying on the floor, a spear made of sun. The room was circular, with black brick lining the walls. Like the night had never left. Save for that slip of sunlight, that one reminder of the light outside. How beautiful was a single shred of light. How beautiful.

On the side of the room, next to the window, was a bed with no covers or pillow. Just a white, starched mattress, lying in wait.

In the middle of the room was a spinning wheel.

The spinning wheel was a rickety old thing, painted purple. She could tell it used to be black because some spots had been scratched off as if by someone with long, cat-like nails. Beckoning her forward, it sat there with a grinning glare.

That was the bad thing, she realized, with a dull pounding of her heart.

The spindle was silver, glinting in the dark. A shimmering toothpick of melted seashells and peppered snow.

Kyra felt her feet lurch forward, her left foot awkwardly stepping like she wasn't in control. The right foot followed, and she was making one clumsy step forward after the other. Her knees bent inward, her arms reaching out and clawing at the door frame but unable to latch on.

I want to go to the spinning wheel, her mind repeated. *My mother wants me to.*

Kyra's body seemed to hate that idea, but soon enough, she was in front of the spindle, staring down at it with a roiling stomach.

Her left hand extended outward, her index finger reaching up to the needle slowly, every molecule in her body begging her to stop.

But her finger, looking long and skinny in her vision, reached up to the spindle.

Kyra pricked her finger on the spinning wheel.

Part Three: Rise

"In those days, the world was covered in night like a blanket.
It was then the Faerie King raised his terrible sword and slashed through the dark sky with its blood-red tip.
'I shall create for my people a source of light stronger than magic!' His orange eyes were ferocious, burning with a great purpose. 'Bow and cower before the new gods!'
The Faerie King created the Sun and the Moon, in hopes that they would indeed be the highest forms of magic.
Perhaps his hopes were found to be true."

—A Faerie Myth, the Grand Storyteller of the Kingdom of Aazagonia

24

Mother Sky Flies High Above

The dungeon stretched long and dark. Rows and rows of empty jail cells, damp and dusty, lined the walls. Water dripped from the ceiling onto the floor and sometimes hit Juniper in the head, wetting her wild curls every few minutes and scaring the living daylights out of her. She watched the ceiling and figured that the moat must line up next to the dungeon. Or maybe the dungeon was underneath the moat! That would be a pretty amazing feat of architecture. Though she wasn't too fond of the idea. Gallons upon gallons of water above her, waiting to come crashing down? No thank you.

She squealed as another musty drop of ice-cold water fell on her. She almost knocked Luca out with a swinging fist before realizing that the thing attacking her was water and not some villainous bug working for the Queen.

"You realize that's just water?" Luca said as Juniper scrambled back into place like a startled deer. She understood, yes, but why should that make her any less scared?

"No, I thought it was a unicorn," Juniper grumbled in annoyance.

"What are we looking for down here, anyway?" Julian inched away from a cell that was oozing with horrid smells. He made a face. "And is there any way I can sit this one out?"

"Cal and Kyra," Juniper said. "We are looking for Cal and Kyra."

Luca squinted in the dark, then pointed. "Wait! I think I see someone."

"That's not a someone. That's a pile of...unnamed something. You know, I don't even wanna know." Julian said, wrinkling his nose. The Winter Palace's dungeon seriously needed better maintenance. Or maybe the smells helped the aesthetic of the room.

"No, up ahead. A person." Luca ran forward in the din, sprinting through rows of cells and clumps of damp, boogery-looking moss. He narrowly dodged a cell before disappearing in the dark. Juniper ran after him, Julian not far behind.

She skidded around a corner to see two cells in the furthest corner of the room.

One had no one in it, the ghost of criminals from long ago still haunting it. Scuff marks on the ground made Juniper wonder if someone had been in it more recently. Shivers ran up her spine in roaring waves.

The other cell had Cal sitting in it. His hand rested on the floor as if reaching out to the other, empty cell. Black hair hung across his face—a shield from the world.

"Cal?" Juniper knelt in front of the cell.

He looked up then. Juniper was scared to see a wild energy in his usually calm eyes. They softened once he saw Juniper and the others, but there was still something lurking under his gaze. "You found me."

Juniper said immediately, "Where is my sister?"

Cal's face crumpled.

Her legs wobbled beneath her, the world's puzzle pieces drifting away. She repeated, "Where is my sister." This time, it was not a question.

"Gone."

Juniper couldn't think of anything to say. She just stared at Cal in weighted silence.

"What do you mean, gone?" Luca asked.

"The Queen put a spell on her. Sent her up to the East Tower. I don't know if she—" his voice cracked. "I don't know if she's okay." Juniper understood what he had been about to say. *I don't know if she's alive.*

"Are *you* alright?" Juniper asked, curling her fingers around the bar so she wouldn't fall over.

"No." Cal shrugged. "But I'm happy you guys are alive."

"That is a silver lining." Juniper cracked a quick smile, but it fell away fast. "Callista didn't hurt you, did she?"

"I'm fine," said Cal. Juniper couldn't tell if he was lying. But she could tell he didn't believe it.

"Well, get him out of there." Julian nodded at Juniper, or, more likely, he nodded at her hands in the confident way only he could.

Juniper did a double take. "Me? I cannot." She crossed her arms, but immediately after she un-crossed them to hold onto the bar again, suddenly feeling very out of place.

"You can do it." Luca put a hand on her shoulder. "You've called up your magic before. I know you and I know you can do it."

"I cannot." Juniper's voice was as soft as the clouds above.

Luca said, "I know you can do it if you just try, Juniper. I believe in you."

"We all do," said Julian. "You just have to believe in yourself first."

"I am no hero," said Juniper, but she felt a twinge inside. Finally, finally, some voice within her denied that statement. Finally, some voice told her she was wrong. Was it not Juniper that had saved them in the giant's den, and Juniper that had fought the Queen the night of the ball? Juniper who had saved Cal in the candy house, and Juniper that had fought the sea faerie?

Heroes came in all forms, she realized at last. And it was not so much about being born a hero as believing in yourself enough to be one. At long last, Juniper finally believed.

She wrapped both hands around the bars, feeling the cold metal underneath her fingers. She felt her magic within, felt it burning bright inside her.

Squeezing her eyes tighter, she clamped her hands around the bars with an even tighter grip. *Help me rescue my friend. Help me.*

Heat flared in her. She opened her eyes and saw that her hands were glowing white, almost lighting up her veins with bright light. It was working!

"You just have to believe in yourself first," Juniper whispered to herself.

And she did. Juniper believed. She had always wanted people to see beyond her, see her for all she could do and everything she was. All along, she had never realized that she had to be the one to see first.

A flash of light exploded out from her, her arms almost translucent as the bars beneath her fingers turned white-hot, melting away underneath her grasp. She gasped as the bars fell away, sinking to the ground in a steaming pile of melted metal.

Cal wordlessly met her gaze from inside the cell, standing up and walking through the spot where the bars had been a few moments ago. Carefully, he stepped over the pool of burning metal. The sizzling puddle hardened in a few seconds, turning into a pile of solid silver. Juniper's own glow died down, her hands turning back to their regular dark color.

A warm feeling lingered within her like the feeling of sipping hot cocoa. She had done it.

The magic had obeyed her for once.

"Told you you could do it," Luca said with a knowing nod.

"Nice work, melty hands." Jules smiled at her. "Explains why you burned me the other day. Light magic can conduct heat. 'Sun's Child,' huh? You can conduct heat."

"What else can I do? There must be a manual I could read," Juniper said.

Cal looked past her as if distracted. "Doubtful. Besides, humans shouldn't be able to use magic, so I think you're on your own for now. Unless..." He trailed off, his distraction turning into pure shock. Juniper could practically see the gears turning in his head, the ideas locking into place.

Juniper looked down in disappointment. "Oh."

"Unless. Humans shouldn't be able to use magic...we need to get to Kyra. Now." Cal's voice was urgent. "The Queen said she was going to the East Tower. That's where Kyra was—is. We need to find her. I think the Queen's more terrible than we thought."

"More terrible? Is that even possible?" Luca asked incredulously.

"Care to let us in on your thoughts?" Julian asked. "Some of us are slower. Not me, of course. Just some of us."

"Not enough time. It's a *long* story. Juniper, take us to the East Tower, preferably a way that no one would find us." Cal was already walking, his long legs carrying him at double the pace Juniper walked. She scurried to keep up.

"I know a way." Juniper set her shoulders in determination.

* * *

They burst through the door in the East Tower, panting and flustered. The door had rusty hinges, so it had taken a harsh shove from Cal for it to open wide.

Juniper felt her world spin off its axis as she saw Kyra lying down on a small bed, her eyes closed peacefully and her hands clasped on top of her. Her golden hair was sprawled out around her like rays of sunlight.

"She is alright," Juniper said, relieved. Then she groaned. "How could she be asleep at a time like this?"

Cal knelt beside the bed, gently shaking Kyra. "Wake up, crazy. We have to go kick some royal butt."

Kyra didn't stir. Normally, she was a heavy sleeper, so that wasn't an issue. Juniper began singing anxiously at the top of her lungs, "MOTHER SKY FLIES HIGH ABOVE, AND ALL THE BIRDS SING HER PRAISE—"

"That's it; she's lost it!" Julian threw his arms up in the air incredulously.

Luca was covering his ears and wincing in pain. "Eardrums! Rupturing!"

Cal was looking at her in his funny perplexed way. "She's trying to wake her up. It should've worked. That would have woken anyone up."

Julian complained, "I think it woke up the entire kingdom."

"Boo-hoo," Juniper said, then turned to her sister. "Why is she still asleep? Is it a part of the spell...?"

She trailed off, her eyes landing on something in the middle of the room. A spinning wheel sat centered like a lead actor frozen in monologue. It was purple and daunting and gave off supremely eerie vibes. The spinning wheel resembled the one her father had owned, back when he was a tailor. In fact, it looked exactly like her father's old wheel. Her thoughts were thankfully interrupted when she saw a splash of color besides purple.

Crimson dripped from the needle.

Blood. Her stomach lurched as a drop splattered to the floor, speckling the black brick red.

Impulse guiding her more than logic, Juniper reached out to the asleep Kyra.

"What are you doing?" Cal didn't stop her.

Juniper wordlessly turned over her sister's hand, showing a calloused palm with hard lines. *The hand of a tree-climber*, Kyra would laugh.

Kyra was not laughing now. Her face was deadly still, her chest rising and falling slowly. The only indication that she was alive. Surprisingly, it was the calmest she had ever looked. All the energy and life had been sapped from her.

Juniper's eyes darted down to her sister's palm, then rested on her index finger. It was slightly curled as if protecting an injury.

There, stark and red against her tan fingertip, was a tiny point of blood. It was about the size of a needlepoint. It looked like it would fit perfectly against the spindle of the spinning wheel.

I am keeping you two alive because I need you.

The mark of blood on Kyra's finger dripped down suddenly, tracing a trail of crimson down her finger, her hand, her arm, then finally falling to the blank white mattress of the bed.

The last thing Juniper saw before the world went dark was that shining trail of blood, as red as the lips of the Queen.

25

Sweet Dreams

Seas of blood surrounded Juniper.

Trickles spurted from Kyra's fingertip like roaring rivers rushing to the sea. It was an unnatural amount of blood from such a small wound. It covered the bed, dripped down to the floor, and formed a puddle next to Juniper's head as she slowly batted her eyes open.

"Did I faint?" Juniper asked groggily, rubbing her eyes and hoping the blood before her would disappear like a trick of the light. It did not.

Julian was sitting on the floor next to her, looking uneasy. "Only for a few minutes."

"So Kyra bled this much in a *few minutes*?" She gestured to the blood around her and scooted away from it as the pool expanded.

"It's a Blutverbraucht spell. Bloodworn. I recognize it from my course in Magical Studies last summer," said Cal. "Once the victim is hit with it, they bleed until they're dead. Kyra's going to bleed out unless we can figure out how to stop it." His voice was calm and collected, for the most part, but there was a hint of panic laced underneath.

"So how shall we do that? Magic?" asked Juniper. As she looked at Jules and his weary stare, she remembered that magic was not the answer for all things. It could not save everyone. And she knew that magic could not save her sister now. She didn't know how she knew. But she did.

"Someone's coming." Luca's head had picked up like a dog's when it smelled someone approaching.

The door to the East Tower banged open. A figure stood silhouetted in sunrise. Juniper's heart wrenched like a carriage spinning out of control.

Tora casually leaned up against the doorframe, his snake-like eyes gleaming gold and green. "Princess," he said, giving a nod her way.

"Jerk," Juniper spat out, making her posture tall to look like she wasn't scared.

"I see you've found our Moon's Child." Tora grinned lazily, ivory canines sharpened in fangs. "Quite the heavy sleeper, isn't she?" He indicated Kyra, asleep on the bed. Blood still seeped from her pricked finger.

"How do we wake her up?" Cal's voice cut through the thick air like a knife.

"That's what I'm here to tell you. Her Majesty sent me to say that not only is her daughter under a Bloodworn spell, but a Dreamscape curse as well." Tora recited the words as if he had heard them repeatedly before.

"Dreamscape?" Luca asked, his fingers worrying at the hem of his shirt. "What's a Dreamscape curse?"

"I thought you'd never ask, wolfie." Tora winked. "Dreamscape is pretty fun, if you love being tortured. Kyra is locked away in her worst nightmare. The only way to get her out is to find her. And if you go in her mind to get her out...there's no guarantee of coming back."

"Pass," Julian tried to joke. "Imagine being stuck in Kyra's mind for eternity."

"All we need to do to get her back is face her nightmare?" Juniper asked, not looking at Tora. She had her eyes trained on the floor, trained on the blood pooling there. It seemed simple enough. Nothing life-threatening. So why was the Queen putting them through it?

"Ooof, so close. You need to face her nightmare...then face all of yours. And if you don't...well, Kyra here is looking awfully pale. My, my, is she losing that much blood? Shame if you didn't follow her into her mind. She would bleed out in minutes!" Tora said mockingly.

"Why are you telling us this?" Cal asked Tora.

"Can't say. I promised." Tora paused, his smiling eyes turning hard and cold. "See you later. This has been truly a riveting conversation, but I fear my brain cells are depleting with each passing second."

"Utter stupidity cannot be lessened, " Juniper said slowly, keeping her gaze cool and calm.

"Comebacks really aren't your thing, Princess," said Tora. "Now if you want to save your friend, all of you have to touch her forehead where her pea-brain is at the same time."

"Thanks for the help," Jules said sarcastically. "You waste of space."

"Seeing as I can tell when I'm not wanted," Tora said, putting his hands up in a wave, then edging backward out the door, "See you later." He winked again, and then was gone. No footsteps gave him away—nothing to signify that he was ever there at all. Shadows were louder than the Snake Prince.

"The nerve of that guy. Middle parts are *my* thing," Julian sulked.

"You made out with him?" He stared at the place Tora had just been with hatred.

"Lapse of judgement," Juniper said, but she kind of felt good about the annoyed look on Jules' face.

"Is everyone on board to enter Kyra's mind and fight our worst nightmares?" Cal asked, already standing as if it weren't even a question.

Juniper said, "It sounds quite easier than fighting a giant."

"Or a house made of candy," Cal said.

"My personal least favorite was the demon wolf pack," added Julian.

"But I think we can all agree the ball was the most torture." Luca grinned.

"Let's do this." Cal's voice was grim.

"Whatever it takes." Luca nodded.

"What he said," Julian smirked and rose to his feet, standing next to the others.

"Okay," said Juniper. "Here goes nothing. Or everything."

They each reached tentative hands out to Kyra's forehead, placing their fingers on her cool skin.

Nothing happened for a moment.

And then, everything was spinning, and the world went white with a blinding burst of light.

* * *

The most annoying sound of all annoying sounds rang in Kyra's ears.

She sat up and was surprised to find that she was in a field of green grass and flowers, sweet-smelling and bright. A ring of oak trees surrounded the field, forming a neat, round area like a faerie circle. She sat up and pressed her fingers into the thick grass, treasuring the warmth seeping into her skin. The sky was bright blue, blue like Cal's eyes.

Where was Cal? And where was she?

She remembered pricking her finger on a spindle...she groaned suddenly. The Queen must have put her under a spell, because Kyra remembered thinking that her stepmother was the most awesome thing since chocolate cake. She even had thought of Callista as her mother. Disgusting. That was enough to get her to despise magic forever.

Kyra stood and saw that there was someone lying in the grass a ways away, half-buried by flowers pink and blue.

No, not just one person, but four people, sleeping in the grass.

She inched closer, almost afraid for some reason. But that was silly. Why would she be afraid? She was Kyra. Not some wuss who got scared of napping people.

Their faces were terribly familiar.

Juniper. Luca. Cal. Julian.

They all had blank looks on their faces, eyes murky white and unblinking. Vines wrapped around their limbs like chains holding them to the dirt. Flowers grew over them, holding hands with leaves and soft petals.

Kyra's stomach clenched in horror. What...? *No.* Scrambling backward, she slammed into someone.

Cal stood there, holding his arms out for her to steady herself.

"Cal? But, but, you—" Kyra cut off, looking frantically between the Cal before her and the eerily asleep Cal on the floor.

"That's not me," he said urgently. "You have to get through this. Face your fear. If you do, everything will be okay. I promise."

Kyra nodded and stepped away from him. She didn't understand what he fully meant, only that she trusted him enough to follow what he was saying. Face her fears. No matter where she was or what situation she was in, that was good advice. She had been following it her whole life. She could do it now.

She walked forward to her friend's lifeless bodies, taking a deep breath.

Kyra opened her eyes, and she willed herself to not be afraid.

The scene before her swirled away to blank nothingness, white walls like an empty canvas.

Cal was still there, and Juniper was, too, along with Julian and Luca. And that awful ringing sound was gone. That was almost better than the welcome sight of her friends before her.

"This is Kyra's mind?" Julian asked, looking around at the blank walls. "Cool."

"Shockingly empty." Cal grinned.

"Hey! My mind is intelligent and blooming with thoughts!" Kyra fumed, but it was a happy fuming. She was very glad to see her friends were all okay and not lying in a flower field of doom. She backtracked. "Wait a second, my *mind*? Feeling like I missed something important."

"Kinda hard to explain. But yeah, we're in your mind, and that scene you just faced was a nightmare. The queen put a spell on you that can only be reversed by each and every one of us facing our worst nightmares," Luca explained.

Yeah, that sounded about right.

"What ever happened to true love's kiss?" Kyra muttered. "Julian, why didn't you try that? We're engagedddd, after all." She poked him in the ribs a bajillion times on the word 'engaged,' and batted her lashes.

"Yikes. Forgot about that." Julian grimaced. "Consider yourself dumped. It's not you, it's me, and all the works."

Kyra feigned surprise. "I thought we were in love! Julian, how could you?" She threw a hand up to her forehead and pretended to look distressed like she had seen actors in plays do. "Everything is a lie!" Swooning? Was that what that was called? Maybe she should look that up in a dictionary. Although, the second she whipped out a dictionary or even read was the second she would jump off a cliff with her eyes closed. "Love itself is a lie!"

Juniper rolled her eyes. "You will overcome it." Kyra could see a glint of joy in her sister's eyes, however, and Kyra cast her a look that meant, *Go ahead and fall in love with my ex-fiance while we're in my mind. I won't judge.* Something told Kyra that Juni didn't understand all that from a mere look.

"For real though, did I miss much?" Kyra questioned.

The look on everyone's faces told her that she did, indeed, miss a lot.

Juniper gave an innocent smile. "Not...much."

"Just a giant thorn hedge, duping some guards, another glowy time, and finding you asleep with lots of blood as your nap partner. So no, not much," Julian said, gesturing with his hands excitedly.

"Did I snore?" Kyra asked, giving a pointed look towards Cal.

"You did," Cal said, at the same time Juniper said, "You did not."

Luca offered, "I was a great actor."

"I helped." Juniper smiled sweetly.

Julian said, "*You* almost killed us all with your 'acting.' There's a difference."

"I don't even want to ask," Cal said. "Thanks for the update, but we have some nightmares to face."

"Don't even try to make that sound better, Calais." Kyra wagged her finger at him. "Even your annoying optimism can't change the fact that this is gonna suck, big-time."

"I wasn't trying to—"

"I know you weren't," Kyra admitted.

Cal raised his eyebrow in amusement. "A new nightmare is forming."

It was true. The white walls of whatever type of room they were in were falling away, taking the shape of a forest again. But this forest wasn't intertwined with daylight and flowers.

This forest was dark and cold, with no stars shining through a thick layer of clouds. Only the moon was visible, a slip of red light against a salt and pepper sky. The forest had tall trees that Kyra had never seen before, limber and reddish-brown in the night.

"Whose nightmare is it?" Cal asked.

"This doesn't scare me," Jules said.

Juniper shrugged. "Could be me. I am scared of most everything."

Suddenly, a howl echoed through the night, a howl that sent the hair on the back of Kyra's neck standing straight up.

Another howl cut through the night. Sharp and vicious.

Luca's face turned deadly pale.

He looked up at the red moon, then down. "I know whose nightmare this is."

"What do we do?" Juniper asked, panicked.

Cal shook his head. "We have to let him conquer the nightmare."

I never asked to be a Dämonenwölfe.

"Do this adorably like I know you will." Kyra looked at Luca quickly, grabbing his shoulders impulsively and pulling him into a tight hug. He was surprised for a moment before wrapping his arms around her. Kyra whispered, "Remember, it's not real."

Luca nodded against her collarbone, then stepped out of the hug.

Preparing himself, he crumpled his hands into fists and stepped away from the others, intense determination written across his face. Luca stood tall and proud, his feet firm on the ground. His purple eyes gleamed, his hands arced in a claw-like pose.

The howls came closer then, and a huge, snarling grey wolf burst through the trees. It pounced.

It reminded Kyra of that night that felt so long ago, when the Dämonenwölfe pack had attacked them in the Southern Forest—when Kyra had pushed Juniper out of the way, dooming Luca.

On that night, Luca had cowered. Tonight, he stood tall and proud. Ready for whatever came next.

Tonight, he looked like a true hunter of the night.

The wolf clawed out at Luca, who side-stepped it with a small splash of fear on his face. The wolf came at him again, howling and baring its sharp teeth. Violet eyes gleaming, its grey fur rippled in the night air.

"I wish we could help," Juniper whispered to Kyra as they watched the scene take place. Luca still looked terrified, unable to muster up much of a fight. He was on the defensive, barely scrambling out of the wolf's sharp grasp.

"What's his fear? Dämonenwölfes?" Kyra asked, narrowing her eyes.

"No." Juniper's eyes went dark. "That wolf that's fighting him...it's himself."

So that was what Luca was afraid of. Not fights. Not even wolves.

Kyra squeezed her eyes shut, digging her nails into her hand and forming small crescent-moons in her palms. The little huntsman was scared of the wolf inside him. That was a tragedy caused by Kyra, by her impulsive need to always protect Juniper.

"Face your fear, little huntsman!" Kyra found herself shouting out at him.

Luca met her gaze, looking like a flustered wild animal. As the wolf prepared to strike again, Luca was already morphing into a wolf, his muscles rearranging, his eyes turning into slits, his small, delicate stature turning strong and formidable.

It was the first time Kyra had seen him as a true wolf. It was glorious and terrifying all at once. Like the night itself.

Luca, in wolf form, attacked the other wolf. They engaged in a ruthless struggle for power, claws scraping out at each other, fangs being bared and fur shining silver in the scarlet moonlight.

Suddenly, Luca lashed out one claw, striking the other wolf in the stomach. The wolf crumpled to the ground, whimpering and hurt. For a moment, it looked like Luca. But that moment disappeared in an instant as Luca rose over the limp body of the other wolf.

He turned back into his human form, brown hair damp with sweat and claw marks lining his body.

Luca looked down at the wolf, breathing heavily as he regarded it. "I'm not afraid of you. Not anymore," he said. Kyra was sure he was not only saying that to the wolf before him. "I never asked to be a Dämonenwölfe. But I am. At first I was afraid of myself, but that fear has passed." He met Kyra's gaze and smiled a little. "Most things do."

As soon as he said those words, the scene began changing to a large banquet hall, the tall trees falling away and being replaced with mounting piles of food.

Kyra and the others stood at the end of the table, looking on the pleasant scene warily.

The banquet table stretched out across the dining room of what looked to be a castle, and laughing nobles filled the tables. Candles flickered about and filled the room with a warm and happy glow. It didn't look like a nightmare at all unless someone was scared of delicious-looking food.

Julian sat at the head of the table, a gilded crown atop his head. He held a glass of blood-red wine in his hand as he stood to give a toast.

The table fell silent as he began.

"Welcome, everyone. I'm so lucky to be surrounded by so many whom I love."

The wine glass in his hand shook. Shook and then was still.

Julian coughed, then continued. "I'm very pleased that you all could make it to celebrate my eighteenth birthday here with me."

"Oh, no," Juniper whispered, eyes round saucers.

"What?" Kyra hissed, longing to know what was so terrible about this nightmare. It looked like a dream, a happy memory of some sort. With candles and...was that cake? Sunbeam above, it was chocolate cake. How could this be bad?

Julian faltered, brows furrowing. "Eighteenth birthday..."

Luca and Juniper gave a quick, worried look to each other.

Kyra murmured, "Whatever. Don't answer. I'll see in a second."

"That's what I'm afraid of," Juniper said darkly.

Julian continued with his toast, grabbing at his stomach with his free hand like he had an ache. "Feeling a bit—" He coughed again, clutching at his arm. "I'm feeling a bit tired now. Think I'll turn in for the night."

Whispers floated around the room at his words, nobles nudging each other. Some pointed and laughed at the prince.

"Yes," Julian said sharply, face turning pale. "Turning in. Really sorry, everyone, enjoy the rest of your ni—"

He cut off, falling to the floor with a bang. His body was concealed by the table. Kyra leaned forward to get a better look, her pulse racing. With his fall, the wine glass had jerked from his hand, flowing everywhere. The wine spilled out over the tablecloth, soaking the white with red.

A hand suddenly clutched at the tablecloth from the floor.

A red hand.

Covered in wine?

On a closer look, Kyra knew with a sickening feeling that it was blood. Juniper whimpered next to her as Julian stood up, his entire body slicked crimson. She reeled back, horrified.

Blood seeped from his head to his toes, his green eyes the only color visible amongst the red; his golden curls matted down with the sticky substance.

"Sunbeam above," Kyra said, stomach lurching.

Julian stumbled around as the banquet hall was filled with shouts of fear and disgust. He desperately tried to wipe the blood off, even using the tablecloth, but it stuck fast. And the places he managed to wipe off were only filled with more blood.

"I," Julian grunted, struggling with the words, "am not afraid."

Nothing happened. Blood kept pouring from him.

Juniper ran forward then, putting both hands on his blood-slicked shoulders. Kyra was shocked. Normally, Juniper wouldn't go anywhere near gross or scary things. But she put both hands on his shoulders and whispered to him:

"You have to mean it."

"You were right." Julian took a shaky breath. "This is terrifying. How will we ever find a way to stop it?"

Tears rolled down Juniper's cheeks as she pulled him into a hug.

Luca was sprinting over to them, then, and throwing his arms around the two of them. His shirt got drenched in blood as soon as he did. Cal was there in an instant, gently wrapping them all up. Kyra stood there for a second, frozen and staring, feeling like she was out of place. But then she ran over, too, and enveloped the four of them in her arms.

The blood began disappearing from Julian's arms and legs as he hugged them all back.

"I'll never have the life I'm supposed to," said Julian.

Juniper said, voice cracking, "A wise boy once told me that no one really does."

The blood disappeared all at once, and so did the elaborately decorated banquet hall.

They were now in an all-black room, with no doors or windows. Black walls, black floors, and a black ceiling. A void of darkness.

Was someone afraid of the dark? Juniper was, so was this her night-mare?

But then a figure stepped forward from the dark, a figure shrouded in gold and pink.

It was Kyra herself, a wry smirk written across her face. The not-Kyra said, "Halbling. Fae. Inhuman. You're revolting." The not-Kyra grinned, catlike. "Wait. That was a pretty big word. *Revolting*. I'm on fire today. You revolting faerie."

"Cal, don't listen to her, that's not true—" Kyra started, but he was...

Laughing.

"She has a point," said Cal, and Kyra despaired. How could he be-lieve those awful things the not-Kyra had said? The corner of Cal's mouth quirked up. "Revolting is a pretty big word for you."

"Wait, what?"

"I know, Kyra," Cal said. "That's not you. Look at the eyes."

Kyra stared at the not-Kyra and saw that the girl's eye color was morphing from grey to black, grey to black, grey to black, over and over like the twisting chain of a necklace flipping from one side to the next.

Another figure stepped forward, a short old woman with her hair tied up in a loose bun. She had smile lines on her eyes and blue eyes—the same as Cal's. The woman must've been Cal's grand-mother.

"Grandma," Cal said. "You're a long way from home." The boy could take everything in the world seriously but his own worst fear.

"Don't call me that. You are no grandson of mine. Your blood is of thieves and the conquerors of our ancestors. The blood of the fae. You disgust me, Calais," The grandmother hissed, her pale blue eyes morphing to black every second, roiling and changing color. A stormy sea.

Cal crossed his arms. "Nice try. My grandma would never call me Calais. She hated the name and hated my mother for naming me that. Grandma always said it was a name for a pretentious piece of—"

"Calais." A new figure stepped from the shadows. It was Julian—an un-Julian, though, a wicked Julian with black-and-green-eyes and a creepily wide grin. "You think you are my best friend? You are nothing but a servant, and no friend of mine would ever be half-fae, nonetheless." Un-Julian laughed, a sharp and beautiful sound. Nothing like the real Jules' laugh. "I hate you."

Kyra put a hand on Cal's arm. She didn't say anything. But now, at least, he would know that she was there. An Un-Luca and Un-Juniper could be seen walking steadily forward to begin a new attack of insults.

The real Julian chortled nervously. "Freaky...but do I really have that nice of a jawline? No wonder all the ladies love me!"

"Your jawline is undeniably sharp and well-proportioned," Juniper earnestly agreed.

"Well proportioned? Keep 'em coming!"

"Focus, guys," Kyra said. "Cal is going through a life-changing nightmare trauma right now, and he sat through all of your life-changing nightmare traumas. Show a little respect."

"No, they're fine," Cal said with a smile. "I'm not afraid of these wannabes," he gestured to the un-Kyra and un-others. "They'll never live up to the real thing."

And with that, the scene washed away, and a room awash in gold was in its place.

Burnt orange hues decorated the walls, the very air lit in hazy reds and pinks. Like a dream half-remembered, or a memory long forgotten, the room reveled in the ghosts of the past. Sunlight was often inviting, warm. But the hue of this peach room was cold, a frozen river of darkness lurking beneath the icy surface. The room was unfurnished save for a small wooden vanity.

On it sat a golden mirror.

* * *

This was Juniper's nightmare. It had to be. She was the only one left. What would pop out of the inky glass surface of that mirror? Spiders? Snakes? A circus clown wearing a toupee? For some unknown reason, toupees were a great fear of Juniper's.

Nervously, Juniper inched forward, a thousand thoughts ricocheting around her brain. Now was not the time to think. Now was the time to face her fear.

"That's sweet. Juniper's afraid of mirrors. Reflections are the worst, 'specially when you just wake up in the morning, amiright?" Kyra did not wait to hear if she was indeed right. She just repeated, "Reflections."

Reflections often were sobering examples of truth. Due to that, they were indeed the worst.

Juniper sat down at the vanity, her anxious fingers curling around the wooden stool. What fear? And how terrifying would it be? Courage, she remembered, was bravery in spite of fear. She would be brave because she had to be, and because she knew she could.

The mirror's surface swirled into a milky white color before speaking at last. A voice from the mirror said, "Princess Juniper of Day. I know you better than you know yourself. To what do I owe the pleasure?" Hmm. And here she was thinking the mirror only spoke in rhymes and riddles. Good. Juniper was scared she would have to rhyme on the spot. That would not end well for anyone.

Juniper said, "You are my fear. I am supposed to be scared of you."

"Child of the Sun and Stars." The mirror laughed. "You will be."

"Now is not the time for playful words and vagueness. Either show me what I am here for or let me leave."

"Arrogance does not suit you."

"Neither does self-doubt, I have found, so I am done caring what others think of me. I alone decide." said Juniper. "No mirror, however prettily they speak, will tell me how to live."

The mirror was silent for a moment, and Juniper could almost hear her heart beating out of her chest. At least she had not cried. Though, there was still time. The others, standing stock still at the edges of the room, had their eyes trained on her. All their breaths were held in stunned silence.

The mirror spoke again. "Tell me, what is it you most desire?"

"Why should I tell you?"

"Princess, I thought you had no time for meaningless exchanges."

Juniper swallowed hard, her throat chalky. What did she most want in the world? She could think of a lot of things. Freedom for her people. True freedom for herself, too. In more ways than one. All the knowledge in the universe. Her friends and family to be safe forever. Julian. Her father back. Juniper thought and thought until she finally decided on an answer, even if it barely scraped the surface of all the things she desired.

"I desire an answer."

"To what question?" The mirror gleamed with pink light.

"If you truly know me, then you know."

The golden mirror paused, then said, "The answer is no. Never."

Smiling, Juniper unclenched her hand. "I am not afraid of you because I know you lie. Reflections hold truth. And you have given me none."

"But-but—"

"Goodbye, mirror. Mother Sky delights upon our parting." Juniper stood as the mirror swirled away to that blank white room again, the gold and orange hues fading away like water washing away paint.

The others were silent as the white room reappeared, shuffling their feet awkwardly. Juniper was thankful it was not her for once shuffling awkwardly.

"Okay, so," Julian said, "what just happened?"

"None of your concern. We are running low on time, and we must make it to the coronation to stop the Queen for good. Let us go back, out of Kyra's mind," Juniper said, avoiding his fervent gaze. Her heart was a lock that she did not want to open. Not now.

The boys shrugged then ran over to Kyra to touch her forehead again. Once they did, they too faded away like mist on an autumn morning. Kyra remained.

"All this forehead touching is gonna give me bad acne," said Kyra with her signature grin.

Juniper said, "Karma for biting your fingernails."

"Uh-huh. Juniper," said Kyra, serious now, "What was the question you asked? The one you knew was a lie?"

"I asked the mirror if the people I love love me in return. When the mirror said you do not, I knew it was lying. I know it lied because I know you. You are my sister, Kyra, and my best friend. No matter our fights and our bickering, I always know that you care for me."

"Now you're getting vain. How do you know I still love you, Sun's Child?"

"Because the sun and moon orbit each other. Because we always look out for each other."

"You're gonna make me tear up." Kyra mock wiped away a tear, then said, "But enough with the touchy-feely stuff."

"I love you, too. Let us go save our kingdom."

"Lead the way."

Juniper nodded and crossed over to her sister, reaching up on her tip-toes to touch her forehead. The room crackled like electricity before falling away to pure nothingness.

Juniper gasped, opening her eyes and sitting up from the floor.

Sprawled around her were the others, opening their eyes blearily and sitting up.

"Those," Julian said, "were some crazy dreams."

"More like nightmares." Juniper put a hand to her head, then pushed her tight curls out of her face.

"At least we didn't die," said Luca.

Kyra pinched Luca's cheek. "Always looking on the bright side."

Kyra rolled her eyes, mocking, "Golly-gee, I'm so gosh darn glad! At least we survived!"

"For the rest of my life, I'm gonna be seeing Cal's psycho grandma with demon eyes." Julian put his fingers at his temples.

"At least you saw your proportionate jawline in the flesh," Juniper pointed out. "That should very well be a win."

"Facts." Julian scraped a finger along his jawline. "Ouch, I'm cutting my finger on the sharpness!"

"Nice one, Juniper, now his ego's never going to deflate." Luca shook his head. "We're all doomed."

Julian whined, "Come on—"

"No matter how much I love making fun of Jules, I think we have something to attend to," Cal said, looking out the window. The sun was high in the sky, directly above. "The coronation is today, right? Looks like noon."

"Lucky us. Time to finally punch Callista in the face. Then the gut. Then the face again, for fun." Kyra stood up, pulling Juniper to her feet. "It's high time we get to the punching, though, 'cause I honestly haven't punched anything this whole trip."

"I have punched," Juniper said meekly. All eyes went to her, and she smiled sheepishly. "Tora."

"Oh, sick."

"Fair enough."

"Good."

"Love that for you."

"Thank you," Juniper said. "Now it's time to stop the Queen."

Kyra nodded. "Once and for all."

The five teenagers raced down the stairs, Juniper carrying her dress around her in fistfuls and hating that she ever even chose to wear a dress to take down her mother. But what do you wear to that occasion, honestly? She thought her fashion choice was fine, but practicality might have missed the mark.

They reached the bottom of the stairs in a rush, and Luca swung the door open.

"Wait a second," Kyra said, a nervous look coming over her sharp features. Juniper froze. Kyra never looked nervous. What could have happened to her? "You guys go ahead. Wait for us in the hallway. I need to talk to Juniper for a second."

"About what?" Luca asked, curiously regarding her. "Secrets, secrets, are no fun—"

Kyra responded by picking him up by the back of his collar and placing him in the hallway. The other two boys nodded and went out of the stairwell, the door slamming shut behind them. Before he left, Cal and Kyra shared a look. A look of understanding. What had they seen in captivity?

"Is something amiss?" Juniper asked. Same question, and soon she would have the same answer. Nothing could have prepared her for what Kyra said next, though.

"Something," Kyra said, shaking her head miserably. "Something's very wrong. The Queen...I know why she learned magic and why she wants all the power for herself."

Juniper rubbed her lips together in a nervous habit. "No point in keeping me waiting."

Kyra hesitated, then continued. "Just so you know...we won't let this happen. I promise. But she learned magic because...it's because...it's because she's trying to raise Jakob from the dead. And she needs two magic catalysts: one of light magic and one of dark. It's logical to assume that you're the light catalyst. It would explain why you have magic in the first place. Callista put this weird vial in your dinner one day...she gave you the magic specifically for this spell. The dark catalyst could be anyone, though," said Kyra, and the weird look that flitted across her features happened so quickly, Juniper thought she had imagined it.

Juniper felt like she had been struck in the chest by a huge weight. She put one hand against the door behind her to hold herself up. She heard her dad's laugh, his kind smile, the way he sewed with the gentlest care. "My...my father?"

"Yes." Kyra swallowed hard.

Juniper's father's voice resonated in her ears—a voice filled with warmth and joy and comfort. *Would you like to make flower crowns, my dearest Juni-tree?* A voice she had thought she would never hear again. "My dad...might come back to life?" The question was like a confused wish, words she never thought she would say.

"Yeah, but—"

"But it would not be him, not really, correct? A zombie or ghost?" Ghosts. Those seemed to be in large supply these days. Past hauntings crept up far too often lately. *Down by the Juniper tree.*

"I don't know."

"We will not let her. I will not let her alter the course of life." Juniper couldn't put any strength in her voice. She sounded weaker than she wanted to. "No matter how much I wish to."

"We won't let her," Kyra said, then slammed the door open wide. The boys stood in the hallway, blank looks on their faces as if they had been standing right by the door, listening.

Luca scratched at his collar. "Er, we weren't listening."

As they ran through the halls, Juniper dully wondered if she should be mad at her mother for what she was trying to do. For what she had already done. But Juniper didn't feel angry at all, just pity for her wayward mother. She wanted to be upset, truly, but she couldn't bring herself to be angry. That made her mad at herself instead. Why couldn't she get upset with her mother, who had done nothing but horrible things to her ever since her father died, and who was altering so many lives to get what she wanted?

One thing stopped her from being upset. Juniper understood her.

They had both lost Jakob.

The group burst out into the large courtyard that was the centerpiece of the Winter Palace, where the coronation was taking place.

Chairs were set up facing a large stage, not unlike the stage in the square of Aazagonia that night of her own funeral a week ago.

The chairs were...they were...empty. In fact, the entire courtyard was empty, cold air whistling through wood. The stage was empty, too.

Everything was empty.

"Where is everybody?" Juniper voiced the question she knew everyone was thinking.

The Queen walked out of the shadows. Crossing from the other side of the courtyard, a flowing violet dress following in loyalty. Her hair had little purple beads twisted in them, braided in little strands like how she used to do Juniper's.

Her mother waved. "Hello, everyone. You know, I was just thinking of how rude it is of you to miss the coronation."

No. They couldn't have missed it. It couldn't be over. The Queen couldn't have won. Not after everything.

"Dang it, Tora!" Julian ran his hands through his hair. "The Dreamscape spell..."

"...Was a way to keep us away from the coronation," Cal realized.

"A distraction. While we were busy fighting our nightmares, the Queen was crowned."

Callista said, "You five make it almost too easy."

"Give it up." Juniper raised her chin to meet her mother's gaze. Remembering her manners, she added a squeaky, "Please."

"Don't think I will," The Queen said. "That's cute, though, darling."

Juniper said, "Father would not want this."

"You don't know what Jakob would want!"

"He was my family too. He wouldn't want to be raised anew. For you to consort with the fae. For you to give me magic against my will!"

"Poor girl. He was not your father...he still *is*. Jakob can be with us again. We can be a family once more, like we should have been. I promise, you will forget every ill thought as soon as you see him." For a moment, Callista looked less like a monster and more like a human. Like her mother. For a moment, Juniper almost believed her.

"On the topic of fathers...where's mine?" Kyra asked, something hard-set in her gaze.

"Safely back in Aazagonia."

Kyra's relief was almost palpable in the air. "You didn't execute him?"

"Sadly, no."

"Sunbeam above, how awful can one person be?"

The Queen snapped her fingers, and Kyra was silent, struggling to speak as if her mouth was sewn shut. "There. I like you much better that way. Now, there's one more thing that needs to happen before I can enact the spell to raise my beloved..."

Callista put her arms out on either side of her, chanting unintelligible words.

"Oh no." Recognition lit up Cal's face.

"What do you mean, 'oh no?' Kyra demanded.

"A summoning spell. I've read about these before."

"Too much to hope she's summoning a sparkly pink pixie?"

"Look."

Juniper looked up into the sky where Cal pointed and saw a small spot of white against the blue sky. A cloud? No...it wasn't a cloud. Juniper was able to make out what the shape was as it neared. It had beating wings and—and...

"What is it?" Kyra asked. "I have bad eyesight!"

"It's ..." Juniper found her voice suddenly, looking up into the sky with fear. Her stomach turned over in terror. "...It's a dragon."

26

Fire, Fly

Once it got a little closer, and Kyra could actually see without squinting, she saw it.

The dragon. It was an ice dragon, and the first (hopefully last) ice dragon she would ever see. Kyra had seen a lava dragon when she was a kid on vacation west, and all she had remembered was heat and bad breath that stunk like hot tamales.

The *ice* dragon, however, was extremely cool looking. Not just because it was, you know, actually cold. And it would be significantly cooler if it wasn't headed right for her with a gaping jaw.

The dragon roared, spreading its wings high across the sky. It had a bluish-white underbelly and icy-looking breath, lighting up the sky with hues of white and grey. Its teeth were sharp, large icicles gnashing. Mesmerizing scales pulsed with the frigid cold of ice-covered lakes. White and silver like a waterfall of snow, the dragon's horns looked sharp enough to impale even the sternest powder-topped mountain.

The dragon watched with an uncaring stare, like it was waiting for them to make the first move. Hyperventilating noises could be heard from Juniper.

Kyra was doing fine, actually, sort of in a trance at the pure awesomeness of the creature. The others seemed okay, too, all poised and ready to fight the magnificent creature like a band of cool-looking ninjas. Everyone stumbled a little as they steadied themselves. Maybe not ninjas. But close enough.

"It's majestic," Luca said, a giddy smile written across his face. "I've never seen a real live ice dragon in my life—or any dragon, but this one is just magnificent."

Kyra whirled on him with a look that she hoped looked like *Are you out of your precious little mind*? "It's not *majestic*. It's going to kill us! That's what it is!"

"It's going to kill us?" Juniper asked with a nervous look on her face.

Kyra backtracked, "It's not going to kill us."

"May I sit this one out?" Juniper asked queasily.

"No."

"Can I faint?"

"Not allowed," Kyra said. "We need you to do the magic hand thing. Now, get going." She shooed a flustered Juniper forward.

"Why must I fight the dragon?" Juniper worriedly looked between the others. "Am I really our best option? Think about what you are saying here!"

Julian, quiet up until this point, stepped forward, his ebony sword at the ready. He looked as if he had been pulled straight from the pages of a fairytale, the hero come to save the day.

Julian said, "That's where I come in. I'm the Dragon Warrior." He took a deep breath. "This is my battle."

"Yeah, nope." The Queen interrupted the heroic moment.

With a quick flick of her wrist, Julian, Luca, and Cal were flung to their knees, shackles of stone rising up from the floor and locking up their legs and arms. They were pinned to the ground in milliseconds. The boys gave muffled shouts as slabs of stone twisted up around their mouths to keep them from speaking.

"Let them go," Kyra almost growled.

"Do you ever listen?" the Queen inspected her fingernail, stepping up onto the stage. "I said, there's one more thing that needs to happen."

The dragon flew down from the sky, its tail whipping through the air, wings beating up and down in slow movements. It landed where the chairs were, sending them scattering like tiny chess pieces. (Although Kyra had never played chess in her life and never planned to, thank you very much).

"You and I must fight the dragon?" Juniper inched backward, looking at Kyra with wide eyes.

"We're royally screwed."

"We may be royal, but we are not screwed," Juniper said, and her hands began to glow a bright white. "Have hope, Kyra."

"Yes! The magicky hands!" Kyra pumped her fist. "Always coming in a clutch."

The dragon lumbered forward, silver and white irises gleaming as frost came in swirls from its nostrils.

"It's not attacking us. I will not strike it until it strikes us," Juniper decided, and the white glow of her veins fell away.

Kyra grunted. "Why do you have to be so good and moral all the time? Bad deeds every now and then are not so terrible!"

The dragon reached forward with one claw, smacking Kyra to the floor and sending her skidding across the stone, her dress getting mussed with snow and dirt. She groaned and sat up, rubbing her side where the dragon's claws had connected.

Kyra found that she was lying in front of the boys in their rock chains. She tossed up a little wave. "Hey. You guys look stone-cold right now." The boys all rolled their eyes, their mouths still covered with stone. Kyra winked and scrambled to her feet, readying herself for another blow from the dragon.

"How are your bad deeds treating you?" Juniper's eyes danced with humor, and she crumpled her hands into fists, turning to face the dragon. Her veins glowed and her hair swirled around her head in thick, curly strands as she aimed a current of twisting light at the ice dragon.

The thin burst of magic hit the dragon in the chest but did nothing to deter it from its course. It was headed straight for Juniper, ice and snow curling around its mouth and forming a cloud of breath. Because while lava monsters breathed fire and lava...ice dragons breathed pure cold.

Ice-breath spiraled at Juniper, encasing her in a frozen block that stretched from her feet to her neck. Freezing over in snowflake spirals, Juniper was unable to move.

The Queen leaned forward from her perch on the stage as if intrigued.

Juniper's eyes suddenly turned from brown to pure white, irises and pupils glowing blindingly. She screamed and her entire body erupted in magic, sending the block of ice scattering in shards. Kyra watched in awe, jumping to avoid the blocks of ice cascading towards her.

Juniper sent another blast of light magic at the dragon, hitting it square in the jaw. She sent two more—quick jabs of light that hit the dragon in the neck, then a wing. In the places it hit, the magic left steaming burns. As if heat played a role in light magic.

The ice dragon snarled before it beat its wings a couple times and flew into the air. Landing on top of one of the many columns lining the courtyard, its claws sent stones and pieces of roof scattering. It flapped its wings again before letting out a loud roar of pure hatred.

"Interesting," The Queen said from across the courtyard. Her head was placed in her hands giddily as if she were watching a play and not her daughters fighting a terrifying monster.

The dragon froze. Its eyes were locked in a trance with Juniper. Nostrils flaring, the dragon began forming another small flurry of ice and snow in front of its mouth. Aimed directly at Juniper.

"Look out!" Kyra cried, and was already running to shove Juniper out of the way of the oncoming ice-blast. But Juniper just watched with determination, her entire body pulsing with light magic, dress billowing around her as if gusts of wind had suddenly appeared.

Kyra was too late. The cold breath hit Juniper in the chest, encasing her entire body in a block of ice and sending her careening to the floor. Her face was still frozen with that determined look, for once not scared. Kyra pounded on the ice, desperately trying to crack it open with every bit of strength left in her. The ice block didn't budge, but Kyra's knuckles did. They bled into the cracks and calluses of her hands. When Juniper's glow faded, Kyra knew it was over. She was soon left staring down at a blank, unmoving Juniper encased in cold. Barely seen through about a foot of solid, murky ice.

Kyra whirled on the dragon, fury clouding her vision. "Take the ice off her immediately!"

The dragon's eyes slitted as it began to breathe heavier, another cloud of ice forming. It would hit her, and she would suffer the same fate as her sister.

She wouldn't be able to save anyone. Not even herself.

Not *ever* herself.

The Queen smiled.

Kyra clenched her hands into fists, not taking her eyes off the ice dragon before her, its eternal gaze riveted on her as it breathed and snarled and made a huge flurry before it.

Kyra remembered the words of the old woman in the clearing suddenly, words that she had written off as nonsense. *You will learn to harness the light and use it for your own, child, remember it. You and your sister are strands of cloth, moon and sun, woven together. Do not forget this.*

"Two strands of the same cloth, huh?" Kyra said for no one but herself. She shook her head, almost smiling at the floor. "Of course."

Callista called out, "You can't intimidate the dragon by simply staring at it, darling. I'm trying to help! You need to make it afraid of you. And if I'm not scared, then the dragon certainly isn't."

"I'm the Moon's Child," Kyra said. "You should be."

Kyra raised her palms to the sky.

And suddenly, all at once, she was transported back in time, flying and racing and stumbling through the years, remembering a time when she had no fear because she had nothing *to* fear.

The memory came to her like the flash of a summer wind, beckoning and whispering and stiflingly hot. Kyra remembered sitting in her father's lap one warm night, the night of his wedding to Callista. Pink silks had been draped across her shoulders, flowery perfumes and glittering jewels adorned her. She remembered that dress, and she remembered the fireflies. She and her father had giggled as they watched those fireflies float in the jet-black sky. Twirling and whizzing through the air, tracing lazy patterns of light and dark along the breeze, the fireflies twinkled like the diamonds on her hem. They were little glowing pinpricks of light that danced for them. It felt like their own personal show, a celebration of the night and of the world. The air had been muggy and hot, her father warm, too, yet Kyra hadn't cared; she only wished to be as close to him as possible. Her father had been her everything. She was eight, and he had been all she had.

"Kyra," he had said, tugging uncomfortably at his tight crown, "How do you like your new stepmother?"

Kyra had frowned, fingers that had traced the constellations moments before now sitting quietly in her lap. "I like her just fine."

"Me, too," said her father. Something told Kyra that it was not true.

"Why do we have a new family?"

"I suppose because we need one."

"No, really. Why?"

What she liked best about her father was that he never lied to her. "Well," said her father, "Callista's parents have incredible wealth." That was all he said about that.

Kyra asked, her voice the trace of a whisper, "How much do you love her?"

"Not much, Kyra. Not much at all."

They went silent for a few moments.

"Father, does this mean that my new mother will watch the stars with us?" Kyra had asked. Mere handfuls of memories of her real mother were left with Kyra, kept locked in a secret box somewhere inside her. One of these memories was the knowledge that her mother had loved the stars; she had drawn sprawling maps of the sky as if it were the sea, something to be braved and explored. The world, to her, was a blank map: waiting for her to learn its secrets and claim it as her own.

That is until the sickness of Godfather Death had gripped her like the entwined branches of the aspens above, squeezing the life and love out of her mother until nothing remained but remembrances. Remembrances that ached with unlearned secrets of stars and snow and parchment with unwritten adventures.

Her father had gone silent. "No," he said finally. "I don't think your stepmother likes the sky very much."

"Why?"

"Well...she thinks the sky is too far away to be bothered with."

"I agree with her, I think. Why people care about the dumb old sky is beyond me," said Kyra, though disappointment was blossoming. "I miss my old mother. She had a nice face and sometimes when

she laughed it made me laugh too. I think her laugh was funny sometimes. I think I liked her more than the new one."

"Her laugh was funny, wasn't it?"

"Yeah. Like a donkey crossed with a chicken."

That struck her father as irrevocably funny. He burst out into a
bellowing fit of laughter. Kyra grinned, then joined in on the un-
restrained laughter with joy that she had not felt in a long time, it
had seemed. They laughed and laughed until Kyra was clutching her
tummy because it hurt from the laughing. It seemed as if her mouth
was going to fall clean off, she was smiling so wide.

Eventually they went back to watching the fireflies again.

"My new sister said something funny, too. Juniper. She said the
world brought our family together like in one of those books she
reads. That's an odd thing to say, right?" Kyra's only meeting with
Juniper thus far had been at the wedding. They had sat at the same
table while all the adults danced in the ballroom, dancing and dancing as if the world were ending that night. Kyra had been trying, to
no avail, to get Juniper to laugh, but the girl would barely even meet
her eyes. "She's odd."

"On the contrary. I think that's very wise. Your mother used to
say that books often hold truths." It was true. One of her secret, bittersweet memories of her mother was of her clutching a book close
in the library, a calm smile on her face. She had said to Kyra that
books held the best adventures. There were some things that Kyra
was reluctant to believe. Because if fairytales were real, then why
wasn't her mother sitting next to her then, naming every star and
exploring the unknowns of the world?

Kyra settled into herself but became restless with the ringing
thoughts in her head. She said the first thing to come into her mind.
"Some girls in the village say I'm odd."

"Do they now? You must know that everyone is odd. If anyone
pretends they are not then they are fools."

"Fools means dumb, right? Yeah, that's right." Kyra was still troubled. "They called me ugly. Am I ugly, father?"

Her father's worn face became lined with something that Kyra was too young to understand. "You are beautiful, Kyra. Like your mother. Don't let anyone tell you any different. It's you who decides, alright?"

"Alright." She looked at the floor.

"If you are at your lowest low, deeper than the seas to the South or colder than the mountains in the North, know that it is you who decides your destiny. So decide. Are you going to let the world happen to you, or are you going to happen to the world?"

Kyra had felt as if she were filled with the light of every firefly in the sky, shining within her in passion and adventure. The lights of this reflected in her father's eyes, and she saw, with a burning sense of knowledge, that he already knew what she was capable of.

In the present, Kyra was again filled with that sense of purpose that she had been filled with on that hot summer night, the purpose that fueled the fire in the throats of dragons.

Rushing through every bone in her body was a feeling of infinity, of cold winter air and sand so hot it burned the trespasser's feet. It was the flame of anger that had kept her going when no oil was fed to it, when no douse of water could quench its everlasting thirst.

The fire within her was stronger than it had ever been because she was stronger than she had ever been. The only difference was the call inside her had a name: magic.

Of course, it all made sense now. It felt like a homecoming, like a celebration of fireflies in the night sky, the feeling of weightlessness in that moment immediately after jumping out of a tree. Like instead of falling, she was flying and instead of dropping, she was rising.

Are you going to let the world happen to you, or are you going to happen to the world?

In that moment, Kyra decided once and for all.

Dark magic ripped out of her hands, heading in jagged bursts towards the dragon and hitting it in the head, sending it falling backward and crashing through the roof. Tumbling bricks fell in its wake.

Kyra's veins were black like the night, oddly visible against her pale-looking skin. Her hands emanated with magic, dark light rippling in waves off of her. Hands bent into claws as the dark magic tore from her body, it sent a crashing wave of agony through her limbs, and she knelt to the ground. Yet through that pain came the most jaw-droppingly wonderful rush of power she had ever felt. Like armies of the undead would bow to her with the flick of a finger. Like if she simply winked, the world around her would crash and burn in a flurry of flame and snow.

She was vaguely aware that the dragon was lying still on the floor, a section of the roof caved in from the impact. The ice around Juniper had melted, and Kyra could feel her gaze and the boys' gaze locked on her, wordlessly staring.

Kyra took heaving gasps of air as the dark glow melted away.

Callista was no longer smiling, but she looked pleased nonetheless. Her voice cracked as she rose to her feet. "Finally."

* * *

Juniper said nothing as she raced to Kyra, falling to her knees next to her sister.

"What? Are you? What?" Juniper fumbled for words, but nothing could encompass everything she was feeling. Kyra had just used dark magic. Kyra had dark magic! "*What just happened?*"

Kyra looked up, and Juniper saw that her eyes were fading from a black color that had filled her entire eye socket, turning back to the stormy grey they had always been. Her hair hung across her, gold strands falling into her face as her head hung low.

"We're the conductors, Juniper. Light and Dark. Callista needed two humans that had magic. She used us. She infused magic into our blood, poured vials of it into our meals. I figured...you have light magic. So Callista chose me to be the catalyst of dark magic. For her spell. She wants to use us...to raise your father." Kyra said this calmly. But Juniper could finally see that beyond that mask was a scared girl.

"It's going to be alright, Kyra."

"Didn't know you went deaf. Did you hear what I said?"

"Yes, I did. But none of it matters, not right now. Just because you have dark magic doesn't make you—"

"Sunbeam above, Juni, okay!" Kyra slowed her down. "Okay." And maybe she believed it.

"G-i-rlsssss!" The Queen called them in a sing-song voice. And suddenly, Juniper felt something cold wrapping around her wrists, wrenching her away from Kyra. Purple strands of light had coiled themselves around them, tugging her across the courtyard to a place next to the boys. The magic bound her to the ground. Kyra was next to her, too, held tight to the floor in makeshift chains of magic.

The Queen walked over, dusting off her fingertips and standing before the five with a deranged look of glee.

"Are you three alright?" Juniper asked the boys, and they all nodded yes hurriedly.

"Fine, you can talk again. More entertainment." Callista snapped her fingers, and the slab of stone covering the boys' mouths fell off, leaving them able to speak again but still keeping them tied to the ground with huge stones.

The second the stones fell, Luca was screaming at the top of his lungs, "SUNBEAM ABOVE KYRA HAS DARK MAGIC AND THAT DRAGON—"

"Stop. Screaming." Cal's teeth were gritted in defense of his eardrums.

"WHAT THE ACTUAL—!" Julian shouted hysterically.

"What part about 'stop' do you not understand?"

Juniper and Kyra shared a look of: *Put the slabs back on, please.*

"Don't make me regret my choice," The Queen snarled, giving the boys murderous looks.

"We're fine," Luca said, his face not looking fine at all as he gave worried looks to pretty much everything around him.

Callista sighed. "Next one to talk gets turned into a ferret."

That shut everyone up really quickly.

"Perfect. Now that I have your attention, I have a spell to complete," Callista said, her eyes softening as she pulled something from her pocket.

Juniper sucked in a sharp breath as she saw what it was.

It was a small, shriveled-up pink lily flower. Old and barely even recognizable. It would be absolutely unrecognizable to anyone else, but Juniper had seen that flower before. It was the very last flower her father had given to her mother the day before he died. They had danced around the kitchen all night long, singing underneath the starry sky of their thatched roof.

Callista held the flower gingerly, as if scared it was going to snap in half. She looked at it with glassy eyes as she set it gently on the floor, its petals drooping downwards.

"First ingredient: check," The Queen said, then looked up at Juniper and Kyra. "Second and third ingredients: check. And the fourth ingredient..." Callista grinned. "Coming."

Juniper's eyes widened as she struggled in her bonds, realizing what she was about to do. Raise her father...raise Jakob. She stopped struggling for a moment. What she would give to hear her father sing to her one more time...she would turn the world upside down to do it. Of course, her mother would, too. And she was.

Before she could stop herself, Juniper said, "Mother, don't do this. Dad would not want to be—to be here again because of dark magic. You know he loved natural beauty, natural things like flowers. This is unnatural!" Tears announced their presence in the corner of her eyes. "No one is able to bring back their loved ones! Why should we?"

"We will be together soon, Juni-tree. We will be a family once more. A family where we will sing and dance again. Like we used to. Don't you want that, Juniper? Don't you want your family back?" Her mother said hopefully.

Tears brimmed in Juniper's eyes as she slowly shook her head. "I know you miss Dad more than anything. I miss him each day. But you and I could have been a family. You did not have Dad, but you still had me. You became obsessed with beauty and magic and things you could triumph over because the only thing you could not win against was grief. You never once asked me if I missed him, too. All the while, I was able to move on thanks to my sister. Because everyone has to move on at some point, and you will, too someday. You have made me miserable this past week, but I love you and I will help you if you just give this up. We get one life, mother, and we cannot waste it mourning what we have lost." The tears spilled over all at once as she pleaded with her mother. "Instead, we must see what we have gained. *Mom.* I am begging you to reconsider this."

The Queen was deadly still, her eyes flickering like candles. She almost looked regretful as she stared silently at the dead flower on the floor. It looked like she was considering what her daughter had said, maybe even considering facing her grief instead of running from it. The Queen spoke at long last.

"*No.*"

Juniper's head hung low.

The Queen continued, sneering, "If you don't want to be a part of our family, then Jakob and I will be together alone." Flames flickered in the Queen's eyes, and Juniper knew that the woman before her would never go back. "Now call up your powers. Kyra and Juniper! Now!"

"Why did you do this? Why did you try to have us killed so many times if you needed us for this spell?" Juniper found herself asking, ever the curious.

"Isn't it obvious? Magic must be catalyzed. You couldn't have simply called up the magic yourself; something had to enable it. Like dangerous situations, dear. Your magic came quicker than Kyra's, though, so I had to keep sending obstacles your way in hopes that the magic would be enacted. I would have kept trying if the dragon didn't do the trick, and I'm afraid I would have gotten a lot less nice."

The Queen had been nice thus far? Juniper didn't want to know what her mean looked like.

"How did you know we weren't going to die?" Kyra asked.

"Faith."

"How sweet."

"Not in you, twerp. In my planning and my skills. Why do you think I had the huntsman's apprentice sent after you instead of the senior one? Why do you think that every danger sent your way had a way out? I never doubted for a second that your magic would not show itself. And it did, and I have prevailed," Callista gloated, unable to hide her glee.

It was all coming together. The pleasure on the Queen's face when Juniper had volunteered to go with Kyra to the 'Winter Palace,' the different quests that they had conquered against all odds, every unanswered question was suddenly made clear and Juniper was wishing that it wasn't.

The Queen said, "You have your answers."

Kyra asked warily, "Why did you answer? Villain monologue and all."

"I wouldn't want to see all this planning and winning go to waste. This has taken me years upon years of concocting, and it has all gone exactly as planned. Years of studying you girls' reactions and minds, years of putting every piece of my plan into work, all to end up not shared with anyone but my Jakob? I want you all to know how stupid you are, and just how intelligent I am." The Queen chuckled. "And villain? I hardly think so."

"It's possible your vocabulary isn't large enough."

"Get going on the glowiness, girls. Spell time!"

Juniper dully let her hands begin to glow, the power rippling through her barely registering as her veins turned white. There was nothing left to say. The Queen's mind would not be made up. Jakob would rise from the dead and hate her for it forever.

"Kyra. Magic. Now." Callista's gaze darkened.

"No! You can't do this! I won't let you!" Kyra yelled.

"Oh, I think you will." The Queen smiled maliciously, and she looked to something beyond Juniper's shoulder.

Tora edged out from the shadows, a silver knife shining in his grip. He held it over Cal's throat, getting dangerously close to the skin. Juniper ignored the terror in her belly at the sight of him, ignored it for the fear for Cal.

"You don't have to do it, Kyra," Cal said, "Once she raises Jakob, she'll hand Aazagonia over to the Fae King. He'll have the power of an entire kingdom, Kyra, the King will—"

"Tsk, tsk, halbling. You talk too much." Tora grinned and sunk the knife deeper into Cal's collarbone, prompting his silence.

"Now I think you have some magic to call up!" Callista tilted her head in waiting, her smile flickering on and off like a lightswitch, one moment calm and the next a delighted lunacy.

Kyra hesitated, looking at Cal. Then her veins were running with black streams of light, her fingertips glowing dark.

The Queen's smile widened, real and pure. For a moment she

looked incredibly young. She raised her palms to the sky, purple light filling them in huge bundles. Wind picked up all around them, a small cyclone in the courtyard. Leaves and snow whipped around them, roaring in Juniper's ears.

"Dark One near, king of every wishing well, be summoned here to complete my spell!" Callista half-shouted into the sky, purple light whipping out and crackling like lightning bolts.

Nothing happened for a moment.

Then:

"Your Majesty."

A man with a shock of white hair and amber-orange eyes walked into the courtyard, wearing a long black cloak. Juniper felt like she had seen him before, and the feeling made her sick. His ears were slightly pointed. With a jolt, she realized that the man was faerie.

In fact, based upon the "Your Majesty," he looked to be The Faerie King.

Julian began, "No way—"

"Ferret," The Queen reminded. Julian clamped his mouth shut. "My liege." The Queen bowed giddily in the direction of the Fae King.

The King offered an off-putting grin. "I'm not here to discuss anything. I'm here to take my place as ruler of Aazagonia."

"And you will, Your Majesty. As soon as we raise Jakob," The Queen said eagerly, curtsying to him. She looked up at him with hopeful eyes, glancing back and forth between him and the flower.

"I'm glad to meet your daughters at long last." The King brought his amused gaze to Juniper and Kyra, still glowing with light and dark magic. "I've heard so much about you both, Sun and Moon. I wonder if we will ever meet again."

"Hopefully not," Kyra grumbled.

"Um, hopefully so!" Juniper tried to smile at him. He was a faerie and a king, and he was about to take over her kingdom. Better to be on his good side.

"And a halbling in our midst. Interesting," The King regarded Cal with a thoughtful look. "A halbling has not been heard of for many years. Who is your sire?"

"I don't know," Cal responded quietly.

The King said, "Hm. We will find that out soon, yes? Now, Callista, let us get on with the spell so you can have your desire and I can take your throne. Long have I waited for this day to come. It is a joy that it has finally arrived."

"After you, my King," Callista said, bouncing on the balls of her feet in anticipation.

The Faerie King raised his palms, and red light began coursing through his entire body, turning not only his veins but his entire body a dark crimson, devoid of any light. Dark magic. Faerie magic. His amber eyes flickered out like a candle to be replaced by the bright scarlet of blood and apples.

Callista closed her eyes and took his hand, her purple magic mixing with his red in flares of color. The King reached out a hand to a fearful-looking Kyra. Kyra looked at Cal, with the knife still held to his neck. She took the King's hand, her dark magic mixing with his. It burned even brighter. The Queen gave her hand to Juniper, who unwillingly stared up at her with a mix of sorrow and fear. Juniper took her mother's hand, thinking for a long moment of her father's kind eyes. Her white magic swirled together with the Queen's purple magic, and the circle was complete.

The magic intensified, twisting around the four and meeting in the center of their circle, purple and white and black and red. Forming huge bonded tendrils snaking their way around, it enhanced the day with blurry glowing colors.

In the middle of the circle, where the magic met, was the shriveled up lily.

The lily lifted into the air, rising to meet the magic. As soon as it did, it burst into a rainbow flame. Juniper wanted to reach out and save the last thing her father ever held, but she could do nothing but watch as it fell to the floor in pink and purple ashes.

"Dark one here!" The Queen shouted. "In the hall!" She lowered her voice suddenly as the ashes drifted down. "Raise my beloved. My most beloved of all."

The magic swept away the ashes, flying up into the air as the glowing left Juniper's body, her veins and eyes returning to normal. Her breath hitched as the sky turned golden.

And then.

Floating from the sky was her father.

27

A Thousand Times Fairer Than You

Jakob floated down from the heavens as if walking on air, his simple clothmaker clothes turned white. Gold emanated off him like a glowing lantern. His hair looked soft and combed, cleaner than it had been in years.

His eyes were not the kind eyes Juniper remembered, however.

They were hardened with sorrow as he set foot in the courtyard. All gazes were locked on him as he straightened his back to face the Queen. Juniper watched in bittersweet agony, wanting to run to him and throw herself in his arms, but unable to move. She was still chained up by purple strands of the Queen's magic.

"Callista," Jakob said, his face crumpling. He held out his arms to his wife, and the Queen ran to him, tears of joy overflowing from her as she wrapped him in a tight embrace.

The pair held each other for a long moment, foreheads resting against each other. Callista trembled slightly, like a flower in the wind. Unable to speak, they just clutched at each other like if they let go, the other would slip through their fingertips like sand.

Jakob did not let go of his wife. His voice was hoarse. "It cannot be."

"It is, my love," Callista spoke with unhindered joy. "I've found you again." She placed a gentle kiss on his lips, caressing his face with loving affection.

"We found each other. Like a compass needle, you are my North until the end of time," Jakob said with a smile. His eyes crinkled around the edges just like they used to. "Where is our Juniper?"

Sourness crossed the Queen's face. "Over there." She raised her chin at the spot that Juniper lay, chained to the floor and wide-eyed.

"Juniper!" Her father exclaimed, running to her with open arms. Juniper let out a sob as his eyes met hers for the first time in an eternity. Jakob's eyes clouded with confusion as he faltered, stopping short. "Why is she tied up? Who hurt her?"

"I..." Callista swallowed hard. "She wasn't ready to bring you back. She was sure it was not what you wanted. But Jakob, listen to me."

The Queen ran forward, reaching out to him.

Instead of connecting with his arm, though, her hand fell through his body like mist—a ghost.

When the husband and wife had moments before been hugging as if the world was ending tomorrow, now they gaped at Callista's hand as it passed through Jakob's body yet again. Unreachable divides had sprouted between them in seconds. In more ways than one.

"What's happening?" Callista asked the Fae King, panicked. Jakob just quietly crossed over to kneel before Juniper.

The King shook his head silently, amber eyes filled with something unrecognizable. Maybe it was a new emotion, an emotion only reachable after living for infinity. Perhaps that emotion was under-standing. Because Juniper did not have that. Not yet.

Juniper looked up at her father, a small smile coming over her face as he reached out and wiped a tear from her cheek.

"Father," Juniper said, resting her cheek against his hand.

"My dearest Juniper." He smiled back. For a moment, he flick-ered, turning transparent. Then he was there again, his warm hand nestled against her hair. "How I have missed the fairest apple of any tree."

"I have missed you, too." She thought back to that cool night in the clearing, after she had escaped from the giant's lair. When the little bird had tweeted and when she had wished. "Even gone, your wisdom has helped me throughout my journey. I-I have sorely missed you."

"I wish you could tell me all about your life—and everything I have missed. I have missed...so much. But knowing that you have turned into a kind, strong, and fearless young woman is enough. You are so brave, my daughter, so incredibly brave. I love you more than every leaf of every tree, more than every drop of water in the ocean, and more than every note ever sung. Further than the end of the galaxy."

"But the galaxy is infinite."

"Exactly." Her father kissed the top of her head. "Infinite."

Jakob turned to Kyra then, looking at her with an equally fond expression. "Thank you for being the best big sister to Juniper. The stars shine down on you proudly."

Kyra nodded, a sort of calm on her face. "I wish I could've known you outside all of this. You seem like a good man. And a great father. I know that because you raised Juniper. And she turned out pretty great, no matter how concerned with my nail biting she is."

"I am afraid I passed that bad habit on." Jakob smiled down at his short, bitten nails. He turned to the boys, who were staring at him in pure awe. "You three are quite something. Thank you for helping my daughter to see that she is worthy of believing in. I thank you endlessly for that, each of you."

"Thank you." Cal nodded at him. "Truly."

"She's easy to believe in," said Luca with a smile.

Julian stood a little taller. "I'm glad to meet you, sir. Your daughter is one of a kind."

"She is, is she not?" Her father mused. "They both are." He looked down at Kyra with a grin, taking her hand and squeezing it.

Then, he stood up, hugging Juniper one more time before turning back to a bewildered Callista. He said, flickering for a moment, "The time has come for me to go."

"Go?" The Queen asked, and Juniper's heart stopped as if a knife had been plunged into it. "You can't go! I brought you back to life, my love! So that we can be together again, like we are meant to be!" Her voice cracked, her composed features tumbling down and replaced with an animalistic desperation. "We are a compass, remember? We are the two brightest planets at night, we are the two sides of a mirror, and we are two hearts welded as one! Jakob, we are the true lovers of legends of old!" She clutched at her heart as if it were truly breaking inside her, scattered shards impaling her skin. "I—we deserve a happy ending! I love you!"

Jakob stared at the stone floor slowly becoming wet with his tears. "And I loved you, too, Callista. But the woman you have become...I cannot love her."

The Queen fell to her knees soundlessly, expression twisted in grief as if she had been impaled. "You don't mean that. You can't."

"I do."

"But...you can't go back!" She stood and whirled on the Faerie King with anger. "You can't let him go! Our deal won't stand unless you force him to stay! He will remember our love if I just have time!"

Time. There would never be enough.

Jakob watched with sad eyes as the King drawled, eyes sparkling, "It's not for me to decide."

The knife twisted further in Juniper's heart, threatening to cease its beating forever and ever. To lose her father once was enough. Losing her father twice would be unimaginable.

"What do you mean?" Kyra asked fiercely. "Of course he can. Jakob, you can stay! You don't need to be anywhere near Callista if you want! You can come and live with me and Juniper! We'll go far away from here, I promise!"

The King shook his head. "That is not what I meant. Jakob cannot stay because the laws of magic dictate it so. The spell was not completed in perfection."

"I did everything right," The Queen said. Her voice was tired. Defeated.

"Sometimes that is not enough," The King said with the wisdom of centuries hidden in his peaceful gaze. "You did not have the right ingredients."

"You should have told me! What did I do wrong?" The Queen demanded, hair spilling out in waves.

"You recited the spell, yes?"

"Yes!"

The King said, "That is where you went wrong. The main ingredient for the spell was simple: the person enacting the spell must be the person the deceased loved most in the world."

Callista clawed at her dress, moaning. "But that's me!"

"No." Jakob's voice was heavy. "The person I loved most in the world was my Juniper tree."

Juniper felt her heart soar. She slid down a little in her chains, wordless.

"You!" The Queen snarled, standing to her feet. "You wretched girl! You have taken *everything* from me! First, you stole my beauty. The kingdom's love. And now you steal the person I most love!"

Juniper searched for words, but nothing came. She just stared at her mother with a mix of grief and pity. Pity for what, she didn't know. But she just sadly stared at her mother, who had been left with nothing but mascara-stained cheeks and a tilted crown.

"A parent's love for their child," Jakob interjected sadly, "is stronger than most anything. You would know that if things had been different, Callista." He turned to the King. "I am ready. My time on the ground is up."

"No!" Juniper and the Queen cried out at the same time, a cry that sounded as if it were being ripped from their very souls. They had both lost him before. They both didn't want to lose him again.

"Please," Juniper pleaded, tears welling up in her eyes. "Do not leave again. I cannot do this alone again..."

"Juniper." Jakob brushed a stray curl out of Juniper's face, smiling down at her lovingly. "You can." He hugged her again, then stood. "I love you."

"I love you, father. I love you," Juniper choked out.

"And you are not alone. As long as the birds sing their praise, I will always be with you."

Her father smiled, and then he was gone, fading away in drops of sunlight and stars. Rays of gold and yellow drifted off into the sky like flower petals, wafting away with the gentle breeze.

"And I shall be with you." She watched the rays trace swirls in the sky and then disappear.

Juniper smiled with the sun, tears falling down her cheeks.

She smiled because she had something that she never had before.

A goodbye.

28

The Magic Within

Crows scattered as shrieking filled the noon sky.

The Queen shrieked, screaming and clutching at her face in agony, pounding her fists against her sides. Kyra silently watched as Callista groveled at the floor, moaning as if she were bleeding out.

Kyra almost felt bad for her. If Callista hadn't done a hundred horrible things to her. If it was ninety-nine horrible things, that would be a whole different story.

She averted her eyes, feeling like she was watching something not meant for her to see. Callista had always had a nice mask of her emotions, a perfectly crafted partition that hid her innermost thoughts from the world. But now, it was crumbling around her, cracks splintering and streaking across the mask like spiderwebs. Mascara ran down her cheeks in bold, dark lines.

Callista grabbed the King by his collar. "Bring him back!" she wailed.

"No," The King said.

"You liar! You scheming little fae!" The Queen snarled angrily, flexing her fingers inward and outward in rapid succession.

"I never lied," The King said. "I did not warn you of the terrible faces of magic. But I never lied. Now hand over your crown, Queen Callista."

"Answer this, Kol: why do you want my kingdom?" Callista said, sounding solemnly brave. Kol. The King's name was Kol. A very faerie-sounding name. Kyra remembered her tutor teaching her that syllable. It meant night.

Kol, the Faerie King, smiled. "The same reason most people do."

"And that is?" Kyra's voice came before she even knew what she was saying.

His gaze collided with hers like an eclipse, like asteroids crashing into each other with the force of a thousand stars.

In that moment, Kyra saw the beginnings of something yawning larger than the dusty plains of her homelands. Kol would be her worst enemy or her best ally. Nothing in between. When someone's stare locks on to someone else's like that, it means something. And Kyra knew she was not ready for what it meant.

"Mortals believe the fae folk are less. Worse beings than you because we have magic and have used it against you in the past," said Kol. "But I know the truth. Mortals should not look down on faeries." His gaze darkened. "They should be afraid. Faeries can accomplish most anything with magic, and it's time we come out of our long wait. It is time we show humans what the fae can really do. It is time that the mortals cower in fear once more."

The words chilled Kyra to her core, sending goosebumps up and down her arms. She knew that Kol would be a force to be reckoned with. A force that carried dark magic. Just like her. She shuddered.

Callista twisted her lips into a cruel, mocking grin. "You think I'm still gonna hand over my kingdom to you, after you tricked me like this? Not gonna happen. Get out of my sight, or I'll send you to the bottom of the sea to scum it with the merfolk! If you don't help me raise my husband again, I'll find someone else who will!"

"No person can be raised twice, little queen."

Callista roared, then raised her hand as if about to cast a spell, but the King was faster. Strands of red magic rippled outward from his fingertips, grabbing at the crown on her head and placing it on his own.

"If you and your daughters are to tear each other to pieces, kindly do it out of my sight." The King fluttered his fingers in a wave, then snapped.

The chains fell away from Kyra's wrists, and she rubbed them soothingly as she stared up at the sky where Jakob had faded away.

The King snapped his fingers again, and the castle fell away too.

Kyra found herself in the Southern Forest, the tall trees kissing the sky and casting dark shadows down. The sun had fully risen, light and warmth blanketing the green moss and leaves. Birds sang somewhere, bittersweet notes of a song Kyra didn't know the words to.

The others were all around her, too, blinking at the daylight and rubbing their limbs where the chains had fallen. Juniper, Luca, Julian, and Cal. All safe and together.

As Kyra rubbed her own wrists, she stared at her palm in silence.

She had dark magic within her. Magic that could shake mountains and part seas. Magic that she had dreamed of her whole life.

"Wait," Julian complained, butting in through her brooding, "None of us got to punch anyone."

"Seeing as we're alive, I'm alright with that," said Cal with his signature grin.

Luca frowned. "It would've been pretty cool to punch someone..."

"Oh, trust me," Kyra said, hearing footsteps. "We will." She turned and rose to her feet, facing the sound of the footsteps head on.

Juniper said, "I do not like the sound of that."

Cursing could be heard through the forest and the sound of heels on stone.

"That's either gonna be an angry witch who wants to eat us, or the Queen," said Luca, careful to keep his voice low.

Julian groaned, replying, "I'd prefer the cannibalistic witch."

His preference was not taken into account, as emerging from the thick blanket of trees came the Queen, with Tora trailing right behind her.

The clearing rang with silence as the two groups faced each other, no one daring to make the first move.

Kyra dared. "Upsetting that Kol decided to drop us all off in the same spot. You think he's watching from somewhere and eating popcorn? Placing bets with his faerie watching party?"

Tora let out a chuckle at her words, his slithering tongue snaking its way out. "Then Kol won't be very entertained. This should be pretty quick."

"Or have you forgotten?" Callista asked, features dancing with a crazed fervor, hair wild and breathing heavy. Her nostrils flared in anticipation, deadly stare fixed with something dark and dangerous. "I never harmed you because I needed you girls. But now that I don't...I have nothing holding me back."

"You're in luck, then," said Cal. "Because neither do we."

The Queen leered wickedly. "You think you can win against me and my snake?" her veins flared up with purple fire. Tora flicked out sharp fangs that dug into his bottom lip and drew blood. It didn't seem to bother him, however. He just sneered with menace. "No weapons you wield can defeat me."

"Oh, *Mother*, forgetting something, are we?" Kyra spat, anger flaring inside her. "You forged the greatest weapon of all."

Kyra pleaded with her dark magic to heed her call. It answered, seeping through her veins. All her life, she had had this anger burning holes within her like melting moons. All her life, dark magic had been winding through her core, lurking and roiling and pent up inside.

And it wanted to be freed.

Black, lightning-like bolts shot from every inch of her skin, throwing the Queen to her feet and sending Kyra slamming backwards into a nearby tree. Her back struck it with an awful crunch, and she tumbled into the grass, gripping it like a lifeline. But the raging pain in her back dulled to a steady throb, and then was silenced by the need for revenge burning inside.

She steadied her shaking hands as she saw that her stepmother had sustained more damage than her, lying still in the grass as if asleep, her loose black curls splayed over her elegantly awful face. Kyra was at first loath to see that Callista was still breathing, even though she wasn't moving. Unconscious, then. Good. Kyra wasn't finished with her yet.

Kyra launched to her feet, running at the queen with every ounce of her being flaring with magic and rage, complementing each other in spite of warring within her, each fighting for control. The anguish threatened to overpower, sending her crashing to her knees in turmoil, conflicted sides of her wishing to break loose. One side wanted her to lay down and cry for all the hits she had taken, the life that had been stolen by her stepmother.

But the dark magic's fury proved stronger. It kept her going as she rose, and she ran forward, stuffing every ounce of grief, pain, and loss deep within. She had to keep going. If she stopped, she had no idea what would happen to her, if she would even be able to go on.

The fall to her knees had given Tora time to prepare for an attack, and before Kyra knew it, he was in front of her, fist reared back in a claw, swinging at her and catching her cheek. A deep gouge cut across her face. The pain didn't register. It just was shoved inside with the rest of it, the magic inside growing and numbing it. Numbing it all. How ugly.

Ugly. Ugly. Ugly. She roared, a deep guttural sound, and swiped back at Tora, striking him across the face with a closed fist. Dancing sparks of blackness spiraled at his chest, knocking him backward and crashing to the ground. Tora's mouth opened in a surprised O before he skidded across the stone and moss.

The exertion blew Kyra herself backward, and she found herself knocking into an astonished Cal.

He looked at her frantically. "Kyra, stop it! Let go! Let it all go!"

For a moment, she stopped. Her veins returned to normal, her vision cleared as she looked at him. She breathed heavily, looking at the awed and horrified looks on all of her friends' faces.

Juniper knelt beside her softly, and Kyra was reminded of that morning a week ago when their lives had been normal, and she had run with the wind. When everything seemed in her control, even though it was far from it.

Juniper spoke quietly. "What are you doing?"

Kyra closed her eyes. "What I have to."

When she opened her eyes, she knew they were pools of darkness. Her hair swirled around her, though no breeze whistled through the treetops.

Tora was rising to his feet, astoundingly calm.

Kyra suddenly saw why. His smooth, pale skin had disappeared and been replaced with green scales covering his entire body, thick with slime and disgusting mucus. A long, whip-like tail had surged from his back, cutting through the air like a knife. His eyes had slit further, gold and green poisoned daffodils in a dying meadow. Huge flaps of skin that could only be described as a cobra's hood reared up from his neck as Tora hissed.

Kyra reared back her fist, dark magic crackling and popping across her knuckles in rapid flying movements like electricity.

Lightning bolts of magic whipped forward from her palms, striking Tora in the leg and sending him sprawling on the ground. He was trying to shimmy away from her, and his face was poised in terror.

Kyra calmly walked over to him, raising her left hand high in the air. A roiling black ball of magic built in her palm, twisting and turning over itself as it grew.

"End me," Tora spat, a deranged boy speaking deranged words. "End me. I know you won't. You don't have it in you, little princess of the night. Scars prevent you from ever healing your aching heart." He no longer looked to be the calculatingly calm fae prince Kyra had come to hate. Now, he just looked like a scared boy scrambling for his life.

All the hatred and grief wrung up inside her fell away in an instant. She couldn't hurt him. Even after all he had done, she could never do that. In that moment, Kyra let it all go. Her sword of anger inside clattered into her heart, and her shield of hurt fell away.

"That's where you're wrong, jerk. I would punch you into tomorrow." Kyra grinned, and she knew it was identical to that of her stepmother's. It didn't bother her as much. "Lucky for you, I have a sister who would think that very rude."

She let the ball of magic drop and whipped out Julian's sword from its sheath, bringing the hilt down on Tora's head and rendering him unconscious in one fluid movement.

"Is it my turn?" The Queen said from the floor, finally awake again. "Though I'd guess I'm not gonna end up like poor little Tora here."

Callista rose to her feet, purple flames dancing across her arms like a holy crusader.

"I wouldn't bet on that," Kyra said coldly. "I wouldn't bet on you."

Juniper walked forward then, her voice cold and level. "I would not either. There are five of us, mother, and one of you. A faerie,

a Dämonenwölfe, a Dragon Warrior, and two—excuse my frank-
ness—two very peeved girls who have been waiting a long time for
this moment."

And then Cal was standing next to Kyra, and Jules and Luca,
too. They stood tall and together. They stood with the weight of all
they had been through displayed proudly on their faces. Kyra stood
with power. It was almost like you could hear that power humming
through the five of them, the power of the fae and magic and of each
other. The thrum of their togetherness was so loud in Kyra's ears, it
was like a chorus of voices crying out in song.

The Queen looked between the five of them, seeing this power,
and Kyra saw something in her stepmother's eyes that she had never
seen before.

Fear. A flash of it, strange and foreign to Callista's face. An emotion that Kyra had never seen in her stepmother. Fear like ice, cold
and chilling and evident in the crease of her brow and the barely visible bead of sweat dripping down the beautiful slope of The Queen's
nose. Her breathtaking lashes did not close over her eyes, open wide
with fear. Kyra recognized all this in her stepmother, and it made
her shiver.

And then the Queen spoke, the flash of disorder fleeing from her
face. Her voice was quiet.

"See you all very soon. Next time, I will not underestimate you.
Expect an army teeming with magic and mischief and sparkling uniforms. Expect me."

The Queen disappeared in a flash of purple and black, a blooming lily in her place. A reminder of Callista's promise...or threat. *See
you all very soon.* The small flower mocked them with future tribula-
tions, but none of that mattered to her.

Because instead of thinking of that, she was throwing her arms
around her friends, pulling them all close in a group hug. Thoughts

of Callista could come later. Right now, she was just happy they were all okay.

Juniper looked even better than okay. She looked at peace.

Kyra squeezed all her friends close, closing her eyes tightly shut.

"Well," Kyra said. "It's safe to say this was the worst trip of my life."

Everyone burst into fits of laughter, though Kyra suspected it wasn't because her words were actually funny. More like everyone was sleep-deprived and exhausted from almost dying a million and one times. Still, she was chalking it up to her fantastic sense of humor.

They let go of the embrace, and she met Cal's eyes from across the hug. He smiled at her with hints of something a little hopeful and something a little sweet.

She took his hand as the others dived into a hurried and loud conversation about everything that had just happened.

"Cal?" Kyra said, feeling heat rise into her cheeks.

"Crazy?" Cal asked with a knowing smile. His nose scrunched in that endearing way.

"I found a new favorite color," she said tentatively. Sunbeam above, she didn't know how to do this.

"Oh?" Cal asked.

"It's blue," said Kyra, rapidly blinking as if faced with a bright light.

"Blue," Cal repeated. The corners of his mouth quirked up. "Remember mine?"

"Grey, right?"

"Grey."

"That's a dull color."

"I disagree," Cal said. He smiled then, and Kyra swore the sun rose with it. "The color grey reminds me of a certain someone's eyes."

Kyra pinked a little, brushing a stray strand of golden hair out of her face. "The day we met in the clearing. You rode up on your horse, and I held a knife at you."

"I think I remember that, yeah. The knife part is a little foggy...want to go over that again?"

Kyra rolled her eyes. "Absolutely not. Besides, I solemnly swear to never hold you at knifepoint again unless you threaten to feed me vegetables."

"Noted. No vegetables." He grinned.

"That day...you accused me of staring at you," said Kyra, biting her lip. "The thing is...maybe I was. Staring at you, I mean."

"That's good to know," Cal said, a huge smile coming over his face. "Because I might have been staring, too."

The dragon's nest inside her fluttered, and Kyra wondered if maybe she understood what it meant. That Cal meant something to her. That was a scarier thought than any wicked queen or giant. But Kyra was learning to open up; to forgive the world around her as well as herself. It was time to face the fact that she was not invincible, unbreakable and fearless. It was time for Kyra to face the unknown.

Kyra flashed a dopey smile, feeling like a sappy idiot but not really caring. Cal smiled back, just as dopily and sappily, making her feel less like an idiot and more like the luckiest girl in the world for him to be smiling at her like that.

Suddenly, she noticed a silence had overcome the others, and Kyra turned to see what the fuss was about. When she saw, she hurriedly wished she had stayed entranced in Cal's dopey smile.

The Faerie King stood, leaning lazily against a tree, inspecting his fingernail. He met Kyra's gaze.

"Hello, younglings," Kol said pleasantly. "I see you have apprehended the...*former* Queen of Aazagonia. Well done."

Rage did not make its way into Kyra's heart. The fiercest of storms was not burning in her anymore. Kyra said calmly, instead of calling him names or kicking him like she would have liked to, "Please leave."

"You are right not to call me trivial names. Names are powerful, you see. They are the essence of the soul." Kol almost looked amused. "You know my name just as I know yours. But I do not think you understand what kind of power we have over each other."

"Cut the fanciness. I don't know or care what you're trying to say."

"I am prepared to make a deal with you."

"How kind," Julian said curtly.

Kol smiled without mirth. "The deal is such: You five will travel to the great city of Yen-Sing, across the desert and seas of Bayuma. The Sultan of the Sand Kingdom has something that I seek to have returned to me. If you bring me back this item...I will help you in your battle against the Queen."

"Yen-Sing? That's...that's..." Luca said. His body tensed, like a dog alerted to danger. Once he realized all eyes were on him, he forced a smile. A flash of panic quickly concealed. But why? Luca hastily said, "Yen-Sing. The desert kingdom. That's doable."

Cal asked, "How will we know you won't go back on your word?" His mouth was twisted in a taut line.

"A faerie's promise is unbreakable," Kol said. "You of all should know this."

Cal went quiet.

"Let me get this straight," Juniper said slowly, "You wish for us to retrieve something? What is this something? And why aren't you going to Yen-Sing to get it yourself?"

"I'm glad to see someone focusing on the important things," said Kol. "I cannot set foot in Yen-Sing. The Sultan has placed wards against faeries around the perimeter of his kingdom. There was a certain mishap four hundred years ago that involved me and a particular massacre of thousands. I was in the right, of course."

"Um." Juniper gulped. "Yeah. Anyways—"

"My staff. The five of you will retrieve my staff."

Julian snorted. "You want us to risk our lives in order for you to get a stick?"

"This is no ordinary *stick*. It is...special to me. Every King of the Fae is entrusted with this staff. Unfortunately, an enemy of mine stole it from me a long time ago, and I want it back, you see. I need it back."

"Why is that?" Kyra asked, her throat squeezing inward. For some reason, she did not want to hear the answer.

Kol's eyes glittered. "A north wind is coming, Princess. Something far greater than you will ever understand. It will shake the heavens with its power, and I will be prepared. Go forth, to the west end of the world, to Yen-Sing. Their Sultan has my staff. Bring it to me, and I will help you. I swear it. I swear by every universe that winks down from above. I will deliver unto the Queen her undoing. The Queen will have her judgement day, if only you retrieve my staff."

Kyra looked around at all the others, meeting each of their gazes. Each nodded in return.

"We'll do it." Kyra nodded at Kol. He grinned, his pointed ears perking up in delight, and his long fingers reaching out a hand to shake. A twinge of dread flickered through Kyra, yet she reached out her hand, ignoring it. He said he would help them bring down her stepmother. Even if the man was evil, he could not break his promise. That had to be enough.

Kyra reached out a hand to shake his.

"Wait!" Juniper said frantically. "Pinky promise!"

"Excuse me?" Kol cocked his head in confusion.

Juniper flung out her pinky. "I said, pinky promise me! It is the only way I will accept."

Kol reached out his pinky, and the two interlocked them in a bizarre little exchange. Never in a million years did Kyra think she would see Juniper engage in a pinky promise with the King of the Fae. Hey, almost as weird as Kyra having dark magic and Juniper's father being raised from the dead!

Next, Kol shook hands with Kyra. His hand was surprisingly warm, like a field of grass spread out in the sun for hours upon end. Like a beam of sunlight.

"May I have a word with Princess Kyra?" Kol asked. He coughed as no one moved. "Alone, perhaps?"

The other four got the clue, wandering off in a thick huddle, possibly discussing their upcoming journey. Kyra smiled against her will as she watched Cal's black head bob away.

Her attention was pulled back to the Fae King.

Kol's ever-so-joyful demeanor was even less lighthearted now. His heavily lidded eyes now cast long shadows over his cheeks. He reminded Kyra of a paper doll. Eerily waiting in the dark of a forgotten dollhouse, dust gathering on its sewn-on smile.

"Oh, no need to jump right into things. Go ahead and keep staring creepily," Kyra muttered.

Kol said, "The time has come for me to impart something to you. A prophecy told to me millions of years ago. Only now do I understand."

"Lemme guess: Two sisters, one awesome and one nerdy, woven of the same quilt or something—"

"No," said Kol. "Do not assume you are the center of gravity, Kyra. This prophecy does not concern you. It is foretold of the Sun's Child."

Kyra felt her blood run cold. She felt as if all the air in the world had suddenly been sucked up through a tunnel, away from her desperately needing lungs. "I don't suppose the prophecy is that she'll be blessed with a thousand sweets and unicorns?"

"Unicorns are not real." Kol, the King of the Faeries who could do literal magic, scowled at her. "And candy has no magical properties."

Kyra blinked. "Tell that to a magic house that tried to eat me earlier."

"Do you want me to impart the prophecy or not?"

"By all means," said Kyra. Her voice quivered slightly.

"*Many trials will haunt the Sun's Child in the land of sea and sand, and the group brought together will be broken again.* I expect your time in the desert and sea of Bayuma will be rife with more challenges. But I have watched the five of you closely on your journey. If anyone can face these challenges, it is you five," said Kol. Sunbeam above, Kyra was glad. That prophecy didn't sound too bad.

And Kol was right. Each in their own way, they brought something to the table that when put together, formed a team.

Kol turned away, then turned back as if remembering something. "And Kyra?"

"Yes?"

"...Keep your sister away from apples."

* * *

Everything felt right in the world.

Juniper smiled. The five of them had begun their journey across the world, all the way to the desert kingdom of Yen-Sing. They were going to retrieve the staff and then finally defeat their mother, for good. No more nightmares of the Queen etched into her brain. No more nights fearing for another tribulation coming her way.

As the snowy forest around them disappeared and with it, the cold, Juniper swore she could feel a desert wind and taste the salt of sea on her tongue. New beginnings were coming...soon.

"Is it too much to hope that getting this staff will be easy?" Julian asked, kicking at a rock as he walked.

"I thought you'd know by now that nothing we do is easy," tutted Kyra.

"Did you hear Kol say something about a war brewing amongst faeries?" Luca asked. "That doesn't sound good."

Cal was definitely thinking about this. He said, "Definitely not. The Queen…I think she's going to garner strength from the different factions of the Fae. You heard her, right? 'Expect an army full of magic and mischief.' That's the fae, right?"

"That's the fae. But are we forgetting the sparkly uniforms part?" asked Kyra. "Because that's what I took away from the goodbye speech."

"Can we get sparkly uniforms?" Julian raised his hand in excitement.

"Is that even a question?"

"Yes! I mean, no!"

Luca rolled his eyes. "Count me out."

"Luca, you darling baby goat. Never in a million years." Kyra ruffled Luca's hair. "Yen-Sing. The city of starlit nights, yeah? Sign me up."

Juniper asked, "How are we to cross the great desert and sea, infiltrate a palace right under the Sultan's nose, and retrieve a magical staff? All while hoping to evade the Queen? It seems rather impossible."

"Possible is my middle name." Kyra's eyes twinkled.

"Your middle name is Rose."

"Always ruining the joke, Sun's Child."

The group fell into a comfortable silence as the laughs trickled away. Juniper could not help but muse about the task ahead and what it would require. The Queen would want revenge, and soon. If she had a whole army of faeries behind her, what could stop her from taking back Aazagonia...or even more kingdoms to get to the five of them? Juniper shuddered. Worrying was suffering twice, yet there was one more thing she had to ask of the others. One more nagging impulse that would not yield until addressed.

Juniper fell quiet. She said, "You three do not have to come with us, you know. It is not your battle to fight."

The boys gaped at her like she had grown a second head.

"You're right," Luca spoke up, and everyone around him fell into a stunned stupor. Juniper felt her heart quake. To lose Luca would be horrible indeed. But she would let him go if he truly wanted to. Love, she was beginning to find, was more complex than she had ever imagined. And sometimes love meant doing what was best for those in your life, no matter the price.

"It seems the little huntsman has gained some much-needed wisdom. Care to lend me some?" Kyra asked, but her brows were knitted. "You wanna leave this all behind?"

"We will not stop you," said Juniper. "It is your decision to make."

"I meant you're right. This wasn't our battle to fight." Luca said with a shake of his oakwood brown hair. "But it is now. It is now because we're friends with you, and we need help if we're going to find our way in this world. The Fae King promised he'd back us if it came down to a showdown with the Queen. And I'm willing to see it through. It's not your battle alone. Not anymore. It's all of ours, now."

"Princesses, it's been an honor. But the Queen will be back, and now that she doesn't need you for her spell, we can expect that she'll want revenge," Julian said, crossing his arms. "And I think a certain Dragon Warrior with an amazingly proportional jawline and impeccable curls will come in handy when that happens."

Juniper began, "His curls are very impeccable—"

"Not the point," Cal interjected. "The point is, the five of us are a group now. When the time comes to face the Queen, and maybe some angry, sparkly faeries, we'll do it together."

"Because that's what we do," said Luca, smiling. "We fight and we win. Together."

That settled it. That, Juniper thought, was the first puzzle piece in her grand quest for understanding. It began with standing by your friends even when they were threatened by their wicked mother and a possible battalion of sparkly faeries who wanted them dead.

Their next journey had begun.

Every passing second was another second that Juniper had peace. A goodbye from her father. A place in the world. Friends who loved her. That was all she could have ever wanted.

It felt like a closure, the last chapter of a fairytale. Who knew what tomorrow held? Right then, it felt like anything was possible.

The end was near, and it felt as if the very world hummed with this knowledge.

A nearby bird tweeted the coming of day, as warm summer light washed over her face. For once, she did not dread what the day would bring.

For once, she hummed the words of a song she never knew she could sing. For once, tears of joy pricked at her eyelids. *Down by the Juniper tree...* Kyra always said that the birds sang for her. But it didn't quite feel like that anymore. No, it was different now—the birds no longer sang for her.

Because, as she raced to catch up with the others, the birds sang *with* her.

29

The Other After the Moon

The fallen Queen knelt, desert winds whipping her skirts around her like phoenix wings.

A single tear glistened against her cheek before falling, a diamond against glittering tan grains. It sparkled for a moment against the sand before fading away forever. Lost to time. Or maybe lost to something else.

The Queen knew loss. She had lost her kingdom. Her husband. Her hope. She had lost everything. It had been taken from her by her daughters—insufferable little fools who deserved pain like no other. They deserved to watch the world around them crumble while being buried by the weight of grief.

Callista had endured pain like no other. It was time for the Sun and Moon's child to suffer as well.

She reached a tentative hand out to the sand, grabbing a fistful of it as she thought. It slipped through her fingers, soft and thin. Revenge was the sweetest of delicacies, the warmest hug of pleasure and comfort Callista could have. The only thing she had ever counted on before was love. She knew better now. Now, she knew revenge, the ultimate truth, could be the only thing to make her smile once more.

The Queen regarded herself as glass now, forged in fire and fury. What once had been soft was now haunted by years of waiting, then hardened by the loss of her husband for the second time.

Revenge was coming the only way she knew how. Her daughters would pay.

And so the Queen spoke softly. Her voice was carried far away with the desert wind.

Maybe carried to a world above the clouds, or a pack of wolves hunting in the night.

Maybe her voice reached out to a glittering glass slipper or a house made of candy.

Her voice might've found its way to an eerie spinning wheel or an apple soon bitten.

A group of five teenagers embarking on a new beginning might be passed on its way.

Maybe her voice rode the wind to a golden mirror, dark and old, growing dusty far below slumbering servants in a kingdom overtaken by a new king.

"Mirror, mirror, on the wall...lead my daughters to their fall."

THE GOLDEN MIRROR

Acknowledgements

I'd like to start by thanking David Varela for designing the amazing cover. You were so supportive throughout the whole process and I am so thankful for your encouragement and beautiful design. Thank you for bringing my ideas to life; without you the cover would still be a hastily scrawled doodle with a mirror that looked more like an octopus.

To the marvelous editor Christina Hill, thank you for your amazing edits and advice, and especially for teaching me that the word 'stepmother' doesn't have a hyphen in it. I'm sure that tiny dash caused us both a lot of grief.

I'm lucky to have such wonderful family members who have been waiting a long time to read this book. Lulu and Papa, you have been a steady source of encouragement and unconditional love throughout my life. Grandma and Grandpa, thank you for constantly supporting me throughout my education and showing me from a young age to always shoot for the stars.

Thank you to Angela Morrow, for being my first fan. Your excitement for my writing has been a huge source of motivation for me over the years.

For my best friends, Grace Banning, Katie Cunningham, Emma Trueman, Nathan Morrow, Reyna Sakakine, Dylan Mills, Mia Kienle, Morgan Llewelyn, Grace Nolet, and Lilly Nolet: thank you for listening to my endless rants about writing and believing in me throughout the years. This book has a major theme of friendship. Without you all, I would never be where I am today. Thank you for being wonderful friends!

To my twin sister, Taylor. Gosh, where to even start? You have been an endless source of support, inspiration, and most of all, love. This book is, at its core, a story of two sisters trying to find out what it means to be heroes, not only for themselves, but for each other. I would be lying if I said you didn't inspire parts of both Kyra and Juniper. Thank you, Taylor, for being not only my fantastically weird sister, but my amazing friend as well. You are the sun to my moon and the moon to my sun.

And a huge thanks to my dad. Thank you for being the first reader of this book and the first person to share this world with me. Your excitement and enthusiasm for this story encouraged me to keep working towards my dreams. I wish I could impart how much it means to me that you were the first person to know my characters and hear my story, but I think Juniper's father said it best: *more than every leaf of every tree, more than every drop of water in the ocean, and more than every note ever sung. Further than the end of the galaxy.* Infinitely.

Lastly, thank you to my amazing mom. Holy cow, we did it. Thank you for the many hours of discussing book covers, formatting, editing, and the entire process as a whole. I mean it when I say without you, I would never have been able to publish this book. You gave me an endless amount of love and support throughout this entire journey, by spending a countless amount of time in an area in which we were so out of our depths. The main mother in this book, Queen Callista, is heartless and cruel. I am so lucky to have such a wonderful mother that the only thing I needed to do to write the character of Queen Callista was to make her the opposite of you. It's unbelievable to me that I am so lucky as to have such a patient and dedicated mother who stood by my side throughout this all. Thank you, Mom, for helping me share my story with the world. I love you.

Brooke Fischbeck is a senior in high school and is eighteen years old. She has been writing since the second she could form letters. She wrote this novel during the infamous year of 2020, spending hours a day to get the first draft done. Brooke lives in Dana Point, California, and spends her free time writing and reading. When she's not writing or reading, she can be found on a tennis court or at the beach.

CPSIA information can be obtained
at www.ICGtesting.com
Printed in the USA
FSHW020100180821
84143FS